Mistress of Netherfield

JULIA WINTER

GLASS HAT
PRESS

DEDICATION

With love and gratitude, this book is dedicated to Claire and Sally, who helped me polish my version of one of the world's greatest love stories and without whom this story would never have flown.

Gratitude too, to Megan Reddaway, whose wonderful editing skills found all those pesky little errors. Thank you!

A worshipful genuflection to Miss Austen. I can't help but wonder what she would make of the reverence with which she is held by any lover of literature, and if she would be surprised by how many—countless—people have agreed with her over the last two centuries, that Elizabeth Bennet is indeed "as delightful a character as ever appeared in print". It is appalling cheek, of course, to use even a fraction of her little bit of ivory, but I hope she will forgive me. My only excuse is that of all literary heroines, Lizzy Bennet is the one I wanted to be. This is the closest I shall ever come.

CONTENTS

ACKNOWLEDGMENTS

Editing : Megan Reddaway

Cover Art: Detail from a portrait of Madame Philippe Panon Desbassayns de Richemont (Jeanne Eglé Mourgue, 1778–1855), painted by Marie Guillelmine Benoist in 1802. The painting is in The Met Fifth Avenue, and the image is available in the public domain for unrestricted use.

.

CHAPTER ONE

A Truth Universally Acknowledged

It is a truth universally acknowledged that on escaping an unhappy marriage, a young widow will be delighted to remove to the dower house and lease the marital abode to a single man in possession of a good fortune, provided he looks elsewhere to fulfil his want of a wife.

"For if I lease Netherfield to a single man," remarked Elizabeth Grayson to her companion, Charlotte Lucas, "an assault on his bachelorhood is assured. Our mamas will have my tenant in their sights."

"They will certainly view him as the rightful property of one of their daughters."

Elizabeth glanced at her mother. "And there sits the Vestal Matron and High Priestess of this doctrine. May the Lord have mercy on the poor man, for Mama will show none."

For having once successfully made Elizabeth the beneficiary of her matchmaking skill, her mother was eager to extend her expertise to the four remaining Bennet girls, all of them unmarried.

"For just look at our Lizzy, will you!" Mama fanned out the cards in her hand and frowned at them. "She would be a spinster still without me, much less own a manor as fine as Netherfield Park! Given Jane's beauty, I am sure I cannot fail but to secure a baron at the very least. For Lizzy's looks are nothing compared to Jane's, you know, and it always astonished me that Mr Grayson gave her the preference."

The usual set of families were gathered at Longbourn, the home of the Bennet family, for cards and supper. The servants had thrown open the glass doors from the drawing room leading to the gardens beyond, admitting the soft, summer air. The evening breeze brought the scent of roses and honeysuckle wafting over the whist table where Mama sat with three other ladies.

At her pronouncement, the three matrons glanced at Elizabeth, who sat nearby with Charlotte. Elizabeth, used to unfavourable comparisons with her elder sister Jane, looked serenely back.

"It is true that Jane is a beauty, Mrs Bennet," said Lady Lucas, the neighbour whom Elizabeth's mother usually described as 'my most particular friend'. "But Elizabeth is very pretty and lively. Sir William always says she is a jewel."

Sir William Lucas stood across the room, talking with Papa and Mr Harpur, who was rarely coaxed from seclusion since the death of his lady two years earlier. If Mr Harpur's chuckles, the bloom on Sir William's cheek and Papa's unusual sociability were any indication, they drank something far stronger than the ratafia Elizabeth herself was sipping. She hid a smile. Sir William was a dear favourite of hers.

The remaining two matrons, one of them Elizabeth's own Aunt Phillips, murmured agreement with Lady Lucas.

"What is more, I know my John has always admired her." And here Lady Lucas directed a simpering smile at Elizabeth.

Elizabeth pretended not to see it. She was fond of John, who had been a childhood playmate, but had no thought of him beyond friendship and the memories of more innocent days. Lady Lucas's hints and winks about her eldest son had increased when Elizabeth's husband left her Netherfield Park, the aforementioned marital home, and Elizabeth had transformed from the near penniless second daughter of the local squire into a wealthy widow with her own estate.

Elizabeth's mother ignored the hint as well as Elizabeth herself did, and raked her maternal gaze over the remaining Bennet girls: sweet, gentle Jane, undoubtedly a great beauty, making shy Miss King welcome; Mary eyeing the piano with eagerness, clutching a sheaf of music; Kitty and Lydia romping noisily around the room with young Maria Lucas, Pen and Harriet Harrington, and Mrs Long's two visiting nieces, who were so indistinguishable that Elizabeth could never recall their names. The younger girls darted in and out to the garden at will, stirring the fluttering silk curtains with their loud laughter.

"The other girls should all do as well as Lizzy, if not better. They all know how important it is to marry well. I've brought them up to know their duty. I know you will understand, Lady Lucas, with two grown girls yourself—"

"Maria is barely fifteen years old! The same age as your Lydia."

"It is never too early to secure their futures." And here Mama affected to lower her voice, though it was but a token effort. "Or Maria will suffer poor Charlotte's fate and remain unmarried until she, too, has to take a position—"

"Mama!" Elizabeth spoke so sharply even her mother started. Charlotte's presence as her companion allowed them both an independence they would otherwise be denied, and she would not permit Mama to jeopardise the beneficial arrangement. "Charlotte does not have any position other than that of my friend. I am grateful that she has been such a staunch one these last few years, and her company not only lends me respectability, it gives a great deal of pleasure."

Charlotte's hand rested briefly on Elizabeth's arm in thanks, while Lady Lucas, red-faced and thin-lipped, fanned herself with vigour, glaring at Mama in a manner that gave their particular friendship an antagonistic tinge. This surprised neither of their daughters. Such discord happened at least twice a month.

"Oh, if you put it like that, then I suppose it must be so," was all Mama would concede.

"I do, indeed." Elizabeth nodded at Lady Lucas. "I hope you know, dear ma'am, that Charlotte's company is a blessing and I am ever grateful for your indulgence in loaning her to me."

Lady Lucas's returning nod was stiff, and Elizabeth foresaw another few weeks of discomfort for poor Charlotte. Her parents had come late to the rank of the gentry when Sir William received his knighthood on making an address to the King, and gave up his trade in consequence. The Lucases were more attuned than most to the subtle condescension of the older landed families in the district around the market town of Meryton, and no one would ever describe Mama as subtle. It was only through a great deal of tact and persuasion that Charlotte, already considered a likely old maid four years earlier, had been allowed to live with Elizabeth in Nether House in Meryton, the dower house of Netherfield Park, following James Grayson's death. Charlotte's companionship was granted only on the strict understanding that no payment would be given. To this condition, Elizabeth had consented. And if she put money aside for Charlotte and invested it as carefully with her Uncle Gardiner in London as she did the sums intended to increase her sisters' dowries, then that was between her and Charlotte. It was unlikely Charlotte would marry now, since she was almost twenty-eight, but at the least she would have some security and income if Elizabeth had anything to say about it.

Mama sniffed loudly, before returning her attention to her daughters. "I am certain to secure good prospects for my girls. Lydia is so very lively and gay, all the gentlemen admire her. She quite reminds me of... well, enough of that."

"Yes," said Mrs Long, another neighbour, much older than Mama and not as well circumstanced. There was no Longbourn in the narrower life following her husband's death, only a small house in Meryton and straitened means: Mrs Long was Mama's fears made manifest. "Lydia puts me strongly in mind of you as a girl, Mrs Bennet."

At that moment Lydia danced up to the card table. "Mama! Have you heard the news? The ___shire Militia is to winter in Meryton and will arrive at the end of August. A regiment, Mama! Soldiers!"

Mama squealed and held out both her hands for Lydia to clasp while Lydia jumped up and down on the spot. "Redcoats! I was always fond of a redcoat and now we shall have an entire camp of them. What an opportunity, my dear Lydia!"

"Oh." Lydia stopped jumping and snatched free her hands, to clasp them at her breast. "So many officers! They will all fall in love with me, I am sure. I shall be quite the regimental favourite."

And on that note, she drifted away to rejoin her cavorting companions. All the younger girls joined hands and danced out of the doors into the garden, singing nonsense about redcoats and laughing. Papa met Elizabeth's glance and rolled his eyes. Elizabeth wished he would take stronger action than that, since Lydia was spoiled and silly, and would soon be beyond all amendment. The thought of Lydia and a regiment of redcoats could not amuse her.

"Very strongly in mind," Mrs Long said, and Elizabeth looked quickly down at her slippers to hide her appreciation.

Mama preened. "Well, I will admit to having had my triumphs! Lydia will make a magnificent match, I am sure. She is certain to catch the eye of a handsome young colonel, for you know she is pretty and lively, and will be popular with the officers. Kitty is well enough, too, when she is not coughing." And with pursed lips, Mama added, "If only Mary would make more effort! And Lizzy herself might remarry, of course. If she can. She is a young widow, after all."

Elizabeth had been a very young widow. "You bestowed upon me such a notable husband, Mama, that I have no desire to make a second venture into matrimony. I thank you for the favour, but I am unlikely to be so fortunate twice."

Charlotte, whose ear was as well attuned to irony as to condescension, again laid her hand on Elizabeth's arm.

Mama sailed serenely on, unheeding, though none of the other ladies at the card table would meet Elizabeth's gaze. "Oh that is all nonsense, Lizzy! Of course you will remarry. Some widower seeking a mother for his children may come into the neighbourhood one day, you know, and he may not cavil at taking a widow to wife. However, none of that is to the purpose! Now you are seeking a new tenant for Netherfield, you must consider only the richest, most handsome young men to be worthy to lease your estate. No more married men like the last tenant, if you please! You must be certain of it, and meet him yourself. You cannot trust to your steward to make the right choice. For, you know, once you have such a man at Netherfield, you may then throw Jane in his way. Dear Jane deserves only the very best."

Twenty-one years had been enough to inure Elizabeth to much of her mother's nonsensical ramblings, and of a certainty, continued argument would end with Mama suffering a fit of the nerves that would have her rushing to her room wailing about her second daughter's ingratitude and selfishness, and calling for Longbourn's housekeeper and whatever remedy the long-suffering apothecary had recommended last. Elizabeth retired from the field of battle without firing another shot, but without conceding the war.

She would not further her mother's ambitions.

The day the prospective tenant came to view Netherfield Park, Elizabeth left Nether House and decamped to visit her Uncle Gardiner in London. She took Charlotte with her. The visit had been long planned to allow her to visit galleries, museums and theatres, and spend time with her Aunt Gardiner, more of a mother to her than Mama had ever been. Charlotte had the added joy of indulging her love of children by spoiling the Gardiners' brood shamefully. That Elizabeth did not rearrange the visit served to signal her disinterest in her mother's schemes. The gentleman might come to look at her house whenever it pleased him, and he would doubtless feel more comfortable talking of business matters with her solicitor and her steward, rather than with a gentlewoman. She would be spared the necessity of soothing her mother's vexation.

"I leave that to you, dear Jane," she said, the day before she left, having called at Longbourn to make her farewells at a time she knew her mother would be in Meryton visiting friends and gossiping. "I am sorry to desert you to deal with Mama's nerves, but I do not have your patience and sweet temper."

"You are not sorry at all," Jane retorted, but she was smiling. She tucked her hand into Elizabeth's arm and they took one final promenade around the garden. "But I will not betray you. I will say nothing to Mama about your perfidy."

"You truly are the perfect sister. Mama has the right of it, and you deserve my rich tenant to be your doting husband."

"Mama's solicitude is for our happiness and security. She means well."

"She is concerned for security, certainly. But I will have a care to make sure my sisters find happiness." And Elizabeth kissed Jane and flitted away to farewell her father before her mother and her other sisters knew of her visit.

In all likelihood they passed each other on the road, the widow and the rich young man. The thought amused her all the way to Gracechurch Street.

CHAPTER TWO

A Fair Prospect

Charles Bingley brought his roan to a stop, and leapt from the saddle to stand and stare at Netherfield Park. The house stared back, its windows glinting in the late morning sun. "What do you think, Darcy?"

Fitzwilliam Darcy dismounted from his chestnut, giving the house a more measured look, raking his gaze over the frontage from attic gables to the half windows at ground level. "A handsome place."

Indeed it was a decent-sized, relatively modern building constructed on Palladian lines from mellow stone. A well-balanced tetrastyle portico crowned with a pediment graced the frontage, giving it a rather grand air for its size. The portico was flanked on either side by lofty Venetian windows spilling light into what must be the principal rooms behind. Altogether, a fitting choice for Bingley to take his first taste of country living, should the inside live up to the promise of the elegant exterior.

They had been watched for, it seemed. A groom ran around the side of the house to take their horses. The front door swung open and a man approached, descending the broad stone steps to meet them.

"One of you shall be Mr Bingley, I'm thinking?"

Well, he was a long way from his Scottish home, the burr in his voice softened by distance or time. He was neatly dressed in gentleman-like clothes that were not of the finest quality. Not the owner, then.

Bingley bounced forward with his usual wide, cheerful grin. "I am Bingley. Mr Muir?"

"I am, sir. I am the factor here."

"I am pleased to meet you, Mr Muir." Bingley turned and went on, "Darcy, allow me to present Mr Muir, the steward of Netherfield. Mr Muir, this is Mr Darcy, of Pemberley in Derbyshire, which is a fine estate. He has come to offer me his advice."

They exchanged bows.

"You are both of you very welcome." Muir swept out a hand to indicate the door. "Will you no' come indoors, gentlemen? I have refreshments ordered, and Mr Phillips, Mrs Grayson's legal man, is awaiting us in the smaller drawing room."

They followed Muir up the steps and in through a front door of such capacity they could have ridden in with ease, with plenty of room to admit their horses and without the need to duck their heads. Muir gave them a swift history of the house as they went.

"Old Mr Templeton built it, in the year '60. He owned Nether Park, and gaining the adjoining estate, Lynfield, on his marriage, he combined the two. He tore down the old Nether Park house and Lynfield, and built Netherfield from the stone and brick of the two older places. 'Tis a fine house."

It was indeed. The inner hall was well proportioned, floored and columned with pale marble that lent the space a lightness and airiness. The staircase swept around to the upper levels in a graceful curve that would not have disgraced a mansion of much greater consequence. The paintwork was fresh and clean.

The room to which Muir led them was decorated in a rosy hue that matched Mr Phillips's suspiciously red nose. Darcy hoped for the sake of Mr Phillips's client that insobriety did not affect the lawyer's practice of his trade, but for all the signs of a fondness for strong drink, Mr Phillips was sober as the judge he would surely never be.

The gentlemen shook hands and, the courtesies over, turned to the promised refreshment. Coffee and cakes were a welcome restorative after their long ride from London that morning.

"Mrs Grayson would prefer you take on the staff," Muir said, when Bingley complimented the cook's skill. "But of course, if you have your own domestics to accommodate…"

"I have none. I am just beginning to set up my establishment, although my sister will bring her own maid and I have a manservant, of course. Are the upper servants well recommended? I will retain 'em, if so." Bingley demolished another small cake in a single bite, adding indistinctly, "The cook has a neat hand with sweet things."

"Aye, that she has. Mrs Nicholls is a rare guid cook. Allen and his wife are butler and housekeeper, and have been since old Mr Templeton's time. They are all weel respected, and keep the house in tip-top condition. Mrs Grayson will be fair pleased that you will keep on the senior staff if you take the lease." Muir put down his coffee cup. "Well, sirs, shall we continue?"

Bingley agreed, and secreted a cake or two in his pocket to fortify himself for the ordeal of being shown over a large country house. Darcy would not do such a thing himself, but he owned he was tempted. Mrs Nicholls was mistress of her craft.

The rest of the house had the same understated elegance as the hall and drawing room, having been redecorated by the previous tenant a twelvemonth earlier.

"Although he didnae get the benefit," Muir said. "He came into an unexpected inheritance and vacated early, though he's paid the rent until the quarter day. As ye'll fathom, it's left the house in fair condition for a quick reletting from Michaelmas."

Very fair condition, indeed. As they wandered through the house, Muir continued his history, telling how old Mr Templeton had died more than five years before, in late '06, not long after Muir had come to the estate as steward. "He lost his own child years before and never had another, so he left Netherfield Park to his godson, a Mr Grayson, who wasna known around here. He himself did not live much more than a six-month after inheriting—"

"He died in July '07. A little over six months." Mr Phillips added, "He had no children. He left the place in trust to his widow."

"It has been let ever since," Muir chimed in.

"The widow does not choose to sell?" Bingley asked, with more eagerness than Darcy cared to hear.

"Nae, sir. She is adamant about keeping Netherfield. The estate is no' for sale."

"Then it is odd she has chosen not to live here herself." Darcy turned from his study of the principal bedroom.

"She spent a part of her mourning here, but prefers the dower house in Meryton itself. Nether House. You will have passed it as you came through the town—an older house than this, from Queen Anne's time, set well back from the street behind high walls and a garden. A pretty place, and for all that it is in Meryton, a private one." Over the course of the negotiations, Mr Phillips had proved to be sharp as a tack, dealing with all Darcy's enquiries with a shrewder wit than Darcy had first given him credit for. "Nether House, being smaller, suits her. She has lived there these last four years."

"'Tis but three or four miles," Muir added. "Mrs Grayson is able to care for and visit her tenants just as well from there, and I am on hand in the steward's house if needed."

"Good Lord!" Bingley turned a look of wide-eyed consternation on Darcy. "Visiting tenants is not something I have ever envisaged Caroline doing!"

"Nor she, I would wager."

"There will be little need," Phillips said. "You will have the management of the home farm, Mr Bingley, if you take the house, since it supplies all the victuals for the house and the surplus will go towards its upkeep, but the other farms are outside the lease. You have the liberty of the manor, though, with the right to shoot game in season."

Which remark launched them into a thorough discussion of Bingley's responsibilities and rights as a tenant which lasted until it was almost time to return to Town.

"We will not stay, I thank you," Darcy said when their business was concluded and Phillips offered a noon meal. "We bespoke a quick nuncheon at the White Hart in Meryton as we passed, and will be off as soon as possible. I would like to reach Town tonight."

"Of course, of course." Phillips nodded genially. "And will we hear from you, Mr Bingley?"

"I will have my solicitor contact you, Mr Phillips, within a very few days." Bingley shook hands with hearty good will, and paused in the hall as all four walked towards the door, to turn on his heel in a slow circle and take one last look at the place while their horses were brought around. "It is a very fine house, gentlemen. Very fine."

"And so it is," he said several minutes later, as they rode down the drive to return to Meryton and the quick meal that was all Darcy's timetable would allow them. "I am mostly resolved to take it."

Darcy checked the chestnut's inclination to pirouette. They had been a mere hour inside the house. There was no excuse for Alastor's fidgets. "As Muir said, it is admirably situated for you, with Town barely half a day's journey. It seems a good prospect to give you a taste of what it will mean to be a country gentleman, and yet allow you to visit Town easily."

"I suppose I may profit from the opportunity for learning an estate owner's duties."

"Yes. Even if all you have to practise upon is the home farm, it will give you some insight into the tasks that will face you when you have your own estate. Muir seems a solid enough man, and will help you, I dare say."

"I am such a tyro, the home farm will be more than enough!" Bingley nodded. "Do you think Caroline will like the house?"

Darcy hunched the shoulder nearest Bingley. "It is elegantly set up, and neat. I do not see what she would have to cavil at."

"There will be something. Caroline is nothing if not adept at finding something to be displeased about." Bingley blew out his cheeks in a sigh. "She has already grumbled that Hertfordshire is not the most fashionable of counties."

"There are fashions in counties?" marvelled Darcy, despite himself.

"You are very well aware of my meaning." Bingley added, slyly, "She would never make that complaint of Derbyshire, of course."

"Of course not."

Bingley laughed, and they rode in silence for a mile or two until they were on Meryton High Street, picking their way between dray carts and delivery boys.

Bingley pointed to their left, where a tall, redbrick wall shielded a house from the street. Its roof rose above the wall coping, and at the tall gateway, they paused to look through the scrolled ironwork onto a lovely, roseate house from the time of Queen Anne, set in pretty gardens.

"That must be Nether House," Bingley said. "'Tis but a fraction of the size of Netherfield."

"But as Phillips said, enough for a childless widow. A handsome building."

"The Widow Grayson is a lucky woman to have two such pleasant dwellings in her possession. You know, I think I will rent Netherfield. I wish I could take up the lease before September."

"It is but six weeks. Not worth seeking out the previous tenant and buying the remaining portion of his lease."

"You are right, of course." Bingley gave his roan a gentle nudge with his heels and they walked on towards the inn. "Will you come and stay with me when I am the, albeit temporary, lord of Netherfield Park?"

"I will be glad to."

"Bring Miss Darcy, too, if you like. I dare say she will be glad to get out of Town again."

Hooves echoed briefly as they passed under the inn's archway to the courtyard beyond.

"I will consider it, though she will be back from her holiday at the seaside in a few days and she will have already missed several weeks of attention from her music master." Darcy allowed his mouth to turn up in a smile, as he slid from Alastor's back. "Her other masters too, of course, and I do not wish her to neglect her education. Still, I will mention it to her when I see her—tomorrow evening, God willing. If we get back to Town tonight, I can leave first thing in the morning. I look forward to seeing her again."

"You will forgive me for observing that is understandable, since your sister is far more amiable than mine." Bingley raised a hand as mine host bustled towards them. "Is our nuncheon ready, my good man? Excellent. Lead on!" And to Darcy, "I do not recollect where she is taking the sea air? Caroline did tell me, but I am afraid I cannot remember exactly. Was it Margate?"

"No," said Darcy, following Bingley into the inn's private parlour. "Ramsgate."

CHAPTER THREE

A Cunning Jade

Fitzwilliam Darcy was never the butt of other men's jokes.

He was, after all, Darcy of Pemberley. Rich and well connected, he was reserved in the company of any outside those very few he counted as friends. He did not doubt that the more boisterous in society were amused by his reluctance to make a fool of himself, and perhaps indulged in the odd wager intended to bring him down to their level. The clubs were full of men who counted themselves as wits and wags, who abhorred anything serious or decent.

Now, in his quiet library in the town house on Grosvenor Street, the young man before him colouring and embarrassed, he could only wonder if this current situation was the outcome of one such wager.

The young man in question met Darcy's gaze. "I am not jesting, sir."

"You are a gentleman who wishes to pose as my valet, and yet you are not jesting."

Matthew Grayson, who could not be more than two or three and twenty, flushed a deeper red. "No. I am quite serious. You recall my brother, surely?"

"Of course. James was a very dear friend at Eton, and remained so even though our paths diverged when we left school. He was the best of good fellows."

"He was proud to count you a friend, I know. That is why I am seeking your help, sir. He did not deserve what happened to him!"

Darcy frowned. "What did happen? He was here in England, I know, but I have heard no particulars of his death. I saw him only once after he was injured in battle in the year six, very briefly at your London house. It must have been early August, as I was summoned home to Pemberley a day or so later and arrived just in time to attend my father's deathbed. I was… distracted after that, and had no opportunity to see him again. I wrote once or twice, I remember, with no reply. When I heard of his death, I assumed he had succumbed to his injuries."

"I do not know what happened to him, and that is the rub! I was out of the country when James died." Grayson put down his coffee cup, all the better to run both hands through his hair, fashionably cut *a la Brutus*. "I am making such a mull of this. If I may start again, sir?"

Darcy nodded.

"Thank you. As you know, James was wounded severely enough to be invalided home from Italy after the battle at Maida, although by the time you must have seen him in London he was on the road to recovery." Young Grayson's face scrunched into a grimace. "So my mother tells me. I was in the West Indies. We have some property there that needed attention, and since I had left my school and was in need of some occupation—a university life was not for me!—I went with my father's steward to see to it. My father was lately deceased, and we left the family estate, Graymead Priory, and Mama in her brother's care. My uncle Rufford—the Earl of Rufford, you know—was pleased to take on the charge. I liked the life on Antigua very much, and at my uncle's urging I remained even after James's death and I inherited Graymead. My mother was sorry to have me far from home, but she agreed with her brother. I knew the estate was in good hands, and I was yet underage and could not take command, so… Well, I was content to follow my uncle's advice."

Ah yes. Many a troublesome scion of a wealthy family had been sent to Antigua to cool his heels and his hot head. James had often grimaced and shaken his head when his younger brother was mentioned. The young man had to have been particularly trying to his more sober family members to be sent from home so close upon his father's death, and for his uncle to delay his return.

Grayson's gaze slid away, the blush deepening. "That same year, James unexpectedly inherited a property from his godfather. There was some difficulty about his living at home at Graymead. I know not what the difficulty may have been. My mother says only that he was not himself, and wanted some distance from the family to recover himself. My cousin, Viscount Kirton, told me he had visited James more than once, but had not been made very welcome."

"I had difficulties of my own that year with my father's sudden death, and had no opportunity to visit James. I am sorry for it now. I know Lord Kirton, from my club and Jackson's boxing saloon. A true gentleman."

"Cousin John is a Trojan. Except… but I get ahead of myself. James went to the new property and kept silence for some months, I am told, and the next news heard of him was in the early summer of '07. He was dead." Young Grayson swallowed visibly. "He is supposed to have had a fall on the stairs of his house, and broken his neck on the floor below. Mama was distraught, as you might suppose, and Uncle Rufford and Cousin John went straight to Meryton—"

Darcy nodded, his suspicions confirmed. Though he had not made the connection with the Grayson name five weeks earlier when he and Bingley had viewed Netherfield House, the appearance of this young man was too much of a coincidence to discount. But since Netherfield belonged to a widow now, that meant James must have married… But to do so without a word to his friends? It sounded a most havey-cavey business.

"—and there they found, to their astonishment, that James was married. Some country girl had clapped him up in parson's mousetrap, and he left her the house and lands there. Of course, she is a fortune-hunter, and"—Grayson's tone took on a bitter, angry timbre—"a damned successful one, since she tricked a sick man into marriage! She could not touch Graymead itself, of course, which is a much greater prize, as that is entailed under strict settlement and came to me as James's heir. But she has done very well out of it. Netherfield Park must bring in a clear three thousand a year, perhaps nearer four. She is a wealthy woman now."

"Now I see why you have come to me. Bingley."

"I know of him, and that he is a friend of yours, but I am not acquainted with him myself. I chanced to be at Watier's yesterday, and he was a guest at a nearby table. I overheard him telling of his taking a lease on Netherfield Park. The name caught my attention, as you might imagine. Bingley said you and Miss Darcy intended joining him there next week, when he takes possession."

As indeed Darcy was. But not, now, taking Georgiana with him. Not after Ramsgate. No. Georgiana would remain in London where his uncle, the Earl of Ashbourne, would take good care of her. She could, perhaps, begin to recover in the comforting company of their aunt and her cousin Lilian. She had need of more solace than Darcy himself could give her. He needed it himself. Thank God he had arrived in Ramsgate in time to prevent an elopement that would have been the ruin of her. They had come so close to losing her forever, and the sad pale ghost of a girl existing in Ashbourne House was a shadow of her former self. That devil, Wickham! Damn him!

Darcy had grown accustomed to the sick roiling in his stomach when he thought of Ramsgate and the disaster only narrowly averted there. He did not think any of it showed on his face, and he kept his voice steady and calm. "Yes, I am going to Netherfield Park."

"This is the best opportunity I have to know for certain what happened to James. I cannot be easy about it, Mr Darcy. I cannot be at peace without knowing what that woman was about when James died. I do not deny I harbour suspicions—"

"What do your uncle and cousin say?"

Young Grayson's mouth twisted. "That I should let it lie. That the story is unedifying and not to James's credit. I cannot believe that. Dammit, sir, he was a gentleman and a gallant hero! He was imposed upon somehow by the chit. What use would James have for a penniless girl like that as a wife? He could have had his pick of the Season's beauties—"

Darcy nodded solemn agreement. James had not been a Darcy of Pemberley, to be sure, but had had higher expectations than some red-cheeked country lass. It sounded a most unequal marriage, one that might have materially reduced James's standing were it known. Quite deplorable. "She is not a lady, then?"

Grayson snorted. "From such a neighbourhood? Her father has an estate, I am told, but I know not what it is. Paltry with respect to Netherfield Park, I do not doubt. And after all her machinations, to have cozened John and my uncle so completely... well, it shows how very skilled at deception she is. A cunning jade indeed!"

"Have you met her?"

"No. My mother refuses to countenance her at all and, well, I have not had the opportunity."

"I understand. Do you wish me to ask Bingley to proffer an invitation? That I could do, most willingly, and Bingley is a convivial, obliging character. He would not cavil at you joining us as a guest."

"Thank you, sir, but no. I would like to see her without her knowing who I am, so she may not get the chance to playact as she must have done for John and my uncle. She must not know I am James's brother. I hoped we could find a way for me to be at Netherfield without my identity being known. That will give me the opportunity I need."

"Will Bingley not recognise you, if you have both been to Watier's?"

"I do not think so. I am not always there, and I had my back to him yesterday. It was the name of Netherfield that caught my attention, but I do not think that Bingley noticed me at all. Will you aid me, sir?"

"I will consider it, though I am uncertain about your plan to pose as my valet. Deception does not sit easily with me. Are you sure she will not recognise—" Darcy broke off, and shook his head. The young man before him was as pale-skinned and fair-haired as Bingley, with a stocky build, while James had been taller, thinner, and darker. "No. You do not bear a great resemblance to James."

"I am my mother's image, I am told, favouring the Ruffords, who are all fair. James favoured the Graysons. I think we are sufficiently dissimilar in looks and colouring that she will not realise we were brothers."

"What is her name and family?"

"Elizabeth. Elizabeth Grayson, though I should not grace her with our name. Elizabeth Bennet, as she was."

"And what will you do if you find she had some hand in your brother's death? That is what you fear, is it not? That James died unnaturally."

Young Grayson nodded, his face pulled into the lines of premature age with grief and anger. And guilt, perhaps, at being four years too late to do anything for his elder brother's health and happiness. "If she is responsible for James's death, then she will pay. I will see the damned jade hang."

CHAPTER FOUR

The Widow

"Mr Charles Bingley is a young man from Yorkshire." Uncle Phillips looked up from the parchments spread over his desk, to stare at his niece and her estate steward over the top of round, gold-rimmed spectacles. "Hailing from the town of the same name in the West Riding. He is a man of some substance, although his fortune derives from trade. His forebears made their money in the textile industries then invested in the building of the Leeds and Liverpool Canal."

"They have a lock on the canal named after the family, I believe." Murdoch Muir, Elizabeth's steward, allowed his mouth to lift at one corner into a wry grin. "Or maybe after the town. I dinnae ken which."

"Oh, famous!" Elizabeth returned his smile.

"Of course, I have looked into his references," Uncle Phillips resumed his reading from the papers. "He is worth around five thousand a year and banks with Coutts, who give him a glowing recommendation. His account is in good standing, and he appears to discharge his debts with promptitude. My enquiries have failed to unearth any major financial encumbrance. He is active in society. Not the highest levels, of course, given his roots, but he and his sisters have been participating in the Season for several years now. He is said to be considering making a purchase of an estate to cement his family's progress."

"I will not sell Netherfield."

"We made that clear, ma'am." Mr Muir pursed his lips, thoughtfully. "He is looking on it as a taster of country life, having lived in towns, 'til now."

Elizabeth did wish he would not call her 'ma'am'. It made her feel older than her mother. But Muir had never been able to bring himself to call her 'Miss Elizabeth' as the neighbourhood did. He thought it disrespectful to refer to her by her childhood name, when she was a widow and his employer. She had given it up as a bad job, and now said only, "Good. What else do you know of Mr Bingley, Uncle?"

"He is no longer actively involved in trade. He is a young man, aged four and twenty. Unmarried. I believe a sister will keep house for him."

Elizabeth glanced at Mr Muir. "And he was quite satisfied with the house, and the shooting rights and so on?"

"Oh, aye, ma'am. The companion he brought with him is a gentleman of some considerable property, I understood, and also from the north. A Mr Darcy, who was a very sensible gentleman, if more reserved than Mr Bingley. A little older, I ken. He it was who had all the questions that needed to be answered, while young Mr Bingley concerned himself most about whether the drawing rooms and the grand saloon would meet his sister's demand for fashion." Mr Muir kept a straight face. "I told him that all the public rooms were refurbished by the last tenant only a twelvemonth ago, and the bedrooms a mere three years since. Surely fashion disnae change so quickly?"

"Not here in the country, no," Elizabeth agreed. "But if his sister is desirous of cutting a dash, then Mr Bingley must understand that the charge will rest entirely upon him for changes to the decor of the house."

"Oh, aye, I was clear on that point." Mr Muir gave a decisive nod. "And that anything more substantial than a painter's brush

Papa smirked. "The north is the place for breeding rich young men, it seems. 'Tis a fact of geography."

Elizabeth had no opportunity to reply. The door to the library burst open to admit her mother with all the speed and haste of a bullet from the gun.

"Mr Bennet! Mr Bennet!"

Papa started, dropping his scone face down on his coat. "Good God, what is it? Is the house on fire?"

"House on fire? On fire?" Mama's voice sharpened. "Oh, what nonsense! No, indeed. I hope I am a better manager than to rule a household that might set itself alight at any moment! 'Tis Lizzy's tenant. My sister Phillips tells me he is a rich man from the north. What a fine thing for our girls!"

Papa dabbed at the butter stain with the napkin Lizzy handed him. "How so? How can it affect them?"

Lizzy rose and offered her chair.

Mama threw herself down into it. "How can you be so tiresome! You must know that I am thinking of his marrying one of them."

"Is that his design in settling here?"

Mama fanned herself with her hand. "How can you talk so! His design, indeed. Of course… well, I do not know, but he is a young man and rich and must be in want of a good wife—"

"As are we all," muttered Papa, but either this sally went over his wife's head or she ignored it, as she did so many of his more sarcastic speeches.

"—but it is very likely that he may fall in love with one of the girls, you know. Indeed, I very much wish him for Jane. Therefore you must visit him as soon as he comes."

Papa lifted the napkin and looked ruefully at the greasy stain on his coat. "I see no occasion for that. I have no desire to run hither and yon to court young paragons for my daughters. Let them come here, if they wish to marry. I do not doubt the girls will welcome them."

"But you must consider Jane! It would be a wonderful establishment—"

"As Lizzy can attest, since it is hers."

"Do listen to me, Mr Bennet. You may count upon it that the Lucases will visit on that account, and the Longs, and the Harringtons. Not to mention the Gouldings—"

"You do not mean to name all our neighbours, I hope, Mrs Bennet?"

"They will all see Mr Bingley before we do, if you do not stir yourself on your daughters' behalf. You have no compassion for my poor nerves."

"No, no! You are quite mistaken there. I have a very high respect for them. They are my old friends."

"Oh, you delight in vexing me!"

"I do, I own."

"Papa," Elizabeth said softly, but it was a mistake to have drawn attention to herself.

Mama's glare would burn iron. "You are no better, Missy! You should have met him when he came here to see the house, and we could have stolen a march upon all those who have unmarried girls to turn off! He is your tenant. You must do what you can to put Jane in his way. You should have been there."

"I could not meet him, Mama. Gentlemen do not do business with ladies, and you would not want to give him a disgust of our family before he even meets Jane. There will be opportunity enough to make his acquaintance. I have no doubt Sir William will introduce us all at the next assembly."

"I have no reliance on that at all. He will try to secure Mr Bingley for his own two plain-faced girls. As if Charlotte Lucas compares to my dear Jane! Heavens, Lizzy, she cannot compare even to you."

"That is not kind, Mama. Charlotte has very pleasant looks."

"And you vex me as much as your father, sitting in here with him and smirking at my efforts to establish you all creditably. When he is dead and his cousin Mr Collins turns us all out into the hedgerows because of that wicked, wicked entail, you will not be smirking then!"

"Indeed, Mama, you know very well that you will always have a home as long as I have Netherfield Park and Nether House."

"I believe your mother regrets the loss of the hedgerows," Papa remarked. "They added such distinction to her complaints."

Mama's nostrils flared. "For once and for all, will you visit Mr Bingley when he takes possession of Netherfield?"

"It is more than I engage for."

Mama took a deep, wavering breath and stood, smoothing down her skirts with both hands. Her mouth was pulled into a hard and unforgiving line. "Well, then. When Charlotte Lucas steals our daughter's rightful husband, do not say I did not tell you so."

"Depend upon it, I will not."

And on that final dismissal from her husband, Mama flounced out as energetically as she had flounced in.

Elizabeth regained her seat opposite her father, and picked up her cup of tea. It was sadly cooled, but she sipped at it anyway. Tea could not be wasted. "You will visit him, I assume."

"A day or two past Michaelmas, I think. We must give him time to look about him a little, though not too much time and allow Sir William the victory. One scone remaining. Pass me the jam, Lizzy, and I will consent to share it with you."

CHAPTER FIVE

An East Wind

September continued wet, and the Michaelmas Quarter Day dawned with a violent tempest. Flashes of lightning, rolls of thunder and the heavy pounding of rain threaded through the entire day, increasing in ferocity by evening and bringing a gale as vicious as if it were winter's winds biting at the land rather than the mere tail end of summer.

After dinner, Elizabeth and Charlotte ensconced themselves in the drawing room of Nether House, sitting close over the fire. They were, Charlotte remarked, quite cosy even though the wind made the chimney smoke. Just as Elizabeth opened her mouth to agree, a loud bang sounded above her head followed by a deep rumble as if a dozen cannonballs were rolling down the roof. Another crash, even louder, and a cloud of soot and smoke billowed into the room, accompanied by the rattle of stones and falling masonry. All the candles were snuffed out in an instant.

Letting out a shriek that she would later deny had ever passed her lips, Elizabeth leapt up to grasp at Charlotte, and together they plunged towards the door through the choking darkness. Elizabeth flung open the door and she and Charlotte fell through into the

wind was just too much for it. We have a hole in the roof big enough to put a carriage through. The rain's not letting up yet, either, and what the roof didn't bring down with it, the rain will. The attic floor is sopping." Thomas jerked his head towards the door. "I had a quick look outside, but it's fair dark now."

"Oh," was all Elizabeth found to say.

"Miss Lucas's room is pretty dirty with some of the mess that came down to you in there." Thomas nodded in the direction of the drawing room. "Your room's fine on the west side—"

"What about the girls' quarters?" Elizabeth's hands ached. When she glanced down at them, she was wringing out a towel so tightly it was turning on itself. She put it down, and stretched out her fingers. "From what you say, the floor above the main bedrooms is the one likely to suffer the most damage."

"The ceilings won't hold against the wet. Any room on the east side of the house better not be slept in tonight, and that's the truth."

"Oh," Elizabeth said again. Just for a moment, she was almost overset with the longing to be no more than Miss Elizabeth Bennet again, the carefree second daughter of the local squire with no responsibilities for anything and anybody other than herself and her ties to her family. Netherfield Park and everything associated with it had brought nothing but anxiety and heartache. Her chest squeezed tight again, as if she were trapped in a carpenter's vice.

She blew out a long breath and straightened up. The Rances had two rooms on the ground floor of the kitchen wing and would be safe from harm or damage. The three maids, though, all slept on the floor beneath the attics, and from the looks of alarm on their faces, were worrying about their belongings. It was the work of a moment to send them upstairs to move Charlotte into one of the guest rooms on the west side, and themselves and all they possessed into the other. The maids would be crowded, but safe.

Elizabeth finished her instructions with "As soon as you can, Thomas, send a message to Mr Muir."

"I'll walk down to the White Hart afore bed, and get them to send their young 'un first thing. He can call in at Longbourn on the way back and tell Squire Bennet. I was thinking Mr Muir'll likely have to send to St Albans. There's no builder closer as can handle such a big job. At the least, we'll need some tarred canvas to cover the hole and stop the worst of the wet."

Elizabeth sighed and nodded.

"Come through to the sitting room, Miss Elizabeth. Everything will be better with a morsel of tea inside you, and some of my fruitcake." Mrs Rance ushered Elizabeth and Charlotte through to the large room that did duty as the servants' sitting and dining room, and sat them at the scrubbed pine table. She served them tea shortly after, bringing a bottle with her and putting a generous splash of brandy into each cup. "Settles the nerves, it does. Medicinal like."

"Give some to the girls, too. They will need it. This is a horrid mess to clear up."

"Don't you worry, Miss Elizabeth. They'll have their share and we'll all do well enough tonight. We can't do a mite of work to clean up until the rain's kept on the outside where it belongs. Tomorrow's soon enough to think about that."

"I would rather not think about it at all," Elizabeth said, when Mrs Rance left them alone. "Dear heavens! The house is a calamitous mess and it will be even worse by morning. I cannot even begin to think—"

"Then do not." Charlotte sipped her tea, brightening visibly as the brandy did its work. "As the Good Book has it, sufficient unto the day is the evil thereof. While the message from our Lord could have been expressed with more clarity, I believe He intends us to know that you may give way to anxiety tomorrow. Tonight we give thanks that no one is hurt."

"The rector would tell you to take Holy Writ as it is… well, writ." Elizabeth managed a faint smile, then sighed. "This will be expensive. It is likely to wipe away the gains I should have made by leasing out Netherfield. I can only hope I do not have to touch my reserves."

"Tomorrow, Eliza. Today's evil is enough." Charlotte scowled, lifting one hand to scratch vigorously at her scalp. "Goodness! I have more soot in my hair than seems possible from only one chimney!"

"I know. Mine is the same. My sister Mary would say ruined hair is a judgement on me for defying propriety and convention by refusing to wear a widow's cap, but it seems unfair that you should share my punishment."

Charlotte's laugh lacked its usual hearty good cheer. She reached for the plate of fruitcake Mrs Rance had left on the table. "We must look for the gold in all this dross. Only consider, you can rebuild the chimney so it does not smoke."

Elizabeth stared, and before she could prevent it, the burning, choking tightness surged up into her throat and nose. "Oh Charlotte! My little house... I have felt so safe here and... and happy, despite everything. And now... Now it... My pretty room... Oh Charlotte!"

She pushed her face into her hands to try and hold back the sobs. Misery and strain snorted out of her, making her shoulders shake. Charlotte allowed her to cry for a moment or two, then pushed a fresh cup of tea across the table top. Elizabeth gulped and choked, and stammered out an apology, despising her own weakness. Once she had vowed never to allow herself to be powerless again, never to allow control to slip away. And yet here she was, worse than a veritable watering pot.

"Forgive me. I am being such a fool! No one is hurt, and that is all that matters. Everything else is reparable. I am such a ninny, turning into Mama with her nerves!"

Charlotte, dear, kind Charlotte, took Elizabeth's hand and pressed it. "We are all permitted moments to grieve. This is your haven. Your own philosophy helps here, you know. Look for the brightness, however small, in the clouds." Charlotte squeezed her hand again and released it, sitting back and picking up her refilled tea cup. "For instance, Mrs Rance left the brandy, and there is now a considerable amount of it in your cup. Drink up. Everything will be better in the morning."

"Or I shall be so overcome with drink, the morning will be infinitely worse!" But Elizabeth picked up her cup, and took a healthy, and very unladylike, swig. "If the roof and chimney need to be rebuilt, I fear the house will be uninhabitable and very dirty for some time."

"Yes. I had better go to Lucas Lodge, and you to Longbourn. We will look on it as our usual Christmas arrangement, brought in a little early."

"Three months early!" Elizabeth's chest tightened again, and she rubbed a hand against her breastbone. Longbourn, almost certainly for some weeks. How was it to be borne? The noise, her mother's fidgets... she sighed, then brightened, because Jane and her father would be there.

"I shall find it hard to return to being merely the eldest, unmarried daughter at Lucas Lodge."

"Yes." Elizabeth found herself looking at her hands again. "It is a diminishment, a return to places where we are dependent and insignificant. I hope I can bear the irritation with grace."

"A state of dependency is my lot, unless I marry and secure an establishment of my own. I am not sure that I regret a husband so much as the chance for children. Since, sadly, the children are consequent upon the husband, I will likely have neither."

"You will always have a home with me."

"But you are very young still and you may yet remarry. My life is narrower. The only remedy for ladies of our class is marriage and that is unlikely now. I will make the best of it, but I do sorely rue how confined and... and lacking my future may be."

"Charlotte—"

"You have greater immediate vexations in having to give up your own establishment, even if just for a while." Charlotte's sly smile was back, and her shaken head told Elizabeth she would not discuss this further. "I quite understand you would wish Mr Bingley to perdition until, perhaps the Christmas quarter day. We could have returned to living at Netherfield."

"I do not like Netherfield." Elizabeth pleated the soft muslin of her dress between her fingers. "I suppose Longbourn is the better option, though I abhor its noise and busyness."

"And living again with the family."

Charlotte understood all too well. Elizabeth could not match her smile for smile, but they nodded at each other.

"Yes. You know what I fear in this prospect of spending so many weeks in my father's house."

She left it unsaid. Charlotte leant forward to put her hand on Elizabeth's shoulder.

Living in Longbourn for any length of time would test Elizabeth's fortitude to the utmost. She would have to guard her tongue, and show nothing of what she felt. For even after almost five years, she feared that she would never forgive her mother.

Never.

CHAPTER SIX

Madam, Will You Dance?

By the time she dressed for the assembly, Elizabeth had been at Longbourn for three days.

In some ways, she had fitted back into the household as if she had never been married and widowed, as if she had never left. She slept in the bedroom that had been hers since she left the nursery. She was her father's confederate and the sharer of his sardonic amusements. But to her mother she was still the daughter who was not as beautiful as Jane or as good-humoured as Lydia, and she had been greeted with a careless press of Mama's cheek against hers, and "Well, what a to-do! And so you are back with us for some weeks. Well, that is how it must be, your father says."

Jane, of course, had welcomed her with open arms, embraces and murmured sympathy at her plight. It was a delight to spend more of her day with Jane. Mary had smiled a welcome, but soon returned to her reading—Fordyce's sermons, again. Lydia and Kitty met her mostly with indifference, but not meant, she thought, in any spiteful way. It was purely that Longbourn had ceased to be her home when Lydia was ten, and Kitty not quite twelve. The younger girls did not know her well.

The day she arrived, Lydia and Kitty had blown in with all the vigour of the previous night's storm, having spent the morning in Meryton with their mother's sister, Aunt Phillips.

"Here you are, Lizzy!" Lydia bounced at Elizabeth to bestow a hasty kiss on her cheek. "Are you quite ruined?"

"Ruined?" Elizabeth turned to greet Kitty with a smile and a kiss.

"Aunt Phillips said it will cost a great deal to repair Nether House," Kitty said. "It looks quite dreadful from the street, you know."

Elizabeth did indeed know. Her poor little house! "It will be expensive, but I do not believe the poorhouse awaits me quite yet."

"Captain Carter and Lieutenant Denny escorted us to see it." Lydia bounced away from Elizabeth to drop into a chair, and only straightened, slowly and reluctantly, when Jane suggested in her habitual mild tone, that Lydia should be mindful of her deportment and posture. "We looked from the street. Thomas would not let us through the gate, which I thought was very high-handed in a servant."

"I was not receiving visitors, Lydia. No great surprise, after all." Elizabeth gave her a sharp look. "You have not said anything to the officers about me, I hope?"

"La, no, but I do not doubt they will find out soon enough. After all, they know now that you live at Nether House." And with her usual carelessness, Lydia turned away to relay her aunt's gossip to their mother. "Mama! Did you hear that Mr Bingley will attend the assembly with a party of twelve ladies and seven gentlemen? Sir William told Mr Harrington, and Mrs Morris overheard and told her servant, who told our aunt's maid. Is that not a pity? Far too many ladies! It would be much better the other way, you know."

Elizabeth was apparently forgotten. She did not repine.

She met Charlotte inside the assembly rooms. Neither had any need to say anything: a glance and a shared, rueful smile was enough.

"This too shall pass," Charlotte said. "John is likely to ask you for the first dance."

"He often does."

"Yes, but Mama is becoming more insistent. She feels that Netherfield would do nicely to cement the family's position in the gentry."

Elizabeth only smiled. She and John Lucas were of one mind on that subject, and she accepted his petition for the first set without a qualm. They talked with the ease of old friends throughout the two country dances, their chatter interrupted only by the demands of the dance.

The Netherfield party arrived as the first set ended. Elizabeth, rosy with the effort required by the second, more energetic, dance of the pair, had made her way to Jane's side when the assembly room doors were flung wide by the enthusiastic footmen and the Bingleys entered.

Despite the rumours of many ladies and gentlemen, they were a party of merely five—Mr Bingley and his two sisters, a Mr Hurst who was the husband of the elder, and another young man, tall and darkly handsome, whispered to be Mr Darcy.

"Mr Muir told me he came with Mr Bingley to view the place," Elizabeth said to Jane, while behind them Lydia was loudly proclaiming her relief at the small number of ladies in the party and bemoaning the paucity of gentlemen.

Sir William bustled forward to greet the newcomers with all the fulsome courtesy at his disposal.

"They are very fine." Jane turned an admiring gaze to the ladies' exquisite clothes. "Those dresses... such rich silks, and wonderful colour. And so much lace."

"And feathers. They have a great many feathers. Yes, very fine birds indeed."

"You have gowns as fine, Lizzy. Are you envious?"

"I have one or two, of last year's fashion. But no, I am not envious." Elizabeth laughed softly. "I would not wear such finery to a simple country assembly, lest my neighbours think I believe myself above my company."

Jane smiled and demurred. "You could never believe that!"

It was entirely possible she took Elizabeth's words at face value, and Elizabeth did not persist. She continued to think however, that the Bingley ladies were overdressed for the occasion, probably with deliberation and forethought, and she smoothed down her own pretty, embroidered muslin while thinking ruefully of those one or two grander dresses in her closet.

Mr Bingley returned Sir William's greeting with grace and courtesy, introducing his companions. The Bingley party wore their best company manners along with their fine London clothes, but it was very soon apparent that all the true amiability belonged to Mr Bingley himself. His sisters talked to each other behind their fans, but those pretty trifles—also befeathered, Elizabeth noted— were insufficient to hide the sneer from one and the anxious, down-turned mouth of the other: the Bingley ladies were not pleased by their new neighbours and the social delights offered by the town. Mr Hurst went straight to explore the possibilities of the punchbowl set out at the side of the room, and Mr Darcy stalked about, unwilling, it seemed, to speak to, or even acknowledge, anyone else in the room. He had not escaped an introduction to Sir William, but he was adroit at avoiding everyone else. Elizabeth felt a flash of sympathy, for whispers of his income and prospects were flying about the room faster than he could outstalk them, but it was tempered by his obvious disinclination for company and disdain of his surroundings.

She turned away and held out a hand for Edmund Harrington to take as he led her into the second set of the evening. A few yards away, Charlotte joined the dancers, her hand in Mr Bingley's, and she and Elizabeth exchanged warm smiles. In the distance, Mama fanned herself with indignant vivacity, and turned away from a triumphant Lady Lucas. Elizabeth could only laugh and give all her attention to the intricate steps she and Edmund trod through a hornpipe. Poor Mama!

Somewhat later, Mr Bingley, who had danced the third set with Jane, asked Jane for the supper set as well, showing obvious enjoyment and an admiration that warmed Elizabeth's heart. Still he found a moment to take Mr Darcy to task. The latter had continued his disapproving striding around the room throughout the assembly. "You had much better dance, Darcy. There is a preponderance of ladies here, and it would be a neighbourly kindness."

Since she was nearby, forced to sit out the current dance due to the lack of partners, Elizabeth heard, and could only applaud, this amiable suggestion.

Mr Darcy, however, would have nothing of it. "Certainly not. At such an assembly as this, with people such as these, when I am particularly acquainted with none of them and dislike dancing so much? No. Insupportable. Your sisters are engaged, and I will dance with no one else. There is not another woman in the room with whom it would not be a punishment."

"Good Lord, you are far too fastidious! There are many pleasant girls here this evening. I never met with so many in my life. All fresh and charming, and some are very pretty indeed."

"You are dancing with the only handsome girl in the room." Mr Darcy turned his gaze towards Jane as she awaited her partner with a patience only Jane could possess when the two fiddles and the viol were limbering up for *The Countess of Pembroke's Fancy*.

"Lord, yes! Miss Bennet. The most beautiful creature, is she not? Utterly divine. One of her sisters is sitting just behind you, who is very pretty too. Do let me ask Miss Bennet to introduce you."

"Whom do you mean?" Mr Darcy turned and looked at Elizabeth. They exchanged glances, but the instant he saw he had caught her eye he turned away again. "Tolerable, I suppose, but certainly not handsome enough to tempt *me*. I will not give consequence to young ladies slighted by other men. I am not in the humour for it, and not so altruistic."

"I am wasting my time, I see. I shall return to my partner, and leave you to your scowls. At least Miss Bennet smiles, Darcy. You might try it."

And with this, Mr Bingley returned to Jane's side and led her into the lines of dancers. Mr Darcy walked off in the opposite direction.

How mortifying to have her mother's opinion of her inferiority to Jane so carelessly confirmed by a stranger. How ungentlemanly, for him to say so aloud where any might overhear! Elizabeth looked around, seeking signs that others had indeed heard Mr Darcy's damning opinion, half expecting commiserating looks or sniggers only partially hidden by fans. Nothing. Perhaps only she had been close enough. Well, it was a striking example of eavesdroppers learning no good of themselves, though in her own defence it had been most unwittingly done.

When she found Charlotte and relayed Mr Darcy's words, however, she contrived to laugh, adding, "It is as well I do not seek his good opinion, and I am confident I do not require his notice to enhance whatever consequence I have."

"Indeed not!" Charlotte said, stoutly. "Poor Eliza! Only tolerable."

"I wonder if our proud Mr Darcy realises how much he is in harmony with my mother's opinion, and what he would say to finding himself in confederacy with her. I wonder if that would prick his pride? I cannot deny he pricked mine."

She and Charlotte looked from Mr Darcy, who stood across the room staring at them, his face dark and forbidding, to Mama fluttering around and blessing herself and loudly proclaiming Jane's triumph in attracting Mr Bingley's notice. And this time when Elizabeth laughed, she meant it. Most heartily.

CHAPTER SEVEN

Deceit Is My Abhorrence

Matthew Grayson arrived at Darcy's house after breakfast, hefting a small trunk out of the hackney that had conveyed him to Grosvenor Street.

Darcy eyed the trunk and Grayson with a similar sense of foreboding, but he was committed now. "Bingley is expecting me sometime after midday. He knows I have confidential business in the area and you will be acting as my temporary secretary. As we agreed, I gave your name as Saville."

Grayson merely nodded. He had said, when Darcy had agreed to this mad venture, that it was his mother's family name, given to him as his second name, and familiar since his family often called him that in fun. All Darcy could promise at the time was that he would endeavour to make it sound easy and unforced, while earnestly hoping Grayson would think better of the scheme. Sadly Grayson had not, and Darcy's foreboding grew as they settled into the coach, riding through the jerk as the horses started off.

"Thank you," Grayson said.

"Do not thank me. You will indeed be acting as my secretary, and I have a deal of correspondence from Pemberley at this time of year. That way I can, to some extent, salve my conscience." Darcy allowed his amusement to show. "You seem suitably dressed for your role."

Grayson looked the part, indeed, in clothes that appeared to ape those of a gentleman without being of the finest fabrics and cut, nor being in the first stare of fashion. "These are things I had made while in the West Indies." Grayson plucked at his jacket, pleating the sober black superfine with his fingers. "The tailors there did the best they could, but of course they were unable to keep abreast of the most recent fashions nor to command the finest materials. The clothes are serviceable enough, I suppose. I cannot think why I did not dispose of them when I came home, but they serve their turn now."

"Yes. Your clothing gives the effect of someone who dresses to the best of his means, and who cannot shuffle off good garments because of a trifling change in fashion. Precisely what I would expect of someone born of a minor landed family—a third or fourth son, perhaps, required to make his own way in the world. A fitting explanation of your role as a secretary. Do you have evening dress of the same stamp?"

"I do."

"Excellent. Then provided you can keep your pride in check and accept the condescension and patronage of those who will believe themselves your betters, you should carry this off."

"I am grateful for your help, Darcy, whether you wish to be thanked or no."

"*Mr* Darcy." Darcy smiled at Grayson's quizzical look. "I am to be your employer. I am not an unreasonable one, I hope, but I do expect you to be respectful in front of the Bingley family, otherwise this enterprise will fail before it can start. You have a part to play and you need to practise."

Grayson smiled widely and nodded. "Mr Darcy." His smile faded. "It will make it more difficult for me to see her, perhaps."

"I will try to ensure that you attend some social functions. Do you have a likeness of her?"

"No. Nothing." Grayson huffed, his mood changed. "Look for the over-dressed fortune-hunter flaunting her ill-gotten wealth. I have no doubt she is shameless enough."

"There are many who show no restraint in their spending," Darcy said. Bingley's sister, for one, measured social success in ells of silk and the curl of ostrich feathers. "I take it she is of my age?"

"Younger. She is one and twenty, I believe."

One and twenty? But she had married James Grayson five years earlier. Five years! She had been only sixteen? Georgiana was barely that, a child on the cusp of womanhood and disconcerted by both states, one moment a merry girl—or she had been, before Wickham—and the next putting on the airs of a matron twenty years her senior. Even if Elizabeth Grayson had been more at ease, more confident, than was Georgiana, Darcy found it hard to believe such a young girl could be a practised, predatory fortune-hunter who threw all thoughts of decency and morality aside to catch herself a rich husband.

Darcy sat back and regarded the young man on the seat opposite. There was a petulance to the downturned mouth that the easy smiles of earlier had hidden. Well, he was committed now, but without consideration and proof of wrongdoing, he would not be rushed into a hasty judgement of the widow Grayson. No matter how much her brother-in-law wanted it.

He took his book, and with a nod at Grayson, applied himself to reading it. Apart from their short stop, they had precious little conversation. Darcy read, Grayson stared moodily at the sights of the Great North Road.

Darcy stirred just short of their journey's end, and gestured out of the coach window. "Meryton. A small market town of no great significance."

"It must be quite a dozen miles from the Great North Road." Grayson shifted uncomfortably.

The roads from Hatfield had been damnably rough, riddled with potholes that had even Darcy's well-sprung carriage lurching from side to side in places. They were better on the approach to larger villages, but out in the open countryside, the surfaces were furrowed with ruts only partially filled with broken stones.

"Netherfield is some three miles farther on."

Grayson turned to him. "She lives here, you said?"

"There, on the right. The wall bounds the garden. It is a handsome old hou—" Darcy broke off. Frowned.

The ruin of Nether House's roof was starkly visible from the road, the forlorn remains of a chimney stack clawing up out of an expanse of tarred canvas.

"The storm on Wednesday, perhaps. The house was undamaged when I saw it several weeks ago."

Grayson blew out a hard breath. "Damnation! While I am indifferent to any vexation my brother's widow may have, I had hoped that at least we would be able to find her easily when it came to confronting her. I doubt she will be living there, not with such damage."

"You said she has family nearby? Perhaps she is with them. We can do nothing until enquiries are made." Darcy settled back against the seat squabs. "I have no doubt that such an occurrence will be a topic of much conversation and speculation. Mrs Grayson's whereabouts are most likely well known." He observed Grayson in silence for a moment or two, noting the younger man's flinch at his mentioning the widow by name.

No matter. Little as Grayson liked the appellation, it was one the woman carried. Darcy returned to his book for this final leg of their journey, but he stared at the pages without ever turning one. It would be up to him and Grayson to determine if she deserved the honour. He hoped he would judge fairly. It was the least he owed his old schoolfellow.

Quite the last thing Darcy wanted on his arrival at Netherfield Park was to find Bingley almost vibrating with excitement, eager to throw himself into the social life of his new neighbourhood. Darcy had been on the road from London for over three hours with only a short stop to rest his horses and take a bite to eat, and he had hoped for a quiet evening with his friends. That, it appeared, was not to be. Bingley had accepted an invitation for the entire Netherfield party to attend the Meryton assembly that night, despite having been in the country a bare three days. An assembly! In such a district, with no knowledge of the kind of people who lived there... Bingley was quite incorrigible. After a journey during which he had become increasingly uneasy about the deception he was to practise, Darcy was unsure he had the fortitude to cope with Bingley at his most ebullient.

Despite his protests, Darcy found himself following Bingley into the Meryton Assembly rooms that evening, dressed in clothes that, given the stares and whispers of the population, were somewhat finer than this simple country dance normally saw. He was, of course, attired correctly in pale breeches, silk stockings and dark coat. Most the men present were; only not with similar quality. As he had expected, the Bingley women had dressed as if for a society ball or Almacks—not that they had the entree to the latter, given their origins in trade. With their feathers, even the shorter Louisa contrived to look tall and richly elegant; and against the muslins and cambrics worn by the local women, they looked like tropical parrots.

"Goodness," Caroline Bingley breathed in his ear. "Look at them! Those dresses are at least two years out of date!"

To this he made no answer, but flattened his *chapeau-bras* hat and jammed it under his arm, allowing Bingley to lead the party across the dance floor to where a local worthy waited to welcome them with such fulsome periods as to make Darcy envy young Grayson who was kicking his heels back at Netherfield. Grayson had been disconcerted to find himself overlooked for the high treat of a country assembly. The Bingleys had no idea of his joining them, and at this early stage of the venture, Darcy would not upset their preconceived notions of the proper place for a secretary. Young Mr "Saville" had been told to remain and make what subtle enquiries he could of the upper servants without raising suspicion, while Darcy sallied grimly forth to make merry with the local populace.

"Goodness," Miss Bingley said again, when they were released at last by Sir William Lucas, for such was the verbose gentleman's name.

"Indeed." Darcy glanced toward the dais where several musicians sat and scraped at their violins. Duty called him.

He bowed, and offered his hand for the set of two country dances, just then forming. She simpered and accepted. He endured the dance as well as he could, and, returning her to her sister's side, adroitly avoided several of the local matrons and their daughters. He retired to the edge of the room in order to survey it undisturbed.

He was methodical about it, studying each woman in turn. Most were fresh-cheeked country maidens, clear skinned and bright eyed with good health and energy. Some had far too much energy. That pair of chits cavorting with the militia officers should still be in the schoolroom. Only in a country assembly would children be allowed to display such atrocious, improper behaviour. The tall one with corkscrews of silvery-blonde hair laughed loud enough to put a neighing horse to shame and gambolled about like a colt. She looked to be of an age with Georgiana. He would be mortified if his sister flouted propriety in such a way.

He tightened his mouth against the knowledge that Georgiana had almost done far, far worse than dance boisterously in the top-floor rooms of a country inn. It was by the grace of God alone that the very worst had not taken place. She was injured, but unsullied; heartbroken, but still pure. He could only hope Aunt Ashbourne could help her as he could not.

He pushed it all to one side, and raked his gaze over the room again. With no real idea of Mrs Grayson's appearance, and only her brother-in-law's prejudice to guide him, he looked for a woman who used rich silks and laces to glory in both her dubious marital conquest and, presumably, her widowhood. No such person revealed herself. There were matrons aplenty in the richer, darker hues appropriate to their married state, but none with the youth he understood Mrs Grayson to possess. Naught but unsophisticated country girls in simple muslin dresses. Bingley was making a cake of himself over the only outstanding beauty in the room, who, since society was wild for tall, willowy blondes, could take London by storm. She was the right sort of age, but as simply dressed as the other girls and not sporting a widow's cap. It was unlikely she was the one he sought. Given the damage to her house, it was, perhaps, likely the widow was not present. In which case, this assembly was even more a waste of his time than he had feared.

He danced once more, this time with Louisa Hurst, and his stultifying duty done again, returned to his retreat against the wall. Just before the supper set, Bingley importuned him to dance more. Did Bingley truly know him? At an assembly such as this, it would be insupportable, an absolute punishment to dance with such rustics. He rejected Bingley, and the lady to whom his friend threatened to introduce him, in the firmest, most unequivocal terms.

Bingley shook his head. "You are a bear at times, my friend. I shall return to my partner. Miss Bennet is an angel, Darcy."

"Yes, yes. Of course she is. When have you ever not discovered an angel, even in such uncelestial places as this? Return to her smiles, Bingley, and leave me be. I will not dance again tonight, making merry with these people."

"Miss Bennet is far more congenial company than you in such a temper. I shall leave you directly," Bingley said, and walked back towards the beauty at something faster than his normal pace.

"Good Lord," Darcy murmured. "A puppy could not be more eager."

He turned away, catching the expression on the rejected lady's face as he did so, and for an instant, he faltered. Had she heard him?

He watched her for several minutes. She turned her face away, presenting her profile to him, and she persisted in avoiding his gaze. When she rose and went to join another, slightly older, lady on the other side of the room, he concluded that he had been a little hasty in describing her to Bingley as unhandsome. She was pretty enough, he supposed, in the fresh country manner, and moved with lightness and grace. She was the right age, but as with most of the ladies, she wore no cap and dressed unpretentiously.

He glanced to where Bingley danced with his beauty. Wait! Miss Bennet, Bingley had said, had he not? The widow's family name. The matrons were gathered in a gossiping group near the tables set out with the evening's repast. He moved closer. Yes. That one was the Bennet mother, a typically brash, husband-hunting virago with more hair than wit, loud with boasts of her daughter dancing with Bingley. He had escaped further introductions to the daughters she had called to her side when Sir William had taken Darcy and Bingley over to her. Perhaps that had been a mistake.

He blew out a sigh and glanced again at the Bennet sister with whom he had refused to dance. She and her friend turned and both looked boldly and directly at him, and shared a laugh. They were not laughing at him, surely? They would not dare. He watched them for some time, but could not fathom the topic of their conversation. It was an amusing one, in all events.

"An opportunity missed," he said aloud, though softly, not to be overheard. "I should have danced with the beauty's less handsome sister, and asked about the widow."

Subtly, of course.

"What an appalling way to spend an evening." Caroline Bingley sank gracefully into a chair in the smaller of Netherfield's saloons, where a light repast awaited the revellers returning from the assembly. "What a collection of unfashionable, rustic oddities!"

"Too true, my dear," Louisa Hurst murmured, but then, of course she would support her sister. They were hand in glove, those two, always, Miss Bingley being the dominant hand shaping Mrs Hurst's pliant nature, glove-like, to her benefit.

"Barely a handsome woman amongst them, too!"

That stirred Bingley. "Oh I say! Miss Bennet—"

"I grant you she is a prettyish sort of girl," Miss Bingley conceded. "But sadly unfashionable. So simply dressed!"

"She smiles too much," Darcy said.

Miss Bingley simpered to show her approval. "I thought so too, sir! I understand her sisters are accounted beauties."

"I thought they were charming, indeed. All the ones I met, from eldest to youngest. Although Darcy was of a different opinion when I tried to introduce him to one sister." Bingley smirked.

In Darcy's mind's eye, a bright, laughing face turned towards him. Laughing at him, he was sure of it now. She had been mocking him. Making sport of him. Such disgraceful impudence! How dare she! Did she not know who he was? She was barely fit to be called a gentlewoman, certainly not of his standing, and she dared—! "She a beauty? I would as soon call her mother a wit."

Miss Bingley and Mrs Hurst tittered in the polite, restrained way women of the *Ton* had of showing their amusement. The Bennet girl had laughed heartily. The Bennet girl had none of the tiresomely refined manners of the *Ton*.

"The mother is dreadful," Mrs Hurst agreed.

"So are the younger sisters." Caroline pinched her mouth into an unattractive moue. "They were far too loud. Did you see them romping like children, flirting with all the officers and gentlemen? So coarse."

Bingley tut-tutted, shaking his head. "I will not dispute with you because I do not like argument, particularly after a tiring night's dancing. But I will say that country manners are not the same as Town and I do not expect them to be. I found our neighbours to be simple and charming, and we must not forget that they gave us a kind, hearty welcome. There were many lovely girls, even the youngest ones, who may have been high-spirited but appeared to be cheerful and good-natured. And Darcy, I thought Miss Bennet's sister Elizabeth to be very pretty, indeed." He jumped up, giving an exaggerated yawn. "I am for bed, and will leave you to your disputes. Goodnight!"

He was gone before his sisters could do no more than utter a protesting "Charles!", while Darcy could only look after him in chagrin.

Elizabeth? Truly? The one who laughed at gentlemen who were far above her?

That was the widow?

CHAPTER EIGHT

Town Bronze

"Well, I have seen her. We were not introduced." Darcy forbore to explain why. "She was referred to as Miss Elizabeth, not Mrs Grayson."

"She does not use my brother's name?"

"I cannot say. She dressed as simply as an unmarried girl, and when our party was introduced to the local dignitaries on our arrival, she was not among them."

Grayson's snort conveyed his opinion.

"I would have expected that she would be." Darcy sharpened his tone. "Netherfield Park is the most prestigious property around Meryton and as its owner, she must rank as one of the foremost gentlewomen in the town. Yet she did not push forward to be introduced. "

"A pity you did not speak to her," Grayson said.

Darcy regretted that himself. "There will be other opportunities. Now I know which she is, I will ensure it."

Grayson had been waiting in the sitting room attached to Darcy's bedroom, eager to learn what Darcy had discovered. Now he pulled down the corners of his mouth and brooded in a manner that would put Mrs Siddons to shame. "Does she pretend to be a maiden to cozen more men into her coils, do you think?"

"I have no notion. She is popular, with open and cheerful manners. She danced most sets, but I saw no flirtatious or improper behaviour." Darcy considered a moment. Not from her, in any event, although the younger Bennet girls had been unrestrained in their enthusiasm for Cupid's games. Perhaps the elder sister had merely learned discretion as she matured. "What did you learn here?"

Grayson cast off his Tragedy Jill airs. His expression suggested he was pleased with himself. "I dined with the upper servants, maintaining my guise of a poor, but genteel, young man eager to gain his new master's approbation by gathering intelligence of the locality. The Allens—the butler and housekeeper—have been here for twenty years, long before my brother became master, and they know everything about the district. I hope that they may be induced to tell me more about James's time here."

Darcy nodded. Yes. They could be an invaluable help. "What did they say?"

"I approached it in a roundabout way, asking about all the genteel families in the Meryton area. There appears to be nothing particularly noteworthy about most of them—the Gouldings, the Harringtons, and more whose names I do not remember. Families such as they, owners of small estates with no more than half a dozen tenants, will be found in any district. There is one oddity. Did you meet a Sir William Lucas?"

"I did," said Darcy, with a painful remembrance of the voluble gentleman who had welcomed their party to the assembly, and who appeared to imagine his flourishing courtesies to be the manners of court.

"Knighted ten years ago, after making an address to the king, and bought himself a small estate on the strength of it. Before that, he owned several shops in towns around about. I would have thought he would have taken himself off to Hatfield or St Albans." Grayson smirked. "Far easier to pretend to be gentry at a remove from where you are best known as the town's foremost draper."

"He was accepted by all at the assembly."

"By those who are not so very high above him, and who know no better!"

Darcy said nothing. He was not so high in the instep as to scorn all those who became landed. He would hardly count Bingley as a friend if he were, since the Bingleys were the first generation removed from trade.

Grayson did not wait for a response. "The foremost landowner in the district, deemed the squire despite Netherfield Park being the larger estate, is Mr Bennet at Longbourn. Her father. Landowners since some Tudor king or other gave them the land, Allen said."

"Longevity trumps newer families, no matter how rich."

As Grayson must know. His family had held their estates for no more than three or four generations. Unlike the Darcys, who had held Pemberley for longer than the Bennets had owned Longbourn, and who considered the Tudors mere upstart Welsh *parvenus*.

"Bennet is respected. Mrs Bennet is a gentlewoman only by marriage—she was the daughter of the local attorney. Her brother is a Cit, in trade of some sort in Cheapside. Her sister is married to the current attorney, a man called Phillips, who inherited his father-in-law's practice. I was most interested in the Bennets, of course, and so paid more attention than I did to the other families mentioned."

"I met Phillips when Bingley came to view the estate in August. He was competent."

But it was another mark against the widow, to have such low connections. It would explain the mother's loud vulgarity and the improper behaviour of the younger daughters. Having married above her class herself, such a woman would see nothing amiss in trapping a rich young man like James Grayson for one of her daughters.

"Bennet is the last of his line, Allen said. He has only daughters—five of them!—and his estate has been entailed in strict settlement on male heirs since his great-grandfather's time. A distant cousin will inherit, it seems."

"Unfortunate for his family." Darcy nodded. That may account for the Bennet woman. Desperation allied with her vulgar background... Yes. That explained her somewhat.

"There is no entail on Netherfield."

"James could not have inherited if there were."

"And she granted him no opportunity to add Netherfield to the Graymead entail." Grayson looked around the room, as if surveying its unpretentious, yet comfortably elegant, decor. He showed his teeth, the way a bad-tempered dog showed his.

"And you feel cheated?"

Grayson reddened from the neck up, the flush rising to his hairline. He smoothed out his expression. "I do not deny that I would welcome the extra income. What man would not? I am not so foolish as to dissemble. But I assure you, Darcy, that I am far more concerned to understand what happened to James, and what that woman had to do with it."

Darcy regarded him in silence for a moment. Young Grayson's motives, it seemed, were mixed. "Did the servants have anything to say of Mrs Grayson?"

Grayson's earlier cheer had vanished entirely. He was sullen, opening a mouth that had pinched itself together to mutter, "Nothing to signify. She seems well regarded."

Darcy lifted his brandy glass to his lips and savoured the fineness of the spirit. Better not ask how Bingley had managed to find the real French article in the midst of the long war with Buonaparte. "Do none of your brother's personal servants remain? His valet?"

"Not in this house, I am certain."

"I see." Darcy mulled it over, before turning to more practical matters. "We are invited to Sir William Lucas's, three days hence. It is an informal occasion comprising music, cards and supper. I will speak to Bingley and ensure you accompany us."

Grayson's tightly drawn mouth softened. The tension of muscles in his neck and shoulder eased visibly, and he sighed, rolled his shoulders as if to force the stiffness from them. "Thank you. The chance to observe her, to take her measure… that is all I ask."

Was it, indeed? And did he think Darcy was so mutton-headed as to believe him?

Darcy, Grayson and Bingley all rode to the grandiosely named Lucas Lodge, leaving Bingley's carriage to the ladies and Hurst. Given the informality of the evening, Sir William had assured them there was no need for formal evening attire. Darcy, not without some misgiving that he was improperly dressed, had been glad to avoid the close confines of the carriage. Miss Bingley was tolerable only when he had avenues of escape.

They rode past Longbourn on the way. Darcy had the impression of a good-sized house, but the thickening twilight hid all but a few distant, lamp-gold windows.

A mile farther on, Lucas Lodge blazed with lamplight. An Elizabethan farmhouse at its core, a new wing had been built to the side to give the house a large, commodious drawing room. It was nothing to Netherfield, of course, but it was a pleasant room. Better than Darcy had expected.

Sir William greeted them heartily, making no distinction between the gentlemen and the *soi-disant* secretary, giving Grayson—*Saville*—a genial welcome. He made a point, indeed, of introducing Grayson to his elder daughter, the rather plain lady with whom Elizabeth Grayson had been laughing at the assembly. She greeted them all with pleasant equanimity. She had none of the verbose, elaborate courtesies of her sire.

The Bennets were there in force, with even Mr Bennet in attendance. Darcy had no recollection of seeing the darkly saturnine gentleman at the assembly. He would have remembered the wry twist to Mr Bennet's mouth as he eyed the guests, his wife fluttering at his side. His younger daughters were more circumspect than when Darcy had last seen them. That was a welcome improvement.

Bingley, of course, went to Miss Bennet's side as the moth to the candle flame. Hurst was equally enamoured of the punchbowl, and the two Bingley hens clucked, and scuttled after their errant cockerels to safeguard them from the twin disasters of Cupid and Dionysius. Darcy remained with young Grayson, half listening to his polite conversation with Miss Lucas, half intent on finding his quarry.

Taller than most, Darcy viewed the entire room with its groups of people who moved and coalesced and moved again, as did a shoal of minnows. There she was, coming towards them. Good. He touched Grayson briefly on the arm to gain his attention, and cut a glance in Elizabeth Grayson's direction. Grayson tensed instantly. The man had no self-discipline at all.

"There you are, Eliza." Miss Lucas put out her hand.

Mrs Grayson took it, smiling. Now Darcy looked more closely, her clothes were deceptive in their simplicity. The finest pale green jaconet, embroidered all over with a thin silver thread under a blond gauze... that was no *ingénue*'s garb. Accustomed to seeing the bills from Georgiana's dressmaker, he would estimate its cost to be twice as much as most of the dresses worn by the local women, though nothing compared to the Bingley ladies' silks, of course.

Darcy bowed. "A fine evening, ma'am, and an equally fine company assembled here tonight."

She arched one eyebrow. "I do not believe we have been introduced, sir."

Darcy brought his lower jaw up with a snap. The temerity stung as sharply as her clear dismissal.

She half turned as she spoke, presenting him with the profile he had studied at the assembly. She was not the equal of her sister for beauty, but he doubted the smiling blonde lady currently allowing Bingley to worship at her feet had such a biting quality. That one looked to be made of spun sugar.

Aware that Grayson was staring, eyes almost as round as pennies, Darcy bowed. "Remiss of me! Miss Lucas, may I request that you do me the honour of introducing your companion?"

"Indeed, I am hers, sir," Miss Lucas said, which incomprehensible comment had him staring as if he were as all-a-mort as Grayson.

The widow turned her face towards him again. Those damned eyebrows were still arched, and the eyes below them remarkably fine in their size and colouring; an unusual dark grey, the colour of the sea in a winter storm. With her pale skin and dark hair, those eyes were startling.

"I had the impression, Charlotte," she said, "that Mr Darcy was reluctant to make new acquaintances."

Another blow intended to sting, though she softened it immediately with a smile so sweet, it melted away the sharpness of Darcy's offence. He bowed again, before Miss Lucas could speak. "Alas, I do not perform well to strangers, ma'am. I must pray you not judge me too harshly."

She held his gaze. "Well, it behoves me be generous to the stranger among us, then. Very well. Charlotte, if you would be so kind?"

"Of course. Mr Darcy, I present Mrs Eliz—"

"Oh there you are, Mr Darcy!" Caroline Bingley insinuated her hand under Darcy's arm and pressed a great deal closer than he liked. "Miss Lucas. And you, I believe are Miss Bennet's next sister, Eliza?" She ignored Grayson entirely, a secretary being beneath her notice.

"I am." The widow bobbed a curtsey that Miss Bingley acknowledged with one equally shallow in return. "Although—"

"I have been making fast friends with your sister, Miss Eliza. Such a charming girl." Miss Bingley showed all too many teeth. Her brow creased slightly as she looked Elizabeth Grayson up and down. She had probably priced that dress to a sixpenny bit.

"I cannot disagree with that, Miss Bingley. Jane is exceptional, I think. However, I should corre—"

"Indeed. One rarely finds such beauty and such simplicity combined. Quite charming. There really is no other word to do her justice."

Really, she might as well call Jane Bennet a milkmaid and be done with it. Darcy turned to Charlotte Lucas. "Miss Lucas, if you plea—"

"I came for you, Mr Darcy, to pray you join us. I have a most particular reason to seek your counsel." Miss Bingley spoke with a thrumming sort of urgency in her tone.

"Good heavens," Elizabeth Grayson said, alight with mirth. "At an evening party, Miss Bingley?"

"Gentlemen of Mr Darcy's breeding... rather unusual in these parts, I believe? Well, Mr Darcy has ever been willing give aid to those of his friends who require it, no matter the time or circumstances." Another showing of Miss Bingley's teeth. Indeed, she had all too many. "It is the mark of a true gentleman."

Miss Lucas and Mrs Grayson exchanged glances, both mouths tightening. To hide smiles, Darcy suspected. Or perhaps to prevent a retort that would be uncivil.

"I suspect such amiability must be the mark of all gentlemen, Miss Bingley, no matter how lofty—or low—their breeding," the widow said. "If, that is, they are to deserve the appellation at all. Along with showing a courteous manner to acquaintances, old and new, and, perhaps, shouldering duties they may find onerous in order to smooth society's workings." And again, the unmistakable bite was sweetened by the widow's smile and the merrily-arched brow.

Had she heard him at the assembly? Damnation! And yet, she showed no sign of resentment. Perhaps it was his general reserve that she criticised. "As I said, I was remiss. Miss Lucas was about to introduce me. And Mr Saville." Darcy took a small side step, but Caroline Bingley had a bulldog's grip, and refused to relinquish her prey. "Miss Luc—"

"And now I have performed the office for you, and we all know each other!" The tug she gave his arm belied Miss Bingley's bright tone. "If you will, Mr Darcy?"

"But I must tell you, Miss Bingley, that you are under a misapprehension—" Miss Lucas tried, but once again no one was successful in completing a sentence, because at that very moment, her father bustled up to them.

"Ladies, gentlemen! I am come to tell you that Lady Lucas is opening up the piano, and has sent me to beg you, Miss Elizabeth, to favour us with a song." He flushed deeper and looked at Elizabeth Grayson in the manner of an appealing puppy. "That is, I should say, perhaps... Mrs..."

The widow laughed and put her hand briefly on his arm. "Your kindness ensures I will always be happy to sing." And here she looked solemnly at them all. "Indeed, there is no denying that I can fudge my way through a song with more finesse than I can a sonata, where my laxity in practising will be all too apparent. Come and play the accompaniment for me, Charlotte, I pray you." She inclined her head to them. "Miss Bingley."

Miss Bingley nodded back.

The widow turned her gaze to Darcy and his "secretary". "Mr Darcy, Mr Saville. We must consider ourselves introduced, it seems. Perhaps in the Town manner, but needs must suffice."

She hooked her arm through Miss Lucas's and the two gave a joint curtsey and walked away. They had their heads close together, Miss Lucas saying something in a low voice that had Elizabeth Grayson laughing aloud.

"Whatever did she mean? The Town manner? However would such a country girl know?" But it was a matter of no importance to Miss Bingley, for she shook her head and tugged Darcy towards the spot where her brother and Miss Bennet were in conversation. "These rustics! Not a particle of Town bronze amongst them. Come, sir. I am concerned that Charles is showing the Bennet girl far too much attention. Do come and help me direct Charles away from such an unworthy prospect."

CHAPTER NINE

Every Savage

"Good heavens, Eliza, Miss Bingley most certainly believes herself to be our superior and that it was for her to control the situation. Have you ever seen the like of her refusal to allow me to make a proper introduction?"

"Perhaps she is convinced that we here in the country could not possibly know how. Town manners appear to be very different."

"They are, indeed." They had reached the piano, and Charlotte took the pile of music to rifle through. "They cannot realise who you are."

"It was not for want of trying to tell them! Well, she shall discover her mistake in her own good time, in all probability when she sees I take precedence over her at formal occasions." Elizabeth took a deep breath to quell her irritation at the bumptious Miss Bingley. "I cannot imagine she will like that."

"No, indeed. And what of Mr Darcy? He seemed more eager for an introduction this evening."

"Heaven only knows. You know what he said at the assembly."

"He appears to have repented his opinion. You, however, are not usually so tame. I expected you to depress Miss Bingley's pretensions."

Elizabeth glanced across the room. Miss Bingley clung still to Mr Darcy's arm. She had pulled him over to her brother and Jane, and was talking to them in a merry, energetic way that had Jane and Bingley overrun and silent. Mr Darcy stood stiffly beside her, staring in Elizabeth's direction. Their gazes met briefly. His expression suggested he was afflicted with toothache.

She returned her attention to Charlotte. "I do not think Mr Darcy has changed his opinion, if his countenance now is any indication. His dark scowls would curdle cream. I must assume he looks for further fault in me." She chuckled at Charlotte's arched eyebrow. "It is of no consequence. Jane's interest in Mr Bingley is more important, and I would not make an enemy of his friend or his sister."

"Jane and Mr Bingley?" Charlotte raised the music to hide the fact she was staring at the Bingley siblings and Jane. "Yes, I can see that he is all admiration—with his open countenance, he does not hide it. But she is as serene as ever. She had better show it more, you know, for she is a deal too reserved and guarded. If she conceals her affection, she may lose the opportunity of fixing him. In these cases, it is better to show more than she feels, in order to secure his interest."

"Secure his interest? I doubt Jane thinks of him in such terms. And affection is far too strong a term given they are so lately acquainted. She told me after the assembly, however, that she considers that him to be amiable, handsome and pleasant."

Charlotte gave a most inelegant snort. "She should be thinking of him in such terms, if ever she wishes to marry. There are so few prospects in the district that she should not hesitate to establish herself with an eligible man."

"You do not take into account, then, the need for her to fix her notion of his character before attempting to fix his interest? I had no chance to do so, as you know. I would never wish Jane the same infelicitous discoveries I made, when it was too late to do anything about it."

Charlotte pressed Elizabeth's hand briefly. "Your circumstances were unhappily different. I do not think that Mr Bingley is another James Grayson."

Elizabeth tightened her lips and nodded.

Charlotte patted Elizabeth's hand and returned to her perusal of the music. "I wish Jane every success, but we both know that happiness in marriage is entirely a matter of chance. It is better to know as little as possible in advance, of the defects of the person with whom you are to pass your life. It is then, perhaps, easier to learn to make the best of it."

"I cannot agree. It was not so for... I wish I could laugh, but this touches me too deeply. What you say is not sound. You know that you would never act in so unfeeling a way yourself."

"I am merely more practical than you are. I am not romantic, you know."

Elizabeth took a deep breath. "Nor am I. Not now."

Last to exhibit, Elizabeth's sister Mary thumped through one movement of a Beethoven sonata before being ordered by their mother to play dances in lieu of tackling the remainder. Herr Beethoven was, Elizabeth had heard, rather hard of hearing. She felt that offered no great impediment to appreciating Mary's playing, which was correct when it came to notes on the keyboard, but lacked emotion.

Mary obeyed their mother, of course, though her expression conveyed her distaste for the cheery Scotch and Irish airs that served to accompany the jigs and reels so beloved of the younger guests. Within two bars of her starting, Lydia and Kitty were galloping away with a pair of pink-faced militia officers in tow. It did not take long for Maria Lucas and Mary King to follow, the Harrington and Long girls rushing to join them.

Elizabeth bit back a sigh. She was fond of dancing, but if Sir William's drawing room could hold more than eight couples in comfort, she would be astonished. She smiled, however, when she saw Jane drawn into the dance by Mr Bingley. Excellent. Mr Bingley could have no more graceful partner, and it gave them another half hour's conversation to learn more of each other. An astute move on his part.

She turned her head, startled to find Mr Darcy stood nearby. Goodness, that expression!

"Charming! Charming! Dancing amuses the young people so..."

Elizabeth had not realised Sir William was also close, but he was speaking to Mr Darcy not her.

"... one of the refinements of polished society, do you not think, Mr Darcy?"

"Certainly, sir. It has the advantage also of being in vogue amongst the less polished societies of the world. Every savage can dance."

Elizabeth gave out a little gasp. The disdain and contempt cut like shards of broken glass.

But kind Sir William merely smiled. She could only hope that Mr Darcy's meaning had passed him by. "Your friend performs delightfully with Miss Bennet, I see." And before she could move away, Sir William took two or three steps towards her and caught her hand, drawing her closer to Mr Darcy than she ever intended. "My dear Miss Elizabeth, you should be dancing, too! Mr Darcy, you must allow me to present this young lady to you as a very desirable partner. You will not wish to refuse to dance, I am sure, when so much beauty is before you."

Elizabeth was hard put to it not to laugh aloud at the surprised expression on Mr Darcy's face. He did, indeed, start to reach out to take her hand as Sir William held it out to him, but she smiled and disclaimed, and shook her head. "Indeed, Sir William, you are very kind, but I will not dance tonight. Mr Darcy has no fondness for the art, as we saw at the assembly, and it would not do to force his acquiescence—"

"Not at all, madam. I should be delighted." Mr Darcy bowed, with all the animation of a life-size mechanical toy.

If that was delight, then heaven spare her from his dismay! She allowed her smile to widen. "You are all politeness, sir. I thank you, but excuse me, I beg. I have no mind to dance." She squeezed Sir William's fingers and drew her hand away, dipped into as graceful a curtsey as she could manage, and with a nod and another smile bestowed indiscriminately on both of them, she turned away.

Good heavens, what an escape. The last man in the world with whom she wished to dance!

Mr Darcy did not dance with anyone else. Instead he repeated the behaviour shown at the assembly: walking around the perimeter of the room, speaking to no one, and staring at her from wherever he fetched up. She was stared at from the buffet table, from the punchbowl, from the door to the saloon where the card tables were set up, and from the windows overlooking Lucas Lodge's small formal gardens. Heavens, the man did nothing but stare. His expression was stern. Forbidding. She could only think her little joke earlier to Charlotte was plain, unvarnished truth: there was indeed something so very wrong with her in his estimation that he looked at her to see confirmation of her faults. It was most uncomfortable.

Once, when Elizabeth was at the buffet table with Mrs Long, she lost sight of him for a moment. Looking about the room for him, she spotted him talking to Miss Bingley. For a moment that lady too had stared at Elizabeth, her expression one of astonishment, until she saw that Elizabeth had caught her gaze, and she smoothed her face into the splendidly null serenity that seemed to be mark of the well-bred society lady. Whatever was that about? She had no doubt they were united in their dislike for a confined country society. Possibly in their dislike for her personally? Well, it was of no consequence whatsoever.

"A pleasant evening," said an unfamiliar man's voice from behind her.

It was a relief to turn from Mr Darcy's dark gaze, to see who had spoken to her.

"Mr Saville." She inclined her head in greeting.

He bowed to Mrs Long when Elizabeth made the introductions and treated her with courtesy, offering both ladies glasses of wine from the buffet table.

"That is very kind of you, sir. Thank you." She took the wine and sipped it gratefully. It was cool and refreshing. Sir William had retained many of his previous contacts in trade, and had an admirable circle of suppliers of life's small luxuries. "How are you enjoying your stay in Hertfordshire?"

He stared almost as intently as Mr Darcy. "As much as I can expect, when I am not here at my leisure... Miss Elizabeth." There was a slightly interrogative note to his voice when he said her name. "Duty has me here, rather than pleasure. I am Mr Darcy's secretary, you know."

"So I understand. Is he an exacting patron, Mr Saville? He gives the impression that he might be."

"Lizzy." Mrs Long widened her eyes at Elizabeth in unmistakable warning.

Elizabeth gave her a tiny grimace. Mr Darcy had, of course, approached from wherever he had been standing and staring last, and now stood behind her. In unmistakable hearing distance.

She turned and smiled. "And there you are, Mr Darcy! Here to defend yourself, I see."

"Do I need to do so?"

"I dare say you do not, against such poor darts as I have in my armoury."

Darcy accepted the glass of wine Mr Saville handed him with a quiet word of thanks. "I am aware that you have a sportive nature."

"And do you know me so well already, sir? I am all astonishment and might ask which of my neighbours I must chastise for gossiping. However, I shall merely say that I hope, Mr Saville, that you will have some leisure to look about you. Hertfordshire is a tame county, perhaps, without the grandeur and wildness of others. But it is my firmest belief that we are the lucky inhabitants of one of England's most pleasant places, and our woods and fields offer many charming vistas for those who are of a mind to be pleased."

"The little I have seen, I would agree is very pleasant," Mr Darcy said. "Without, as you say, the wildness of my own home, but a very congenial place."

She rewarded him with a smile.

"Perhaps I will have the opportunity to explore more widely. It will depend upon my business... Mr Darcy's, I should rather say, since I am here to support him." Mr Saville sipped his wine, pale blue eyes regarding her over the glass. "I have seen little other than Netherfield Park. You must know it, of course. A fine house."

And what, indeed, could she say to that most unwelcome observation other than "I know it well. Everyone in the neighbourhood does."

"Mr Bingley is a lucky man, to lease the place."

"And we are lucky that he has brought a party with him to swell our small society. It is always agreeable to have new people in our community—is it not, Mrs Long? We are fond of our neighbours, gentlemen, and live with them in general amity, but new acquaintances offer variety, and that is always welcome."

"Indeed." But Mrs Long glanced at Miss Bingley, then looked at Elizabeth with a small smile that told her that the variety was somewhat uneven in its quality.

"I understand the previous owner is dead. I suppose that is how Netherfield came to be available," Mr Saville said.

Odd, how the cold had invaded the room running bony fingers down Elizabeth's arms to chill her. The autumn had been very cool thus far. She scooped up her shawl, which she wore holding it loosely in her elbows, to cover her arms and shoulders, and forced a smile. "Yes. Some years ago now."

Mr Saville trained her gaze upon her. "I believe he was a young man. It must have been most unexpected. And his heir does not choose to keep his house. Hmmmpfh."

Elizabeth would have welcomed a change of topic. "It is the way with many houses of its kind, is it not? It proves too large and costly for its family, and they must find a way to turn it to account."

"And that is the case here?" Mr Saville asked. "How sad for the house, to have an owner whose only thought is to profit from it!"

Elizabeth could only stare. How very judgemental of him, when he had no knowledge of the circumstances! It spoke to some private resentments there... perhaps it explained his obviously reduced circumstances, that he had had some expectations that had come to naught, and that made him bitter. His contempt stung, even though it was of no account. He could have no idea he was saying it to anyone who had any concern in the matter, much less the most. They did not know, thanks to Miss Bingley's officious interference. His barb could not be aimed at her.

Mr Saville and Mr Darcy exchanged a glance. Elizabeth could not see precisely what was to be read on Mr Darcy's face, but Mr Saville grimaced slightly. She met Mr Darcy's gaze as directly as possible, and lifted her chin. The silence was a little too long.

She kept her tone as light as she could. "It is wrong to judge circumstances of which nothing or but little is known. If not for the lease, you could not enjoy Netherfield."

"And, of course," dear Mrs Long added, "we here in Meryton would not have the pleasure of making the acquaintance of you all."

Though the pleasure, like the variety the Netherfield party brought, was very uneven in its quality.

CHAPTER TEN

Four and Twenty Families

Mrs Bennet was inclined to boast about the social nature of the neighbourhood, reminding everyone that they dined with quite four and twenty families.

"I could wish," said Elizabeth as October wore on, "that it were fewer. Or that they would not all desire to entertain so often. A few days without a rout, or an evening party, or drinking tea, or cards would be most welcome, if I may then escape our new neighbours."

"Nonsense! You are the most social creature of us all." And Charlotte Lucas, to whom she was giving vent to her dissatisfaction, laughed heartily. How anyone could see that and call her plain, was quite beyond Elizabeth.

"I do love society, I own. But, Charlotte, consider." Elizabeth looked around the Gouldings' drawing room. "This is to be the first formal dinner."

"A more elegant evening than usual. Can Meryton reach society's standards, do you think? At least, tonight you are as well dressed as either of the sisters are likely to be."

Elizabeth smiled her thanks, and smoothed her skirts, made from a deep amber silk. The dress was overlaid with silver net on the bodice, and although it boasted but one flounce around the hem, it was fashionable and pretty, and matched the amber aigrette set *en tremblant* in her hair. Elizabeth deemed the ensemble eminently suitable for a widow, showing she was no green girl. "Thank you! You are a very useful sort of friend to have, Charlotte. So comforting to my vanity."

Charlotte laughed. "Your first opportunity to wear it, I believe, since, as you say, none of our neighbours has dared risk such a formal occasion."

"Indeed. Mama has been afire to see Mr Bingley seated at her table, but Papa hates such evenings, as you know, and would not be moved into hosting a full dinner since Mrs Goulding sent out her invitations for this evening several weeks ago. He refuses to suffer in his own home, as he put it, merely to steal a march upon our neighbours."

"Mrs Goulding is to be admired for her courage."

"And courage it is, too! Mr Darcy and Miss Bingley will find us sad rustics with no sense of fashion. In some cases, I hear, Town dinners do not begin until eight, or even later."

As one, they glanced at the clock on the mantel. It was barely half past five.

"Of course we dine at this time at Longbou—" The flurry of noise and the appearance of the Gouldings' butler in the doorway heralded the arrival of the Bingley party, the only guests still awaited. "Well, they are here at last. Mrs Goulding will be relieved. She must have feared her dinner would be quite spoiled."

They watched in silence as Mr Darcy bowed to his host and hostess. He was impeccably dressed, in the sober but elegant style that the fashion periodicals, when they wrote of men's fashion at all, imputed to the influence of Mr Brummell. His dark blue coat was perfectly fitted, and his cravat impressively tied into a waterfall of starched muslin. Beside him, Messrs Bingley and Hurst were paler imitations. Mr Saville was not present.

"He does look every inch the gentleman," Charlotte murmured, as Darcy's gaze swept around the room. "I dare say every other man here is regarding him out of the corners of their eyes and wondering if they fill their coats so well, or if they can emulate his style of tying his cravat. Oh look! Mr Bingley has gone straight to Jane's side."

"Then she will be happy." Elizabeth returned stare for stare with Mr Darcy, before withdrawing her gaze and looking to see Mr Bingley's eagerness as he crossed the room to Jane, as quickly as might be. "Goodness, Mr Bingley is a touch cavalier in his civilities to the rest of us!"

"It is love, then."

"I hope so. He does not even notice the rest of his company in his ardent desire to be with Jane. It is said, is it not, that a general incivility to others is the very essence of a gentleman in the throes of love?"

"Said by whom? You?"

Elizabeth laughed aloud. "Perhaps! I speak as the most sensible, intelligent person in the room, of course, seeking to dazzle with the brilliance of my wit and humour."

"But of course! Oh, excuse me, Eliza. I see Mrs Harrington beckoning me." Charlotte, who had been nodding and smiling her acquiescence at Mrs Harrington, flitted away.

Elizabeth walked towards the sofa where Mrs Long sat patiently awaiting the call to go in to dine. A glance around the room showed her Mr Bingley had somehow dispersed all the bees droning around Jane, and had her to himself. Jane's smile was softer than usual. Mr Hurst had joined Elizabeth's father and the other gentlemen, and held a glass in his hand.

Elizabeth had to pass Mr Bingley's sisters and Mr Darcy on the way, aware of Mr Darcy's watchful gaze as she approached him. The sisters were dressed as if for dinner with a duchess. Or, perhaps, several duchesses. Elizabeth's dress was, she hoped, elegant. But theirs were made by a modiste of the first stare. Both wore turbans of the same shimmering silk as their dresses, capped by plumes of ostrich feathers.

Elizabeth did not stay to talk, although she did pause long enough to dip into a curtsey and murmur a greeting. She moved on to join Mrs Long, feeling the pressure of three pairs of eyes watching her progress, and doubtless criticising her air and carriage, and deriding her cherished pretty dress as quaintly bucolic. She would chastise herself for her folly for allowing the thought to rankle, as soon as she returned to Longbourn. There was no time then. Mrs Goulding bowed to Louisa Hurst, and as soon as that lady was moving toward the dining room, Elizabeth offered her arm to Mrs Long with a smile she hoped was as cheery as could possibly be.

"Let you and I follow in Mama and Lady Lucas, Mrs Long. I vow I am half famished! I walked a great deal today, you know, and since I am a healthy country girl"—this for Mr Darcy and Miss Bingley's ears, since they were close by—"and Mrs Goulding always sets an excellent table, my appetite is likely to be something prodigious."

Mama chattered happily with Lady Lucas, who walked at her side, next after Mrs Hurst. Elizabeth followed her mother, arm-in-arm with Mrs Long. She glanced over her shoulder as they went, in time to see the expression on Miss Bingley's face. Good heavens, what a look of blazing affront! Did Miss Bingley think she should take a place ahead of the wives of the local landowners? An unmarried girl? Surely not! The way that Miss Bingley lifted her chin and flared her nostrils in disdain suggested otherwise, but before Elizabeth could consider it further, Jane—dear, dear Jane—came to Miss Bingley's side.

"Come, Miss Bingley! Shall you and I go in together?"

Jane's sweet smile would have disarmed Napoleon himself. Miss Bingley unfroze her lips to essay a small, frigid smile in return, and joined the ladies' line as they processed into the dining room. She and Jane walked first amongst the unmarried girls, as was proper. Elizabeth hid a smile and turned her attention back to Mrs Long.

The table was splendid. A haunch of venison took pride of place, surrounded by platters of roast partridge and duck, roast lamb, trout and salmon, and a host of other accompaniments in the sort of pleasingly artistic pattern that proved Mrs Goulding had studied her cookery books most carefully to create a display that would be as pleasing to her guests' eyes as to their palates.

Elizabeth took Mrs Long to a place near their hostess and helped her into her chair. As she straightened, Miss Bingley barrelled past her and went to a seat near Mr Goulding's end of the table, close to her own sister, taking the place that, by rights, Elizabeth should have.

Elizabeth and Mrs Long looked at each other. Mrs Long's eyebrow had almost disappeared under the edge of her lace cap, and her lips were pursed. Elizabeth did not shrug, because not even Mrs Long, who liked her and was indulgent, would allow that to pass without comment. Instead, she took a seat nearby, leaving one empty chair between them for a gentleman to take.

"You are a good girl, Elizabeth," Mrs Long said, reaching over to deliver a pat on Elizabeth's hand. "A very good girl."

Which was kind of her, but evidently not a sentiment shared by Mrs Goulding who, as she came in the last of the ladies, just ahead of the gentlemen, gave Elizabeth a look of some exasperation at finding her at such a distance from Mr Goulding's end of the table. Nor did the sentiment seem to find a home in Mr Darcy's breast. He came in with Elizabeth's father, first of all the gentlemen. Taking the seat of honour for the gentlemen, at Mrs Goulding's right hand, he found himself beside Elizabeth. From the rigidity of his jaw and the set of his mouth, lips drawn into a thin line, he did not think her good at all.

She glanced up as the chair on her other side was taken. Oh, how delightful! John Lucas. They exchanged greetings under cover of the rest of the gentlemen finding seats, although Elizabeth was not so distracted as to miss Mr Bingley drawn to Jane's side as a pin to the magnet. That too, was delightful.

"What are you doing at this end of the table, Eliza? The honour is likely to put me off my feed."

"How ungallant of you, John."

"Pah. You have made me walk the plank too often for gallantry, my girl!"

Once they had been shipwrecked pirates, or Crusaders, or explorers setting off to follow great rivers to their secret sources. They had, of necessity, become more formal with each other as they left childhood behind, but John remained a very good friend. Elizabeth had no qualms at leaving her hostess to entertain Mr Darcy while she and John had a comfortable coze together.

They were interrupted when the two footmen removed the soup and the fish, whisking away their used dishes and plates. The usual flurry of servants bringing in new platters to replace the tureen and fish, and disposing them prettily on the table, halted their conversation. Mrs Goulding abandoned Mr Darcy for the nonce to oversee everything with an anxious eye, and that gentleman turned to Elizabeth with a somewhat tight-lipped expression that may have been an attempt at a smile.

"I hope you are well, Miss Elizabeth?"

"Very well, sir. And you?"

"I am always so, I thank you." He glanced at John Lucas. "Will you do me the honour of making me known to your companion?"

Elizabeth could only express delight, and comply. The two gentlemen inclined their heads and murmured the conventional words to denote their mutual pleasure and honour at the acquaintance.

"I should not interrupt, perhaps," said Mr Darcy, "and it is even more discourteous to admit that I overheard a little of your conversation and found it most intriguing. You walked the plank at Miss Elizabeth's behest, did you, Mr Lucas?"

John's laugh rang out. "Indeed sir. Miss Elizabeth may not look dangerous, but I assure you she was the most ruthless pirate in the whole of Hertfordshire. She must always be the captain, with the rest of us merely her minions. If I were not walking planks, I recollect I was swabbing decks."

"A pirate with an obsession for cleanliness, then." And Mr Darcy relaxed the hardness of his mouth.

The way his eyes crinkled at the corners startled Elizabeth. "You would not say so, sir, if you saw the state of my pinafore each time I was let out to play. My mother would always claim my obsession was with grime and dust!"

"And climbing trees," John said.

"You traitor! Would you make public all my indiscretions?"

"Why, what else are old friends for?" And John smiled devilishly.

Luckily Mrs Goulding then reclaimed Mr Darcy's attention. No doubt, he was considering how heathenish and uncouth she had been, to play at pirates with the boys instead of tending her needlework. How vexing. He did not need further fuel for his disapprobation, after all.

When the second course had been removed, and the dessert course was little more than half-empty dishes on the table, Mrs Goulding determined that it was time for the ladies to retire to the drawing room and leave the gentlemen to their port.

"Oh dear," Elizabeth murmured, placing her napkin upon the tabletop while Mrs Goulding garnered the attention of the ladies. Both John and Mr Darcy turned towards her, and she said, brightly, "Well, I must leave you to the weighty discussions usual to gentlemen. You, doubtless, will enjoy yourselves with politics and wondering if banknotes will ever replace the guinea in our affections, or debating if the Battle of El Bodón is to be accounted a dreadful reverse or merely a skirmish allowing General Wellesley the chance to regroup and return to attack the French at Ciudad Rodrigo. I must content myself with needlework, the servant problem, or if I am lucky, an account of Princess Charlotte's latest dresses."

Mr Darcy stared, his eyes rather wide.

"Life is very unfair," was all John said, and, when Mrs Goulding rose with the help of Mr Darcy, he leapt up to aid first Mrs Long, and then Elizabeth, from their chairs. "Perhaps Mr Darcy and I should discuss piracy?"

"A flogging at the very least, Pirate Lucas," Elizabeth pronounced. "In the absence of a convenient plank."

John threw back his head and laughed heartily, before bowing with a flourish of his napkin. Mr Darcy's eyes were still wide.

Mr Bingley, being closest to the door, went to hold it for the ladies and bow them out. Elizabeth hooked her arm through Mrs Long's and fell in line behind her mother. She ensured Mrs Long was seated near the warmth of the fire, and sat beside her, determined to keep her company for a little while at least. The various ladies settled themselves into chairs and sofas to spend the time in gossip until the men joined them. In her own house, she and Charlotte would spend the interval between dinner and the advent of the tea tray taking a brisk walk or even doing some desultory shopping on Meryton's high street. At Longbourn she could usually coax Jane out into the gardens for a stroll. Here, though, she must be all ladylike sociability—"do the pretty", as her father described it.

Mrs Goulding was a careful hostess. Whilst her guests had dined, servants had spread the small tables in the drawing room with bowls of fruit and shelled nuts, and glasses of ratafia and orgeat, and between them were piled several editions of *La Belle Assemblée*, the *Ladies' Monthly Museum* and the *Lady's Magazine* to give direction should the conversation flag. Some ladies brought from their reticules small items of "work"—purses they were netting, or handkerchiefs and a small array of silks for embroidery—so they could claim the virtue of hands as busy as their tongues were likely to be. Elizabeth was fond of embroidery, but not of doing it in public where every lady present would be casting critical eyes over her stitching. She reconciled herself to an hour of inconsequential social chit-chat.

She had reckoned without the Netherfield ladies. Miss Bingley, ensconced on the largest sofa with her sister on one side of her and Mrs Goulding on the other, opened by complimenting her hostess on her dinner, and then, with such brazen impudence that even Elizabeth stared, went on an offensive General Wellesley might envy.

"I was much struck by the Marquess of Lansdowne's dinner just before we left Town. He had the gentlemen take in the ladies in order of precedence. It is quite the newest fashion, rather than have all the ladies process in together and leave the gentlemen to find their own places when they follow. Such a civilised and decorous way of proceeding, do you not think, Louisa?"

"Just so, my dear." Mrs Hurst spoke with less conviction. She appeared to find her bracelets fascinating, and her chin quivered.

"One can then be certain of ensuring that each gentleman and lady has the most appropriate company and it quite encourages the harmony and tranquillity of the evening. One is so often imposed upon by the most unsuitable people otherwise. Have you thought of instituting the practice here, Mrs Goulding? You could lead the way, you know, in bringing Meryton's customs up to date. It would give your little dinners the stamp of the highest fashion!"

Mrs Goulding was rather pink in the face. "I prefer to give my guests precedence, Miss Bingley, and follow them in to dinner. It is perhaps, old fashioned to show them honour this way—"

"Oh, it is of little account here in the country, I dare say. But in Town, of course, it would never do to be behind the latest fashion." Miss Bingley glanced around. She must have noted, as did Elizabeth, that every eye was upon her. She had the audacity to pat her hostess on the knee, a familiarity that Mrs Goulding's friends of many years standing would not think of claiming. "It is quite understandable that you have not the means here to know how to go on, ma'am. I beg you do not trouble yourself over the matter. Dinner was delightful!"

Elizabeth put a bright eagerness into her tone. "You attended a dinner hosted by a marquess, Miss Bingley? How wonderful an experience that must have been! Do tell us about it. We will insist on every last detail, will we not, ladies? For we are all agog to know how such eminent and fashionable people go on."

One or two covert smiles, and many nods. Some ladies were quite genuine; Jane, for one. The expression on Charlotte's face, as with others, held the same challenging humour Elizabeth felt herself.

Just for the instant, Miss Bingley froze. The smile never slipped, but her eyes narrowed as she met Elizabeth's gaze. "I attend many dinners, Miss Eliza. I assure you that the marquess, while doing everything in the most fashionable and convenient way, is not alone in this. Most of our circle are quite *comme il faut* with society's best practices."

"Indeed?" Elizabeth smiled. "Well, I have no doubt the *Morning Post* had a brave account of the evening. It usually does, does it not? How exciting it must be to read an account of such a fashionable gathering and find one's name listed there for all to see! I expect Papa still has a copy in his study. He is a sad hoarder of newspapers, Miss Bingley. He complains that if he does not hide them, his daughters whisk them away to make fire spills and curl papers!"

Miss Bingley's smile became fixed. Her eyes glittered. Her sister looked much as a rabbit would when faced with a fox.

Mrs Goulding caught Elizabeth's eye, smiled, and shook her head slightly. Being far more polite and forgiving than Elizabeth could ever be, she complimented the Netherfield ladies on their gowns, and turned the conversation neatly onto fashion and the strictures of *La Belle Assemblée* in relation to the number of flounces appropriate for a ball gown in the latest Russian fashion.

Elizabeth sat back in her seat, prepared to let the topic of marquesses and precedence pass. Miss Bingley spared her a look that was part distrust, she thought, but mostly hearty dislike. Elizabeth, with a glance at Jane, forbore to return it in kind. Jane did not deserve to have her acquaintance with Mr Bingley soured by her own sister's failure to cease baiting the newcomers, no matter how deserving they were of scorn for their pretension. Besides, Mrs Hurst looked miserably apprehensive, twisting her fingers in the skirt of her gown.

Elizabeth accepted a glass of orgeat from the maidservant, and caught Mrs Hurst's gaze. She, poor lady, started, when Elizabeth smiled at her. "Tell me, Mrs Hurst," she said, seeing how both the Bingley women stiffened, "You are more *au fait* with London than we are. Is it true that Princess Charlotte has been seen wearing lace-edged drawers that showed below her hemline? Was it very shocking?"

Mrs Hurst stared, but the tension ebbed away into a buzz of chatter about royalty's penchant for wearing lacy pantalettes. And after a moment, Mrs Hurst gave Elizabeth a tentative smile in return.

Elizabeth took a sip from her glass. Excellent. Jane was saved, that night at least, from the consequences of her sister's sharp tongue. Sometimes doing the pretty was its own reward.

CHAPTER ELEVEN

Fine Eyes and Fidgets

Hurst awaited Darcy and Bingley in the vestibule at Netherfield on their return from the Gouldings' dinner. "I have been here this age! I wish I had come back with you."

"I am just glad Darcy took his own carriage as well. A fine notion that, my friend, that you did not wish to crush the ladies' finery." And Bingley's sweetest smile had both gentlemen grinning, although George Hurst's expression was, perhaps, closer to a grimace.

Hurst drew them to the side of the hall, out of the immediate line of sight of anyone leaving the saloon. "Next time I, too, will be as considerate. Caroline is in a rare temper. I suspect she did not make quite the impression she planned tonight. She had a great deal to say about fine eyes and pert manners, but at times she was too affected with temper to speak with coherence. I could not catch the detail of what transpired." He lifted one shoulder in a slight shrug. "I gave no sign of interest of course. Goulding had some very fine port, did he not? So far as Caroline is concerned, I dozed for the entire journey home to sleep off my potations." He added, in meditative tone, "I have become adept at appearing a trifle disguised, these days."

Fine eyes.

Darcy would never hear the end of that, he feared. A moment of admiration at Sir William Lucas's evening party for Elizabeth Grayson's unusual dark grey eyes and the life and vivacity they gave her features, followed by unthinking folly when he confided his admiration to Caroline Bingley... the consequences of that indiscretion were likely to be uncomfortable and, apparently, unending. Miss Bingley had been both snide and arch about the widow ever since, even though Darcy had been careful never to mention the woman again. He could wish himself at Jericho at this moment, rather than enter that room.

Bingley's blithe countenance showed no real distress. "Caroline will be insupportable until she is permitted to tell us her woes."

Hurst snorted. "One consolation is she may do so in a more lady-like manner than we might otherwise expect." He nodded at Darcy. "For which I thank you, Darcy. Without your restraining presence she would vent her spleen in far more trenchant terms."

"I am glad to be of service. However, I should not intrude on a family matter..."

"Oh no." Hurst caught Darcy's arm. "That is doing it much too brown. Caroline's bristles have been well and truly set up, and I tell you that is a matter this member of the family has no wish to deal with!"

Bingley, though, widened his already beaming smile. "No, Hurst. Darcy almost has the right of it. What do the high emotions of ladies have to do with any gentleman? They need another female in whom to confide and who will provide much better consolation than we poor males might venture. They are finer creatures than we, after all."

The three looked at each other, and, as one, glanced in the direction of the door to the smaller saloon behind which Miss Bingley was doubtless wreaking the same havoc as a famished lioness descending on an undefended sheep pen. They shared a knowing smile.

"Poor Louisa, though." Bingley's mock solemnity fooled neither of them. "It is an imposition on her good nature."

Hurst snorted. "Why do you think she has so many pretty gewgaws? She has her eye on a sapphire necklace. I will send to Town for it tomorrow."

Bingley beamed. "Excellent! Then we may safely leave Caroline in her hands. Where shall we go?"

"The billiards room?" Darcy suggested.

"The first place Caroline will look," Hurst said.

"That puts the library out of bounds, too," Bingley pointed out. "Particularly if she's looking for Darcy."

"She may not think of the gun room," Hurst said, but almost immediately shook his head. "No. No room on the public floor will be safe. She will not hesitate to enter even such a masculine domain if she is searching for prey."

"Well, then, the small sitting room adjoining my bedroom, and a bottle of brandy, perhaps? Miss Bingley will not venture there." Darcy allowed his smile to widen. "I can assure you that if she tries, Simms—my valet, Hurst—will defend the inalienable right of a gentleman to privacy in his chambers. She will not pass him." He did not add that Simms was under orders always to guard his chambers from Miss Bingley. Darcy would never permit her to leg-shackle him with a compromise.

Hurst and Bingley nodded at each other. Bingley bespoke the brandy bottle from the footman, before the three of them escaped up the staircase with more dispatch than decorum.

Darcy had time that night for only a few moments conversation with Grayson, after Hurst had gone yawning to bed around midnight and Bingley had followed.

"I had dinner with the upper servants again tonight," Grayson said, after revealing he had been loitering around waiting for Bingley and Hurst to depart. He looked less than pleased at the exigencies of his situation. Graysons, Darcy suspected, were unused to being kept cooling their heels while others enjoyed a very fine brandy. "To no avail. The Allens were close-mouthed." He ran his hands through his hair, until its *à-la-Brutus* curls were all confusion. "I am doing no damned good at all really. Did you find anything?"

"Not a great deal. When the ladies retired, I made careful enquiries of several of the gentlemen under the guise of seeking more about the history of the house. Most turned the conversation onto something else—the sport to be had on the estate, or listing other large houses in the county that might be of interest to me." He hesitated. "Sir William Lucas, however…"

Grayson, nursing a glass of brandy, cocked his head to one side.

"Sir William said, and I quote him exactly I think, 'We could do nothing. A man cannot interfere, you know. It is not done. I wish…' And there he stopped and would say no more."

John Lucas, a more educated, more sensible man than his father, had given Darcy a very direct stare when he had heard Darcy's enquiry. Lucas had tossed back his port and risen from the table, as though to put some distance between him and Darcy, pausing by Sir William only to put a hand on his father's shoulder.

Sir William had stuttered to a halt, and he had shaken his head. "Quite right, John," he had said. "Quite right."

And the normally voluble, sociable knight said nothing more to Darcy for the entire evening.

Grayson scowled at this recital. "Some mysterious regret on Sir William's part does not take us very much further forward."

"No. We should make more formal enquiries, Grayson. I am not at ease with the part I play here."

"Perhaps. If there is no other way." Grayson tossed off the brandy, scrunching up his face against the burn. "But not yet. I would like more opportunities to talk to the woman myself, first. If she is to be caught out in lies, I should like to be the one to do it. I owe James that much, at least."

Of course, they did not escape Miss Bingley entirely, but a night's repose had blunted her ire. A little.

When Darcy entered the breakfast room next day, she was holding forth to the rest of their party, including Grayson. As a result of Darcy's request, his so-called secretary joined the family at breakfast and, when they dined at home, at the dinner table. The various slights bestowed on Grayson were not malicious, arising as they did from the perceived difference in the social level inhabited by "Mr Saville" in relation to that of the Bingleys. Grayson professed himself able to bear the small indignities with grace and humour, but his mouth was often thinned with resentment.

"Ah, there you are, Mr Darcy! You are not usually so late abroad in the mornings." Miss Bingley withdrew her attention from Grayson with such rapidity that Darcy half expected to hear the air snap and crackle.

"I broke my fast some hours ago, Miss Bingley."

"This is a second breakfast," Bingley said, the last of the party to appear. He went to investigate the dishes laid out on the sideboard. "Darcy and I rode several miles this morning, and oh, it is wet and chilly! Invigorating, I can tell you, and it provokes such an appetite! I could eat my own horse."

Miss Bingley glanced at the windows. The panes were running with rain. "Out in such weather? You will catch cold, Mr Darcy." And when he did not reply beyond a short bow, she sighed and returned her attention to Grayson. "As I was saying, Mr Saville, you suffered no loss by not accompanying us yesterday evening. An insipid affair, with the most beetle-headed rustics masquerading as gentlefolk—"

"They *are* gentlefolk, Caroline. And I thought we had a fine dinner." Bingley, his plate loaded with fried potatoes and devilled kidney, took his seat at the table.

Darcy, essaying little more than bread and butter, and a great deal of coffee, felt impelled to offer a more tepid observation. "The food was well done, and the wine was excellent."

"Goulding's port!" came from a reverent Hurst.

"The food was adequate," Miss Bingley conceded. "Hearty and countrified. In keeping with their position in life, I imagine. But it was hardly fine! Why, the Gouldings do not keep a French chef."

Bingley glanced up from his plate. "Nor do we."

Miss Bingley's mouth looked rather tight, as if she were keeping the words confined inside it with an effort. "No, indeed, Charles. We do, however, have a keener notion of how to go on in fashionable life, and the cook here takes direction well enough to produce dishes for more refined tastes."

Her smile for Darcy left no one in any doubt whose tastes she meant. Nobody else at table would meet Darcy's gaze, except for Grayson, who actually smirked at him. If Grayson had in truth been Darcy's secretary, he would have been dismissed and looking for a new situation.

"And your company, Miss Bingley?" Grayson asked.

"Dull-witted and with no conversation to speak of. Barely one step up from the peasantry," she answered.

Even Bingley, for all his sweet temper, could not stomach that. "Caroline! Enough! Our neighbours are gentry."

She merely lifted her chin. "I speak as I find, Charles. Why, what old-fashioned nonsense when we went into dinner! All the ladies to go in first? Why, no one does that these days. It is positively primitive! And when I hinted how they may go on, I was most rudely accosted by Eliza Bennet—"

"It is still a very common way of showing courtesy," Darcy said, breaking into what he suspected would be a tirade against the widow. "You may find the tradition countrified, Miss Bingley, but it is an old one, allowing the hosts to give precedence and honour to their guests. Many people still consider that to be important."

"Perhaps so, sir. But you must agree in your turn, that it ends in a most indecorous scramble where no person knows their place and people who have no right to it, push themselves forward to take places of honour."

"This is a well-established neighbourhood. I have no doubt the ladies know precisely where they stand in the order of things."

Miss Bingley tensed so much that the cords of her neck stood out. "Indeed? And yet Mrs Bennet was quick to follow in my sister, and her second daughter immediately after her. You cannot say that is a proper order."

"But it was, Miss Bingley. Mrs Hurst was asked to lead in the ladies since she, the wife of a gentleman, was the principal guest of the evening. As the foremost lady in the district, Mrs Bennet would usually lead—"

"Foremost before the advent of my sister and myself, I think!"

"No, Miss Bingley. Netherfield Park may be the largest estate, but Longbourn is the most senior. It is several centuries older, and the Bennets take precedence. That has not changed because your brother has leased Netherfield."

Miss Bingley turned an unhealthy shade of orange-red. Georgiana had purchased a bonnet with ribbons of that precise hue, Darcy remembered, to take with her to Ramsgate. Coquelicot, she had called it. It was not flattering on either lady.

"And Eliza Bennet?" Miss Bingley asked in more subdued tones.

"Is a widow, not an unmarried girl. She walks ahead of her sisters, even Miss Bennet—as is proper."

"A widow?" Louisa Hurst stared. "Truly? But everyone calls her Miss Elizabeth. She does not wear a widow's cap. Surely you are mistaken, Mr Darcy."

That earned her an admonitory glare from her sister. "Mr Darcy is never mistaken, Louisa! Though, to be sure, she was introduced to us as Miss Elizabeth. How did that come about?"

"I do not believe," said Darcy, in the interests of strict fairness, "that the introduction was properly completed."

Miss Bingley snorted. "But I am certain that Miss Lucas introduced her to us. You must remember it."

"As I say," Darcy murmured. "It was incomplete. She is, I believe, more properly Mrs Grayson."

Bingley's attention had been on his plate, but at that he looked up quickly. "Grayson? I say—"

"How outrageous then that everyone refers to her as if she were unmarried! How disrespectful to her husband." Miss Bingley's coquelicot flush faded to a more becoming rose-pink. "To my mind, such a dismissal seems to dishonour him."

"I quite agree," Grayson said, earning himself an approving nod from his hostess. "Not at all the thing."

Bingley tried again. "The point is—"

"An impecunious widow forced to live with her parents again." A cat with a canary could not have smiled more widely than Miss Bingley.

"Caroline, she is not—" Bingley put down his fork.

"The gown she wore yesterday evening was very fine," said Mrs Hurst, in more doubtful tone. "It did not suggest to me an impecunious widow."

"One who must have wasted her jointure, if she is reduced to her parents' charity again. That is perhaps, why she is so thrusting in society." Miss Bingley tapped her chin in a manner intended, Darcy thought, to indicate thoughtfulness. It did not. She merely looked as though the canary's feathers tickled on the way down.

Bingley looked upward for an instant. Perhaps calling upon some deity to grant him patience. Perhaps admiring the fine plasterwork on the ceiling. "She is—"

"Her impertinence is intolerable," Miss Bingley said. "She was most rude yesterday evening when I attempted to convey how one went on at such a dinner in Town."

"Perhaps you should not have hinted that you were a guest of the Marquess of Lansdowne." Beside Hurst, his wife started and grimaced slightly, giving her sister a look of such guilt that there was no doubt of the source of Hurst's intelligence.

The glare Miss Bingley directed at Mrs Hurst would have shrivelled Netherfield's beautiful wrought iron gates to piles of rust. She mouthed an admonitory "Louisa!" at her sister, lifted her chin and stared down her nose at her sister's husband. "I did no such thing! If Eliza Benn— If Eliza whatever her name is, is so dull-witted as to think that is what I meant—"

"Dull-witted? Quite the last thing I should call the young lady in question. You implied you dined with Lansdowne, Caroline, and she did not allow your pretension to go unchallenged. She was not the dull-witted one, my dear. She has your measure." The smile Hurst directed at Miss Bingley was pure malice, but then he had a lot to endure from that quarter.

Miss Bingley cast imploring glances at Darcy, seeking support, no doubt. He kept his attention on buttering a fresh slice of bread and slathering it with strawberry jam. It was difficult to be certain who looked the most pained at his concentration on his task: Miss Bingley, who rated herself more highly, or Hurst, who was very fond of strawberry jam.

Miss Bingley returned to the fray. "I am not to be blamed if I was misunderstood by those... those ninnies! Eliza is the one with all the pretensions, only she pretends intelligence with nothing more than fine eyes to support her!"

Darcy gave his bread a critical look, and smoothed out the jam more evenly. She would keep harping on that. Tiresome.

Miss Bingley drew in a long breath, and half turned away from Hurst. "She is not worthy... no, I must not be unkind to the unfortunate."

Bingley took his gaze from the plasterwork. "Caroline, please listen to me—"

"How sorry I feel for her! To be so reduced.... It is very sad. Having escaped Longbourn once, and haled back there by poor circumstances! We must have compassion on her, I suppose, for all her shabby, opinionated ways and her determination to be noticed by everyone, so pitiably eager to be the cynosure of all eyes."

Bingley threw up his hands and returned to his breakfast. He caught Darcy's gaze, and lifted one shoulder in the merest shrug.

Miss Bingley raised her hand to her mouth and tittered in that irritating way society women had. "You must be careful, Mr Darcy. I noticed she contrived to be seated next to you at table." More high-pitched hee-hee-ing from behind her hand. "She will be desperate to snare herself another husband!"

"Good Lord, sir, yes," Grayson said, all long-faced sincerity while his eyes were lit with mischief. "You should be very careful of such a lady, sir."

Dismissal without a recommendation, that was what Grayson deserved.

Darcy took a bite of his bread. It tasted of summer, the sweetness bringing to mind the sensation of a hot sun warming the burgeoning fruit, and chasing away the chill of the squally late-autumn rain gusting against the breakfast-room windows. "I do not believe that I am in any danger. Mrs Grayson made no attempt to attract my notice. Indeed, she spend the entire dinner talking to the gentleman on her other side."

"Oh." Miss Bingley's look was that of the cat seeing a second canary. "I expect those country people had more in common. What did they discuss? Turnips, perhaps? Or potatoes?"

Darcy allowed through the chuckle that had been threatening ever since Hurst had exposed Miss Bingley's pretence. "Alas, nothing so bucolic, Miss Bingley. They spent their time recollecting their shared experiences of piracy. From what I heard, they believe the standards of swashbuckling skulduggery have fallen mightily since their day." He reached for his coffee, aware Miss Bingley and Grayson were both staring. He looked from one to the other. "I think they were merely looking at the wrong sort of buccaneer."

He raised his coffee cup, and ignored the bemused glances. He did not wish to be the object of a widow's coy advances. Of course he did not. But it was galling, all the same, that she had given all her attention to John Lucas. Ridiculous, when the conversation of a man of the world, a more sophisticated man than that rustic, could have been hers for the asking if she had but turned her head and invited him into the debate.

Miss Bingley looked closely at him. He had no idea if she saw what she looked for, but at last she sat back and signalled to a footman to refresh the teapot, returning to her breakfast.

"Well, Mr Saville, perhaps we may absolve her of that, at least. For my part, I will continue to think of her with pity for her circumstances. Poor thing! Poor, poor thing!" She smiled. The second canary had evidently ventured close enough to be dealt with as pleasurably as the first. "I am resolved to be very kind to her." Another smile. "In all conscience, I could do no less."

Malice was by no means as sweet as strawberry jam. Darcy rose, bowed to his hostess, murmuring something about the library, and left Grayson congratulating Miss Bingley on her magnanimity. He was aware of her gaze, as calculating as a cat's, all the way to the door.

"Very kind," Miss Bingley repeated. "It is the least she deserves."

CHAPTER TWELVE

The Middling Sort

Bingley, his left hand forming the bridge for his billiard cue, did not take his eye from his ball for an instant. He drove the cue forward, cannoned off Hurst's ball and neatly potted the red, gaining himself enough points to net the game. His skill had improved markedly over the summer. He must have been practising.

"Miss Bingley seemed unaware of who Mrs Grayson is," Darcy said when Bingley and Hurst had shaken hands, and Hurst had handed over his two shillings wager.

"I did try to tell her. Four or five times, at least. She did not wish to hear me. What more am I to do?"

"I meant," Darcy said, "that she did not recognise the name of your landlord."

"Landlord!" Hurst stared. "You jest! That chit of a girl owns this house?"

"Yes. At least, a Mrs Grayson is my landlord." Bingley frowned. "I do not know if I ever mentioned it."

"You did not," Hurst said. Several tall-backed chairs lined the walls of the billiards room. He took one, nodding when Darcy came to join him. The stare he directed at his brother-in-law was sharp and alert, with nothing in it of the somnolent sot whose mantle the man apparently chose to don in other company. "Good Lord."

"Indeed," said Darcy. "I would have thought that you would have mentioned it when you talked with Miss Bingley about taking the lease."

Bingley eyed him with obvious amusement. "Do you discuss business with your sister?"

Darcy bobbed his head to concede the point.

"I thought not." Bingley returned his attention to his cue, reaching for a leather pad to burnish the sides. "There was no necessity to discuss the lease with Caroline. I told her all she needed to know—that I had found a house I liked, and that it was a convenient distance from Town. I may have mentioned it was owned by a widow... that, I do not recall. Caroline was more interested in the house than its owner. Louisa and Hurst were at his estate in Norfolk at the time. When I wrote to invite them, the issue never arose."

Hurst's snort was most ungentlemanly. "Bingley, you might have written her name half a dozen times, but your writing is so blotted and indecipherable, I would never have known it. It was all Louisa could do to determine that we were invited to join you." He added, with a faint smile for Darcy, "I make Louisa translate his letters."

Darcy returned the smile. "I have no Louisa, unfortunately. Bingley's correspondence is more enigmatic and perplexing than the Delphic oracle."

"I write with spontaneity, that is all." Bingley glanced up. "I confess, the day we came to view the house, I rather imagined the owner to be a wrinkled old crone, not someone like Miss Elizabe— Mrs Grayson, I mean. Why do people call her Miss Elizabeth? I am sure Sir William Lucas does. Others too."

"Perhaps because she is so young. She can barely be of age," was Hurst's opinion. He frowned. "Yet, she cannot be recently widowed, either. She wears neither mourning nor a widow's cap."

"The steward said something of when her husband died. Can you remember?" Bingley asked Darcy. "I confess I cannot. I was more interested in the house."

"Summer '07."

"Good God." Hurst was patently disgusted. "She must have been little more than a child. Sixteen, at most. How abominable!"

Something in Darcy's chest tightened around his heart like a carpenter's vice. The same age as Georgiana. Dear God, the same age... Elizabeth Grayson had once stood in Georgiana's shoes, but no one had arrived in time to save her... No. She may have been complicit, in a way Georgiana had not— Yet Georgiana had not been entirely innocent. She had known full well that to elope was wrong, went against everything she had been taught. How had she forgotten that? She had connived with Wickham, with that cur of a mongrel, almost to the point of her own destruction. Could youth mitigate folly?

The hand he passed over his mouth trembled, the fine tremors in his fingers fluttering over his face. He forced his breathing into a calm serenity he could not truly feel.

He wrenched his thoughts away from Georgiana and back to Elizabeth Grayson. However much a child she had been then, she was not one now. Her role, though... her guilt or innocence... that was the question, when considering why James Grayson had married her. But however that marriage came about—through her mother's machinations, no doubt—it was indeed abominable that a child should have been used in that way. What in heaven's name had Grayson been about, allowing himself to be caught?

"Yes, that was it—the year seven. I recall now that her husband had inherited this house less than a twelve-month before. How do you remember these things, Darcy?" Bingley was lightly amused.

"I pay attention."

And knew when James had died.

"You had better rein in Caroline, brother," Hurst cocked an eye towards Bingley. "She has taken a dislike to Miss Eliz— Mrs Grayson. That could be awkward."

Bingley sighed and placed his cue on the edge of the table with exaggerated care. He came to join them, taking a chair on the other side to Hurst. "I will try."

"Miss Bingley seems somewhat intense," Darcy said.

This time Hurst cocked that satirical glance at him. "And that surprises you? You are interested in Miss Elizabe— Drat it! Mrs Grayson. Caroline is no birdwit and has two eyes in her head. She sees it."

"I am not—" Darcy stopped, shook his head. "Not for the reasons you suppose. I have a... a business interest."

"Are you after Netherfield to increase your holdings?" Bingley's eyebrows rose so high they almost disappeared under his hairline.

"Not precisely." Darcy could only hope his expression did not betray him. He added, feeling more than usually awkward, "I cannot say more about it at present, as others are involved. I am sorry."

"I assume that is why you have Saville with you?" Bingley nodded. "I thought it must be something unusual for you to engage a secretary. Well, I will not pry. This is a pretty house and a good estate. I could wish for it myself, but the steward was quite clear in his belief, you remember, that Mrs Grayson is not minded to sell."

"I am surprised she chose to return to her parents' home after living here, when surely she might have more independence." Hurst looked around the room. "I am certain Longbourn is a fine house, but not so fine as this."

"She has Netherfield's dower house in Meryton," Darcy said. "Smaller than Netherfield, of course, but a good, commodious house. It was damaged in the big storm at the end of September. I can only suppose she has returned to her father's house while hers is repaired."

"Oh ho! Then she owns two houses of quality? That will stick firmly in Caroline's craw. However, it is not only Miss Elizabeth that concerns her." Hurst's expression turned thoughtful, brow wrinkling. "I suspect Caroline had hopes of finding a place where she could belong by right."

Bingley jerked up his head sharply, and turned to his brother. "I do believe you have the right of it. She feels, very keenly, the injunction laid on me by my father to improve the family's standing and achieve landed status. She knows it would bestow a... a legitimacy that we do not have."

"Bingley!"

"No, Darcy. You have been a very good friend, and without you we would not have reached as high as we have. But the truth is, that we are received on sufferance in many places, as adjuncts of you."

"Which is ironic, since I do not truly enjoy society."

"That is how it is. Louisa married well—if you will forgive me for putting it in such terms, Hurst."

"Not at all. The match was to the advantage of both families." Hurst's smile had a ruminative quality. "My family has never been more than minor Norfolk gentry, landed for several generations now, but not too high. We are of a similar kind to the gentry in this district." He chuckled, and shook his head. "To Caroline's disgust, I should add. She is as dismissive of the district around Chamnhurst as she is about the people here. Chamnhurst, Darcy, is a good estate of something over two thousand a year. With care, I can afford most comforts in life consonant with being a gentleman, but I do not have the means to bespeak every last luxury. Louisa's dowry enabled me to extend my holdings and increase our overall income. In return, she is a gentlewoman by marriage. We both gained by the arrangement."

Hurst was sharper than Darcy had ever seen him. That he hid this thoughtful, considered manner under the guise of a man whose only thought was food and drink, was startling.

"We Bingleys were more than content with that." Bingley's nod at his brother showed affection and a respect Darcy had never suspected. "After all, we are not gentry, but of the middling sort. We anticipated a similar match for Caroline."

Hurst laughed outright at that. "When Bingley became one of your circle, Darcy, the move from trade to lower gentry was no longer enough for her."

"And yet that is the natural progression. Her sights should not be set too high, if she is not to be disappointed." Which was, Darcy hoped, an unequivocal statement of his position vis-à-vis marriage and Caroline Bingley.

Bingley's grimace was answer enough, a counterpoint to Hurst's cheerful grin.

"Yes," said Hurst, with a nod. "But you will understand, Darcy, that the point you made this morning, that the ladies of the district all know where they stand in local society, rankles on her like a sore spot under a saddle. She must realise that despite her dowry and Bingley's income— which is twice mine, by the way—she has no more secure a position in this district of people who have no footing in the London society we move in, than she has in the *Ton*. She had high hopes of taking a leading role here and, I think, finally coming to a place she could call her own, where she could draw breath freely."

"I am astonished that you understand this much of your wife's sister," Darcy said.

"I listen to them while they talk." Hurst's mouth twitched. "Caroline seldom moderates her voice, even when I am there. I have cultivated her belief that I am usually insensible and sleeping off my potations, and that makes her incautious. Louisa knows better, but also knows that curbing Caroline is a waste of her breath." He chuckled. "Wellesley would benefit from a mind such as Caroline's in his war room. She plans campaigns against the bastion of the *Ton* with more aplomb than the War Office manages against Boney."

"But with about as much success." Bingley sighed.

"True," Hurst said. "But while I find her something of a trial—I lose my wife whenever the two are together, since she swallows up Louisa as the whale did Jonah—and only brandy helps me tolerate her, I grant her the virtue of persistence."

Belatedly, Darcy felt this discussion went beyond matters to which even a family friend ought to be privy. Hurst merely laughed, when he said so.

"You have two good eyes too, Darcy. I do not doubt that you see Caroline as she is and what drives her. Still, you are right in that we ought not, perhaps, to discuss this so openly. Leave her to me, Bingley. Or rather, to Louisa. I will ensure they both have a better understanding of Mrs Grayson's position. It would be a great pity for Caroline to waste the kindness she is so determined to bestow."

"Poor Louisa!"

"Poor Louisa is not in it, Bingley. I am about to write to Town for the sapphire necklace." Hurst directed a sharp smile at his brother-in-law. "You may buy her the earrings."

Bingley winced, and sighed. "Very well. Ask them to send the bracelet, too. I might as well be hanged for a sheep as a lamb."

Darcy was surprised to find that he was looking forward to witnessing Elizabeth Grayson's response to Miss Bingley's new knowledge of the widow's true status.

They met at a card party hosted by the Harringtons a few days later. As ever, Miss Bingley and her sister—to whom she appeared reconciled after Louisa Hurst's indiscreet gossiping with her own husband—dressed for Town, rather than a less formal country invitation, and swept into the Harringtons' house in finery intended to intimidate.

He stayed close to Miss Bingley, finding a distance that meant he could hear her conversations without being so close that she herself would take heart from it and read into it a softening towards her. He walked a fine line so long as he and Bingley were fast friends. Darcy must accord Caroline the deference and attention warranted by her being related to Bingley, but not accord so much it would give rise to expectations that he had no intention of fulfilling.

Elizabeth was with her elder sister and Miss Lucas, who always seemed to be close by. Bingley, of course, went to Miss Bennet's side with the speed and dispatch of an arrow loosed from Cupid's bow. Darcy refrained from rolling his eyes, though it was a close-run thing.

Miss Bingley and Mrs Hurst hurried after their brother. It was difficult to see if Miss Bingley's eagerness was to patronise Elizabeth with her warm feelings, or snatch her brother from an entanglement she had no hesitation in stigmatising as beneath him.

Bingley could probably do better in monetary terms than the near-penniless daughter of the local squire, but Jane Bennet was above him socially. She could not offer him advancement, but consolidation of the level he had reached: he would bring money into the union, easing her lack of dowry, while she dispelled the scent of trade. That was not to be dismissed out of hand, but Darcy's main concern was that the girl showed no sign of returning Bingley's ardour. And that mother... Darcy regarded Mrs Bennet. She sat in the midst of a group of middle-aged ladies he recognised as her particular cronies. Lady Lucas was there, and Mrs Goulding... those two he knew. The others he had seen at various social gatherings but had no recollection of being formally introduced. Mrs Bennet's air of smug satisfaction was almost palpable. She saw the value of a son such as Bingley. She would be very loath to allow him to slip from her grasp, and that milk-and-water elder daughter of hers would, Darcy suspected, do as she was told.

Bingley could do better in terms of social advancement, and would not thrive in a marriage without affection. Darcy would remind him of that.

He took a step sideways, where the draped curtaining of the full-height windows gave him some cover, and turned his attention back to the ladies, only a few feet away. Elizabeth and Miss Lucas had risen and come to meet Miss Bingley and Mrs Hurst. Darcy could not but admire their strategy. They had handily cut off Bingley and Miss Bennet, leaving them in some privacy and preventing his sisters from interfering. Really, very neatly done.

The ladies murmured greetings and dipped curtsies at each other. Miss Bingley took a step forward holding out both her hands to Elizabeth, who, after an instant's delay, extended her own.

"My dear Mrs Grayson," Miss Bingley said, grasping Elizabeth's hands. "I fear you must think us sadly rag-mannered! We have been so remiss... We had no notion, I assure you, that we were referring to you in such a disrespectful way."

Oh, how neatly did Miss Bingley cast her criticism at the local families, not one of whom had called Elizabeth "Mrs Grayson" at any time the Netherfield party had been present. She had painted them all in an ill-mannered, ill-bred hue and at the same time limned herself and her sister in a far more polite, refined light.

Elizabeth's smile looked less brilliant than Darcy was accustomed to seeing. "It is true, Miss Bingley, that my neighbours are very kind, and most do refer to me by my girlhood name. I have thought for some time that I have done you a disservice by not insisting on your being introduced to me properly."

Darcy could not see Miss Bingley's expression fully, but doubtless it reflected her disgust at the thought of being the lesser in any such introduction, that she would be the one presented to Mrs Grayson and not the other way about. A masterly riposte on Elizabeth's side. It paid Miss Bingley back in full.

"It is of no moment, however," Elizabeth went on, "and has caused no injury. I am not offended, and there is no necessity for your apologies. The oversight was ours. We are known to each other now—"

"Indeed," Miss Bingley said, nodding so emphatically that her feathered headdress looked likely to take wing. "I understand the circumstances completely, and of course, one should not expect the highest... the manners here are rather different to those I am... Whatsoever the cause, I am glad to have this misunderstanding behind us. I would not add to your sorrow for the world by not acknowledging the dignity of your position."

Elizabeth appeared to bite her lip. "It has been some years, Miss Bingley. I have had time enough to grow accustomed to my lot."

"But I imagine the regret is unending. The loss of standing, if you like. The diminution from wife to... Oh, I should not speak of it! I do not wish to cause you pain. And now, I hear, further misfortune has fallen upon you. I understand you removed from the marital home and it is let. That must have been a sad day for you! And now your house is in disrepair, I am told. How hard it must be!"

"Well, one must hope it is only a temporary displacement, Miss Bingley." Elizabeth's gaze dropped until she was staring at Miss Bingley's satin slippers.

Beside her, Charlotte Lucas snapped open her fan and used it to cover the lower half of her face. Above its scalloped edge, Miss Lucas's eyes were very wide.

"As you correctly surmised," said Elizabeth, "it is not something of which I can easily speak—"

"Of course, of course! I did, though, wish you to know how thoroughly I sympathise and to say how much I regret the misunderstanding on our part." Miss Bingley squeezed Elizabeth's hands and released them. She glanced at Bingley and Jane Bennet, who were in close conversation. "I will not speak of it again, of course. And I must go and greet some of the other ladies." She curtsied. "My dear Mrs Grayson."

"Miss Bingley." Elizabeth curtsied back, Miss Lucas following suit a second or two behind her.

Louisa Hurst hesitated, while her sister bustled away to harass their brother. Darcy could see nothing of her expression, but Elizabeth gave her a nod.

"Mrs Hurst," she said, and curtsied, rather more deeply than the slight dip she had bestowed on Miss Bingley.

Louisa Hurst's grip on her fan left her fingers white. She curtsied back and hurried after Caroline.

Charlotte Lucas, though, caught Elizabeth's hand. "Did I dream that?"

Elizabeth's face was downcast again and Darcy could only glimpse it. When she looked up, she was biting her lower lip until it was white under the pressure. She and Miss Lucas stared at each other. Quite suddenly, Miss Lucas let loose a small snort of laughter, and Elizabeth relaxed her mouth into a blazing smile.

"Oh lud!" she said. "I do wish Papa could have witnessed that! It would have kept him amused for a month."

"Indeed! I do not know how you kept your countenance, Eliza! What was she about, do you think?"

"We will assume the best, and believe she truly wished to redress the mistake under which she laboured rather than seek amusement at my expense. It was... kind of her."

"If you say so."

"Truly, I do not think Miss Bingley so devoid of proper feeling as to make sport of widowhood. She dislikes me, I know, but that would be more than improper. It would be vicious. While I do not like her any more than she likes me, I do not believe her capable of that sort of malice."

Another choke of laughter from Miss Lucas. "Well, perhaps you are right."

"I think I am. I do not think we are the sort of people she is used to, and so she is not comfortable here in Meryton. I would rather believe she is trying to make herself so. She does not want open enmity." Elizabeth glanced at her sister and Bingley. "Until she must."

"You are kinder than I, by far." Miss Lucas snapped her fan shut with a flick of her wrist. "Now all the social niceties are correctly observed, shall you and I go and preserve Jane's peace?"

Elizabeth tucked her arm into Charlotte's. "We shall. But only, my dear, in such a way that I do not compromise the... what was it? Ah yes. The dignity of my position."

She turned her head and looked directly at Darcy. For an instant she seemed startled at his proximity. He kept his expression blank and unmoved, he hoped, despite having been caught so rudely observing her, and bowed. She narrowed her eyes at him, then blazed him to ash with her smile. She favoured him with a nod and a curtsey.

Darcy watched her rejoin her sister. She was laughing again.

Damn the woman! Was she laughing at him?

Again?

CHAPTER THIRTEEN

Sporting Gentlemen

October did not so much as wear itself out, as it was washed away in rain and squalls. A persistent chill wind gusted from the north-east.

Darcy, Bingley and Hurst did a great deal of shooting, ranging across Netherfield's preserves where pheasant and partridge were in abundance, sometimes joining with other gentlemen of the neighbourhood and the militia officers on larger shoots across a neighbour's lands. They met more of the local worthies by this means, shooting across their preserves by invitation. One such new acquaintance, Mr Harpur, the local magistrate, was pleased to welcome them to his house, the great house at Stoke, which was even more impressive than Netherfield. A cousin of the Harpurs at Calke Abbey in Derbyshire, he had been well acquainted with Darcy's father, and they discovered many other mutual connections. The shoot over his lands had taken copious numbers of birds, but Darcy treasured most the memories Harpur shared of

George Darcy at similar shoots at Calke. That had been a particularly fine day.

On the first of November, they were invited to the season's inaugural run with the Puckeridge Hunt, only a few miles to the east, rising in the dark before dawn to reach the meet at Furneux Pelham Hall. As with the shooting parties closer to Netherfield, Darcy ensured Grayson joined them, Hurst kindly lending a suitable hunter from the string he had brought with him from his Norfolk estate. It was the life Grayson was born to, after all, and it was little enough to do to stop the boy's long face and sighs of martyrdom. The Hunt was a subscription pack of the kind the lower gentry favoured, and it was unlikely they would encounter anyone who knew Grayson and could give the game away. Grayson was suitably grateful for the consideration shown him.

Or so he said.

"A wonderful day!" was Bingley's verdict when they arrived home again, wet, tired, and aching from head to toe.

At least, Darcy was. Bingley seemed to have more energy than an entire pack of foxhounds, somehow even more vibrant after a day's hard run after the fox. Grayson was similarly animated. He and Bingley were of an age, both of them three or four years Darcy's junior. More in Grayson's case.

Not that he was old. They were merely very young. And untried.

Puppies.

At each meeting, with each new set of neighbourhood faces, Darcy had made discreet enquiries about the history of Netherfield.

The closer neighbours—Goulding, Harrington, Sir William Lucas and his son—had proved close-mouthed, returning enquiries with shrugs or platitudes, or, in the case of John Lucas, a hostile, stony stare. Those from farther afield did not appear to know anything beyond the mere fact of the house's existence. They might remember the original owner—James Grayson's godfather,

Thomas Templeton—or the tenant who had rented Netherfield since. But James, it seemed, had made no firm impression upon the wider neighbourhood. He had been there barely a six-month, after all.

"I do not think I ever met him. Died pretty quickly after the old man, did he not? Drink, I heard," was the contribution of one landowner from near St Albans, so quite out of the district.

"Got riveted to a local girl," another said, this one from an estate on the other side of Hertford. "Something too smoky by half about that, I fancy, but damned if I know the particul— Wilkinson!" The gentleman waved violently at another man across the room. "Forgive me, sir, but I must speak to Wilkinson. He has a gun for sale. Wilkinson!"

Old Mr Harpur said only, "Are you interested in buying the estate? A little close to London for you, I would have thought, though I see the value of estates between Derbyshire and London, where you might break your journeys. I do not believe the current owner wishes to sell, though." And, more quietly, almost to himself, "An unlucky house, that one. Templeton was a friend. He took the loss of his son very hard." He sighed. "That is a feeling I share. It does not do to talk about it."

Which, of course, prevented Darcy from asking more.

Propriety and consideration were, at times, damnably restrictive.

The day after the hunt, they enjoyed more excellent sport when, in his turn, Mr Bennet held a shooting party over Longbourn's fields and hosted a meal afterwards.

Longbourn was a gracious old house. Very old—the central portion pre-Elizabethan, Mr Bennet said when asked, with the wings added during that great queen's reign—it was heavy with three or four centuries of history. The dining room in which the repast was served boasted some of the finest oak panelling Darcy had ever seen, its warmth enhanced by the welcoming fire roaring in a chimney breast massive enough to roast the proverbial ox. The room comfortably sat all two dozen gentlemen who had made up the shooting party, and to add to the hospitality, it was attended by all the Bennet womenfolk.

Darcy could ignore most of them. The mother and the two youngest had eyes only for the redcoats, the middle daughter sat in a corner with a book, and Bingley worshipped at the feet of the eldest, leaving her no time to give attention to anyone else. Bingley was well content. Darcy was... well, he was not entirely certain what he was. The remaining Bennet daughter, the widow, was far from meeting Miss Bingley's opinion of her ambition to entrap a second wealthy husband. She greeted Darcy courteously enough but gave him no more of her notice than she bestowed on anyone else. Indeed, she spent more time at Grayson's side, in seemingly earnest conversation that lapsed, once or twice, into Elizabeth's clear laughter.

No hee-hee-hee-ing behind her hand for Elizabeth Grayson.

Darcy moved closer to listen, arriving across the table from them just as Elizabeth's smile changed to that of a lady making polite conversation, lacking the genuine brightness of a few moments earlier.

"Sir William?" Elizabeth said in answer to some sally of Grayson's that Darcy had not caught. "He came to sporting pastimes later than the other gentlemen, but I had not heard he was so poor a shot that your hat was more in danger than Papa's partridges."

An assertion on Grayson's part that had Darcy raising an eyebrow. Sir William Lucas was not the best shot Darcy had seen, but it was ludicrous to suggest that the man put his fellow shooters in jeopardy.

"I suppose one cannot expect better," Grayson said.

Elizabeth's smile had a sharp edge to it now. "Because he is only lately landed, you mean? Perhaps. But Sir William has settled into his role as the owner of an estate—"

"A very small one."

"That true. One cannot deny that in terms of acres alone, the Lucas holdings are smaller than many of the estates in the district.

But it is more than many gentlemen can boast. You are, I deem, a younger son yourself?"

Darcy's mouth twitched as he fought a smile. Beautifully done, and with a sweet archness that tempered the offence she certainly intended to give.

Grayson reddened across the cheekbones. "The second son."

"I thought so. Still, I would never deny that you are a gentleman by birth, despite your current employment as a secretary. Nor would I deny that Sir William has achieved that distinction through his own efforts."

Grayson's smile looked forced. "You defend him very well, Miss Eliz... Mrs Grayson."

"You are country born and bred?" Her own nod echoed Grayson's. "Is it not the case, in your own home district, that there is a permeability between the upper reaches of the trading class and our own? Although perhaps that is more likely here because of our closeness to London, where there is a larger contingent of educated gentlemen in trade—" She inclined her head at Grayson's expression. "Very well, sir! Of gentleman-like men of industry. Men like Mr Bingley."

Grayson conceded the point with a grudging "Mr Bingley is gentleman-like."

"He is not alone. There are many such men. My mother's brother is one of them, and I am very proud of him, for he is educated and enlightened, and as intelligent a conversationalist as any gentleman born. Sir William was very successful in his former trade, and that speaks to his diligence and acumen. It is not that people ignore the differences, Mr Saville, but we accept them. Sir William is one of us now. He has earned a place here."

"He has a witty and beautiful defender."

She ignored whatever compliment Grayson may have intended. "If I defend Sir William Lucas, it is because his kindness to me, at a time when I needed it most, can never be forgotten."

"And yet, he calls you by a name that does not accord you your status."

Elizabeth smiled. "Yes. He is a very thoughtful and good-willed man. Forgive me, Mr Saville, but I should speak to some of the other guests. The duties of a hostess, even a subsidiary one, are taxing, you know!"

She rose to her feet. Grayson, taken by surprise, was an instant delayed in leaping up in deference. He bowed, and with a nod of her head, she moved away from both Grayson and Darcy, going to join her father where he stood with Mr Harpur and... yes, with Sir William Lucas. Her message was unmistakable.

Darcy rose, rounded the foot of the table where Mrs Bennet ruled supreme over several raucous militia officers with her two youngest daughters as her willing acolytes, and took the chair Elizabeth had vacated. Grayson had resumed his own seat, and was staring down at his plate.

"A useful conversation?" Darcy asked.

"Hmmmpfh." Grayson raised his face. "I do not get to speak to her as often as I could wish. It makes my enquiries more difficult. I do not wish to spend the entire autumn and winter dancing at her tune." He glanced sidelong at the widow. "You overheard?"

"I did. Most of your conversation, at least."

"She was flirting with me, do you not think? I expect one such as she cannot prevent herself from doing it." Grayson cast a withering glance at the two youngest Bennets fluttering around the red-coated officers. "It is in the blood."

Flirting!

Darcy managed not to guffaw but could not resist a sardonic twist to his mouth. "I am morally certain you know that not to be the case. Her manners are lively and spirited, and not those of polite society, but not many women would flirt by schooling you in propriety and the courtesy due to those who have offered you hospitality."

Grayson's flush deepened, as indeed it should. He said "Hmmmpfh" again, and turned his attention to his plate and the footman who approached with more of the superlatively roasted beef.

Darcy left him to it. Instead he looked up to fix his gaze upon Elizabeth. He watched as she left her father's company and went to encourage some of the other gentlemen present to take more of the excellent repast. As she left, she briefly touched Sir William's arm, and the two shared a smile. Indeed. She was quite partisan in her loyalties.

He watched her for the next half hour, speaking but little to Grayson and the others near him. He was revolving in his mind what Elizabeth Grayson had said.

His kindness to me, at a time when I needed it most... And *He is a very thoughtful and good-willed man...*

She considered Sir William's calling her by her unmarried name a kindness, a mark of good will. At a time she had needed it. A se'enight earlier, Mr Harpur had said Netherfield was an unlucky house. And had not Sir William let slip at the Goulding's dinner that he had felt helpless in regard to that something that had happened at Netherfield? Was that the reason for his kindness and good will?

It would all bear thinking about. It would bear considerable thinking about.

The recent sporting meetings had done much to win the militia officers acceptance in local society. Colonel Forster reciprocated the only way he could. Though it was widely known he was partial to the elder Harrington girl, he was not yet leg shackled. A bachelor dinner at the White Hart the day after the Longbourn shoot was a neat way of repaying the regiment's social obligations.

Darcy allowed himself to settle back into reserved silence behind Bingley's assured cordiality, as he had done so many times before. Grayson was far down the table, with Phillips, the man of business for Elizabeth Grayson. He suspected young Grayson's motives were not entirely social, but did not interfere. It was why Grayson was there, after all. On Darcy's other side, Hurst was enjoying himself, for once not retreating behind the shield of drink-ridden sot, and was deep in a discussion with Forster on the finer points of staging Shakespeare in the modern theatre. Darcy had suspected neither of them of such intellectual interests.

He sipped at his wine—tolerable, but not the best—and glanced around the table. The usual set of faces, although Elizabeth's father was not there. Bennet was not known as a sociable gentleman. It was astonishing that only his wit and intelligence, and not his taciturnity, had been passed on to Elizabe—

He brought the thought to a crashing halt, covering his sudden confusion by grasping the carafe of wine and splashing more into his glass.

Elizabeth.

When in heaven's name had he started thinking of her as "Elizabeth"?

He could not remember. He was mired neck deep in it, before he knew when it started. Good God, that way lay utter folly!

Well, that had to stop. Yes, she was an attractive woman... not so great a beauty as her elder sister, although with ten times Jane Bennet's spirit. Which was to say that Elizab— that Mrs Grayson was all wit and fire and liveliness and her elder sister, whom so many would say claimed the palm for beauty, was an insipid milksop in comparison. But he could name ten women... twenty... who were more beautiful than Elizabeth Grayson.

And better bred. Much better bred. She might be the daughter of a gentleman, but in truth, all Mrs Grayson could boast were family connections of the worst and most unfortunate sort. And she did boast of them! She had done so to Matthew Grayson. "I am proud of my uncle," or some such, she had said. Proud! Of a man who, unlike Bingley, still practised his trade. At least Bingley was a generation removed from the stink of the shop and taking every possible step into the gentry.

Worse, she meant Mrs Bennet's brother. Darcy took a quick swallow of wine. He could just imagine what a paragon the man must be, the masculine counterpart to that harridan. A vulgar thrusting Cit, without a doubt.

She was proud of that. Proud! Good Lord.

Darcy looked about the table, catching sight of Grayson. That young man was in close chat with Phillips, whose red face betrayed that he was in his cups, if not ape-drunk. Phillips was another uncle, was he not? Another fine relative of whom she could boast! Those sisters of hers, too. Very well, the eldest was refined enough, well bred and unexceptional. In every way, unexceptional. The middle sister was an oddity, to be sure, a rude little savage with no notion of how to go in society and no musical talent whatsoever. Shy, perhaps, but old enough to know better. The two youngest, though... loud, coarse, vulgar and unrestrained. He would be astonished if either of them avoided infamy.

They were, in fact, a cruder version of their widowed sister. She had an intelligence they did not show, of course. But that impertinence of hers... it was merely more refined than their animal spirits. She was not improper, the way they were improper, but she had a high opinion of herself and had no notion of being respectful towards those immeasurably above her.

She had laughed at him. More than once.

No, indeed. There was very little on the credit side to Elizabeth Grayson.

She had Netherfield of course, if a man were in desperate need of money or land. But Netherfield came complete with the animosity of the family of its previous owner. Her dead husband's family. She brought no good connections there, either. If young Grayson proved some irregularity—

No. The circumstances of her marriage and James Grayson's death might be mysterious, but he could not believe she was responsible for anything untoward. Yet, something had undoubtedly happened in that "unlucky house", which did not improve the widow's eligibility.

Eligibility! Eligibility? He was in as much danger of making a cake of himself regarding a chancy widow as Bingley was over the widow's sister. Such nonsense.

He must have had too much wine. He would think of her no more. Not one more thought.

Not one.

With a quiet deliberation, he turned to Hurst and Colonel Forster and joined their conversation. No one could have noticed his sudden distraction. No one would ever notice. He was a gentleman, an intelligent and rational man, who acted always with propriety and prudence, and with an eye to what was due his breeding and his position. He would cede control of himself to no man, and certainly to no woman. Particularly that woman. He was in no danger of giving way to foolishness. He was far too restrained for that.

And he would give serious consideration to removing himself from all temptation until the regular tenor of his mind was restored. This was a trial he was confident he could face. His fortitude would withstand such paltry attractions.

He discovered how far he was to be tested, however, when, at breakfast next morning, an exasperated Caroline Bingley told them that Jane Bennet was in the house, having come for dinner the previous evening and been taken ill over the meal. She had ridden there, while the men had been at the officers' dinner. In the rain. More of the Bennet matron's machinations, no doubt.

It was not that unedifying thought that had him looking around the table, ensuring no one saw the perturbation of his spirits. Jane Bennet had no power to move him. But even as he considered the implications of having an ailing Bennet daughter in the house and the folly Bingley was likely to commit as a result unless he was saved from himself, a footman flung open the door to admit a glorious creature, one with pink cheeks and windswept hair, and whose beautiful eyes were quite brilliant with the exercise of a three-mile walk across the muddy fields.

Elizabeth had come to nurse her sister.

And torment him.

CHAPTER FOURTEEN

A New Favourite

The day after the Longbourn shoot, Elizabeth had met Charlotte Lucas in Meryton to make their weekly visit to Nether House to spend an hour with Mr Muir and the Rances, examining progress with the repairs.

"Well, at least we have a roof above our heads again!" Elizabeth said as they walked away together, afterwards. Nether House had regained its old, pretty shape, with its hipped roof re-tiled and proudly boasting two tall chimneys. "The chimney has been rebuilt so well, I am not able to tell it from the other."

She hid her winces with smiles. The repairs bit hard into the money she set aside each year to enhance her sisters' meagre dowries and support her mother in her widowhood, should it come to that.

Charlotte agreed. "Mr Muir has worked wonders to ensure we will be back in our own snug quarters soon."

Elizabeth eyed the clouds. As she had predicted earlier in the day, rain was on the way, and sooner rather than later. "I shall be very glad to leave Longbourn."

Charlotte merely smiled. "Your mother is trying your patience?"

"I do not have grace enough to feel pity for her fears if she outlives my father."

"Her home taken from her by your father's heir, and her income reduced to a sum that would barely keep her in genteel poverty? Her desire to see the five of you settled in marriage before that fell day is quite understandable."

"That was before I inherited Netherfield from James. Her future now is not so bleak. She knows I will support her despite— that I will support her. But no! Still she toils and plots to marry off my sisters. Her machinations have no surcease and so long as he is reasonably sound in wind and limb, no single gentleman between eighteen years and eighty is safe from her scheming, no matter his suitability, or his own wishes or proclivities. She has not one mite of moderation! And poor Jane must bear the brunt of it."

"The only recourse in life for a woman of our stamp is marriage. The lot of a spinster is an unhappy one." Charlotte did not try to hide her sigh. "I do not relish being sneered at."

"Charlotte—"

"I am content. Truly." Charlotte squeezed the hand Elizabeth had laid on her arm. "Enough of that! What has your mother done to Jane?"

Elizabeth hesitated, but the mulish set of Charlotte's mouth showed she would not welcome sympathy. So Elizabeth said, slowly, "The officers are holding a dinner today, as you know."

Charlotte cocked an eyebrow towards the White Hart on the other side of the marketplace as they walked through it. A carriage rolled towards the Hart. "The guests are gathering as we speak, I fancy. That is the Harringtons' carriage."

"A note came to Jane this morning from Netherfield, inviting her to spend the time with the Bingley sisters. Of course my mother has ensured that Jane cannot have the carriage. Jane is to ride there. Look!" Elizabeth's sweeping gesture took in the lowering clouds above their heads and their threatening load. "She will be drenched. Mama hopes she will be forced to stay at Netherfield for the night, and so see Mr Bingley when he returns from the officers' dinner. And to what purpose, other than to make her appear desperate, and increase his sisters' scorn and resentment? It is most ill-conceived."

"And you could not sway your mother—?" Charlotte caught herself before finishing, and shook her head. "What am I saying? As soon stop a cavalry charge. My mother is no less determined, you know. Perhaps it is the way of all mothers." She sighed, and her mouth twisted. "I wonder if I would be the same, had I the chance of marriage and children?"

"You have too much sense." Elizabeth made a gesture of pushing it all away. "At least, I am free of it myself. I could not hold my tongue if she tried to force me again into marriage. It is a relief that none of those single gentlemen are pointed in my direction."

Charlotte laughed. "I am unconvinced the gentlemen need to be directed towards you, Eliza." She raised the hood of her cloak against the mizzling rain. "Mr Darcy looks at you a great deal."

"As we know from his own lips, Charlotte, it is not with admiration."

"I do not think that gentlemen stare at ladies for many other reasons."

Elizabeth raised one shoulder in a shrug that Miss Bingley, she who epitomised the highest *Ton* standards, would stigmatise as dreadfully uncouth and unladylike. "I am barely tolerable in his eyes. I must assume there is something so reprehensible in me that he looks to find yet more evidence of my faults. Perhaps he and Miss Bingley then catalogue them together."

"It is certain he pays you significant attention. He listens to your conversations, you know, as well as rarely taking his eyes from you. You look at him often, too, I notice."

"I do not!"

"If that is the case, then it is a puzzle to me, how aware of his scrutiny you are." She smiled at Elizabeth's snort. "What is your view of him, truly?"

"He thinks himself much above us, but then he is a rich man and nobly connected. No doubt he considers he has good reason. He is taciturn and unsociable, superior and in general, an unpleasant sort of man. He has not deigned to meet our welcome with grace."

"He is uncomfortable in the neighbourhood's company." Charlotte hesitated in so uncharacteristic a manner, that Elizabeth stopped and drew her to the shelter afforded by the jutting window of the baker's shop.

"What is it?"

"John told me that Mr Darcy and his secretary are asking about Netherfield, its history and its previous owners—and hence, about you. John says Mr Darcy is quiet about it, not too obvious, but he has noted it happen more than once. He stopped Papa from saying too much on one such occasion. You know Papa would never say anything to your detriment, but..."

"I know." Elizabeth shivered as the brisk wind gusted rain into her face. She blinked the water away. "I suppose Mr Darcy may be on the lookout for purchases that may extend his holdings."

"Perhaps. Or perhaps because he is interested in you, and wishes to understand how Netherfield has been left to you."

Elizabeth stared. This was beyond belief!

"Well, despite your contention, Eliza, a man does not generally stare at a woman out of dislike. Whatever his lack of appreciation of you at the assembly, he has proved very attentive since."

"Pffft," was all Elizabeth would vouchsafe to say.

Charlotte's smile had a bitter-sweet quality. "None so blind... I could wish a gentlemen was as assiduous in discounting my charms, I assure you. Think again."

Elizabeth had no opportunity to answer. A blaring call interrupted them.

"Lizzy! Lizzy!"

They both started, and turned. Lydia stood under the market cross in the centre of the square, waving her arm above her head to attract Elizabeth's attention. Kitty made a less vigorous motion of her hand and a faint '..zy' echoed Lydia's bellow. A couple of redcoats and a stranger in gentleman-like garb attended them, which circumstance neither pleased nor surprised Elizabeth.

Elizabeth raised her hand in acknowledgment of her sisters' calls, but did not essay to join them. The stranger's face took on an expression she could only describe as alarm and dismay. He looked past her towards the Hart, and she followed the direction of his gaze. A second carriage had arrived, decanting Messrs Darcy, Bingley, Hurst and Saville outside the doors. When Elizabeth looked again at the stranger, he caught her gaze and grimaced, before taking a sideways step to use the nearest officer to shield him from view, and half turned away, as if to hide his whitened face from notice.

"How very peculiar. Charlotte, did you—" Elizabeth glanced again from the door of the Hart, now closing on Mr Saville's heels, to the stranger. "Oh. It is nothing."

"Do come!" Lydia called. "We are to Aunt Phillips's house, to bear her company while uncle is at dinner with the officers."

Kitty merely waved.

Elizabeth shook her head, and tugged Charlotte away. "Poor Kitty, always overwhelmed by Lydia's... Lydia's largeness. Everything Lydia does has such life and energy to it, that Kitty cannot keep up. She is a pale, feeble copy. One a bright picture in the most vivid colours, the other a watercolour left out in the sun to fade. Mrs Hurst has the same sense of pallor against Miss Bingley's intensity, do you not think? She fades into a kind of insignificance."

She glanced behind her. Lydia stood staring after them, her hands on her hips, brows drawn down over her frowning face. But even as Elizabeth looked at her, she thrust one arm through that of Lieutenant Denny, snuggling up so close to him it appeared her cloak and his uniform jacket had fused into a single red mass. Good Lord, but Lydia could not possibly realise what such brazen behaviour betokened for her reputation! Or her sisters'.

Elizabeth considered shaking Lydia until the chit's teeth chattered and sending her home. But the little group was already walking towards Mrs Phillips' house, trotting swiftly against the increasing rain. Lydia jumped over a puddle, aided by the soldier and the stranger, who had seemingly recovered his countenance.

Each man took one of her arms and swung her across the dirty water. Kitty scurried after, tugging along her own redcoat. Good heavens, they were wild, coarse, unrestrained... How could they act so?

Elizabeth turned away. To create a scene in the village street would do more harm to the family's standing in their neighbours' eyes. She could only resolve to speak to her father. Not that it was likely to do much good.

Charlotte's amused voice recalled her to their conversation. "I have noticed you treat Mrs Hurst with a little more kindness."

"Am I unkind to Miss Bingley?"

Charlotte pursed her lips. "You are a little sharp at times. Less so with Mrs Hurst." She flashed Elizabeth a sideways glance and a swift smile. "Indeed, you have more patience with her, as I have seen you show Kitty. You are more encouraging."

"I must be sure to hide my feelings better. I would not offend either willingly, not while Jane... Well. It would be uncivil in any event. I shall be more circumspect."

"Think of Miss Bingley as a test of your Christian charity and fortitude."

"She certainly is! I am tested most severely."

Only their mother lamented the absence of Lydia and Kitty at dinner. Indeed, she lamented so loudly and so long that even Papa failed to take amusement from it. Whilst he did not rebuke her silliness, his cold, sarcastic responses eventually silenced her, leaving her huffing to herself at her end of the table while Elizabeth talked quietly to her father at the other. She drew in Mary to the conversation whenever she could. Perhaps Mary was glad of the notice, because for once she forbore to make the Reverend Fordyce's sermons the whole subject of her remarks and although nothing of what she said was remarkable, she was sensible. Mary would likely repay genuine attention.

A footman from Netherfield brought a note from Jane as they rose from the table, explaining she would stay the night. That was enough for her mother's huffing to change to a smug delight that Elizabeth found difficult to bear. She took herself off to the drawing room as a preventive measure against speaking her mind, stabbing a needle through her embroidery in lieu of stabbing her wit through her mother. She was alone there when, a little before Hill was due with the tea tray, the rising wind blew Lydia and Kitty in from Meryton. Both were pink-cheeked and merry, so much so that Elizabeth suspected Mrs Phillips had indulged them in a bottle of her husband's best wine. It had done little to moderate their spirits.

"Oh, where is Mama?" demanded Lydia. "I have such news!"

"Oh yes," said her faithful echo. "Such a wonder—"

"Quiet, Kitty! I shall tell Mama. Where is she, Lizzy?"

"She went to her room for something," Elizabeth glanced up from her embroidery. "She will be back when tea is brought in, I expect. Papa is in his study and Mary is practising—"

"Hmmph, I can hear her. She pounds that poor pianoforte as if she were a blacksmith beating out horseshoes."

Elizabeth attempted to quell Lydia's spite with the observation that Mary was most diligent in her practice and that was to be commended.

"Oh, if you say so. We shall tell you the news, then. You should have joined us." And Lydia plumped down hard onto the sofa beside Elizabeth, bouncing her against the springs.

Elizabeth, who had her work tilted towards the candles so she could see to set her stitches, sucked on her needle-jabbed finger. Just as well for Lydia, the linen had not been blood spotted. "Is our aunt well?"

"Oh yes, I suppose so. She was vastly glad Kitty and I went to keep company with her while Mr Phillips was out, was she not, Kitty?"

Kitty had come to lean against the sofa's high back. "Ye—"

"He was still at dinner with the officers, of course, when we walked home, but she set uncle's clerk to escort us." Lydia pulled her face into a disdainful pout. "He is a paltry sort of fellow. I care for none unless he wears a red coat."

"Nor do I," Kitty said.

"You both astonish me."

"But you should have come with us! Did you see the gentleman with Denny? He is to join the regiment tomorrow. He came today to speak to Colonel Forster and sign his papers, but he will not have a uniform until tomorrow and... well I do not understand it perfectly, but it means he is not yet properly a redcoat and so did not attend the officers' dinner. I told him that it was little loss to him, since he went to Aunt Phillips's house with Kitty and me instead, and —"

"He went to her house?" Astonished, Elizabeth jabbed her finger again, and with a smothered exclamation, she bundled the abused handkerchief away into her silk workbag. "He did not dine there, surely! He went to the house, despite the master of it not being there to accept an introduction? You must be jesting, Lyddie!"

"Oh, no one cares about such old-fashioned notions! You are far too fastidious sometimes."

"I may be fastidious, but you are not nearly as fly to the time of day as you think you are! You little ninny, what sort of true gentleman does such a thing, uninvited?"

Lydia dismissed Elizabeth's disbelieving stare with a wave of her hand. "No, no. You do not understand. Aunt leaned quite out of her window to invite him, so far that I feared she might topple into the street. How I should have laughed! Would not you have laughed, Kit?"

"Oh yes! Prodigiou—"

"Well, she did not fall, and she was delighted to invite him in, make his acquaintance and welcome him. She loves company, as you know. He did not dine. He said it would not be proper without Uncle's sanction, although he was very grateful for Aunt's attention. He sat with us only a quarter hour, then betook himself to the inn—the Red Lion, I fancy, rather than the Hart—promising to return with the other officers when Uncle is there and make his apologies for imposing." Lydia beamed. "There! Was that not very gentlemanly and proper enough to satisfy even your notions of good conduct?"

"It has improved my opinion a little."

Lydia sighed. "Far too fastidious, is she not, Kitty? His name is Wickham. He is very handsome and charming, and shall be even more so when he is in his regimentals!" She swayed a little in her seat, her expression rapt and her eyes half-closed. She clasped her hands below her bosom. "Oh, I cannot wait to see him in his red coat!"

"Nor I!" Kitty sighed and clasped her hands in imitation.

Elizabeth contemplated using her own hands to box two pairs of ears, but that office was not her responsibility, though she doubted her father would shoulder it as he ought.

"Pish, Kitty, he will want nothing to do with you when I am there to engage with him. You may forget him entirely." Lydia abandoned her melting looks and dreamy expression to glare daggers at her sister.

"Why should he like you better? That is all—"

"Because I am prettier than you, and livelier, and the gentlemen all do like me better. That is why. Oh do stop crying! You are such a watering pot— oh, Mama! Mama! There you are! Mama, I have such news!"

Mama entered into Lydia's feelings quite as fully as her youngest daughter might wish, and for the next half hour, the room reverberated with their joyous chatter. Elizabeth huddled into her corner of the sofa and sipped the tea Hill brought in a moment or two after Mama had joined them. Not for the first time, she contemplated abandoning the drawing room for her father's study, and the chance of sipping something stronger.

Something much stronger.

When Jane's second note arrived at breakfast, Mama could not quite meet Elizabeth's direct gaze, but busied herself with consuming a prodigious amount of toast and tea. "No one ever dies of a trifling cold, Lizzy. You make too much of it."

Elizabeth pushed her plate aside. "Do you forget, ma'am, that Mrs Harpur took a chill and was dead within the week?"

Her mother flushed an unbecoming crimson. "Mary Harpur was always ailing! Jane has a little cold. That is all."

Papa tutted loudly, and rustled his newspaper at them. "Well, if Jane should depart this life, it will be a comfort to your maternal heart to know she did so in pursuance of your ambitions towards Mr Bingley, my dear."

Mama made a noise that reminded Elizabeth of her Aunt Phillips's asthmatic parrot.

Elizabeth returned her attention to Jane's note. It was scribbled in pencil, Jane's usually fine script untidy and the letters ill-formed. "I do not think Jane is at all well, Papa. She says here that her kind friends at Netherfield"—Elizabeth succeeded in keeping the sarcasm from her tone—"have sent for the apothecary."

"Jones is a good man." Papa lowered his newspaper and looked at his second daughter. "Am I to order the carriage for you, Lizzy?"

"No need, Papa. I will walk. The rain has stopped and I will enjoy the exercise. It is barely three miles." Elizabeth turned her gaze to her mother and waited. She was not to be disappointed.

"Nonsense, Lizzy! There is no necessity for you to go to Netherfield. There is nothing for you there."

"Jane is there."

"You cannot go in all this dirt. You will not be fit to be seen!"

"I will be fit to be seen by Jane, and that is all that matters. I will send word if need be." She pushed back her chair, and to a chorus of clucking admonishments from her mother, she nodded to Papa and took herself off. The rain had curtailed her exercise in the previous week, and a brisk walk over the field paths, clambering over stiles and jumping over puddles, was just to her taste.

She arrived at Netherfield with muddy boots, a splashed petticoat and her face aglow. Mr Allen admitted her with a word of welcome but without so much as a blink of surprise, though he sent for his wife. That good lady fussed over Elizabeth with genuine concern that she would succumb to the same illness as her elder sister. She brushed Elizabeth down as swiftly as may be.

"Miss Jane slept ill, there's no denying it, and she remains abed. Mr Jones says 'tis naught but a feverish cold and cough, but she should not think of removing from here until her fever goes. There. I doubt I can do better with the mud without you change out of those things, and that, I know, we just can't do. Well, we must make the best of it." Mrs Allen used her hands to smooth the wild curls on the sides of Elizabeth's face, and resettled her bonnet. "They're in the breakfast room, ma'am. Well, show her in, Allen, do!"

Allen, with an air of not hearing his wife's reproof at all, did so with great gravity, sweeping open the door and announcing Elizabeth to a subdued chorus of astonished exclamations. Elizabeth blew out a breath, squared back her shoulders and walked inside.

CHAPTER FIFTEEN

Materia Medica

"I vow, Jane, they could not have stared harder had I been an animal in the exhibit at the Exchange."

"Hhhmmm," said Jane.

"Mr Hurst said nothing and his wife looked distressed, although I cannot be sure if that was for you or for the sight I apparently made. Miss Bingley left me in no doubt. She was loud in her astonishment that I had taken the trouble to come at all, and her horrified gaze was fixed upon my muddy petticoats. I think that Mr Darcy, although lacking a swathing of linen bandages, had been embalmed in the Egyptian style—you recall Papa's delight last year at finally obtaining a copy of Mr Hertzog's *Mumiographia*?"

"Hhhmmm," said Jane.

"Mr Darcy, I fear, is no stranger to the embalmer's art, so rigid and unmoving was he. Mr Saville stared agape, his fork suspended in mid-air. 'Twas like a scene from a play, with all of them portraying Astonishment, or Society Confounded or some such. Only your Mr Bingley vouchsafed me a real welcome, and since that must arise from his care and anxiety for you, I could not but see him as the most amiable of the company."

All the time Elizabeth spoke, keeping her tone low and using a sing-song intonation intended to soothe, she passed a cool cloth over Jane's hot skin to wipe away the worst of the fever sweat. She took another cloth from the pile, sprinkled it with lavender oil, and gently pressed it to Jane's temples to help alleviate the pounding headache to which her sister had confessed. Elizabeth hoped the next "Hhhmmm" was one of relief and a sense of increasing comfort.

Mrs Allen bustled in with a night-rail over her arm. "It's one of my own, ma'am, and not of the quality Miss Jane will be used to, but it is clean and fresh."

"That is extremely kind of you, Mrs Allen." Elizabeth caught her former housekeeper's hand for an instant, and the two shared a warm glance.

"It will be odd to have you here, ma'am, as a guest."

"But a guest I am. We must not forget that Miss Bingley is mistress here now." Elizabeth squeezed Mrs Allen's hand and released it. "I do confess it eases my mind that you and Mr Allen are still here to look after the house. I can trust you to care for my sister, too."

"That you may, ma'am. Shall we change her night-rail?" Mrs Allen hefted the cotton gown in her hands and between them, they eased Jane out of the fashionable, lacy confection she was wearing, and into Mrs Allen's nightgown. It rather swamped Jane, but was clean, cool and comfortable.

Jane sighed, and managed to turn up the corners of her mouth into a small smile. "Thank you, Lizzy, Mrs Al—" Her voice was scratchy and hoarse, and the effort of even those few short words had her coughing and pressing a hand against her chest to try and halt the spasms, unable to continue. She was unhealthily flushed, sweat beading on her brow and upper lip.

"Do not talk, dearest. I assure you I can do so for both of us." Elizabeth wiped Jane's hot face again. "Indeed, I welcome the opportunity to hold you captive to my wit for a few hours. I can be as nonsensical as I wish, and you do not have the voice to gainsay me. What could be more pleasant and convenient?"

Jane turned her face into the cloth and sighed again. In a moment or two, her eyes drifted shut.

Elizabeth sat back. "What did Mr Jones say of her case?"

"He thinks it no more than a bad cold, to be sure, but said that since Miss Jane has a tendency for chills to settle on her chest, he would send a composer and a paregoric draught for her, as sleep will be the sovereign remedy. His boy delivered them an hour ago and she has had one dose. He will return tomorrow to see how she does. I dosed her all night with my own receipt for chesty coughs, too, and he said to continue with it. She has taken it well, and finds it soothing, I think."

"I have seen that receipt. It contains laudanum." Elizabeth worried at her lower lip, staring down at Jane. "I do not—" She halted. Swallowed hard against the lump in her throat. "I cannot be easy about it. With your mixture and paregoric, that is great deal of opium."

Mrs Allen, her expression grave, put her hand over Elizabeth's. Elizabeth started under the housekeeper's touch and looked down to see her own hands wringing out the cloth until her fingers were white.

"Oh." She dropped the cloth into the waiting bowl. The lump in her throat was the size of Meryton. A surge of something... shame? Terror? She could not tell. She knew only a pounding heat and a torrid dread that had her throat closing until her breath came short and her heart beat faster than the militia's tympanist could drum out an attack. She had to swallow again before she could speak. "I cannot like it, Mrs Allen."

"She isn't him, dear ma'am. Rest easy. Mr Jones would not give her anything that would cause harm. Recollect that he would not supply opium when he realised the ill-effects."

No, indeed. Mr Jones had stiffened his back against threats and more than once, outright raving, and had refused to supply any opiates. Not that it had truly helped. All it meant was that every other apothecary within fifteen miles had been importuned and not one of them had the same high principles as Mr Jones. They had pocketed their extortionate fees and handed over the poisonous stuff.

"Sleep is what she needs, ma'am," Mrs Allen said, her tone far gentler than Elizabeth had ever earned from her own mother.

"Between the paregoric and your mixture, she will certainly sleep. I would like to talk with Mr Jones about it, but for now I will try to be content and not grieve myself over what cannot be changed."

Mrs Allen squeezed Elizabeth's hand and withdrew her own, returning to a brisk cheerfulness. She started folding the lacy night-rail. "Now then, I shall give this to the girls to launder, and return it to Mrs Hurst."

"Mrs Hurst is of my height, I think. Her sister's nightgowns would have fitted Jane better, since they both have similar tall, willowy figures."

They looked at each other and Mrs Allen merely pursed her lips.

Elizabeth could only smile, with a sort of weary resignation. "It was very kind of Mrs Hurst, and I shall thank her for it when I see her."

"She is a quiet lady, but she was quick to offer what aid she could," Mrs Allen said. "Do not fret, Miss Elizabeth. Your sister shall be very well in a day or two."

"I am sure she will be," Elizabeth said, and when Mrs Allen had left her, she smoothed Jane's coverlet and tucked it more securely around her sleeping sister's shoulders. "I will make certain of it."

Elizabeth's opinion of the Netherfield ladies improved as the morning wore on. Mrs Hurst appeared an hour or so before noon, letting herself into the room quietly and with the minimum of fuss.

"I have come to see how Miss Bennet does," she said, keeping her voice low, "and, if you would like it, to bring you some refreshment."

Elizabeth smiled. "I would be most grateful, Mrs Hurst. It is very thoughtful of you, thank you. Mr Jones's draughts have Jane very sleepy, which is probably all to the good, but I will see if I can rouse her. I am certain she would welcome some tea. It will soothe her throat."

Mrs Hurst returned the smile, and beckoned in the maid hovering in the doorway with a tea tray. She poured the tea with the same quiet grace she had shown when entering the room, and sat patiently as Elizabeth coaxed Jane to take half a cup. Jane swallowed with obvious difficulty, but she managed a faint smile and to croak out her thanks, before drifting away again into sleep.

Mrs Hurst drew Elizabeth over to a set of chairs set near the fireplace, where they could talk with less chance of disturbing Jane. "I know it is a platitude, but sleep truly is the best healer." She poured tea for Elizabeth and herself. "I am so sorry that Miss Bennet has been taken ill. It is difficult to be away from home at such times."

"It is, but you have been very kind. I am grateful that you called for Mr Jones. He has known us all our lives, and knows just what to do to bring Jane back to good health quickly." Elizabeth took the proffered cup with a murmur of gratitude.

"It is always the first day of a cold that is so difficult to bear. One often feels so dreadfully weak and feverish." The smile she directed at Elizabeth was rather sweet. "I confess it usually makes me rather peevish."

"Unlike Jane, I am horrid when I am ill." Elizabeth sipped her tea and sighed. It was very well made. "She has all the goodness between us, as well as the beauty."

"I cannot agree," Mrs Hurst demurred, but could say no more as Miss Bingley came in.

She entered with exaggerated caution, tiptoeing across the thick carpeting to join them. Her sister greeted her with a fond look and an outstretched hand, and for the first time Elizabeth saw the same loving bond between them that she had with Jane. She should not be surprised. Doubtless Miss Bingley showed another side of herself to her sister, her real self, that she did not share with strangers. It was much as Jane's serenity protected her in public, Elizabeth dared say, and Miss Bingley's society manners were her armour.

"How does she do?" Miss Bingley nodded approval at Elizabeth's response, her concern appearing sincere and putting Elizabeth into charity with her. "Mr Jones, I am told, is an excellent apothecary. Mrs Allen sent for him, you know, and has a great deal of confidence in him. I hope he will do your sister good."

"I am sure of it. I cannot tell you, Miss Bingley, how grateful I am for your kindness, and Mrs Hurst's. I do thank you both."

"It is nothing," Mrs Hurst said as her sister settled into the chair beside her.

Miss Bingley refused tea. "I am sorry that our invitation was the means of her illness. I had no notion that she would ride."

Jane had had none either, and Elizabeth allowed an instant's fulmination against her mother's silly plots. "I am told my father had need of the carriage horses elsewhere on the home farm. That would not normally be a problem, as Jane is the accomplished horsewoman in the family and thinks nothing of a three-mile ride. It is unfortunate that she was caught in the rain."

"Very," said Miss Bingley, in such a way as to leave Elizabeth speculating about whose misfortune most concerned her. "We had some excellent conversation over our meal before Miss Bennet was taken ill. She was telling us of your family."

"Indeed?"

"I understand that you have no near family on your father's side, and only an aunt and an uncle on your mother's—"

"We have a large family ourselves." Mrs Hurst laughed softly. "They can be both a comfort and a cross, as I am sure you will realise."

"We are not intimate with many of them now." Miss Bingley's tone was repressive. "Your uncle lives in Cheapside, I am told. Do you go often to London?"

"In Gracechurch Street, rather than Cheapside. And yes, the two families visit with each other a great deal. We are very close."

"Gracechurch Street... Cheapside... It is all the same, surely?"

"Not at all, Miss Bingley. It is an irrefutable matter of geography. The two streets are quite separate."

Miss Bingley covered her mouth with one hand and tittered out a laugh. "Forgive me. It is an area quite outside my experience. We live on the other side of Town, of course."

"My husband has a house on Jermyn Street," Mrs Hurst said, quickly, "We spend a great deal of our time there still, when not at Mr Hurst's estate in Norfolk."

"A convenient address," Elizabeth said, Miss Bingley sinking in her estimation again. "I understand that your family is from the west of Yorkshire. Are they still very involved in the area? I am told there is the matter of a canal lock?" She sipped at her tea again. It was tepid, but still she smiled at Miss Bingley over the rim.

Miss Bingley must be brought to realise that the game she played was not hers alone, and her sudden mottled colour suggested Elizabeth had made her point. But even as Elizabeth spoke, she saw Mrs Hurst bite at her lower lip, and was suddenly struck by her own impertinence and rudeness when Mrs Hurst had been nothing but kind. Elizabeth could play the game as well as Miss Bingley, but in truth she knew better. She should not, would not, descend to that level. Instead, internally berating herself for being such a ninnyhammer as to fall for Miss Bingley's ploys, she turned to Mrs Hurst with a real smile.

"Do you know, Mrs Hurst, I have never been so far north and Yorkshire is quite out of my reckoning. I have heard the landscape there has a particularly wild beauty, and I should love to see the moors for myself. I love the outdoors, as you may have realised, and am a great walker, so do tell me all about it! If ever I should be fortunate enough to travel there, what must I make certain to see?"

Mrs Hurst rallied, and for the next little while, they discussed the sights to be savoured in Yorkshire, and when that palled, Elizabeth encouraged her to talk about her husband's estate in Norfolk. Mrs Hurst grew easy again, and after a little while, Miss

Bingley, accepting the implied olive branch, joined in. The three of them reached an imperfect and unsteady, but perhaps sustainable, level of harmony.

In Mrs Hurst, Elizabeth saw the potential for amity, and even friendship. She could not say the same for Miss Bingley, but then, everyone had their cross to bear. Miss Bingley, it seemed, was to be hers.

She suspected the sentiment to be mutual.

Not long after midday, Elizabeth announced that it was time she returned to Longbourn. Mrs Hurst looked doubtful, although her sister would only say that "Of course, dear Mrs Grayson knew best," and did not hide her satisfaction. But Jane, more wakeful although still weakened and fevered, showed such distress at the thought of Elizabeth leaving her that Mrs Hurst tutted quietly and shook her head.

"You had much better stay, Mrs Grayson. It will ease Miss Bennet if you are here, I am sure." She glanced at Miss Bingley. "I know that when I am ill, Caroline is indispensable to my comfort. Do stay, I beg you."

"Please, Lizzy," Jane begged, hoarse as a crow. Her hot hand clutched at Elizabeth's.

Miss Bingley looked sour for an instant, but Mrs Hurst's words had their effect, giving yet more indication of the good relations between the two sisters. "Louisa is quite right, Mrs Grayson. You must consider yourself quite at home here as long as dear Miss Bennet needs you."

Elizabeth forbore to say that she had never felt at home at Netherfield, but she thanked the sisters for their kindness and consideration. She declined to join them for a nuncheon downstairs, preferring to stay with Jane, although she happily accepted the offer of the tray which was later brought to her by Mrs Allen. While the Bingley ladies went to share the midday meal with the gentlemen, Elizabeth penned notes to her parents, with the addition of one for the Longbourn housekeeper. She had no doubt her mother would happily send Jane's prettiest clothes in the expectation that Jane would dazzle Mr Bingley—although Elizabeth thought even Mr Bingley might not find red eyes and a red nose to be the epitome of charm and beauty—but had no confidence Mama would send what was truly needed by both her daughters. Mrs Hill would ensure that what came would be appropriate, and that Elizabeth, too, would have clothing enough for a few days' visit.

The ladies returned at about four for an hour. Jane tried to rouse herself, but she was not able to converse without her voice deserting her or a paroxysm seizing her lungs. She was persuaded to take a little broth, but refused anything more. She fell asleep again before Mrs Hurst and Miss Bingley left at five to dress, leaving Elizabeth to scramble into an evening dress with a maid's help. The maid was to spend the evening with Jane, under the strictest instructions to send for Elizabeth immediately if there were a need.

At half past six, Elizabeth was called downstairs to dine.

CHAPTER SIXTEEN

Social Niceties

For a simple family meal at home, dinner was very fine and of a quality Elizabeth was more used to seeing at an entertainment. It quite drew the distinction between country expectations and those of Town society. She was seated between Mr Hurst, who greeted her in a gruff tone before returning his attention to his ragout, and Mr Saville, who was more restrained in his manner since last they'd met after the Longbourn shoot. Perhaps he had taken her strictures to heart, and intended to show a less lofty demeanour.

She ran upstairs to see Jane when the ladies withdrew, but Jane slept deeply and the maid was diligent in tending to her. Content to leave her in the girl's care a little longer, Elizabeth returned to the drawing room to spend an obligatory hour or two being an exemplary guest. If she were unwelcome in some quarters, all the more reason not to give them cause to cavil at her behaviour.

Miss Bingley was at the pianoforte when Elizabeth entered, playing with all the skill bestowed by a natural musical gift fostered, no doubt, by the best masters. Elizabeth's own talents were no more than adequate, but she could appreciate Miss Bingley's finesse. She listened with real delight and praised the performance sincerely.

Mrs Hurst looked pleased. "Caroline is very good, I agree, but do not decry your own performances, Miss Eliza— Oh, forgive me. Mrs Grayson, I should say. I do find it hard to remember!"

"My neighbours are all very kind to call me by my girlhood name, and I am not in the least offended. I will answer to either without discrimination."

"Still, it is a difficult situation for you." Miss Bingley took a seat on a sofa opposite Elizabeth, who sat beside Mrs Hurst. "Mr Hurst told us that repairs are almost complete on your little house."

"Yes," said Elizabeth. "It is a great relief. I hope to—"

"Of course, you will be glad to have use of it again. It must help tremendously to stretch a small inco—" Miss Bingley stopped herself, and said, before an astonished Elizabeth could respond, "It is in Meryton, I believe?"

"Yes. A few moments' walk from the marketplace, but quite set back from the road and private. I will be pleased to—"

"I have seen it, I think. Such a pretty house will be easy to let. There will always be some merchant or other to lease it."

"A merchant... yes. Or his descendants." Elizabeth could only wonder at Miss Bingley's lack of understanding. "I should explain—"

"Oh, here are the gentlemen!" And Miss Bingley turned from her as the gentlemen entered the room, and had something to say to Mr Darcy before he had walked more than three steps through the doorway.

Elizabeth turned what she hoped was a pleasant, welcoming expression to the gentlemen. How perplexing! Did Miss Bingley truly think Nether House had been the marital home she now leased to strangers? How had Miss Bingley merely progressed from one misapprehension about Elizabeth's status to yet another? When Mr Hurst had told his wife and sister about Nether House, he must have been so vague as to leave them in ignorance of the whole truth.

She had no time to ponder the riddle. Mr Bingley came to her immediately to ask again how Jane did, and she delighted in his hearty good wishes when she made her report. His concern for Jane was patent. He was called away quite quickly by his sister, and with a rueful smile for Elizabeth, went to attend her. Mr Hurst slumped into the chair beside his wife, while Mr Darcy, ignoring Miss Bingley's siren call, walked to the window embrasure and took up his observation point there. Elizabeth affected to pretend she did not see him staring at her, yet again, and her attention was diverted by Mr Saville following the other gentlemen into the room and coming to sit near her.

They exchanged polite civilities while Miss Bingley and Mrs Hurst busied themselves with the provision of tea and coffee, and the company settled in for a social half hour before deciding on its amusements for the remainder of the evening. After a few moments of such inconsequential talk, Mr Saville changed the subject with some abruptness.

"I am greatly interested in the history of this house, Miss Elizabeth." He kept his tone low, not to be overheard by the others who were discussing when to bring out the card tables, while Mr Darcy stood to one side and stared at her. As was usual. "What can you tell me of it?"

Her breath stabbed into her chest, and she had to look down quickly, as if she were focusing on the fine porcelain coffee can she was lifting from its saucer. "Greatly interested, sir?"

"Very much so." He lowered his voice. "I am here on Mr Darcy's behalf, you understand, to execute some matters of business."

Elizabeth glanced sidelong at Mr Darcy, who had emerged from the window embrasure to stand a little nearer, after accepting a cup from Miss Bingley who had "... prepared it exactly as you like it, sir! I know just how you take your tea."

"Indeed? On Mr Darcy's behalf?"

Mr Saville nodded and smiled, waving his free hand at her in inviting fashion. He balanced his coffee can on his knee, holding it steady with the other hand. "He wishes to know more about the house and estate."

"Does he? Well, I do not know what I can tell you. I have known the house all my life, of course. I was free of it as a girl, since old Mr Templeton was a crony of my grandfather's and my father kept up the connection. He built the house more than fifty years ago, when he married. I am told the only time my grandfather and he were at odds from boyhood to death, was over that marriage." The coffee was bitter, but she swallowed it and took another steadying sip. "He stole my almost-grandmother, you see."

Mr Saville let out a soft laugh. "I am astonished they ever mended the breach."

"I expect they both loved their horses more than any one woman. They were never happier than at Newmarket. They went often together, leaving behind both their ladies." She warmed to her theme. So remote a family history was a safe topic. "My grandfather died before I was born, but Mr Templeton told me of it when I was small. By his end, his memories of his younger days were sharper than those of the preceding week and he recounted the tales often, living in a past before he lost both his wife and his son."

His answering smile was thin, and his gaze was fixed on her. Perhaps he had no turn for nostalgia. "And so the house passed out of the Templeton family, I suppose. Yet I understand the new owner did not live long. A young man and a hero of the war against the French, I heard. His death must have been a sad accident."

Elizabeth put down her cup with a kind of particularity, setting it in the exact centre of its saucer, and moving the saucer to a spot that was the precise middle of the little table before her. She pressed her lips together hard. Just for an instant, to guard against the words that might escape her otherwise, but not so long that she might appear afraid and hesitant. She had no reason to be afraid. None. It was over.

She wound the hand farthest from him into the stuff of her gown. Then she took a deep breath, lifted her gaze and stared him in the eye. "I do not like gossip, Mr Saville. Whatever enquiries you are making, you will gain more by making them elsewhere."

He started, but kept his voice low, mindful there were others in the room who might overhear. "Madam! I—"

"If Mr Darcy is interested in Netherfield or any estate, then I suggest you might better enquire into the condition of the house and its lands. Your curiosity touches on neither."

Elizabeth glanced at Mr Darcy. He stared back at her, frowning. He looked from her to Mr Saville, and his frown deepened. He took a step or two towards her even as Miss Bingley's voice rang out.

"You are being very confidential with Mr Saville there, Miss Eliza— I am sorry, Mrs Grayson. May we have a share of the conversation?"

Elizabeth caught Mr Saville's gaze and held it again. "It is entirely inconsequential, I assure you, Miss Bingley. You could not have disturbed two people who have less interesting things to say to each other." She rose. "I shall return to my sister, if you will excuse me. I have been away too long. Thank you for a most enjoyable dinner, and I hope you all have a very pleasant evening."

The gentlemen all sprang up to bow her out. Mr Saville bowed, his ears a scarlet brilliant enough to rival a militia officer's coat.

When Elizabeth reached the door, she turned for an instant. Mr Darcy had crossed the room to join Mr Saville. They were speaking in close confederacy. She could see Mr Darcy only in profile, and could make nothing of his expression. The waiting footman closed the door softly behind her, cutting off her view of the room, just as she noted that Mr Saville's face was overspread with the same scarlet as had afflicted his ears. Perhaps Mr Darcy was taking him to task for his lack of subtlety.

Good. Mr Saville's performance as a confidential secretary was somewhat lacking. Elizabeth was not surprised that Mr Darcy did not appear pleased.

She was very displeased, herself.

"I have no idea what he was about, Jane, but since he must know who I am and of James's connection to me, I cannot but think it the most unconscionable impertinence. To say such a thing, to me of all people! Outrageous!"

Jane, improved after a night's repose, made a soft clucking noise. She sat up against her pillows, cradling a cup of tea in her hands, her eyes narrowed against the morning light pushing its way past the elaborate curtaining at her window. She got her words out in short bursts, taking a sharp breath between each one, her voice scratchy and hoarse. "He may not... have known... if Mr Darcy is—" She coughed, and took a soothing sip from her cup. "—looking to purchase... Mr Saville's enquiries... understandable."

"They would be if he were enquiring about the condition of the tenant farms, or the rents or some such issue."

Elizabeth was too old to throw herself into the chair beside the bed in a fit of ill humour, but the temptation was so strong she sat slowly and deliberately in order to quell it. Jane lowered the cup and gave her a gentle smile. What she would not give for Jane's peace of mind! She thought, some days, that she had never in her life felt one tenth of Jane's serene contentment.

She had spent the chief of the night at Jane's bedside, even though her sister had slept soundly enough under the twin influence of Mr Jones's paregoric and Mrs Allen's cough remedy not to need her or even notice she was there. Elizabeth had had no inclination towards sleep. She had tried, certainly, stretching out on the bed in the adjoining room that Miss Bingley had allocated to her use, but that had proved futile. She had walked the floor for what seemed a lifetime of hours, turning Mr Saville's questions and expression over and over in her mind. In truth, Mr Saville had said little enough, but any hint coming close to her life with James Grayson cut too sharply for her to think it innocent. When she was weary of Mr Saville, she turned to thinking upon Mr Darcy's staring at her so much. She had thought he did so out of disdain for her person, which she knew from his own mouth had not charmed him, but now she wondered if it were for some other reason. One connected to Netherfield and her own unhappy residence there. When walking did not bring her peace, she had crept into Jane's room and spent the bulk of the night in this self-same chair.

She sighed, and assessed Jane's condition now. Her sister was unmistakably improved, but her eyes were still fever-bright and her face flushed. She suspected Mr Jones would insist on another day or two before he would permit Jane's rising from her bed. Well, Elizabeth would just have to smile and be pleasant, and give Mr Saville as little countenance as was compatible with her being a good and unassuming guest.

She turned over the bulky letter that Mrs Allen had brought along with the tea and yet more of the cough mixture. She had not looked at it until then. "From Papa," she said to Jane, and unfolded it. It had another letter folded within it, in a hand she did not recognise. She read Papa's letter swiftly. Despite feeling languid and stifled when she began it, amusement and appreciation bubbled up within her by the time she reached the end, lightening the load on her shoulders.

"Oh, dear Papa! Do listen, Jane. He writes that he has informed Mama that a guest arrives today, a man he has never met before in the whole course of his life. He reports Mama's nerves are set all atwitter by the knowledge that it is none other than Mr Collins."

Jane's eyes widened. "His heir?"

"Indeed. He writes that of course he reminded Mama that Mr Collins might put her out into the hedgerows the moment that Papa has breathed his last... Really, Jane, he is quite unprincipled in his teasing Mama."

Jane gave her a speaking look, but, Jane-like, would say nothing.

"Very well," said Elizabeth, laughing. "If teasing I may call it. It cuts deep, sometimes. She never can catch when he is funning, and when he is serious, and I suspect he finds that too tempting to resist. However, Mr Collins will arrive at around four o'clock and will stay for a fortnight complete. Papa says that he anticipates nothing but unalloyed enjoyment from the man's company, and as proof of this he encloses Mr Collins's missive. He adds that he is quite out of charity with me, since I have removed myself and cannot join his amusements." Elizabeth unfolded the second letter. "Shall I read it?"

When Jane nodded, Elizabeth read the entirety of the letter in which Mr Collins introduced himself and set out his reasons both for writing, and for proposing himself the satisfaction of waiting on the Bennets and staying with them for some weeks.

Mr Collins was a descendant of a brother of Mr Bennet's great-grandfather who had changed to "Collins" when marrying an heiress of that name. Profligacy and an addiction to French brandy had soon seen the heiress's portion shrink away, and the Collins family had passed into some obscurity. But because of the strict settlement that Longbourn may not be inherited by females, this Mr Collins was, by some convoluted lineage and the scarcity of males in the Bennet line, the only extant male heir. When Mr Bennet was no more, Longbourn would pass out of Bennet hands forever.

Papa had known this man's father, now deceased. The two had heartily despised one another, and Papa confessed to a quite unchristian glee that the elder Collins had predeceased him. *"At least I have the satisfaction of knowing he will never have Longbourn,"* he had written to Elizabeth. *"What the son may be like, I do not know, beyond what may be gleaned from his letter which I enclose for you to see. But I believe, my Lizzy, that he shows promise and I will find the fellow extraordinarily amusing!"*

Jane stared at her when she finished reading Mr Collins's effusions aloud. "Would you read... again what... he says of his father?"

Elizabeth did so: *"The disagreement subsisting between yourself and my late honoured father always gave me much uneasiness, and since I have had the misfortune to lose him, I have frequently wished to heal the breach; but for some time I was kept back by my own doubts, fearing lest it might seem disrespectful to his memory for me to be on good terms with anyone with whom it had always pleased him to be at variance."*

"Hmm," said Jane. "That shows... filial respect... I suppose." She sounded doubtful, as well she might. "He is now a rector... though only lately... ordained? How lucky .... to be... distinguished by... what was the name?"

Elizabeth referred to the letter. "A Lady Catherine de Bourgh, who has granted him the living at Hunsford in Kent. He is profoundly beholden to her, I deem. He puts her claim to 'grateful respect' over his readiness to 'perform those rites and ceremonies which are instituted by the Church of England'." She smiled, her previous melancholy receding. "It would be a queer specimen of a clergyman who performed any other sort of rite! Unless Mr Collins intends to profess himself a Mohammedan."

"Apologising for… entail, and wishes… amends?… Laudable… cannot see how he…. may do such a thing." And Jane had to rush out the last few words before pulling in a long wheezing breath and tapping at her chest as if to loosen it.

"Can you not?" Elizabeth took the empty cup from her and put it to one side. "You had better not speak so much, dearest. Does your chest hurt?"

Jane shook her head and lay back against her pillows, her breathing ever more difficult and rasping. Elizabeth was not disposed to believe her, and rang the bell to call the maid to ask for a bowl of boiling water to be brought. Jane made the slightest moue of the lips when Elizabeth sent the maid on her errand, but if Elizabeth must thrust Jane's head under a towel to make her breathe the steam, then she would do it.

"I share Papa's disappointment in my being absent at the introduction of such a paragon of a churchman to our home," Elizabeth said as they awaited the maid's return. "He will not be such a novelty by the time we return to Longbourn."

Jane held out a hot hand for Elizabeth to grasp. "Instead I keep… you here in… discomfort. … I am sorry… dear Lizzy."

"It is not at all your fault, Jane." Elizabeth glanced around the room, a frisson of ice tingling down her spine and back again to pool between her shoulder blades. "I have never been comfortable in this house."

CHAPTER SEVENTEEN

Thorns and Roses

It sat ill with Darcy that he was caught up in this imbroglio. Very ill. He could not feel more begrimed if he had been labouring in the depths of a coalmine and the evidence of that hot and dirty toil was spread over his countenance and hands for everyone to see.

"The truth is that I do not like this," he told the world outside his window.

Behind him, Simms paused in his task of brushing Darcy's coat for the morning, and when Darcy turned, he caught sight of the man's quizzical expression. Simms had been Darcy's valet for the last dozen years, and knew quite well that Grayson was no secretary and that they were interested in the owner of Netherfield. He was a quiet, trustworthy man, not given to gossip.

Darcy hesitated only a moment. "What think you of the upper servants here? Are they to be trusted in their opinions?"

"Mr Allen is a worthy man, good at his job, sir. I have found him to be educated beyond what is normal for a butler, and sensible. Mrs Allen would rival your own Mrs Reynolds, I think."

"And their view of Mrs Grayson?"

"Respect." Simms said at once. "And pity."

Darcy turned his gaze upon him, but Simms shook his head.

"Perhaps pity is too strong a word. Compassion and sympathy, though, most certainly. They are loyal, and careful to say little." Simms paused. "There is a man called Thomas Rance, who was a footman here. He came here with Mr James Grayson, from his Nottingham estate."

"Graymead."

Simms inclined his head. "As you say, sir. An old Graymead servant. Rance was here for the entirety of Mr Grayson's tenure. He may be willing to speak of it."

"Finding him might be difficult."

"Not at all, sir." Simms helped Darcy into the blue superfine coat, settling it across the shoulders and twitching it into place. He nodded, apparently satisfied that Darcy would not disgrace him. "He is Mrs Grayson's general factotum at Nether House."

"You are not gaining her confidence. Quite the opposite, I fancy." Darcy invited Grayson into his private sitting room with a gesture and nodded to a nearby chair.

Grayson threw himself into the chair with an air that reminded Darcy forcibly of his cousin Lilian's four-year-old protesting that he had been denied a treat by his nursemaid. "Last night was a mis-step on my part."

"Yes." Darcy watched him. "And not the first."

The younger man's face twisted into a grimace. "I had not thought to find her so... clever. I mean, a certain native intelligence and cunning were to be expected but she—"

"Mrs Grayson is educated—if unconventionally so—articulate, witty and, yes, clever. She may not know what you are about, but you have raised her suspicions of you, and I doubt you will make much progress now."

Grayson's scowl would have curdled milk still in the cow. "It was a miscalculation on my part to pose as your secretary. I cannot move freely in society here. I... we need someone who can. Therefore..." He looked sidelong at Darcy. "Perhaps I should return to London."

"It may be for the best, as I fear you can do no good here. Leave Mrs Grayson to me." The only response Darcy gained was a sharp nod and the black look now directed at him instead of the middle distance. "There are other avenues for you, however. I am told a man called Thomas Rance could help."

Grayson's expression changed, his jaw slackening and eyes widening, and his frown now betokening puzzlement rather than rancour. "Rance? There have always been Rances at Graymead, tenant farmers whose sons have worked on the estate while awaiting farms of their own. I heard that James had one of them with him, but it had slipped my memory. I... I do remember Thomas, I think. He would be older than James was. Some five and thirty now, perhaps. I had not realised... He is close by?"

"Very close. He is Mrs Grayson's manservant. So far as Simms has been able to discover, he acts as butler-cum-whatever else is needed in a small household. He lives in Nether House, in Meryton."

Grayson gaped at him, then closed his jaw with a snap.

Darcy lifted a hand to his brow and rubbed away the frown forming between his eyes. "A servant whom your brother brought with him... a servant from a family that has served yours for generations with, I take it, faith and honour?"

Grayson nodded, mute and scowling again. His jaw worked, twitching against his tight-closed mouth.

"Well then, would such a servant would remain with the widow if aught was amiss with your brother's death? It is unlikely that any untoward circumstance could be hidden from servants who knew him so well. It strikes me that others here also speak of her with respect—the butler and his wife, for instance."

Darcy waited. But all Grayson did was glower, his entire body tensed, and raise one heel from the floor to tap his foot against the carpet. He was nervous. What cause had Grayson to be so nervous?

"Perhaps you can seek Rance out."

"No." Grayson looked at him at last. "No. I had better not. He will tell her who I am and ruin all. If she realises I am James's brother, then all is lost. She would not countenance you, either, in those circumstances."

"Very likely not." Darcy looked swiftly away, and when he could command his expression again, he returned his gaze to Grayson. "She may not in any event, after your performance yesterday evening."

Grayson lifted one shoulder in a shrug. Indeed, petulant four-year-olds had better manners.

"I asked you when we first arrived about your brother's valet. You have remembered nothing of the man, nor any thoughts on where he may be found?"

"I do not. He was an old army servant, whom James kept on. Not a man most gentlemen would accept as a valet. I have no notion of what happened to him."

"Well, we should try and discover it. Perhaps Rance knows. You should leave Rance to me, I suppose. I will try and find an opportunity to speak to him." Darcy stood, tugging his waistcoat into place and ensuring his coat sat correctly. "I am for breakfast. You should consider your next steps. You should not join the company tonight at the least—"

"I concluded as much. I will dine in Meryton with the officers."

"Good. I would counsel you to return to London, though. You do nothing here to advance your cause."

"If I have no success by the end of the month, I will go." Grayson's glower would have struck the cow down with bovine staggers.

"That would be best. For all concerned."

Mrs Grayson was not at breakfast.

She had, said the footman, been and gone, saying she would walk for an hour in the gardens. Darcy nodded, and with a glance at the otherwise empty breakfast room—the Bingley family were not early risers—he ran back upstairs and had Simms help him into an overcoat. He wanted an opportunity to speak to Elizabeth alone.

Purely as a matter of the business in hand, of course. For no other reason. What other reason could there be for a man who had himself under good regulation?

She was wandering in the rose garden. Or rather, what would be a decentish sort of rose garden in summer, but in November was little more than winding pathways enclosing patches of muddy earth filled with bloomless bushes already prepared for winter. What thoughts and memories were assailing her there, having returned to the house stigmatised as "unhappy", the house where she had been widowed, and walking in gardens girding themselves for the death of the year?

When he approached her she drew herself up in a manner that could teach his Aunt Catherine, famous as she was for her bad-tempered pride, a thing or two about queenly hauteur. How any man could prefer Jane Bennet's milksop prettiness to Elizabeth's fire astonished him, although at that moment Jane's sweetness might have been welcome. Elizabeth did not smile, but at least she inclined her head in greeting rather than turn on her heel and spurn him.

"Mrs Grayson." He bowed, a little lower than was strictly necessary given her lower social position, but the respect and consideration might ameliorate her ire.

"Good morning, Mr Darcy. You are early abroad." Her tone was cool. Uninviting.

"I hoped to find you. May I join you?"

She gestured to the broad, flagged walkways with one gloved hand. "The paths are wide enough, sir."

Hardly a fulsome invitation, but sufficient. He fell in beside her, but had the sense not to offer her his arm. They walked a few yards in silence, before he cleared his throat and offered a handsome apology.

"I regret, ma'am, that anything my secretary said yesterday evening may have caused you distress. I hope that was not the case, or that it was of short duration. Howsoever, it was much to be deplored."

There. Very handsome.

"Do you regret it?"

He blinked at the doubtful tone. "Mrs Grayson—"

"He is your secretary, sir. I must assume he is acting on your behalf."

Damnation!

"To some extent, he is." It was the most he could say without outright untruth. Dear Lord, he hated such prevarication.

She stopped. He had taken a step before he realised and when he turned, she had both hands clasped at the high waist of her frogged, military-style pelisse. Framed by a bonnet he could only think flattered her face, those fine eyes—such an arresting shade of grey, accentuated by the dark brows and lashes—regarded him in solemn challenge.

And challenge it was, though he disliked that she was having to steel herself to speak. He did not like to see her usual confidence dimmed like that, to see her clutching her hands together as if it gave her comfort.

"Are you looking to buy Netherfield?"

"Mrs Gr—"

"I am told that both you and Mr Saville have made enquiries about the house. That is not unusual, of course, when a large estate is up for lease and in itself does not truly concern me. It is just business. The substance of those enquiries, however, does. While I am uncertain of the tenor of your questions, sir, Mr Saville's interest appears to have a somewhat gossipy inclination, intent as he seems to be on somehow scoring a point against me. He knows who I am, I am sure. His remarks last night were unconscionable. Does he truly think I relish discussing my husband's death with strangers?"

Damn the puppy! Grayson was not just a fool. He was an utter fool. A cork-brained, addle-pated noddy who had obviously said more to vex Mrs Grayson than he had admitted to.

Once again, Darcy prevaricated. While he spoke the absolute truth, the deceit and misdirection he intended with it was bitter on his tongue. "I repeat that I regret the incident. For my own part, I am a prudent man. I seek to extend my holdings wherever that will add to my family's security. However, ma'am, I do not approve of gossip. I have spoken to Saville."

"I would be more reassured if you had chastised him, but I will be content with mere speech. As for the rest, I can only admire that you are so diligent as to continually improve your situation and circumstances, and I could wish every gentleman of my acquaintance was as careful of his family's future. But Netherfield Park is not for sale. You must look elsewhere to exercise your prudent forethought."

Though her tone was civil, it was also quite firm. She was holding him to account! He, who was so far abo— Every muscle tensed, and when he drew in a slow, steadying breath it pushed against the pressure in his chest, and every tendon in his neck and jaw tightened in disagreeable fashion. Damn Grayson to have put him in this position! He would not look away. He would have to accept her rebuke with as much grace as he could muster, but his next discussion with young Grayson would indeed include a large measure of chastisement.

"Call off Mr Saville, sir. I am obliged to the Bingleys, and I would not cause embarrassment in their house while I am a guest, but I will not tolerate such disrespect. If Mr Saville approaches me again, anywhere, I will not acknowledge him."

Darcy had a strong desire to give the nodcock the cut direct himself. He forced control into his voice, keeping himself carefully contained and refusing to allow her censure to rattle him. Nor would he respond in any other way than to show understanding and a measure of contrition. "As I say, I do regret—"

"I am sure." She took a deep breath. "And now I must return to my sister. Enjoy your walk, sir."

She allowed her hands to fall to her sides to grasp the thick stuff of her pelisse to draw it up as she dropped him a shallow curtsey before turning and walking back to the house. Her back was rigid, shoulders stiff. And it was with a moment of shocked insight that he realised her clasping her hands together had not been a sign of insecurity or nervousness.

No. He rather suspected she had clasped her hands to prevent herself from using them to box his ears.

"Is Mr Saville not joining us this evening?" Miss Bingley glanced around the drawing room, gathering everyone's attention to start the migration into the dining room.

"He sends his regrets." Darcy turned to catch Elizabeth's gaze, where she sat with Louisa Hurst. "He dines in Meryton tonight, I believe."

"Oh, that is a great pity." Miss Bingley smirked at Elizabeth. "You and he seemed to be having such a comfortable coze yesterday, my dear Mrs Grayson, I had quite counted on him to amuse you this evening."

"One cannot live one's life in a state of perpetual amusement, Miss Bingley. There would be a sad want of balance. I will weather the disappointment." Elizabeth returned Darcy's gaze and held it.

He bowed slightly, and waited until she gave him a small, acknowledging smile. A little approbation, at last. He went to her side and, to Miss Bingley's poorly hidden chagrin, offered his arm to escort her in to dine. Mrs Grayson took it without hesitation, and spoke quietly as they walked along the hall to the dining room.

"I am to thank you, then, for your action tonight in keeping Mr Saville away."

"I sought only your comfort, ma'am."

She turned her head to look at him. How could eyes the colour of ice hold so much fire? But it was not, it seemed, the passion of anger. Not now, at least. A minute frown creased her brow, and she shook her head as if to clear it. "What a bundle of contradictions!"

He raised an enquiring eyebrow as he took his seat beside her, but she smiled and shook her head again. "It is of no great importance, sir. Now then, when we met at the Gouldings the other week, I believe I left the gentlemen discussing the merits of a new attempt of Ciudad Rodrigo. What think you of Wellesley's strategy?"

Miss Bingley, taking her own seat at the mistress's end of the table, and hence at Mr Darcy's left, was almost arrested in motion, hanging in mid-air for a moment. "Good heavens, Mrs Grayson. What a topic for the dinner table! Or for a lady to discuss at all. I declare I know not what to say."

Elizabeth pursed her lips again, and her smile widened. "Then, Miss Bingley, we will leave such things to the gentlemen." Her eyes were bright with mischief, tiny laughter lines crinkling the corners. "So, Mr Darcy, since the war is forbidden us, what think you of the servant problem?"

Darcy almost choked on his soup and Elizabeth Grayson, damn her glorious eyes, laughed.

CHAPTER EIGHTEEN

Appearing To the Greatest Advantage

Darcy approached the drawing room following the gentlemen's hour apart after dinner with something akin to trepidation, resolved to keep himself under good regulation. The drawing room was quiet. The sisters talked together softly, and Elizabeth had a book in her hands, tilted towards the candles on the small table beside her. She closed it up as they entered. Tea and coffee appeared almost immediately.

"Slops," Hurst said, as he took his coffee from his wife's hands. But he was smiling and they exchanged a fond look, Louisa Hurst's mouth twitching up into an answering curve. "It will keep me awake long enough for cards later."

"Oh yes! I must win back everything I lost to you yesterday, brother Hurst, or I will be penny-pinched for the rest of the quarter!" Miss Bingley flickered a glance at Elizabeth. "Will you play, Mrs Grayson?"

"Thank you, but I shall read a little longer, and then return to Jane."

"Singular," Hurst said. "Do you prefer books to cards, ma'am?"

"Mrs Eliza Grayson is a great reader." Miss Bingley poured the tea. "And quite despises cards!"

"I take pleasure in many things, but tonight I will read."

"You take pleasure in your care for your sister, I dare say." Bingley stepped in then. "I am delighted she is doing better. I hope she will join us tomorrow."

That netted him a quite brilliant smile. "As do I, sir. She is indeed much improved and I think she may venture downstairs for an hour tomorrow."

Bingley beamed.

Darcy accepted his tea from Caroline Bingley. Could not the woman refrain from sugaring it so freely? It made his teeth ache. After a few minutes of inane conversation with his hostess, he excused himself on the pretext of finishing a letter to his sister, and took up position at the small writing desk near a window. From there he could see Elizabeth's profile limned against a bank of warm candlelight, and admire the elegant shape of her nose and chin. Her face might not have the perfect symmetry of her sister Jane's, but Mrs Grayson was a very handsome woman.

His attention was recalled by Miss Bingley, who was listening to her brother's plans for a small ball at the full moon—"in order to repay our new friends' hospitality"—with a horror that Darcy could believe was, for once, unfeigned.

"You cannot be serious, Charles! There are some among us who would find such an enterprise more punishment than pleasure!"

Mrs Grayson's light laugh was musical to hear. "Do you not like to dance, Miss Bingley? I would have thought it one of the great delights of the Season."

Bingley huffed. "It is! And if you mean Darcy, Caroline, he may go to bed early if he chooses! But he said naught against it when I mentioned it after dinner."

"I do not consider it a hardship," was all Darcy would venture.

Miss Bingley threw him a distracted glance. "Indeed!" She turned to Mrs Grayson. "A country ball, my dear Mrs Grayson, cannot compare to one in Town. The company… the refinement and elegance…" She trailed off, but her meaning was inescapable.

"Oh, I quite agree. There is far more elegance and enjoyment when one's company is the friends and neighbours one has loved and known since childhood. They are so comfortable to be with. I do see your point, that one's felicity must be dimmed if one must consort with strangers." Elizabeth's mouth curved up into the sweetest of smiles. "You are to be commended for your finer feelings, Miss Bingley."

"That is not…" Miss Bingley allowed her voice to die away again. Even she must see that she had no argument to make that did not insult their guest.

Elizabeth's smile widened.

"The ball is quite a settled thing," Bingley said with a firmness unusual to him. "As soon as Mrs Nicholls can make white soup enough, we will send out our cards. I thought you would relish the challenge, Caroline."

"Of course." Miss Bingley spoke with flat resignation. "I will do my best to make it a brave success. Louisa will help, I am sure."

"You have made this decision very swiftly, Mr Bingley." Elizabeth turned her smile to Bingley.

"Whatever I do is done in a hurry, Miss Elizabeth. I like to act, rather than cogitate forever upon contingencies as does my friend there. Everlastingly thinking about something robs it of its joy."

Darcy raised an eyebrow. Should he consider that a criticism? "That explains your letters, then. You are too joyful to take the time to make them legible."

Miss Bingley laughed, and said to Elizabeth, "My brother's letters are so carelessly written, he misses out half the words he needs for clarity and his pen drips blots upon the rest!"

"Oh, unlike some, I have no time for pretty writing and pretty speeches, where every word must be of at least four syllables." And Mr Bingley cocked an eyebrow in Darcy's direction and smiled. "As I said, I like to act swiftly." He turned the smile to Elizabeth. "As an example, I took this house very quickly, you know—"

She inclined her head and smiled. "And I suspect would quit it as readily?"

"Well, I do not deny that I set off on journeys almost as soon as I have determined on them!"

Darcy put down his quill. He could not give his letter to Georgiana the attention it deserved. "This impression of haste and energy is all very well, Bingley, but is it not merely intended to make your character seem an interestingly dashing one? You make no allowances for your own temperament. Let us consider your idea of taking a journey. Should I say to you, even as you have your horse brought around, 'Stay another week!', I am certain you would not go, and another word would have you stay a month."

"Which is to say that Mr Bingley's friends praise his sweetness of temper more fully than he does." Elizabeth regarded Darcy while Bingley sputtered out some incoherent protest, her eyes gleaming in the candlelight. "Although I detect some censure in your tone, sir. Do you not think to yield readily to the persuasion of a friend is a virtue?"

"It is no compliment to either, if it is done out of pure sweetness of temper, as you have it, rather than rational conviction."

"You make no allowance for affection and friendship." Elizabeth frowned at him. "Surely, we all yield more readily to the desires of those we love? When a friend desires something of us— oh, let us not say anything of great moment or of dubious morality but merely the normal requests and accommodations our friends may require of us in daily life—there is some virtue if we yield without waiting to be argued into it."

"I would be happy to be given that virtue, that I have a sweet rather than quarrelsome temper." Bingley had seemingly found his voice. "For I dislike anything that smacks of a dispute."

Elizabeth laughed. "And you wish me to cease disputing with Mr Darcy? I am happy to comply, sir!"

"And I shall return to my letter to Georgiana, and leave Mrs Grayson to sing your praises."

Darcy rather regretted mentioning Georgiana's name, since that immediately sent Miss Bingley into one of her raptures over his sister. "Miss Darcy is the most delightful creature, Mrs Grayson! Such manners and countenance! And so accomplished for her age. You admired my playing on the pianoforte, but Miss Darcy is as far my superior as... she is by far the better player."

"I do not know how every young lady in the kingdom has the patience to be so accomplished," Bingley said. "If they are not painting tables, they are singing like angels in perfect Italian, covering screens, netting purses, and are more exquisite artists than any of our Royal Academicians. No lady is ever mentioned without I am assured she is very accomplished."

"I would take such assurance with scepticism." Darcy looked down at the letter, and pushed it to one side. He had lost his train of thought. "I cannot boast of knowing more than half a dozen truly accomplished ladies."

Miss Bingley nodded so furiously her feathers almost took wing from the silk turban wound around her head. "Nor I, for a certainty!"

Elizabeth reached for her coffee cup. Darcy had noticed she preferred it to tea in the evenings. She took a sip, regarding them over the rim of the thin porcelain. "You both must comprehend a great deal in your idea of what makes an accomplished woman."

"I do." He nodded.

"Indeed!" Miss Bingley put down her tea cup, all the better to make her points with energetic gestures. "There is a great deal to be compassed, Mrs Grayson. A mere smattering of music sufficient for a country party, or a few words of French are hardly sufficient. A woman requires a thorough knowledge of music, dancing, drawing and the modern languages if she is to be considered even moderately accomplished. She must be the most attentive hostess, as able to entertain a friend to tea as—" And here Miss Bingley glanced sidelong at her brother, and tittered into her hand. "—as to organise a successful ball at little more than two weeks' notice. And, in addition, she must have a certain quality, hard to define but quite unmistakable, that is evident in her every word and expression, her air, her carriage and comportment."

Elizabeth turned her gaze to Darcy. "Does this accord with your own understanding, Mr Darcy?"

"I suppose it does, and yet to all the qualities, a lady must add something more substantial. No woman is truly accomplished who does not seek to improve her mind through extensive reading." He nodded to the book on her knees.

He could but hope she understood him, but her expression was difficult to read, though her eyes were very bright.

"I am astonished, then, that you know even one accomplished lady," she said.

Darcy leaned forward. Warmth flooded along his breastbone, every nerve was afire... with the delight of debate, to be sure. Debates of all kinds had been his love at Cambridge, but never had he faced such a protagonist. "You are most severe upon your sex, ma'am. Do you doubt the possibility of a woman uniting all these graces?"

"I doubt any woman of sense would spend her life on nothing more than this list of elegant pastimes. I have never seen such a woman."

At this, Miss Bingley protested. She knew, she said, a very great number of ladies who met every one of these criteria. "Although it is true that in such a country place as this, I do not suppose there are so many... I do not think these qualities are gained outside the best ladies' seminaries."

"Such as the one you and Mrs Hurst attended."

Miss Bingley smiled, and inclined her head.

"I see. Well, if those habits of great industry—for to achieve so much, a woman can have no time to do any other task, duty or pleasure—are inculcated in seminaries, I can see why I am so lacking. In your experience, does such application continue after a lady has dazzled a gentleman into marriage? Once wed, how does such a woman carry out the duties of mistress of an estate and household, if she spends all her time learning new Italian love songs?"

Miss Bingley blinked, and Darcy sat back to enjoy the spectacle. A glance around the room showed him that Bingley was attending with a most unaccustomed frown on his good-natured face. Hurst was openly elated, throwing off all pretence of his usual sleepiness. Mrs Hurst, though, was playing with her many bracelets and resolutely keeping her gaze on them, rather than look at the debaters.

"I am sure I mentioned the duties of hostess, Mrs Grayson. Such a woman would be an ornament to any gentleman, and make him the perfect wife, able to manage his household and indoor staff with elegance and grace, support him at every social occasion and entertain friends and acquaintance to the highest levels, and thus assure his place amongst the top rank of society."

"Oh, I do not deny that, Miss Bingley. However, when it comes to the management of a large estate, Mr Darcy will doubtless confirm that a great many souls are dependent upon it being well run, on the care and attention given by the master to its organisation. I suspect he spends a great deal of his time in consultation with his steward to ensure the smooth conduct of estate business with his farms and tenants."

"We correspond twice-weekly while I am absent and meet daily when I am at Pemberley," Darcy acknowledged.

Elizabeth met that information with a decided nod. "The mistress has her part to play as well. If the master's concerns are with crops and yields, with the lambing, and the price of wheat and barley, hers are for the welfare of their dependents—ensuring all have sufficient to their needs in health and sickness, that the women are well cared for in their confinements and the children do not suffer any deprivation. Those will stretch her talents and skills for tact and organisation. That she must also be a good hostess is, of course, quite right, Miss Bingley. But it is a very poor mistress who neglects her duty to the estate to net herself a new purse."

Miss Bingley lifted her chin until she was staring at Elizabeth down her nose. "Surely no gentlemen would wish his lady to carry out such a regime! We are not *missionaries*."

"In fact, Mrs Grayson speaks with great exactness, and has precisely delineated what any man of sense would expect of the mistress of his estate." Darcy had to wonder how Elizabeth had so won him over to her support.

Elizabeth glanced at Mrs Hurst, and her expression became pained. "I think I must accede to your brother's wish not to continue this discussion, however entertaining we find it, but I will say one thing more. I do believe that many women show great artistic talent that is pleasing to everyone around them. That is not to be derided, but praised for the pleasure they give. My only contention is that learning German or painting a screen should not be the totality of a woman's life, nor an indication of her intrinsic worth. Our lives are circumscribed enough by the mere virtue of being female. We should seek what opportunities we may to broaden our outlook and ourselves, and the lady of an estate has the greatest opportunity of all to do this."

Miss Bingley merely stared.

Elizabeth sighed and smiled together. "I should return to Jane. I am sure you wish for a less contentious evening at cards in the quiet of your own family." She rose and dipped a curtsey at them. "Forgive me if I have caused dissension tonight. It was not deliberately done. Good night, everyone."

She had barely quitted the room before Miss Bingley, forgetting everything her seminary had every taught her about posture and deportment, threw herself back in the sofa. "Well! What a performance! Eliza Grayson is one of those pert females who seek to recommend themselves to gentlemen by sneering at her own sex, while attempting to captivate with cheap witticisms and sniping remarks intended to draw attention. It must have succeeded with her husband, I assume, but that sort of ingratiation is a paltry device and a very mean art. Do you not think so, Mr Darcy?"

"There is meanness in all the arts and allurements used by ladies who consciously seek to captivate, since little of it is ever sincere," was as much as Darcy would vouchsafe to say.

It silenced Miss Bingley, however, and he was allowed to return to his letter in a measure of peace while the others eventually got up a few hands of whist. He spent the next half hour staring at the paper before him, while avoiding Miss Bingley's eye and castigating himself for his own folly.

He had given the widow a great deal too much attention. If it were not for the equivocal nature of the cause of her widowhood, and her wholly unacceptable and inferior connections, he would admit, if only to himself, that he was in danger of admiring her more than was proper. It was folly. Insupportable. She attracted him far more than he could permit.

No more. She and her sister might be fixed at Netherfield for a day or two yet, but he would not distinguish her with his notice and conversation beyond the absolute minimum consonant with his being a gentleman. He would not debate with her, not seek her out, nor offer anything but the most basic of civilities.

He must be firm, and overcome this foolish tendency to engage with her. She was entirely beneath him.

CHAPTER NINETEEN

Under Good Regulation

Mr Darcy proved to be the most inconstant, provoking man Elizabeth had ever met.

Whilst the stiff apology he had offered for the offence given by Mr Saville had hardly been fulsome, it had appeared genuine, and his preventing his secretary from joining them at dinner had spoken even more eloquently of his regret. Their exchanges that evening had been lively and entertaining. She had seen him smile more than once, his amusement obvious and his eagerness to engage in debate with her unmistakable. She had returned to Jane cautiously optimistic that Mr Darcy might be more than the proud, arrogant, unbearable man she had first supposed.

Her optimism did not survive breakfast the next day. He had retreated again. The gentleman who greeted her coldly at the breakfast table, and who turned away to continue his discussion with a patently delighted Miss Bingley, was once again the remote, supercilious creature who had stalked around the drawing and dining rooms of the neighbourhood gentry. This was the gentleman little pleased with his surroundings, and disdainful of the people with whom he was forced to consort.

"It is hard to take Mr Darcy's likeness," Elizabeth told Jane later, as they prepared to join the company in the interval between dinner and the appearance of the tea tray. "But I fear my first impression was correct, after all. He is a man little pleased with our neighbourhood and ourselves. We are beneath him, of course, in wealth and consequence and therefore must be disdained and ignored. As Papa says, the rich may give offence wherever they go. And yet, I have seen glimpses of another man, one who enjoys the cut and thrust of good conversation, who can be kind and thoughtful, who would be a good neighbour and acquaintance. I am fatigued from puzzling over which is the true Mr Darcy."

Jane was recovering nicely. She still had a tendency to shortness of breath and coughed if she spoke for any length of time, but her fever had abated and her appetite improved. She was pale after three days' illness. Galling that a Jane who was not in her finest looks was still a very beautiful woman who would merely garner sympathy alongside the customary admiration. Elizabeth placed a thick, warm shawl around her shoulders and offered her arm as support as they walked towards the stairs.

Jane took it, and pursed her lips at Elizabeth's speech, appearing to be giving it some consideration. "I think he is a complicated man, not easily to be delineated in the way in which you and Papa delight."

"Complex characters are the most satisfying to tease out." Elizabeth forced her gaze from the marble floor below as they descended the stairs. She had been uneasy using this staircase for years now. "Every time I find something about Mr Darcy—some new expression, some new turn of countenance, some new conversation—it comes back to his sense of superiority in the end."

"I wonder," Jane offered, "if Mr Darcy is merely reserved in company, and does not quite know how to go on when faced with the conversation of strangers? Such a man would take refuge in distance, I think."

"As you are yourself reserved, you mean?" They reached the downstairs hallway and, with a frisson of something—relief?—

Elizabeth was able to turn away from the area beneath the balustraded landing of the storey above them. "I know that makes you sympathise, yet consider that you are always friendly and gracious when in company. He is a man out in the world with every advantage of sense and education, position and consequence. I do not know his exact age, but he is nearing thirty perhaps. He has had several years to practise being at ease in company, and not treating people with such unfriendly hauteur that he leaves them with the sense he holds them in despite."

They had reached the drawing room, and their conversation must, therefore, come to an end. The Bingley sisters greeted Jane with great kindness. Elizabeth would have liked to believe such solicitousness came from their knowledge of their brother's desires and wishes, but she was not, she told herself sternly, a romantic. She would not harbour hopes when she knew all the bitterness of hope unfulfilled. She took a seat on a long sofa beside Mrs Hurst, allowing Jane and Miss Bingley to chat together uninterrupted, and put the book of sonnets she had brought with her onto a nearby small table.

"It is gratifying to see Miss Bennet so improved." Mrs Hurst poured Elizabeth a glass of orgeat from the delicate bottle on the table.

"She is indeed very much better. Thank you." Elizabeth took the proffered glass and sipped at it. "I hope you will grant us one more day to impose on your hospitality. I am sure Jane will be well enough for the journey home to Longbourn the day after."

"You must stay until she is completely well. It is no imposition."

"Ah, but it is, really. You are very kind, but you must want the house to yourselves and your own party, and not have visitors foisted onto you the way we were. It is unfortunate indeed that Jane was ill, but we have been blessed in being able to rely upon your kindness."

"I would hope," said Mrs Hurst, "that though we are yet new neighbours, we may prove to be good ones. I am sure you would do no less for any of us."

"I hope I would not." Elizabeth was not given to random caresses, but Mrs Hurst's hopeful demeanour and her general air of uncertainty made Elizabeth kind. She patted Mrs Hurst's hand, and was surprised when the lady turned her hand under Elizabeth's to close them together, squeezing gently.

It was swiftly and unobtrusively done, and almost immediately Mrs Hurst withdrew her hand and turned the conversation onto something more general, and she and Elizabeth solemnly considered the merits of Brussels lace over that of Valenciennes, and other questions of equally great import, until the gentlemen joined them.

Elizabeth relished Mr Bingley's expression of joy as he hastened at once to Jane's side. His delight in her recovery and solicitude for her comfort spoke of his interest and engagement as eloquently as his lips, occupied as they were in a myriad enquiries as to the softness of the cushions at her back and the comfort of her chair, assertions that she looked very well indeed, and anxiety that he should have the footman build up the fire so she should not catch another chill. Jane welcomed his attentions with her usual sweet smiles, and soon the two were being very cosy and confidential together, basking in the warmth of the blaze in the hearth.

Mr Darcy settled into his chair with a book, while Mr Hurst sprawled onto the sofa on the other side of his wife. Miss Bingley deserted Jane immediately to sit in the chair nearest Mr Darcy, to pick up her own book and leaf through it while chattering to him without surcease. Mr Saville was still not in evidence. Elizabeth had seen nothing of him since he had offended her. Mr Darcy might be a proud sort of man, but he had grace enough to spare her another encounter with his secretary. She was grateful.

"Have you had an entertaining conversation?"

Elizabeth started at Mr Hurst's enquiry. She glanced at him. There was no sign of sleepiness or the languor she associated with a man satiated on food and drink. His eye was bright, and fixed on her with an expression she found hard to interpret.

"We have discussed lace, sir. I doubt you will have much opinion of it."

"I do not know. I like that frivolous bit of lace Mrs Hurst calls a cap. Vastly fetching, I call it." He leaned forward to look at

Elizabeth across his wife. It was an intelligent look, one she had not expected to see. "You choose to wear no cap."

"No," was all she said.

He nodded. "You were a very young widow."

"I still am, sir."

What was the man about? If not for his wife sitting there looking a little flustered and apologetic, she would leave.

He laughed softly, and kept his voice low. "Indeed. We were concerned, Mrs Hurst and I, that your youth and your generally cheerful manner were used by Saville the other night as an excuse to escape censure."

Elizabeth stared. She did open her mouth, but no sound came out other than a faint "Oh!"

"I was certain he made you uncomfortable." Mrs Hurst's voice was as soft as her husband's.

Mr Hurst nodded along to every word from his wife's lips. "I know not what he said to you, and do not need to, but be assured I will not tolerate the man offering disrespect to a lady and a guest. If my brother Bingley knew of it, he would be just as angered. Darcy has kept Saville from joining us at meals, and I hope that has been enough to shield you from importunity. But if Saville says or does anything to discompose you, know you may rely upon Louisa and me to champion you."

Mrs Hurst's hand closed over Elizabeth's again. "I feared you did not speak because you were putting your consideration for your sister above your own comfort."

Elizabeth's eyes stung, and for a moment the candlelight dazzled and blurred. Her face burned with shame for those past unkindnesses where she had made Mrs Hurst uncomfortable. How was she any better than Mr Saville in that respect? She had been blind too, to this couple. They were not as she had perceived them through the lens distorted by Miss Bingley. She really should cease to congratulate herself on her ability to delineate character. "You are so very kind. Thank you! Mr Darcy has promised I shall not have to suffer Mr Saville's company again. I am content with that."

"Good," said Mr Hurst. "I thought Darcy would act. I am surprised only that he engaged someone that required him to do so."

As one, they all glanced in Mr Darcy's direction. He was staring again, his book open on his knee, one hand lying across the pages and the other clenching and unclenching as if some doubt or ill-temper claimed him. Elizabeth fancied his eyes were on her rather than her companions. Miss Bingley twittered on in his ear, apparently unheeded.

"Your kindness touches me very deeply. Thank you." Elizabeth half turned to Mrs Hurst, and squeezed the lady's hand. "I do not deserve it, for I have not always shown it myself. I am sorry for all those times I caused you distress."

"You never have," Mrs Hurst assured her. "I do not have your lively manner, or quickness, and sometimes it takes me a moment to truly understand what is said when the conversation is so swift and pointed... well, you comprehend me, I think? If ever I seemed ill-at-ease, you have always been very quick to notice and turn the talk to something more comforting. Do not think your consideration went unmarked."

Elizabeth shook her head, unable to speak. She did not deserve such grace and could only hope her smile looked less tremulous than it felt. The Hursts, thank heavens, left the conversation there and spoke quietly together. When she felt tolerably composed again, Elizabeth picked up the book of sonnets and glanced at the others in the room over the top of it. Bingley and Jane had returned to their own low-voiced conversation. Mr Darcy still stared. Miss Bingley, though she continued to talk to him about the books they were ostensibly reading, was looking from him to Elizabeth and back again. He did not appear to notice. That she deplored his inattention was obvious.

Miss Bingley suddenly clapped her book together, and spoke loudly enough to draw the attention of all in the room. "I shall send word to hurry along the tea tray. You gentlemen returned to us early tonight!"

Mr Hurst laughed. "Some of us were very eager to return to the ladies' company, sister." He looked in pointed fashion at Darcy, who remained in his brooding abstraction.

Miss Bingley jumped up to pull on the bell rope and, when the footman appeared, sent him post haste to collect the tea tray. She did not return to her seat, but walked about the room. Her figure was elegant and she had a graceful carriage, but Mr Darcy did not once look her way. Elizabeth, stealing glances from one to the other while appearing fixed on her own book, was amused at her hostess's persistence until Miss Bingley loomed up before her.

"My dear Mrs Grayson, let me persuade you to join me in a turn about the room. It is a refreshment to the spirits after sitting so long in one attitude."

On a little reflection Elizabeth agreed, if only not to sour Miss Bingley's opinion of Jane. She was a little taken aback when Miss Bingley tucked a hand under her arm and paraded her around the room like a trophy. Jane gave her a warm glance as they passed, although the Hursts did not take a great deal of notice. Mr Darcy, however, blinked out of his reverie and turned his gaze from the corner of the sofa that had been Elizabeth's seat, to follow them around the room.

Miss Bingley drew herself up to look even taller and more willowy than she was already. Perhaps to provide him with a contrast, since Elizabeth was somewhat shorter than she. "Will you not join us, sir?"

"I thank you, no. I would not interfere with any confidences you may wish to share, if that is your object. Or if you walk because you believe that your figures appear to the best advantage, then I might admire you better from here."

His tone, however, and expression were anything but admiring. He bore a similar expression to that at the Meryton Assembly, when he had pronounced his poor opinion of Elizabeth's claims to beauty. Miss Bingley, however, was moved to exclaim her shocked delight.

"Abominable man! How shall we punish him, Mrs Grayson?"

"Oh, it is easy enough. You must laugh at him, and tease him a little. You are intimate family friends, I believe, so you must know how it is to be done."

"What, tease such a calm, well-tempered gentleman who is never less than self-possessed? Never!"

"Is Mr Darcy is not to be laughed at?" Elizabeth sent the man in question a speaking glance, for she had laughed at him more than once. "That is a great loss to the maintenance of my own good temper, since I dearly love a laugh."

Mr Darcy appeared to find that a distasteful trait in her, because that was, most undoubtedly, a sneer he gave her. "Any wise, good action may be rendered ridiculous by a person whose first object in life is a joke."

"And do you believe me to be such a one?" Elizabeth halted her perambulation with Miss Bingley and freed herself from the lady's clutching hand. "I hope I am not. I do not like ridicule and derision, particularly when aimed at the wise and good. I do not wish to think myself so petty and spiteful. Folly and nonsense are vastly diverting, however, but these qualities, I suppose, are lacking in you if Miss Bingley cannot find them after so many years' friendship."

"No! Indeed I cannot!" said Miss Bingley.

Mr Darcy's hauteur was almost palpable. "I have taken great care to avoid those weaknesses which often expose a man to mockery."

"Such as pride, perhaps."

The sharp glance he gave her showed he recognised the barb. "Where there is a real superiority of mind, pride will be always under good regulation."

Elizabeth smiled and inclined her head. "Yes. You have always struck me as a man of strong self-control."

"You must admit," said Miss Bingley to Elizabeth, "that Mr Darcy has no defects to attract your laughter."

"I am perfectly convinced of it," Elizabeth answered, without once losing her own control. She would laugh over this later, when she could not offend.

"I have my faults as with any other man," Mr Darcy said, his brow drawing into a frown. "I do not think they are of comprehension and perception—"

Elizabeth allowed through a faint, wry smile, but her tone was, she felt, sincere since she spoke the truth. "No. You are an intelligent man."

"I thank you. No, ma'am, my faults are not of understanding, but my temper is, I think, unyielding. I do not forget the follies and vices of others, and certainly do not easily forgive offences against myself and my family. My good opinion, once lost, is lost forever."

"A resentful temper… implacable rancour… no, I cannot laugh at that. You are quite safe from me."

If anything, his disapproving, disdainful expression deepened. "That is the value of self-regulation. It offers protection."

"Oh, here is the tea tray at last." Miss Bingley walked hastily away to take her place behind the tea and coffee pots. It must have been galling to her that even as she stalked away, she could not garner Mr Darcy's attention.

No. That implacable, resentful gaze was fixed on Elizabeth. Well, all Elizabeth could assume was that if she had been tolerable before, now she was not even that.

An anathema, perhaps.

The next day dragged.

Jane came downstairs after breakfast, well enough to rejoin normal life. She spent much of the day before the fire in the morning room chatting amiably with Mr Bingley and his unmarried sister. She was tempted out for a walk around the garden at one point, so wrapped in shawls and scarves that she was quite double her normal width as she promenaded slowly on Mr Bingley's arm. Miss Bingley went along with them, to play propriety. She hung grimly onto her brother's other arm and was a third in their conversations all day.

Elizabeth spent the hours mostly in the company of Mrs Hurst. They were more at ease with each other than Elizabeth could ever be with Miss Bingley. Louisa Hurst might one day prove to be a friend.

Elizabeth had two things vex her that day. Her mother's response to her note requesting the carriage for the next day was a tart *No! Indeed I will not send the carriage! Do not be so selfish, Lizzy Bennet!*—indignation having got the better of Mrs Bennet's memory as to Elizabeth's married name—*Jane must stay at least a week*—these last words heavily underlined for emphasis—*and make sure Mr Bingley notices her and pays his addresses. He cannot fail but love her, if he can but spend time with her. You must make certain he has the opportunity. I will be extremely vexed*—more savage underlining—*if you spoil her chances of gaining him!*

"I shall take Jane home in my own phaeton," Elizabeth said, putting aside the note with a sigh. Her mother learned nothing from her mistakes.

"Your father's carriage is not available?" Mrs Hurst asked, and when Elizabeth owned to this, answered, "If you are determined to return home tomorrow… and I do understand, Mrs Grayson, that Jane may be more comfortable recovering in her own home—I would be myself! Well, I will ask my brother to lend his carriage for the trip. We will be very sorry to see you go, and though you must do as you think best, I cannot think a ride in an open phaeton will do her good."

Which was the sort of kindness Elizabeth had come to expect from Louisa Hurst. It was a great pity that when in company with her sister she grew smaller, less clearly delineated, sitting in Miss Bingley's shadow with her nervous fingers playing constantly with her bracelets. She was a much brighter light when separated from the irresistible cavalry charge that was Miss Bingley.

That difficulty overcome, Elizabeth went to the library after a bite to eat at noon, and there faced the second of her day's vexations. She was joined there by no other than Mr Darcy, who, although he stopped short at seeing her, did not retreat. Instead, he returned her greeting in a tone so glacial that she expected to see icicles depend from the bookshelves and all the books wearing snowy caps over their spines.

Gathering the cold around himself like a mantle, he took a seat on the far side of the room, and devoted himself to the book he had brought with him. When she quietly slipped out of the room a half hour later, she doubted he even noticed. Unless, of course, the temperature rose from the depths of winter to the dizzy heights of spring when she softly closed the door behind her.

All in all, it was quite a relief the next day to have one of Mr Bingley's footmen hand her down from the borrowed coach onto the gravel sweep before Longbourn's doors. Before she could do more than thank him and turn towards the house, the front door burst open and a tall, heavyset man dressed in clerical garb hurled himself down the shallow steps to grasp her hand and raise it to his lips to slobber over it. An ecclesiastical whirlwind, he spun on one foot to catch Jane's hand and do likewise.

"Oh, my dear cousins! I have been awaiting your homecoming, most anxiously!" He rocked back on his heels to survey them, his large hand still enclosing Jane's. "Oh, your beauty is beyond compare. Nothing I have heard does either of you justice! My dear, dear cousins, I am so happy to see you."

"Mmn." Elizabeth stepped forward until the stranger had perforce to relinquish his hold on Jane's hand and take a step or two away. "And you, sir, I assume, are Mr Collins."

The cleric beamed. "Indeed I am, cousin. Indeed, I am!"

"Mmn," said Elizabeth again, looking him up and down. "How... splendid."

CHAPTER TWENTY

The Benefice of Clergy

Mr Collins was around twenty-five years old, tall, and so well made that corpulence in his later years was not mere possibility, but a promise. Neither very plain nor very handsome, he was the possessor of an ordinary, but not unpleasant, face. The sort of face, indeed, over which an observer's eye skated and slid away again, since there was no arresting feature to catch the interest. Elizabeth's first impressions were that he talked a great deal, and had he been a horse, she might have calculated his age with relative ease, he showed his teeth so much.

He moved with clumsy speed to position himself between his returning cousins to claim their attention and escort them into the house.

"I was prepared to be delighted, you may be sure. But this!" He stopped after only two steps, and turned, first to Jane and then to Elizabeth. "You are both so very charming! I came determined to be pleased, as you might imagine. My gracious patroness, the noble Lady Catherine de Bourgh, was the impetus behind my coming here. 'Mr Collins,' said she, 'a clergyman of your standing should make every effort to heal breaches within his own family, no matter how unworthy the...' But perhaps I should not... In any event, cousins, Lady Catherine encouraged me to do my Christian duty to heal the breach with my cousin Bennet, and here I am."

"Yes." Elizabeth took a step to urge him towards the door. "So I understood from your—"

Mr Collins stopped again. "Lady Catherine is all beneficence and wisdom! I was fortunate indeed, the day I came to her august notice. She is all kindness and affability. Such condescension! Such generosity of spirit!"

Elizabeth tugged him on another step, but she was by far the smaller, and her strength was not enough to stir him from his paean of praise to his patroness. His broad face bore an expression of earnest reverence that would not have been out of place at his church's altar.

"She has taken such a benevolent interest in me, that I cannot conceive how I came to deserve it! She has even visited my humble abode in Hunsford, to advise me on how I should go on, and has suggested so many contrivances and conveniences in its fitting out, that I defy any parsonage in the kingdom to match it for excellence!"

"Mr Collins—" said Jane.

"Do you know, cousins..." He stopped again, several feet short of the door portico. "Do you know how far her kind interest has gone? Why, she inspected the rectory from attics to cellar! She has deigned to instruct my cook on the provision of meals that are most fitting for a man of my circumstances, and pointed out to the maid where the girl has been deficient in her dusting. The maid will not be so negligent again, I promise you! And Lady Catherine said to me, 'Mr Collins,' said she, 'that corner closet in the front left guest room is just the size and shape to be fitted out most commodiously with shelves. I shall send the Rosings carpenter down directly to see to it.' And so she did! That very day!"

"Shelves in a closet? That is indeed commodious." But Elizabeth regretted her impulse immediately. Mr Collins saw nothing of her amused contempt, and she must only blame herself for the folly of encouraging him.

"Indeed, you perceive immediately the cause of my gratification. For her to take such an interest... it is beyond anything great!" His sigh was that of a man in deep ecstasy."

"Rosings?" Jane said, proving she was no wiser than Elizabeth in preventing her cousin's loquacity.

"Her ladyship's house and estate, from which my little parsonage is separated only by a lane. The finest house in Kent... Nay! In the kingdom! Why, the chimneypiece in the drawing room cost eight hundred pounds." He repeated the total, a little pause between each word to emphasise the grandeur of it for their amazement. "Eight hundred pounds. Can you imagine its magnificence?"

Elizabeth bit back the observation that a true profligate would have made it eight hundred guineas.

"As I have said, she is the reason I am here. She encouraged me to make peace with my cousin. 'Mr Collins,' said she, 'it behoves a clergyman to set a good example to his flock in all things, and to show that forgiveness, charity and forbearance that is the mark of the true Christian.'"

"She sounds—" Jane tried, Elizabeth being too busy choking back her laughter to essay into speech.

"What is more, Lady Catherine spoke to me of my duties. 'Mr Collins,' said she, 'a clergyman in your easy circumstances must show your flock the perfect example in every aspect of his life. In dealing with the poor and indigent, in denouncing those who stray from the narrow path Our Lord set before our feet, and using as the most precious example, those who are laudable, excellent Christians in their deeds and comportment—' And in that, cousins, there is no finer exemplar than herself! She said, 'In all these things I expect you to expend unremitting energy in ministering to your congregation. But above all, you should marry. Give your parishioners the example of virtuous living so they may emulate it. Choose a gentlewoman for my sake, and depend upon it, when you are married, I will receive her.' There! What do you think of that? So here I am, my most beautiful cousins. I have come prepared to admire you and what joy will be ours and our dear family's—"

Eyes round with horror, Jane fell to coughing, raising her free hand to her mouth. It was enough to impel Elizabeth from the fascination of drowning under Mr Collins's verbose periods. She twitched her arm from his grasp and tugged at Jane.

"Mr Collins!" Her tone was so sharp, he started and his grip slackened, allowing her to free Jane. She drew her sister away. "Sir, you must be aware that we return home after some days of Jane's being ill in a neighbouring house. She must not be kept out in this cold wind any longer." She dropped him a curtsey and turned on her heel, taking Jane with her.

A bleated "Oh, but you are charming in your concern for your sister!" sounded in her wake, but she did not pause to look back at the ridiculous windbag standing behind her in the sweep. Hill had the door open for them, and in a trice she had whisked Jane into the frail sanctuary that was Longbourn.

Papa stood in his study doorway, his expression one of the liveliest amusement. Mama however, was not at all pleased. She had emerged into the hall from the family sitting room, presumably on hearing the wheels of the Bingley carriage, eyes narrowed in a caricature of vexation.

Elizabeth, relieved to be in the warm house, put a hand in the small of Jane's back to propel her to the stairs and the safety of their own rooms. "Good morning Papa, Mama. I am pleased to see you both in such good health. Jane and I are delighted to be home."

"Well," said Papa when Elizabeth joined him after seeing Jane to her room to rest after the exigencies of travelling three miles. "Is he not a promising specimen, and an even finer gabster? The man has tongue enough for two sets of teeth. I am almost proud to own such a cousin. What a distinction he lends us!"

"I perceive Lady Catherine could hardly have bestowed her notice on a more grateful object. He talked of nothing but her greatness." Elizabeth settled into the chair opposite her father's, both armchairs set facing the hearth and its welcome fire. "What an addle-pate he is, to keep Jane out of doors, merely to chatter about his noble patroness."

"Trying to impress his importance upon you. He has come looking for a wife, Lizzy."

"So I gathered."

Papa barked out a laugh. "He has won over your mother with his plans. Not one mention of the hedgerows since his arrival and his communication of intent."

"She should not concern herself. She must know that I will not allow her to be homeless or in want."

"He is a marital prospect for one of her daughters," Papa said, tone drier than any desert Elizabeth could imagine. "What is more, he is the heir of Longbourn, and that adds to his eligibility for one of you, that he might vouchsafe Longbourn to the family. And no matter what you may offer her, my dear, the business of her life is to see you all wed."

"I cannot imagine he will look twice at Kitty and Lydia, and I hope Jane is safe from him, with Mr Bingley being so promising a prospect. Mary might suit him. She would make an admirable clergyman's wife, and I do not believe she is at all romantically inclined. A marriage of convenience would not disconcert her."

"Well, I agree your mother is likely to steer him away from Jane, and he has already had three days in the company of the two silliest chits in the country... no, he will not consider either of the youngest two. We shall have to see where his interest lies, shall we not?"

"He should consider where best to apply himself, if he is to gain his objective."

Papa smirked. "I await his wooing with some anticipation, then."

"I have no doubt that you do. Mr Collins, however, must study to avoid disappointment."

She and Papa shared a wide smile of perfect understanding.

They were bound for Aunt Phillips's house that evening to drink tea and play cards after dinner. Jane cried off, citing weariness after her recent illness. Papa, too, declined to leave Longbourn, remarking dryly that the social delights offered by his wife's sister were far too familiar to tempt him out of doors on a wet November evening.

As for the rest of the family, those accustomed to readying themselves in a timely manner, as too often happened, cooled their heels in the smaller sitting room awaiting Lydia's pleasure. And, of course, to a lesser extent, Kitty's, since she did nothing that was not in emulation of her younger sister. A full five minutes after the time the coach was intended to depart, they waited still.

Mama, hearing the soft chime of the mantel clock, made an exclamation that started with "Oh, those girls! They are always—" but on her recollecting herself immediately, changed to an effort to convince Mr Collins that her youngest daughters were only taking great care to appear at their best, "For they know very well the honour of having your escort, sir, and the distinction of introducing you to those of Meryton society whom you have not already met. I shall go and hurry them along."

A promise she kept immediately by bustling out of the room, lace lappets flying and hands all aflutter. Mr Collins came immediately to join Elizabeth and Mary, plumping himself down in the nearest chair and dragging it closer while still seated in it, to the great detriment of the polished floorboards.

"My dear cousins, I cannot tell you with what anticipation I view this evening's engagement. What could be more congenial, than an evening spent with family and friends? It is precisely the sort of harmless entertainment, you know, that Lady Catherine must approve."

"My aunt will be pleased to know it, sir." Elizabeth noted Mr Collins's examining her and returned his gaze with a direct one of her own.

He frowned. "Cousin Elizabeth, your respected mother told me that you are, in fact, a widow?"

"I am, sir."

His frown deepened. "You do not look like one."

"Indeed? And is there some particular characteristic of widowhood in which I am deficient?"

He opened and closed his mouth more than once with all the elegance of one of her father's carp in the fishpond. "You do not dress as one, cousin. That is what I mean."

"I am sure my mother told you that my husband is more than four years dead. Did you expect me to be in bombazine and crepe? I put off my mourning over two years ago."

He made an odd "haaa-ing" sound and ducked his head, grimacing. "I meant only that you dress as would any young girl— as cousin Mary here does. There is little distinction..."

Mary glanced up from her book to observe that "Lizzy has better taste in dress than I. And prettier dresses."

"I am barely one and twenty, Mr Collins, so do not dress in the more matronly styles and colours chosen by, say, my mother. Is my gown inappropriate?"

He gestured dumbly to his head, and it was not until she quirked an eyebrow at him that he squeaked out an outraged, "You wear no cap!"

"I do not." Elizabeth caught Mary's fleeting glance and they exchanged faint smiles. Mary's views on Elizabeth's heresy when it came to societal expectations of married women's dress were well understood between them.

"But my dear cousin... the impropriety... good heavens, you cannot understand... so unconventional behaviour... my fear is that a gentleman may be misled about your status—"

"That does not concern me, Mr Collins."

"But that is the effect of... of..." He prescribed a circle about his own head with one hand to explain his discomposure. He huffed out another of those odd "haaa-ing" sounds, that she realised was intended as an indulgent chuckle. "You are greatly charming, and so obviously an innocent when it comes to a man's thoughts and intentions... The expectations of society are there for your protection, my dear, dear cousin. You must see that this is so!"

Elizabeth, who was so far from innocence as to a man's intentions and deeds that Mr Collins's inane words cut to the bone, allowed her tone to freeze like the breath of a winter wind. "How I dress is for me to decide. One's intentions, deeds and morality are not determined by whether or not one wears a lace cap. And in truth, this is a rather improper discussion."

"I am a clergyman, dear Elizabeth—"

"Sir, we are only just met. Please do not use my given name with such freedom."

He deflated a trifle, even his pomposity pricked by her coldness. "It is my duty to speak out about those derelictions when I see them, and I flatter myself I do it with delicacy! I merely point out, *cousin*, that it is more seemly to follow society's dictates on this matter. It is for the protection of innocence and modesty, and to show her respectability and decorum, that a married woman covers her hair."

This assertion had Mary nodding agreement.

"I am sure, my dear cousin, that Lady Catherine would agree with me—"

Elizabeth smiled. "And I am sure that the great lady you have described so minutely would never be so rag-mannered as to offer her opinion on a matter that is so clearly none of her concern."

Mr Collins gaped at her, one of her father's carp caught in the fisherman's landing net gulping in the unfamiliar air.

Elizabeth softened her tone. The noddy was not worth her ire and she would pay him the compliment that he was in earnest; an innocent who saw matters in simplistic terms, rather than a man attempting some ridiculous exercise of an authority he did not possess. "Come, we shall not quarrel. I assure you I followed every convention when I was first widowed with regard to the wearing of mourning and the curtailment of my participation in society. We may agree my lack of a widow's cap now, some four years later, is... unconventional, as you termed it. I intend no deception regarding my status when it comes to gentlemen, and it is purely a personal preference that is a matter for me to decide, is it not?"

He drew his hand over his brow, with another of those odd, rather high-pitched "Haa!"s that this time clearly denoted a discomforted attempt to laugh. "You are perfectly charming, my dear cousin..."

"Well, we are agreed then, and shall be friends henceforth. Oh here is Mama, and the girls at last. John Coachman is waiting at

the door, I believe, Mama. We should leave, or we will be late."
Elizabeth cast her gaze over her two sisters. Lydia's decolletage
was a little too daring for an evening at their aunt's—or anywhere,
really—and she and Kitty had evidently spent hours curling their
hair and pinching their cheeks hard to make them rosy. "Armed for
battle, I see, Lyddie."

Lydia did not even pretend not to understand her. She pulled
Elizabeth up and towards the door. "Officers, Lizzy! The officers
will be there! Come, you laggard, I do not wish to be late." Her
blue eyes met Elizabeth's, wide and bright with life and laughter.
"After all, I have a campaign to win!"

CHAPTER TWENTY-ONE

An Affecting Tale

Childless and comfortably off, Aunt Phillips would deny to her last breath that she ever gossiped, but would claim her interest in the doings of her neighbours was merely a natural and unaffected desire to promote the good of society. Consequently, she was never better pleased than when her drawing room was crowded with friends and neighbours to allow this benevolence full scope. She gave Mr Collins an effusive welcome—new faces were always appreciated—and carried him off to join a whist table.

"Oh! The officers are here!" cried Lydia, and she darted away, pulling Kitty along with her.

Elizabeth and Mary exchanged wry glances.

"There is no point," Mary said. "She does not listen. Mama and Aunt Phillips will not curb her."

"And it is not our place to do so."

Mary smiled, shook her head, and meandered off to the piano. She would spend most of the evening there, playing quietly in the background until Lydia tired of cards and demanded dancing.

Mary's playing was better than usual, less strained than when she was actively exhibiting. If only she would always play in such an unselfconscious way. Elizabeth took a seat nearby, wishing she had remained at Longbourn with Jane.

Kitty interrupted Elizabeth's reverie. "Lizzy, may I introduce Mr Wickham to you? He has recently joined the militia."

Elizabeth had no opportunity to refuse. The man stood before her, and common civility demanded she rise from her seat and greet him, notwithstanding her misgivings over his actions the night she first saw him in the square with Kitty and Lydia, and his going into her Aunt Phillips's house despite her uncle's absence at dinner with the militia officers.

Kitty performed the introduction with surprising grace. Elizabeth made a small curtsey in answer to Mr Wickham's deep bow. He took a seat between Elizabeth and the nearest table, where Lydia was playing lottery tickets and flirting with officers in the most energetic and noisy way ever known to mankind. Kitty scampered off to join Lydia.

Mr Wickham was the happy possessor of pleasing manners, a handsome countenance and a figure that bore regimentals very well. He conversed with ease and friendliness, beginning with an honest declaration that he had asked for the introduction. "I know that you saw me with your sisters the other evening." He made a slight grimace. "I was charmed by their open and friendly manners... Miss Elizabeth?"

His tone indicated some confusion.

"I am generally called so by my neighbours, sir."

"I see." His smile was charming. "I have no family now, you see, and my godfather's family, which once was almost my own... well, that is a sorrow I must bear in silence. Your sisters' hearty welcome was balm and solace. To be honest, I was a little lonely, and had no notion of what I might do that evening to occupy myself. I was only just arrived and could not in all conscience join Colonel Forster's dinner for the local gentlemen when I was not quite a member of his militia. I am sorry that I allowed myself to be tempted into meeting your aunt that night. It was an impropriety."

What a frank admission! Perhaps he was a gentleman after all.

"I did wonder at it."

He smiled. "You will make allowances, I hope, for a man who was most pressingly reminded of his lack of family. Your sisters and your good aunt gave me hope that I would find friends here in Meryton."

"I hope you do, sir." Elizabeth recalled his odd expression when he saw the Netherfield party arrive for the dinner from which his conscience had barred him, but had no expectation that her curiosity on that head would be assuaged.

However, Mr Wickham began the subject himself. "I understand from your sisters that you have been some days from home, staying at a place called Netherfield? Is it far from Meryton?" On receiving her answer, his tone took on a hesitating manner. "Do you know how long Mr Darcy has been staying there?"

Darcy! It was Mr Darcy whose notice he had tried to evade, whose very presence in Meryton had caused him alarm and confusion, if his loss of colour and his expression at the time were any indication. How very intriguing!

"About six weeks. Since the Michaelmas quarter day, or thereabouts." Elizabeth added, "He is a man of property and importance in Derbyshire, I believe."

Mr Wickham nodded. "Pemberley is noble estate, and as you say, an important one. A clear ten thousand per annum. I can speak with some authority, as I have been connected with his family from my infancy."

Elizabeth stared, and his smile grew very wry.

"You may well be surprised at such an assertion, as I am sure you saw that I did everything I could to avoid his notice that evening. Are you much acquainted with Mr Darcy?"

"A little. I do not find him a sociable man. He does not have easy manners. He seems rather…"

"Proud?" Mr Wickham supplied and his smile widened at her nod. "You do not surprise me, but I have known him too long and too intimately to be a fair judge. Is he well liked in the neighbourhood?"

"I would not say so. As I implied, we have found him to be reserved and distant. Of course, none here are of his own circle, and he holds himself aloof."

"Do you know whether he is likely to be in the neighbourhood much longer?"

"I am sorry, no. I heard nothing of his plans while I was Netherfield. Does it affect you, whether he goes or stays?"

"I cannot allow... My circumstances are such that I am constrained to stay. That is, I have no other recourse at present, and my obligations demand that I remain. Darcy and I are not on friendly terms, as you may have realised. His father was my godfather, one of the best men ever to draw breath. Old Mr Darcy was a true friend both to my father, who was his most trusted steward, and to me. But the current Mr Darcy..." Mr Wickham shook his head. "The lesser son of a noble sire. I admit to a sense of ill-usage and regret for his treatment of me. That, I am sorry to say, has been scandalous, and a disgrace to the memory of his father."

Elizabeth could find nothing to say. Mr Darcy was proud and disdainful, but Mr Wickham's words suggested a man whose character was many shades darker.

Perhaps seeing her confusion, Mr Wickham changed the conversation to a more general discourse on Meryton, praising the agreeable attentions and courtesies shown the officers by the local society, ending this encomium with "It was this prospect of sociability, as described to me by a close acquaintance and confirmed to me by Mr Denny, that tempted me to enter the militia. Good society is necessary to buoy up my spirits and help me overcome my disappointments. It is an odd turn that brought me here at all. I was intended for the church rather than the military, and I should at this time have been in possession of a valuable living if it were not for the gentleman we were speaking of just now."

"Indeed!"

"My godfather, the late Mr Darcy, bequeathed me the next presentation of the best living in his gift. He was very fond of me, and I cannot say enough of his kindness. But after his death, when the living became available, it was given to another man—one who had never rivalled the current Mr Darcy for his father's affections."

"Surely not! Must not a bequest be set out in the old gentleman's will? How could any man of honour disregard that! Have you no legal recourse?"

"There was some informality in the terms of the will, a technicality such that I have no hope of legal redress. The current Mr Darcy chose to treat the bequest as conditional, declaring that I had forfeited all claim to it by extravagance, imprudence—in short, anything he did not approve of! And since we are very different men, and his jealous temperament resented his dear father's kindness and indulgence to the mere son of a steward, you may be certain nothing I do can find favour with him. I have striven to mend the breach, although with my warm, unguarded temper, I may have spoken my opinion of him and to him, too freely. Well, the living went to another man and I must bear it, despite losing it through no great fault of my own."

"This is quite shocking." Elizabeth considered Mr Darcy's temper to be the very opposite of warm and unguarded. She could well believe that an open and pleasant man as Mr Wickham would be anathema to him. Despite her indignation, she had to hide a smile. There was a great deal in Meryton that Mr Darcy considered reprehensible. Mr Wickham was in better company than he knew. "How has he avoided public disgrace?"

"I could not... As long as I remember his father, I cannot expose him."

"Very forgiving of you, sir. I have seen him be supercilious, unsocial and disdainful, acting as if he is above his company. Had you nothing but his pride to recount I would not be surprised. But this is a malicious act. I had not suspected him of that... and yet, only a day or two ago, he boasted, almost, that he had an unforgiving and resentful temper."

"I can hardly be just to him, but I do believe that."

"I am astonished that his pride did not prevent him from dealing with you so unkindly. One might even say dishonestly, if he disregarded his father's last wishes."

"I cannot say. He is indeed a proud man, in many ways. And yet that same pride leads him to act in a way that is generally seen as liberal and generous. He assists his tenants, I know, and relieves the poor. He is proud of his sister too, and that makes him a kind and careful guardian."

"You are very good to recognise his better qualities, even if they too arise from his sense of pride," said Elizabeth. "What sort of girl is Miss Darcy?"

"Sadly, too much his sister. She is very, very proud and, like him, easily puts aside the claims of old friends and views them with contempt." He shook his head. "She must be sixteen now. She lives in London, where a lady superintends her education. I am told she is highly accomplished."

"No doubt," Elizabeth said. "I am sorry that Mr Bingley, who is a good tempered and amiable man, has been so misled in his friendship. He cannot know anything of this."

"I doubt it. Darcy could not boast of it, of course. But as for cultivating the friendship of an amiable man, Darcy can be pleasant company when he chooses."

"Indeed? Then the neighbourhood must conclude he does not so choose at our gatherings."

"Among those he considers his equals, he is a very different man from what he is to the less prosperous and—forgive me—the less important."

"Yes. I can well believe his manners are coloured by his sense of his own consequence and standing."

At that moment, the whist party broke up for a general change in partners, and Mr Collins, temporarily freed from his obligations, looked around the room. His broad face brightened when his gaze caught Elizabeth's and she could only feel the folly of looking his way when he lumbered across the room towards her. She introduced the two men and civility required her to ask how Mr Collins had enjoyed the game.

"I lost five shillings," the cleric said, rather mournfully, before saying, in more brisk and cheerful fashion, "Happily I need not concern myself about such a small amount! Thanks to Lady Catherine de Bourgh, I do not need to regard such trifles."

Mr Wickham, who had been smiling at Elizabeth from behind Mr Collins's back, seemed momentarily taken aback, and asked if Mr Collins was acquainted with the family of de Bourgh. Elizabeth widened her eyes and shook her head in warning, but it was too late. It was some ten minutes before Mr Collins's flowery, flowing paean of praise for his glorious patroness came to an end, and it did so only because, to everyone's delight except perhaps Mr Collins himself, Mrs Phillips chivvied him back to the whist table for the next round of cards.

"Good Lord," said Mr Wickham, his expression blank.

"I imagine standing under a waterfall gives the same sensation of being drenched. He is very grateful to Lady Catherine for granting him his living."

"He is indeed." Mr Wickham caught her gaze, and they laughed quietly together before he added, "Did you know that Lady Catherine and Lady Anne Darcy were sisters, and therefore she is Mr Darcy's aunt?"

"No, I did not. Except for a mention in my cousin Collins's original letter proposing this visit, I never heard of the lady before." Elizabeth did not hide her smile. "Though I have heard a great deal since."

"Her daughter, Miss de Bourgh, will have a very large fortune. I have heard Lady Catherine speak often of her daughter and Mr Darcy uniting the two estates and creating a rich and powerful alliance, a match she promotes tirelessly, and speaks of to everyone. I believe that her desires will be met. It is the kind of connection that Darcy would relish—one of riches and family combined."

Poor Miss Bingley. All her efforts must be in vain. So many attentions, so much flattery quite wasted, though the lady should have known her suit was hopeless, given her father was a tradesman, and that of Mr Darcy's mother must have been at least an earl.

"The Earl of Ashbourne," Mr Wickham confirmed when Elizabeth enquired. "The current earl is Darcy's uncle." He continued, "It is many years since I saw Lady Catherine, but I remember that her manners were somewhat dictatorial."

"So I deemed from my cousin's discourse. She takes a very close interest, I think, in everyone's doings." Elizabeth could only marvel at the coincidences that brought so many connections of Mr Darcy's family to Meryton at the same time. "There must be a great family resemblance, in some respects."

Mr Wickham could not but laugh. "I would never dispute it. The family pride is something prodigious!"

Elizabeth joined his laughter, and they continued talking together with mutual satisfaction till supper put an end to cards, and shortly after that, the party broke up. Elizabeth took her leave of Mr Wickham with great cordiality, and the Bennet family squeezed into the coach for the journey home. She found that thinking of the gentleman blunted, somewhat, the competition between their cousin's flow of words on his facility at cards and his losses ("Trifling, I assure you!"), and Lydia's loud happy recitation of how many fish she had won and how very taken with her all the officers were.

Jane, when Elizabeth related Mr Wickham's tale to her next morning, could not believe that a gentlemen she knew, one who had Mr Bingley's regard and friendship, could be so unworthy.

"Depend upon it, they are both mistaken in each other somehow, in some fashion that we cannot comprehend. It is quite inconceivable that a gentleman of Mr Darcy's standing would be so unprincipled, so indifferent to his public character and honour as to disregard his father's will. I cannot believe that his intimate friend is so deceived in him."

"Mr Wickham related this to me without ceremony or ostentation. It did not seem rehearsed, but he laid the facts before me in perfect modesty. He is an open, pleasant-mannered gentleman and there was truth in his looks and expressions."

"I dare say he believes what he says to be true. I would not accuse the gentleman of dissimulation or falsehood. But nor could I accuse Mr Darcy of deceit and dishonesty without great cause. If, as I believe, there is some misconception, perhaps on both sides, some imperfect recollection or understanding, we would be dishonourable ourselves to accuse either one. Just think how such a thing could destroy Mr Darcy's character in the eyes of society! It would be infamous!"

"Oh, I shall not speak of it to anyone other than you," Elizabeth assured her. "There is no one I trust as I do you, and I have no cause to denigrate either gentleman. But consider Mr Darcy's manner. You must agree he disdains those beneath him in wealth and consequence, and he does not trouble himself to hide it. You have seen how he behaves amongst our neighbours. Such a distant, aloof man might well, for those same reasons of hauteur and superciliousness, deride a man born below him and think nothing of denying a bequest that he does not believe—for his own proud reasons—that man deserves."

"To accuse Mr Darcy of such a very grave offence, such base, disgraceful behaviour, I think more is needed than reserve and poor manners on his part, and open and pleasant manners on the part of his accuser. We do not know either gentleman very well, and I, for one, will forbear to judge. I do not know what to think."

"Well, I know exactly what to think!" But Elizabeth touched Jane's hand, when she saw how troubled her sister was. Poor Jane! Never would she have thought such wickedness existed in the world. "But I will keep my own counsel, and I will be as polite to Mr Darcy as I have always been."

Jane merely smiled, but before she could speak, their mother's shrill, excited voice echoed up through the house. "Jane! Jane! Make haste! Mr Bingley is here! Quickly, Jane! Quickly!"

Obediently, Jane hastened, Elizabeth on her heels, and had the ineffable joy of Mr Bingley himself putting into her hands an invitation to his proposed ball to be held the following Tuesday, the 26th. How happy she must feel on his bespeaking the first two dances, and then, quite daringly, the supper dance. From her seat beside her mother, Elizabeth smiled at Jane's quiet pleasure at being so singled out. She ignored Mr Darcy's dark looks from his chair on the other side of the room, where he sat silent and disapproving, while grateful that Mr Collins was out with her father meeting the tenants. Thank heavens! Her cousin would undoubtedly offend with his odd manners, and Kitty and Lydia were vexatious enough in their loud raptures, without giving Mr Darcy another Bennet connection to condemn.

Elizabeth had the felicity of hearing, as a result of Lydia's anxious enquiries, that the militia officers were to be invited, and much as Jane was doubtless happily anticipating her dances with Mr Bingley, she thought with satisfaction of dancing and conversing with Mr Wickham. It would be an added pleasure to the usual delights of a ball.

Elizabeth would encourage Jane to make the very most of this opportunity. She would lend her the seed pearl parure: it would set off Jane's best blue silk to admiration. She would coerce Mary, who was closest to Elizabeth in size and figure, and whose colouring would suit it best, into the amber dress she had worn herself at the Gouldings' dinner. The rest of Elizabeth's more sophisticated dresses were too mature for the youngest two, but she had ribbons, feathers, aigrettes and artificial flowers enough for every Bennet girl to make a brave show.

A ball presented infinite possibilities, and not only, perhaps, for Jane.

CHAPTER TWENTY-TWO

Thorns and Brambles

"Good heavens, Bingley, you visited Longbourn only yesterday. Do you intend to dance attendance on Miss Bennet every day?"

Bingley smiled. "Yes, until I may dance with her in truth. I like Miss Bennet very well indeed."

"So I must assume, since you delivered the Bennets' invitations yourself. Everyone else in the district has had to make do with a mere footman."

"None other in the district has her eyes or face, nor her sweet temper. She is a very pleasant companion and being with her, even if simply for a morning visit, brightens my day considerably."

"The same can hardly be said for the rest of her family."

"I do not intend to dance with the rest of her family—with the exception of Mrs Grayson, who is as pleasant a companion as her sister almost, although a deal too sharp for me." Bingley let out a snort of laughter. "And a great deal too sharp for Caroline! I should feel guilty for finding her responses to Caroline's attempts to cow her so amusing, but I own I do not."

Nor did Darcy, but since he was determined not to consider Elizabeth Grayson at all, he merely grunted and agreed that he would at least join Bingley for the ride. "I shall not go to Longbourn, but you may have my company so far as Meryton."

No, he would not go to Longbourn. The widow had merely nodded at him the day before when he and Bingley had delivered the invitations to the ball that Caroline Bingley had reluctantly penned at her brother's insistence. One cool nod and a very direct look from grey eyes that held no welcome in them, before she turned her attention to her sister and Bingley. Had he offended her? The petty offence Grayson had given had been apologised for, most handsomely. She had no cause for complaint.

She would have to find someone else at Longbourn today, to spear with that glance. It would not be Fitzwilliam Darcy.

Not that Darcy particularly wanted to go to Meryton, either, but it would give his horse a good run if he allowed Alastor free rein on the way back to Netherfield. Perhaps it would make the brute less apt to try and bite Bingley's grooms. With this laudable ambition in mind, he and Bingley repaired to the stables.

They took the most direct route, eschewing the mundane public road for more picturesque fields and woods. The day was chill and foggy, with thick mist curling up from the streams and twisting though the dark tree boles in Netherfield woods where they had to take care and go more slowly on the narrow path. Twice they could give the horses their heads across winter-ready fields, the steaming breath from both men and beasts mingling with the colder fog. Bingley's greatcoat and hat were bedewed with misty droplets, and a glance at his own sleeve showed Darcy he was no less so. This foretaste of winter promised it would be a cold one.

Meryton was less dense with fog, thicker with people. Of course. Market day. Darcy had forgotten. He moved Alastor carefully through the throng. Perhaps he should turn back here, rather than leave Bingley at Longbourn's gates. There was rather too much activity testing Alastor's temper.

"At least we missed the worst of it," Bingley said with unimpaired cheer, bringing his roan alongside so they could talk. "Oh look! The Bennet ladies!"

Bingley urged his roan to the edge of the market square, where Mrs Grayson and the four Misses Bennet stood in conversation with a group of militia officers and, incongruously, a tall black-clad clergyman. Sighing, Darcy followed. At least the youngest two were not romping around like untamed colts... perhaps the presence of their elder sisters held their bad behaviour in check a trifle. A very small trifle. The youngest Bennet chit, the one with those silly corkscrew curls badly cut in the lop-sided fashion favoured by the more frivolous and *outré* elements of society, was side on to Bingley and Darcy as they approached. She hung on the arm of one officer and stared up at him as did a mouse fascinated by a snake. She was not squealing, which was an undoubted improvement on her usual manner, but the vacuous expression of adulation on her face, evident even in profile, was only to be deplored.

Bingley called out a greeting, and Miss Jane Bennet looked up, her pretty face showing her surprise before relaxing into her usual sweet smile.

The officer turned his head to look at them when he heard Bingley's call, and his gaze caught Darcy's.

Wickham.

Wickham! Good God. Wick—

Darcy's chest constricted on the instant, cold fingers clenching around his ribs to crush everything beneath into a pounding, painful, churning mess caused by a heart trying to leap up out of its cage of bone. The cold rushed away, borne on a pulse of heat that had his face burning as if dipped in a volcano. Only pressing his lips together so hard his mouth hurt, prevented him from voicing his hate and fury and guilt.

The noise of the market faded into a distant hum and buzz. Vague shapes moved on the edge of sight, as wispy and unimportant as though they were phantoms the fog had made manifest. Only he and Wickham were there, transfixed, staring at each other with such hatred that the air should have seethed and roiled with it.

Wickham had paled, his face frozen into a grimace that was half dismay, half defiance. Darcy could only hope his own showed no expression at all.

The world had narrowed down to that familiar face, the one he had hoped never to see again. For a moment so long it felt an aeon, he and Wickham stared at each other, then, slowly, Wickham lifted his free hand to his temple to touch the shako perched on his head in a sketch of a greeting. That was too much to be borne. What Darcy wished to do was wrench Alastor around and send him galloping back the way he'd come, scattering the denizens of Meryton hither and thither like chaff. But no Darcy ever cut and ran. And certainly not before a cur like Wickham.

So, instead, Darcy turned away from Wickham as if he had not seen him. As if he had never seen him.

He looked at the rest of the company. Mrs Grayson frowned. She looked from Wickham to Darcy, with that same direct, almost challenging, gaze she had turned on Darcy at Longbourn. The clergyman murmured something and pulled at her arm.

"Please do not tug at me, Mr Collins. I am not a parcel!" Mrs Grayson's tone was sharp.

"Oh, but my dear, dear cousin! It is my privilege, right, and duty to see to your protection—"

Darcy bowed slightly to the Bennet women, ignoring Wickham and the unknown cleric. "Good day, ladies. I hope you are all well. Forgive me for not staying. I will return now to Netherfield, Bingley, so I leave the ladies in your care."

He touched his hat. Another cold I-do-not-see-you glance at Wickham, a curl of the lip to show his contempt, and he turned Alastor with quiet deliberation and rode slowly away, so upright in the saddle that his back and shoulders stabbed with complaining aches and pains.

And all the while, the lava of his hatred flamed inside his chest and gut. It was a miracle it did not melt his saddle and burn Alastor's back.

It was more than an hour before Darcy regained some equilibrium, and by that time, almost every bramble in Netherfield woods had been slashed and beaten back by his riding crop, and he was out of breath and panting, sweating under his greatcoat. He raised his hand to his mouth, and licked away the blood from the thin, scratchy revenge a bramble thorn had wrought upon the back of his thumb... what in God's name had he done with his gloves and hat? They were nowhere in sight.

Alastor was a hundred yards off, tied to the low branches of a bare oak tree. Darcy had flattened every bramble between them, no thicket a match for him. He could have taken a horsewhip to Wickham with the same wild energy. He could have skinned him, and rejoiced in it.

Alastor was in a foul mood. He snapped towards Darcy's arm, though he missed, and danced around as Darcy pulled himself back into the saddle. He settled when Darcy gathered the reins and set him back along the path to Meryton.

The militia officers were billeted in a long house abutting onto the White Hart, opening onto the Hart's busy courtyard and only yards from the taproom door. The house took the overspill from the Hart's more salubrious rooms, which was darkly, amusingly fitting. Wickham was nothing more than the overspill from good society. He had found his level at last.

It was the work of moments to be directed to the right room, and Wickham readily opened his door when Darcy's fist buffeted the oak panels. Wickham nodded. His face showed nothing but a bright interest, underlain with an amusement and unconcern that he had surely not displayed when they saw each other in the market square.

"I expected you would come back," was all the greeting the blackguard offered, but he stood to one side and gestured Darcy inside. "Though I rather thought we would have this meeting before today."

"I would have had it in Ramsgate, but it appears you left the town quite hurriedly."

Wickham grimaced, and stepped aside to allow Darcy into a small, cold, mean room with a narrow bed pushed against a wall. A rough-wood table and two chairs sat before a blackened, empty hearth, a bottle and two glasses ready on the tabletop.

Wickham picked up the bottle. "Not what you're used to, but all my coin will run to. It is a passable brandy." He splashed some into the glasses and waved Darcy into one of the chairs.

Darcy took the chair, but refused the brandy. He needed a clear head. "You knew I was here in Hertfordshire?"

"Not until I arrived a week ago. I saw you, coming here to the Hart that night for dinner with Colonel Forster. You did not see me."

"I have no doubt you made sure of that."

Wickham was more relaxed than he had any right to be, the smug, insufferable wretch. He sprawled in the chair opposite Darcy, legs spread. At his ease. "Of course. I will admit that I preferred to manage our reunion. And yet you caught me by surprise today."

"Why are you here?" By contrast, Darcy sat as tall as he could in his chair, shoulders held back stiffly and his chin raised high. *You must always dominate a discussion, especially when you are uncertain that the advantage is yours*, was one of his father's maxims. *Make yourself look as large as you can. Betray nothing of what you feel. Loom over the other man if you need to, to put him at a disadvantage and, perhaps, affect his confidence and spirits. You are Darcy of Pemberley. That is weapon enough.*

Wickham's expression did not change. "Oh, nothing to do with you, Darcy. At least, only in so far as you have reduced me to these circumstances, where I must seek any employment if I am not to starve. The pay is adequate and the companionship, merry. Both offer some compensation for your ill treatment."

"Oh, spare me the tale of your woes. Save it for those who are unused to your lies and deceptions. I treated you better than you deserved."

"You stole my inheritance!"

Darcy was assailed with all the futility of their interactions since they had reached manhood. Wickham played some game, as ever, and Darcy was not privy to the rules. He never had been. That it was not a game he wished to play did not quell the rancour of bitterness. "Indeed? Do you propose to return the three thousand pounds I gave you when you relinquished the living, so that you may be considered again for it?"

That cracked the smooth facade. Wickham grimaced again.

Darcy nodded. "I thought not. I repeat, Wickham—why are you here?"

"I merely wish to settle to something. Forge a new career."

"That means you have some scheme in hand. You would not be true to yourself—though you are true to none other—if you did not."

Wickham threw up both his hands. "Of course! Of course I do! Heaven forfend that Fitzwilliam Darcy is ever amiss with his judgements and opinions!" He scowled, huffed then said, in less contentious tones, "I am here because an acquaintance suggested a possibility of advancement and opportunity, and told me of the militia—though he did not tell me about you, damn him. I joined last week because... well, my finances are at point-non-plus. The militia provides bed and board enough to keep body and soul in harmony, an officer's pay is sufficient to allow me some small indulgences, and the society hereabouts will suit me. Whatever object I have, whatever opportunities for my future I may pursue, have nothing to do with you and yours, Darcy. You have my word on that."

"For what that is worth."

"It is all you get. I owe you nothing more."

"But that is where you err." Darcy had not taken his gaze from Wickham—*Hold your opponent in a steady gaze; discompose him with a coldness in your glance, an implacability of demeanour,* George Darcy had said—and he followed his father's advice and maintained it still, steady and cold. It was a defence, to appear unmoved and immovable, and one he used often. "Listen to me, Wickham. In another week, after the ball to be held at Netherfield, I am returning to London. Do not find yourself at any social occasion before then where I am likely to be also. I will not hesitate to publicly deny your acquaintance."

"You cut me in the market square," grumbled Wickham. "It was noticed. It will cause remark."

"That is of no concern to me. The officers are invited to the Netherfield ball. Stay away."

"That interferes with one opportunity I have identified—"

Darcy drew himself up to the utmost he could manage. "If you attend, I will have two or three of Bingley's largest footmen toss you out of house and kick you down every inch of the drive to the public road." He paused. "The drive is a mile long."

Wickham poured himself another brandy and sipped it, eyeing Darcy over the rim of the glass. Darcy stared back, keeping himself in that still, quiet implacability that would have Wickham breaking as a wave does against a basalt cliff.

Wickham breathed out a noisy sigh. "Very well. There is merit in my proceeding slowly, and a little disappointment merely increases anticipation... Well, I will bear it, although I shall not be the only one disgruntled by your hard heart. I assure that you though I have been here but a week, more than one lady will miss me at the ball."

"Such as that Bennet child? She is about the age you favour."

Wickham shrugged. "It is an inconvenience not to attend. Perhaps some compensation is in order."

Wickham was quite stupid. He had a sly cunning and a strong sense of self-preservation, honed and sharpened by a selfish disregard for anything but his own interest. But only a stupid man would keep pressing and pressing, pushing against boundaries to test and destroy them, when the advantage did not lie with him.

Darcy stared him down in silence. Wickham's gaze slid away and he gulped down his brandy, his Adam's apple bobbing in a way that almost invited a throttling. Darcy clenched his fists, all the better to resist that particular temptation.

"Not another penny of Darcy money will ever come your way. Quite the opposite. You left a great deal of debt in Derbyshire when you quitted it. More in London. And in Ramsgate. I estimate I own your liabilities to the tune of more than eighteen hundred pounds. A very large sum."

Now. It was time. *When the moment comes to be Darcy of Pemberley, to threaten with all the weight of Pemberley standing mightily behind you... loom*, his father had said. *Be as enormous and as implacable as the rock from which Pemberley was hewn, and as inexorable.*

Darcy moved, before Wickham could react. He rose swiftly to his feet and did indeed loom, leaning over Wickham where the man still sprawled in his chair. Wickham paled, his head snapping back to allow him to stare up at Darcy.

"One word, Wickham. One word. The merest, tiniest whisper of Georgiana's name, and I will have you arrested for that debt. I will bury you in debtor's prison for the next thirty years. You will die there of some noxious miasma, or starvation, or old age. I will be rid of you. I will have you out of my life."

"Dar—"

"Do you understand? Your liberty and your life depend upon it."

This time when Wickham's Adam's apple bobbed, it was not to mark the benison of brandy sliding down his throat.

"Not. One. Word." Darcy left a measurable gap between his words for emphasis.

Wickham gave a short, savage nod.

"Good." Darcy straightened, tapped his riding crop against his leg, and nodded. "Then we are in accord, which is a miracle." He walked to the door, aware of Wickham's staring, furious, impotent glare that would, if Wickham could but do it, burn through Darcy like fire.

"Fitzwilliam, I—"

"No! You long ago forfeited that right. I am Mr Darcy, to you." Darcy stopped at the door. "I take no leave of you, George." He allowed Wickham to see his gaze wander around the bare little room and he smiled. He made sure Wickham saw that, too. "Do not forget. Not one word."

He closed the door behind him, and leaned against it until the moment of relief passed. He smiled still as he went to the stable to retrieve Alastor, taking several deep, steadying breaths on the way. He had not breathed so freely in... oh, in weeks.

Since Ramsgate.

CHAPTER TWENTY-THREE

A Simple Country Dance

It rained for two days before the ball, but to Caroline Bingley's dismay, the day of the ball was fine, promising a clear night with the bright moon almost at the full.

"There is no escaping it," she said to Darcy when the Netherfield party met that evening for an early, light repast. "What joy awaits, with every rustic coming here in their Sunday best, which in Town one would not hesitate to consign to the ragbag!"

With a sigh, she led the way on a tour of the rooms readied for the entertainments. The drawing room and the two large sitting rooms on either side had been opened up to create a very passable ball room. The servants had folded back the tall doors and cleared all the furniture, leaving a shining expanse of polished floor gleaming under crystal chandeliers, with more sconces on the walls lighting the rooms to brilliance. Chairs and sofas were set back against the walls to accommodate those not dancing, and tables at one end of the room buckled under enormous bowls of punch and ratafia to refresh those who were. The piano had been moved to the supper room to entertain the sixty or so guests as they ate. The supper tables were already set, candlelight reflecting from burnished silverware and finely cut crystal.

Darcy complimented Miss Bingley on the arrangements and the decorations. It was, indeed, well done. She preened, and he ran a hand around his collar, easing the starched neckcloth. He had still to decide what to do. Indecision was not a usual trait: a sin to lay at the widow's door.

Night drew in, and Netherfield was a blaze of light from one end to the other. The grooms had lit flambeaux along the length of the drive, and at eight, the first coaches were to be seen lumbering over the gravel sweep to the front door. Miss Bingley shepherded her brothers and sister to the hallway to greet their guests.

"At least we are spared that," Grayson said, as he and Darcy retired to haunt the empty ball room.

"A blessing." Darcy glanced at his *soi-disant* secretary. "You will not approach your brother's widow."

Grayson raised one shoulder in an inelegant shrug. "I have said I will not. I will make myself useful, in accordance with your instructions, and dance with all the... what do the French call them? Ah yes, the *faire tapisserie* who are too plain for partners and hence decorate the walls."

"Good," said Darcy. "I would be obliged."

She was glorious. Her dress was as fine as Miss Bingley's, reflecting her status as a widow of comfortable means. The rich green of the silk, enhanced by a peridot parure, lit shades of answering green in her grey eyes.

Emeralds. She would look splendid in emeralds.

She did not acknowledge his admiration, although she must have noted how he stared when she first came in, as if he were the veriest mooncalf. She dropped him a curtsey and murmured a greeting, but went to join Miss Lucas almost immediately. Darcy stepped back to watch her go, noting the heavyset clergyman lumbering after her, the same man he had seen in the marketplace. Whoever he was, Mrs Grayson gave him scant notice. Her expression showed no more than the civil patience that women of her standing were trained to possess. She introduced Miss Lucas to the clergyman, but the man showed little interest in anyone but the widow or gazing around the ball room to take in its magnificence. The cleric wore an admiring expression on his round face—for Mrs Grayson or Netherfield?

Darcy took up position near the windows whence he could keep his gaze on her even through the growing crowd. She flitted from group to group, greeting friends and acquaintances. Laughter followed her every footstep. This was her *métier*, it seemed, where she could smile and laugh and talk until all around her were at their ease. She included the persistent clergyman only so far as civility demanded.

She glanced Darcy's way more than once. Did she look for him particularly? Did she hope that he would come to her, talk and laugh and invite her to dance? He could not tell. Her expression was open and amused, but she wore that for everyone. It was not assumed to invite him in, but her general air. He could only applaud her discretion at not showing her feelings. Once, it seemed, she quite deliberately sought him out, turning from where she had been talking with some of the red-coated militia officers to meet his gaze with that very direct one of her own. It pierced him. She did not smile.

He was still pondering the meaning of it when at last the small orchestra finished their tuning up, and the first set was announced. Darcy almost never danced the more significant sets of a ball—the first, the last and the supper dance in between. Ladies put much emphasis on gaining those particular dances with eligible gentlemen, and he would not raise expectations. Darcy was surprised to see Grayson lead Miss Bingley out for the dance. He had not thought she would lower herself to a man she believed was a mere secretary... but then, she knew Darcy's habits and could not expect to dance the first with him. He would take her out for the second, and consider his duty done. Bingley was, of course, dancing with Jane Bennet.

Darcy started towards Mrs Grayson to seek her hand in the dance, but the ungainly clergyman was there before him, taking the widow's hand and leading her out to join the forming sets. The clergyman smirked and simpered, looking around the other couples as if pitying them for the inferiority of their partners and turning his beaming countenance onto Mrs Grayson. He gained nothing in response other than the bland politeness a lady was forced to give a man who was not her first choice.

Mrs Grayson did not appear to enjoy the dance. It was doubtful that her partner had anything but the most slender of notions about the steps and frequently went the wrong way, or was standing in the spot that others in the formation required. The man was a danger to every woman there, but Mrs Grayson was nimble enough to avoid injury to her dress or satin slippers. The fool smiled amiably throughout this display of utter ineptitude, but Mrs Grayson gave him no more than the tips of her fingers whenever the dance brought them together and her expression never changed from polite disinterest, no matter what folly the man exhibited. She spoke but little.

Darcy retired to the window again and watched from there, leaning against one of the pillars forming the embrasure, and crossing his arms. That fool may have been swifter in gaining Mrs Grayson's hand, but Darcy would wager she would not grant the man a second set. Darcy would secure her for the third. Perhaps that would redeem him for not being quick enough to save her from dancing with the nodcock. Once she glanced at him—to see if he were watching her, he was certain. He allowed his mouth to twitch into the faintest of smiles in response, and she looked hurriedly away.

He danced the second with Miss Bingley, as he had promised himself, and as soon as it was over, returned the lady to her sister and her duties as hostess, and hurried to where Mrs Grayson stood with Miss Lucas and several other young ladies of the same age. He bowed. Invited her to dance. Waited, allowing his faint smile to show.

She stared at him, her expression quizzical, and for a fleeting moment he held his breath, his heart thudding its apprehension though the pulses of his throat. She would not refuse him, surely!

That would be beyond belief.... But at last she smiled, and once again he could only admire her discretion and control, for that smile showed no more joy than was seemly.

"Why... yes, Mr Darcy. Thank you. Although it must be the set immediately after supper, if you please. I am engaged for the next two."

He bowed again. "Then anticipation can only increase the eventual pleasure. Until then, Mrs Grayson. Miss Lucas."

They curtsied, and with their murmured *Mr Darcys* sounding in his ears, he moved away, all the better to perfect his own control.

Waiting and anticipation would be all very well, if he had not to spend the interval observing the ball, and the follies it manifested.

Bingley saw nothing of it, of course. If he were not dancing with Miss Bennet, he was sitting on a sofa being confidential with her, and there are none so blind as a lovestruck fool. It was all too likely that Bingley would excuse it all, too, thinking the wild behaviour of some mere high spirits—the two youngest Bennet girls being the worst offenders, one squealing and giggling while the other danced around with a militia officer's shako perched on her silly corkscrew curls.

Mr Bennet might brought a halt to the chit's romping and returned the shako to its rightful owner, but he neither offered his daughters chastisement nor ordered any amendment to their behaviour. While it was true that later Mr Bennet stopped the middle daughter in her display of poor musicianship over supper, he did so in a way that must have mortified the girl and certainly did not show himself to any advantage as a gentleman. He evidently took delight in his family's antics, finding a dark amusement in their folly: an indolent, irresponsible, sardonic man. Mrs Grayson had shaken her head at him and persuaded the red-faced girl to play the accompaniment and join her in a light Italian duet, and for a few minutes Darcy was able to ignore everyone around him and enjoy her singing and how she blended with her sister's weaker voice. Not technically the best he had ever heard, but she had a pretty voice and chose her song wisely to show it to advantage. She and her sister could retire to their seats at table to applause, honour and self-esteem restored.

Darcy's satisfaction did not last long. He was only half listening to Sir William's chatter about the coming Petty Sessions at which the knight served as a magistrate, when he became aware that Mrs Bennet sat just beyond Sir William, talking with Lady Lucas. The harridan did not trouble to lower her voice as she predicted her eldest daughter would entice Bingley into parson's mousetrap and hence bring the rest of her girls "...to the notice of other rich men. What a marriage that will be!"

What a vulgar, commonplace mind! An unrepentant fortune-hunter! Everyone must have heard her. That Bingley's sisters had was evident by their expressions: barely controlled contempt on Miss Bingley's part, anxiety on Mrs Hurst's. Bingley himself was too intent on his low-voiced conversation with Miss Bennet to hear anything, while she smiled calmly back at him. If she had a heart to be touched, it was not evident, but Netherfield might have crashed down around Bingley and it was doubtful he would see the ruin unless it was reflected in Miss Bennet's eyes. Certainly, Bingley's gaze was fixed nowhere else. Fool. Darcy must speak to him, before his honour was engaged.

A glance at Mrs Grayson showed her speaking urgently in a low voice to her mother. She caught Darcy's gaze, and quickly averted her own. Her action was futile: her mother waved her away, and an instant later she swiftly left the supper room, her colour high. She did not return.

With the exception of herself and her elder sister, her family had exposed itself in every possible way. She must be so mortified, cast down that her poor origins were so relentlessly displayed. She must fear it lowered her in his eyes, that he would renege on the dance he had requested. A lesser gentleman, one less certain of his own unassailable position, might well do that. A Darcy, of course, would not break his word, even on such a trivial matter.

A few minutes later, the company made a general exodus from supper to return to the dancing. Darcy tugged at his waistcoat, looking down to hide his smile. It would be his pleasure to relieve her mortification, and seek her for the dance. While her relations were execrable, and he would never offer for her, he could at least show her that a true gentleman would act to put her at her ease. And while it was indeed an honour for her to be asked, it would be a delight to dance with her. He could not imagine anything more pleasing than taking her small hand in his and leading her out onto the floor.

An ineffable pleasure for them both.

CHAPTER TWENTY-FOUR

False Steps

Elizabeth stood at the other side of the room, the lumbering cleric bowing and scraping at her side. Her smile was strained, and became even more so when she saw Darcy. The clergyman, too, turned and saw him. The man's broad, round face lit up. Darcy did not catch what the clergyman first said to her, but her alarm was unmistakable.

"You cannot, sir! It is not for you to—"

"It is my duty," said the clergyman, clearly heard as Darcy approached. "You must pardon me, my dear cousin, but though your advice shall in future guide my every action, in this case I consider myself more fitted by education and experience to decide on what is right."

And as Darcy reached him, the clod-hopping, addle-pated nincompoop had the crass ill-manners, the bare-faced gall, to introduce himself. The idiot bowed so low Darcy could almost see down the back of his collar. Across that broad, black-clad back Darcy caught Mrs Grayson's anguished gaze, enjoying the pretty colour on her cheekbones, while the cleric between them proclaimed that he was "William Collins, sir, at your service! I am, sir, the humble recipient of the gracious notice of the most noble, the incomparable Lady Catherine de Bourgh..."

Lady Catherine? Darcy blinked, stared, his expression as cold as he could make it. Mrs Grayson's blush deepened, and she drew her lips together in a thin, hard line.

The cleric, Collins, was impervious to the chill. He fluttered and fawned, talking of his reverence for Darcy's most troublesome relative, deifying her beyond recognition. "I am proud to serve as Hunsford's new rector, as you might imagine, sir! I hope I know what gratitude is due Lady Catherine's generous kindness in offering me the living, and how I must go on to prove my sense of obligation for her grace and patronage. I am pleased to tell you that her ladyship was in excellent health when I left Kent a week or more ago, and that fair flower, your betrothed, Miss de Bourgh. Oh, what a day that will be to have two such noble houses joined. As Lady Catherine herself says, you will unite two impeccable bloodlines with wealth and consequence enough for a Dukedom! Yours will be one of those Great Marriages, she is sure. I know she anticipates the joys of the match with much enthusiasm—"

Darcy took a step to the left and held out his hand, cutting right across the flood of verbiage as if Collins was not there. "It is our dance, I believe, Mrs Grayson. Shall we join the sets?"

The hand she put into his shook a trifle, and her colour had drained away. She said nothing. He led her away to take the top place in the forming set, leaving the silly obsequious little man to bow and cringe behind them. He would not take the trouble to look. Collins was so typical a specimen of Lady Catherine's preferred servant, it was laughable. That his aunt was so lost to propriety as to trumpet her nonsense about a marriage with Anne to such a toadying little man! What vulgarity! Well, she must always be Lady Catherine, immutable in her character. Thank heaven she rarely left Kent.

"Mr Darcy—"

"Who is that man? He called you cousin."

"Mr Collins is…" She pressed her lips together again, before she could go on, "He is a distant cousin of my father's. He is visiting Longbourn partly, I believe, at your aunt's direction."

Darcy grunted out a *Hmmmpfh* to convey his derision. Lady Catherine certainly enjoyed directing the lives of those around them. Only a fool obeyed her. The clergyman's attentions to Mrs Grayson were very marked. "He is very attentive."

A wry smile. "I have known less troublesome wasps plague a picnic! But sir, you must allow me to apologise. I am well aware that to force an introduction—"

"You are not responsible for his lack of manners, ma'am. I beg you think no more of it."

She blushed again, giving him a doubtful, frowning look. "You are very good. I thank you."

The music started then, striking out with *Mr Isaac's Maggot*. He bowed. She curtsied, and the dance began. For several minutes Darcy gave his attention to the dance as he and Mrs Grayson passed each other, reaching out to touch their hands together, made neat fleuret steps as they came towards each other and then retreated… She moved with grace, holding her head erect, her gaze on him. The value of the maggot was its stateliness: the faster jigs precluded speech, on the whole, but this dance allowed some conversation.

She spoke before he could determine how to begin, making that very point. "We should have some conversation, you know. It will look odd if we are silent for the entire set."

"And if I say I am minding my steps?"

Her eyes widened, as if she were surprised that he would, or could, make a jest. "I would presume, sir, that you are seeking a compliment. You are a fine dancer. You should dance more often."

"It is not an exercise with which I am comfortable."

Her mouth twitched into a slight smile. "Yes. I perfectly recall your disinclination to dance at the last assembly."

That silenced him. Had she heard his unkind—and untrue!— words of disparagement for her charms? No. She was smiling more brightly now. He gave himself over to the delight of watching her: the grace of every movement, the fluidity of her step and the gestures with her arms that the dance required, the line of her neck and throat, and how she held her head so proudly.

Beautiful. She was beautiful. He had been a blind idiot at the assembly, ever to have said anything to the contrary.

They were more than halfway down the line—chassé, allemande, fleuret—before she broke the silence. "When you saw us the other day, we had been making a new acquaintance. You know him, I believe."

Wickham. Good God, the man was more pestilential than the pox.

He swallowed back the tirade that would escape his lips if he allowed it. "Mr Wickham makes friends easily with his display of happy manners. It is less certain that his is a character is capable of retaining those of any worth."

The dance parted them for a moment and when they came together again, hands touching, she said, her air troubled, "I believe he has had the misfortune not to retain your friendship, sir, and suffers the consequences."

They parted again. Darcy moved down the line to take position behind the second couple, while Elizabeth mirrored him on the other side of the line of dancers. He found he must unclench his jaw to allow him to speak. What had that cur told her?

When they came together again, he limited himself to saying, "I am confident I made the right decision, Mrs Grayson."

She regarded him for a moment, then inclined her head. They traversed the entire line, and the first dance of the set came to an end. He bowed, she curtsied, and both brought gloved hands together in polite applause for the musicians. They stood close together, waiting for the second dance of the set to be called.

Elizabeth plucked at her lace overdress as if to pull away some imperfection, and then smoothed it flat, her eyes on the floor. When she raised them again, resolution and determination showed in the set of her chin. "You said once that you have what you termed a resentful temper."

"I remember."

"I assume you are careful always to be cautious about that temper being provoked?"

"Yes. Never without cause. Or without thought, and reasoning, and judgement."

"I see."

He hoped that she did, indeed. "Why do you ask?"

Her smile was faint. "I am trying to make you out. To illustrate your character."

He made his mouth turn up in a smile. "And how do you get on?"

"Very badly. There are some... conflicting images that I cannot reconcile."

"I could wish you not attempt it at the moment. I cannot think it would do either of us credit—"

"Quite right, sir. It is not the proper occupation in a ball room."

That was not what he had meant, but rather that he feared she would mistake him, particularly if she had heard Wickham's tales. But before he could explain further, the music struck up with a vigorous version of *A Fig For Buonaparte*, and within a moment or two neither of them had breath enough for conversation. It was an interminable fifteen minutes. She was within reach, but his hesitation kept her at a metaphorical little distance, and by the time he was leading her from the dance floor at the end of the set, the little distance seemed as long as a mile.

Miss Bingley encountered them at the punch table. "Good heavens, Mr Darcy, I did not expect you to dance! You must congratulate yourself, Miss Eliza... Mrs Grayson, I mean. You cannot know what a victory you have achieved there. But I forget my manners. I must wish you joy!"

Elizabeth frowned. "Wish me joy? Whatever do you mean?" She took the cup of punch from Darcy's hand with a smile of thanks.

"I am afraid I overheard your mother speaking to her friends of your impending match with your father's cousin. He is your father's heir, is he not? That is very eligible indeed! It must give you great comfort to anticipate such an improvement in your circumstances."

Darcy's chest tightened so convulsively, it forced a cough from his lungs.

Elizabeth held the cup to her lips, but she did not drink from it. Her eyes were wide above the glass rim. Darcy could wish he too had something behind which to hide his shock. She placed the cup, its contents untouched, on the table beside them. With one glance at her mother, who held court with all her cronies on a sofa on the other side of the room, she turned her attention to Miss Bingley.

"I am all confusion as to why you think a clergyman of moderate means would be an improvement in my circumstances. The truth is that though I do not, it is true, enjoy the sort of society to which you aspire, I am the daughter of one gentleman, the widow of another, and, as an estate owner, a gentlewoman in my own right. By every measure of society, I outrank those who can make no similar claim to the gentry. If I were prepared to remarry—and I am not—I have no need to limit my prospects to any particular gentleman, much less the one you mention."

Miss Bingley was whiter than her own lace. "Estate? What estate?"

"Why this one, Miss Bingley. Surely you understand I own Netherfield Park and your brother is but my tenant? As you said once, there is always some merchant or other wanting to lease good houses." Elizabeth lifted her chin. "Please do not repeat gossip concerning me. I would dislike having to speak to your brother about it, but I will do so, if I must."

Miss Bingley, scarlet now with chagrin, spluttered something, several somethings, in which many a "But Mrs Bennet said…" featured, a contention that Elizabeth ignored.

Instead, Elizabeth glanced around the room. "It is a very creditable ball, and will do much to cement your brother's relations with the gentry class. I do hope you enjoy the rest of it." A swift curtsey to Darcy. "I thank you for our dance, sir. It was a pleasure."

And with a nod, she sailed away, head held high, leaving both Darcy and Miss Bingley staring after her.

"Well!" Miss Bingley spluttered again. "But…! Well!"

Darcy watched Elizabeth go. Good Lord, she was glorious.

Several weeks before, Hurst had undertaken to tell his wife and sister of Mrs Grayson's status. Now he merely laughed when Darcy took him to task for misleading them. Assured that Miss Bingley had indeed looked very foolish and had been the recipient of a dagger-sharp set-down, he laughed again, slapped Darcy on the shoulder and went to find a celebratory glass of port. The man was incorrigible. But then, Darcy might take refuge in the port decanter, too, were Caroline Bingley his sister. Instead, he went to find Grayson, who was kicking his heels in one of the card rooms.

"I saw you dance with her. I dare say it took us no further forward?" Grayson scowled when Darcy confirmed that "forward" was not a direction anyone had taken. "I will settle this soon. I must get back to my own life, and I have rusticated here for quite long enough. I believe I must challenge her face to face."

Darcy quelled the sudden lurch he felt within his chest. "Sir William tells me the Petty Session meets on Friday, to hear cases for the January Assizes."

Grayson started. "Are you suggesting we have the magistrates investigate?"

"I am suggesting that the magistrates would have already done so, when James died. We should speak to them, to discover the outcome of those investigations directly."

Grayson took a moment or two to consider it. "I would speak to her first, and then seek corroboration, or otherwise, of her story from the magistrates. Sir William a magistrate, though? Good Lord. Who else?"

"Mr Harpur. We have met him, you recall."

"I do. Well, at least he is a gentleman."

"Yes," said Darcy, and returned to the ball room to watch Mrs Grayson dance with John Lucas, while Miss Bingley glared at her from where she sat with Mrs Hurst.

Not for the first time, the deception he was practising weighed on him. Mr Harpur was indubitably a gentleman, with all the rectitude and honour that implied. Darcy wondered if his own good intentions and the memory of his old schoolfellow were enough to clear him of the feeling that he himself had failed to meet similarly high standards.

Or what the widow would say, when she knew the truth.

CHAPTER TWENTY-FIVE

A Private Interview

Wearied by their enjoyments the night before, the Bennets all slept late and it was well past ten on Wednesday before the entire family had straggled in to breakfast. Papa departed quickly for his library, rather than suffer his family's raptures over the ball and the account of every dress worn, and who danced which dances with whom.

"No man should have to tolerate lace this early in the morning," he said as he rose from the table. "I confess I am not equal to it."

"There are more important things to discuss." Elizabeth gave her mother a cool look when the door had closed behind him. She had, of course, been unable to speak to Mama in the coach home since it had been crowded with her sisters, and there had been no opportunity since. Her mother had claimed a terrible fatigue the instant she had entered Longbourn's doors, and rushed away to her room before Elizabeth could prevent her.

"Indeed there are!" Mr Collins's tone was hearty. "And I am delighted, my dear cousin, that you are of the same mind as I am on the necessity for a... a significant discussion between us." And as her sisters looked on, their expressions ranging from outright horror (Jane and Mary) to confusion (Kitty) and glee (Lydia), he turned to Mama and simpered. He positively simpered. "I may depend, I know, on your interest with your fair daughter, ma'am. May I have a private interview with my cousin Elizabeth?"

Elizabeth spoke before her mother could. "No, Mr Collins, you may not. I can conceive of no reason for you to seek a private conversation with me."

"Lizzy!" hissed her mother, fanning herself with her hand, her expression now as horrified as Jane's.

Mr Collins chuckled. "My dear cousin! My dear, dear cousin! Your modesty does you great credit, but you can have no real understanding of why I would seek such an interview..." His voice trailed off as Elizabeth stared at him and held up her hand in a gesture of negation.

She looked at the eagerness for a spectacle evidenced in her mother and Lydia, Kitty's slowly dawning comprehension, and the embarrassment shown by Jane and Mary. Jane looked quite anguished, and Mary sat with her head bowed to hide her face. Perhaps she had hoped Mr Collins might look at her... Elizabeth prayed not. She would not have Mary mortified.

"Mr Collins, I am... Very well." She would do everything she could to prevent Mr Collins actually making a proposal, but it was best done in private. She rose from her chair. "If you will follow me, sir?"

Mr Collins spluttered something into his napkin and bounced to his feet. "Now?" He looked down at his breakfast in patent dismay.

"I believe this is a matter we should settle immediately." Elizabeth gave her mother one burning look, and went to the door. A moment of hesitation, and Mr Collins scuttled after her. "The west parlour, I think. We will not be disturbed there."

He followed after her, looking rather dazed. Once in the parlour she gestured to him towards the empty hearth, and turned to ensure the door remained open before joining him near the fireplace.

"My dear cousin," he said petulantly. "This is a matter that requires a gentleman's lead. You are all loveliness and... and everything, of course, but you are not in authority here and it is unseemly—"

"Mr Collins, I am aware of only one reason why a gentleman would wish for a private interview. If there is another, then I apologise for my misapprehension. However, I will state clearly that I will not remarry."

Mr Collins stared. He swallowed visibly. "You are all that is delightful! I am certain that you have marked my interest in, and approbation of, your manifold charms and attractions. The moment I saw you, I singled you out as the companion of my future life. My sentiments cannot have escaped you—"

"I did note them, sir, but I have endeavoured to show you, as gently and as civilly as possible, that I am not similarly affected. I am honoured by your notice, but I repeat that I will not remarry."

He flung his hands into the air as one who is astonished by what he is told. "But I have not explained my reasons for marrying, to convince you of the eligibility of my suit! I have much to offer, cousin! Not only in my situation now, so nobly granted by the continuing notice of Lady Catherine de Bourgh, but also as the heir of your father and the future master of this pleasant estate. That alone must have many calls upon the softer sentiments in your heart, as the place of your childhood happiness! No, cousin, I am convinced that when you have listened to my protestations and my application is sanctioned by your excellent parents, as I am already assured by your mother will be the case, you will quite see your sweet, guileless modesty is—"

She would not allow him to finish even one of his florid speeches. "You appear to think that I am under my parents' authority. I assure you that I am not, and even if I were, my answer would not change. I am a guest in this house, as much as you are. I am a widow, sir, with an establishment of my own. I left my parents' authority when I married almost five years ago. I cannot be cajoled–or forced–into any subsequent marriage by any representations of theirs, much as I honour and esteem them. In every case, I would thank the gentleman concerned for the honour of his regard—and indeed, I do thank you—but I will not remarry."

"But my dear cousin Elizabeth, you must! It is most unseemly for a woman to be left in charge of a property of the extent of Netherfield Park— of any property! It is not a woman's place. The laws of God and man decree it. You are a delicate, gentle flower. You must not be taxed with a dreadful burden that is so clearly beyond your powers. No woman has the mental capacity, the intelligence and education... It must warp her and make her that distasteful object, the unwomanly woman. It is a crime against nature and, I have no doubt, against the Lord since He has decreed that the woman be man's helpmeet. You must be the vine, clinging to your stronger mate and allowing him to carry the weary load on your behalf, as is his duty, honour and pleasure."

Elizabeth was within an ames-ace of decrying the notion that a clergyman with no experience of running an estate thought he would be more successful at it than she was purely because of his sex, despite her being born to country gentry life and managing Netherfield under the approving eyes of her trustees for the past four years. She forbore. She had a sharper weapon than that.

She regarded his broad, reddened countenance, and smiled very sweetly. "Oh, I must commiserate with you, Mr Collins! How difficult it must be for you to deliver this same lecture to Lady Catherine. How does she respond to the charge of being unwomanly, pray?"

Mr Collins's mouth dropped open. "But what can you mean?"

"Why, simply that if it is unnatural and unseemly for me to manage my estate, it is surely equally so for Lady Catherine to manage Rosings. How does she take your chastisement, sir?"

Mr Collins spluttered and choked. "But you cannot... It is hardly... It is very different in Lady Catherine's case! She is... She is all that is great and good and—"

Elizabeth inclined her head. "Indeed, it is different. Rosings is out of reach, is it not? Well, sir, so is Netherfield Park. Content yourself with managing Longbourn when it is yours, and I am sure your wife, whoever she may be, will indeed entwine herself around you as a vine around the sturdy oak. I say again, for I believe the fourth time, that I will not remarry. Honoured as I am by your proposal, and though I appreciate the sentiments which provoked it, I will and must refuse your suit."

"But—"

"I will not discuss this further. A gentleman would not persist." She dipped him a small curtsey, and turned to the door.

The sound of a kettle letting out steam came from behind her. Elizabeth turned back and eyed him as coolly as she could.

Good Lord. He would surely have an apoplexy. His entire body was stiff with outrage, his chest thrust out and his arms set wide, his hands clenching. His jaw was set so hard, the tendons and sinews in his neck stood out like ropes. His colour deepened to magenta, his eyes protruding with the violence of his passion.

They stared at each other, Elizabeth and Mr Collins. It took every scrap of courage she had to lift her chin and wait, when every nerve flashed with lightning and her heart leapt. She could not but help glance at his large, meaty hands clenching, but she would not run. She would not. Running always made it worse when he caught up with you...

Mr Collins straightened up with an air of offended dignity. "I shall discuss this with my cousin Bennet. Ladies such as yourself"—with a withering scowl, to indicate he felt she barely merited the title—"are altogether too ignorant and silly to be know what is good for you, or make decisions for yourselves. We shall see who will prevail."

She stepped back to let him pass. "I will."

His glare should have turned her to ash. He did not quite slam the door behind him, but certainly closed it more decisively than Elizabeth had given him credit for.

She breathed out a slight sigh. Well. That was done. Not as well done as she should like, and she should have preferred to divert him from his determined course, but so far as she was concerned, it was over.

When she returned to the breakfast parlour, five heads swivelled round to face her, five faces eager, and five sets of eyes searching her expression for some indication of what had occurred. Elizabeth, taken with some of her father's deviltry, smiled at them, directing a particularly sweet smile at her mother to mirror the one she had given Mr Collins before skewering him with her words. She resumed her seat.

"Pass me the coffee pot, Mary, if you would. I am sorry to say that my cup has grown cold."

Mama found her voice. "Lizzy?"

"Yes, Mama?"

A glance down the length of the table revealed her mother almost beside herself with agitation.

"Mr Collins! What of Mr Collins?"

"Oh," said Elizabeth. "He has gone to my father, I believe."

An instant of stunned silence was broken by twin shrieks from Mama and Lydia.

"Oh Lizzy, Lizzy! My good, good girl! Oh, we are saved, we are saved! Mrs Collins... how well that sounds!" Mama bounced in her seat, all the better to convey her excitement and approbation. "Oh, my dear, dear Lizzy!"

Jane and Mary stared at her, both round eyed. Jane paled visibly. Kitty had raised a rosy apple to her mouth. It was now transfixed there while she stared wildly over it at the spectacle before her, while Lydia snatched up her napkin to try and hide her exhilaration. Mary pushed the coffee pot at Elizabeth with a shaking hand.

"Thank you, Mary." Elizabeth filled up her cup to warm the remains. "I do not understand your excitement, Mama. Mr Collins has gone to Papa to complain that I refused him, apparently under the erroneous belief that Papa will—or can—do something to force me to change my answer. Papa, of course, cannot, and Mr Collins will have to find a bride elsewhere."

She returned her attention to her breakfast. Kitty stared still over her apple, her mouth open and her eyes wide as saucers, and Lydia sniggered into the napkin she had pressed against her lips. Jane caught Elizabeth's hand with hers under the table and squeezed. Mary, her voice shaking and rather squeaky, asked Elizabeth if she would like more bread and butter.

"What? Lizzy!" shrieked Mama.

"Whatever did you expect, Mama?"

Mama moaned aloud. The sudden crunch of Kitty's teeth into the apple sounded as loud as a gunshot, and Lydia's giggles escaped the muffling napkin. Jane squeezed Elizabeth's hand again.

"We are told that we must honour our parents." But Mary's slight smile belied the mild reproof.

"You should not tease us so!" Jane said, smiling too.

"Oh Lizzy! How could you!" came very faintly from Mama's end of the table, where that lady drooped and wilted against her youngest daughter. Lydia, other than providing a stout arm in support, was so far from sharing her mother's sentiments that she looked on in frank enjoyment.

"Oh, I could very easily, ma'am. What on earth possessed you to push the man in my direction? You cannot possibly imagine I would ever agree to marry such a man! What were you thinking?"

"Oh, what have you done?" Mama wailed. "Oh! Oh! Lizzy, you ungrate—"

"What were you about to encourage that lunacy?"

"I told Mr Collins you would make him such a good wife! I thought... oh, you must remarry. He is a clergyman... Most gentlemen will not wish to marry a widow, but a clergyman need not be so particular, you know. You are too young to be a widow."

"If I married Mr Collins, I would be one again in very short order!"

Mama's face crumpled. "Oh, he will put us out into the hedgerows, when your father dies! Oh—"

"Who else did you tell, Mama? To whom did you speak of it with such unguarded freedom, that Miss Bingley overheard you last night and had the unmitigated temerity to come and wish me joy? I know you spoke to Lady Lucas. Whom else?"

Her mother moaned more mournfully than a ghost and shook her head. "Oh my poor nerves! Nobody can tell what I suffer! Those of us who do not complain are never pitied."

"Goodness, Lizzy, if people are talking of it," Kitty said, "that is not a good thing!"

Lydia trumpeted out a laugh. "Perhaps you will have to marry him. What a good joke!"

The inanities of her two youngest daughters seemed to give Mama courage. "Indeed! If people are talking... Lady Lucas... Miss Bingley mentioned it, you said..."

Elizabeth slammed her cup down into the saucer. It was a wonder it did not shatter. Her pulse was speeding, racketing along faster than a coach with a runaway team, and it hurt to breathe. She pulled in sharp, angry little breaths. The joke had soured to acid. "Your clacking tongue, madam, forced me into one miserable, unhappy marriage. I will never permit you to do that again."

Mama gaped at her. "Unhappy? What do you mean, unhappy? You gained Netherfield Park out of it!"

"At what cost? James was... Mama, you know what he was! How can you sit there and pretend you do not know what it is you did?"

"La, Lizzy, Mama told us how you would provoke him." Lydia crumpled up her abused napkin and tossed it onto the table, still gleeful and laughing. "She says a man does not like an impertinent wife, and it was perfectly understandable that he checked you—"

"Checked me? Checked me!" Heat flared in her until her ears rang and her face felt aflame.

"Lizzy..." Jane said in a small, frightened voice.

"Madam, is this what you said to your daughters about my marriage?"

Her mother looked too bewildered to answer. It was Kitty who nodded, and Mary.

Ice swept down to quench the flames. Elizabeth drew a long breath. By some miracle, she prevented her voice from trembling. "Shall I show you the scars, Lydia, that his *checking* left? Would you think it so droll a thing then? Or you, madam. Before you spout such nonsense to your daughters, would you not like to see the marks James Grayson left on me the night he kicked your grandson out of my womb and tried to toss me down the stairs? Do you think for one moment I will ever forgive you?" She raised her voice over Mama's wordless wails and cries, aware of the shocked expressions Mary and Kitty turned her way. Jane, of course, knew already, and Lydia probably did not care to listen. "Hear me, madam. I will not marry Mr Collins. I know very well you think that if he marries me, he and I will live at Netherfield and you will be left to reign here in Longbourn. As ever, you think only of yourself. But if you are cognizant of your own good, you will not provoke me. If you expect my support when my father leaves us, you will cease at once."

"Lizzy," Jane said again. "Lizzy. Be calm."

"I am perfectly calm." Elizabeth pushed back her chair and started for the door. She took no leave of her mother, asked no permission to go. Her mother deserved no such respect.

Her knees started shaking before she had gone two steps. A moment later and Jane was beside her, winding an arm around her waist to steady her. And a moment after that, Mary appeared at her other side; shy, awkward Mary, who had not Jane's close companionship with Elizabeth to be certain her ministrations were welcome.

Over the weeping and blubbering lamentations from her mother and the shocked sobs coming from Kitty, Mary said, very soft, "I would help if you wish it, Lizzy."

Elizabeth used her free hand to grip Mary's. "Thank you. You are very good."

Mary closed the door with unusual emphasis behind them, and returned to Elizabeth's side. They were halfway up the stairs when Papa crossed the hall into the breakfast room and flung open the door.

He glanced up at them, and gave a jerk of the head to order them to carry on. He raised his voice in unusual sharpness and ire. "Kitty, Lydia—leave at once." And as soon as the two youngest Bennet girls were out in the hall, he went on, "Well, Mrs Bennet! What is this I hear from my cousin, that you have been more than ordinarily nonsensical? Stop that bawling and weeping, and explain to me what madness possessed you to think you might force Mr Collins onto our daughter. Good Lord, madam—"

For the third time that morning, a door closed with a very decided snap of the lock, drowning out his voice and his wife's wails.

CHAPTER TWENTY-SIX

A Woman's Good Opinion

Elizabeth had not wept.

It was far too late for weeping. Jane's hand smoothed over her hair, and Mary deftly arranged tea and plumped cushions, and set the curtains of Elizabeth's bedroom just so to prevent the pale November sun from striking her in the eyes. They offered quiet grace while she shivered and remembered, and overcame the memory of her weakness.

Men, now, were always loath to admit to weakness. They thought it unmanly. Dishonourable. A reason for humiliation and shame. Even when the dreams were blackest, they would repay quiet grace with a curse and a blow—many blows—to prove they were truly strong, untouched, valiant. What real man needed such womanish sympathy? To offer it, was an insult, to be repaid in pain and blood.

James's voice, broken and choking, when she woke him from another nightmare, hammered into her memory... *So many, so many... arms and legs shattered or blasted away... blood. So much blood. Screaming and yelling... Harry's belly is torn open... God, I want to be sick... Shut up, Harry! Shut up!... He cannot hold his guts in... Not even both hands... Begging me. Begging me... I have to do it. I have to... He screams so loud! My pistol... where is my pistol... Forgive me, Harry. Forgive... Stinks and smokes, and men's guts spilling out... There! There! See? Grapeshot. Bloody grapeshot! Tears a man to shreds, rips off arms and heads and legs....They are everywhere, the dead men, holding out their bloody hands... Begging me... I cannot shoot them all...*

No. Men did not like admitting to weakness. They merely enjoyed thrashing it out of others.

"I do not think I can remain here, Charlotte."

Charlotte and Maria Lucas had come to Longbourn to discuss the delights of the previous evening. Elizabeth had drawn Charlotte away from the others to relate to her the agitation of the morning.

The hour spent in quiet reflection had restored Elizabeth to something like equanimity, and she imbued the account of the proposal with a comic air. At least, it was comic until she came to her mother's unthinking wrenching open of old wounds.

"Much of the time I contrive not to dwell on what she cost me. But she does not think, Charlotte. She closed her eyes to it then, and will not acknowledge it now. She told my sisters that I was pert, and husbands were right to object to pert wives."

Charlotte winced.

"I cannot forgive this easily. For a while, the less I see of her, the better it will be for all of us. Nether House will be ready by Friday and I will return home."

"Of course. I shall join you there on Friday, before noon. I confess I have had my fill of Lucas Lodge, too." Charlotte put both hands on Elizabeth's arm and squeezed. "Is Mr Collins still here?"

"Papa set him to rights about things, I believe, but says he is very angry. I am sorry for it, but not sorry enough to change my mind."

"Of course not!" Charlotte looked thoughtful. "Do you think he would care to come back with us to Lucas Lodge? Papa would welcome his company and he can dine there, and perhaps by the time he returns he will have recovered some of his good temper."

"That, my dear Charlotte, is an offer I will close with directly. Do take him away. It will better if he and I do not meet for a few hours!"

Charlotte smiled. "Then I will ask him. It is little enough, to promote peace. Poor man! I will ensure he has a good dinner, and every opportunity to find balm for his wounded spirits."

Charlotte was a good friend. A very good friend.

Elizabeth spent her remaining time at Longbourn avoiding both her mother and Mr Collins. Concerning the latter, dear Charlotte took the burden upon herself and welcomed Mr Collins to Lucas Lodge on Thursday, too—an invitation he was eager to accept. He spent the day there and dined again at Sir William's table. Doubtless he was as desirous as she to avoid a meeting, and on those few occasions when he and Elizabeth did come across each other, his cold bow and averted gaze spoke even more eloquently of his resentment than his most flowery speeches might have done.

Her mother was more difficult to evade, and Elizabeth sat through meals with Mama glowering like a small thunderstorm set at the foot of the table. Elizabeth, mentally interposing a large umbrella between the squall and herself, maintained a sunny, equable climate with her father at the other end of the table, an indifference to her good opinion that had Mama sending occasional crackles of acrimonious lightning at them through the temperate zone inhabited by Jane, Mary and Kitty.

Lydia was indifferent to any variation in the weather. Unless it wore a red coat, not even a hurricane could catch her interest.

"How on earth," said Elizabeth, rather astonished at her ability to subdue her heavy heart and sound brisk and cheerful, "will you bear with the great Lady Catherine de Bourgh?"

"With as much grace as I can muster, I suspect." Charlotte puckered up her mouth into prim merriment. "I must walk carefully, of course. She is Mr Collins's patroness and must be respected on that account, and she is an earl's daughter. That alone commands esteem and deference. But I will be mistress in the rectory, I assure you." She added, a little wryly, "Although perhaps in a very quiet fashion at first until everyone is accustomed to the change."

"Sedition and rebellion! I would not have suspected you of being a Radical."

"It will be a test of all my virtues, I am sure!"

"You have patience, practicality and tact. I—"

Elizabeth broke off as Thomas Rance opened the door and stepped into the doorway. He rubbed a hand over his mouth and chin. The lines between his eyes were deep enough to have been chiselled there by one of the newly departed workmen.

Elizabeth matched his frown. "Thomas?"

"You have visitors seeking admittance, ma'am. A Mr Darcy. Him that has been at Netherfield Park."

"I know Mr Darcy, but you know that I do not receive gentlemen here—"

"Out of the way, Rance!"

Thomas moved quickly, bracing himself against the door jamb with one outstretched hand, blocking the entrance. That was not Mr Darcy's voice. It sounded more like—

Mr Saville loomed up in the doorway, pushing against Thomas, trying to force his way past the arm Thomas used as a shield to prevent him.

Elizabeth sprang to her feet. "Mr Saville! Sir! What do you think you are about?"

"That's just the thing, ma'am. He's no Saville. He's Mr Matthew!"

"Mr Matthew?" Something deep inside Elizabeth lurched and whirled, spinning like a top until she was dizzy. "Matthew Grayson?"

Mr Darcy stood behind his *soi-disant* secretary, more forbidding and remote than she had ever seen him, his distaste so strong it could almost be smelled, rolling off him as if he had been doused in a cheap cologne.

"Aye! The master's brother." Thomas's voice was a low, growling rumble, grinding out the sound of distant thunder.

Charlotte's gasp sounded louder than clashing cymbals.

"Yes indeed, madam." Mr Saville— No. *Matthew Grayson* pushed at Thomas's arm again, and at Elizabeth's nod, was allowed entrance. "The master's brother, and his heir. The heir whom you cheated out of Netherfield." He sketched a short, mocking bow. "Well met, sister."

CHAPTER TWENTY-SEVEN

Accused of Many Faults

Friday had arrived at last, treading on the heels of a long, slow Thursday. It brought with it a crisp, bright air of expectation as if the day knew itself to be one of resolution and the end to subterfuge.

Darcy was up with the dawn and went to breakfast early. Bingley and Hurst were already in the breakfast room, both yawning. They nodded greetings, neither of them alert or cheerful. Hurst because... well, it was Hurst and unless there was shooting, the man abhorred mornings. Bingley's morose unhappiness was of a different stamp. He had received an urgent express the previous evening. Some crisis concerning the illness of the cousin who managed the Bingley family's manufacturing interests, and a loan falling due within the week, demanded Bingley's immediate return to London. He would leave almost as soon as he put down his knife and fork. His main preoccupation, though, was the lack of opportunity to go to Longbourn first.

"Caroline will write to the Bennets on my behalf," Bingley announced, after a short discussion of his impending journey, during which Grayson ambled in for breakfast. "I hope to return within the week."

Darcy indicated Grayson. "We have some business of our own to see to this morning that will take us to Longbourn. I will deliver the note, if it is ready."

Hurst waved a hand around to indicate the environs of the room, of the house at large. "To do with Netherfield Park?"

"In part." Darcy pushed away his plate, his breakfast untasted, and took up his coffee. A dash of cream and a spoonful of Lisbon sugar were stirred in carefully, with Darcy aware of his companions' thoughtful gazes while he focused on the slow movement of the silver in the delicate porcelain coffee can. "I cannot yet speak of it. The business is not entirely mine."

"Is that so?" Bingley dropped his cutlery onto his plate and sat back, regarding Darcy with the oddest expression on his face. Amusement? Certainly, that was there. But also a little bafflement. "We had, of course, noticed your interest in the widow."

Darcy stiffened. "I have none beyond the resolution of this enterprise."

Hurst laughed aloud, damn him. "Of course not. There is no reason at all for Caroline to be in such a twitter about her."

"Hurst!" Bingley cut a glance at Grayson. "Do not speak of Caroline in such terms."

Hurst smirked as he turned away. Darcy was mildly grateful for Bingley's firmness. He would have been more so if Bingley could convince his sister of the value of a similar discretion on her part.

Darcy downed his coffee and went to pour another. He did not deign to respond to Hurst's provocation. There was nothing he could say that would not make things worse. He had hoped that he had been circumspect enough for his interest in Elizabeth Grayson to escape notice, and was chagrined to realise his mistake.

Not that he had any interest. He did not. None.

She was beneath his touch. She was not worthy of him, or of Pemberley. Even with Netherfield as a dowry, her questionable past with her husband and her ridiculous family weighed heavily against her. She could bring no connections to a marriage other than a Cheapside merchant, and those excellent relations she might have claimed in her late husband's family—the Earl of Rufford as an uncle-by-marriage was not to be sniffed at—were obviously hostile to her pretensions. Netherfield aside, she had nothing to recommend her but a pretty face, a sharp intelligence, and pert manners.

It was not enough.

Miss Bingley handed over the note, intricately folded and sealed. The superscription read *Miss J Bennet* in a very fine hand: Miss Bingley's exclusive Ladies' Seminary had no need to be ashamed of its teachings in penmanship.

She appeared slightly mollified when told Darcy and his secretary had business at Longbourn, and were not calling for any other reason. She waved off her brother in his coach, and even before it was out of sight down the drive, turned to Darcy. "I would speak to you on your return, sir. It is important." And at his cool regard, she tutted audibly, and added in an impatient tone, "About Charles, and her." She nodded to the letter Darcy was in the act of enclosing in his pocketbook. "If you please."

Darcy considered, and nodded. He rather deplored Bingley's need to attend to a business he ought to have put behind him, but it was as well, perhaps, that he was to be separated from Miss Bennet for a while. While it may be true, as some Roman poet once said— Darcy had neither time nor inclination to meditate on the reference until he remembered it exactly—that love's tide flows stronger towards an absent lover, it was equally possible that Bingley would benefit from a return to his previous life and habits. Absence might well enable him to see that he could do much better than allow himself to be leg-shackled to the near-penniless daughter of a minor gentleman who showed not a particle of affection for him. That Jane Bennet would marry Bingley to oblige her family was inarguable.

Darcy, though, would prefer Bingley not to be disobliged in the process. He and Miss Bingley were united in that, if in nothing else.

He and Grayson remained at Longbourn only for so long as was needed to hand over the letter, and, on Darcy's part at least, wonder briefly at the fleeting look on Jane Bennet's face when she realised Bingley was not with them. He dismissed it almost immediately when she surveyed them with her usual serene expression, which did not falter when they asked to speak with Mrs Grayson. She showed no curiosity, telling them the widow had returned to her own house in Meryton, and bade them a courteous farewell after a strained ten minutes.

They arrived at the Meryton house swiftly enough, but the large man who opened it to their knocking was not disposed to allow them entrance. He wore a pleasant expression initially, greeting them with civility and explaining Mrs Grayson did not receive gentlemen callers outside of arranged social events, although he would take her their cards... his voice trailed off and his expression changed, slowly, to a narrow-eyed contemplation of young Grayson.

"Well. If it isn't Mr Matthew. There's a surprise. Let you back from foreign parts, have they?"

"You are a long way from Graymead, Thomas Rance."

Rance met Grayson's glare full on, raising his chin and drawing himself up. He looked away from Grayson, took the card Darcy held out and glanced at it. "Mr Darcy. I heard you were staying with the tenant at Netherfield."

Darcy inclined his head. "We would like very much to speak with your mistress. Please take my card and ask her if she will be willing to admit us. It is important."

"Does she know about Mr Matthew being here?"

Darcy shook his head.

Rance snorted. He had a very direct gaze, and brown eyes, harder than boiled toffee, raked over Darcy from head to foot. In the end he grimaced, and stepped back a couple of feet to allow them into the hallway. "I look to you to keep him in bounds." He spoke directly to Darcy, as if Grayson was not there. "He's loose in the haft, and always has been. Please to wait here while I speak to Mrs Grayson. If she refuses you, you will leave."

"We will. And return when her father or someone she trusts is here, if that is her wish." Darcy looked as sincere as he knew how.

Another of those raking glances, and a sharp nod. "I'll hold you to that, sir."

Rance turned his back on them without further ado, went to knock upon and open a door to the right of the stairs, and announced Darcy. What the widow said in response was impossible for Darcy to distinguish, but her surprised tone was unmistakable.

Grayson's fragile patience snapped. "Oh, be damned to this!" He rushed forward. "Out of the way, Rance!"

Darcy went after him, too late. A few moments of shocked exclamations from Mrs Grayson, and a wickedly savage greeting from Grayson, and he was in a pretty drawing room, still in Grayson's wake, his dislike of the man heating itself into real hatred for being dragged into a contretemps that was not of his making.

Elizabeth Grayson stood before one of a pair of sofas set before the fireplace, her body angled towards the door. Her creamy skin always had a natural pallor, but now she was salt-white, a statue with both arms held stiffly down, hands curled into fists. Seated behind her, Miss Lucas drew down her brows, giving her plain, pleasant face an almost fierce aspect.

"Matthew Grayson." Elizabeth brought her head up proudly. She and Grayson stared at each other, but she spoke to Rance. "Thomas, you will stay, please."

"Ma'am."

Elizabeth swept a cold glance from Grayson to Darcy. She did not curtsey, though Darcy offered a correct bow, and she did not resume her seat, forcing them to remain standing. Even Grayson did not flout that convention, although he grimaced. Miss Lucas, as though to reinforce the lack of a welcome, rose swiftly to stand behind Elizabeth and put a hand on her shoulder.

Mrs Grayson's gaze never left Grayson and Darcy. "Well, I suppose this explains the particular interest you have had in Netherfield. I am at a loss, though, *gentlemen*"—and the scorn stung more viciously than a mad wasp—"to understand the reason for your deception."

"Our deception!" And Grayson huffed out a laugh he no doubt intended to make just as scornful.

"What else would you call this masquerade?"

"Necessary, madam, in order to discover the truth." Grayson shifted to one side, but for all that it was him speaking, it was Darcy she kept skewered on her gaze. "To know and understand the manner of James's death."

She looked away from Darcy at last to pierce Grayson with the same proud look, and Darcy drew what felt like his first breath in several minutes.

"James's death?" Her voice rose a semitone or two. "Yes. I can tell how that has weighed on you, sir, since your first words were about being cheated of Netherfield. James's death, indeed. Your uncle and cousin know what occurred. Did you not ask them?"

Another huffed out, would-be scornful laugh. Grayson had no aptitude for the stage. "What? When you beguiled them into believing your lies, as you beguiled James into that sham of a marriage?"

"I have never seen or spoken to either of them. My father has, but I assure you he was so very angry at the time I am certain he quite failed to be beguiling. I can tell you they discussed everything with the magistrates."

"And all us servants," Rance cut in. "Those who saw Mr James fall and gave testimony to the magistrate when he came. On the Bible, it was, and all written down and signed to. Me, the Allens, and Mr James's valet Brownlee. We all swore and signed, and told the earl."

Why in Heaven's name was he here? This was agony. Darcy swallowed and turned to Rance. The servant's hard, inflexible gaze was fixed on Grayson. "You saw him fall, Rance?"

"Tell them, Thomas." Elizabeth should not have been able to draw herself up higher, to seem taller, nor hold herself more stiffly. But somehow she did.

"Oh no!" Grayson, the thrice-damned fool, just would not be still and *listen*. "From your own lips, madam."

The look she gave him should have felled him. "I cannot oblige you there, Mr Grayson. I did not see it happen. James took very badly the news I gave him that morning, and he made his displeasure known." She raised a hand to her cheekbone, and let it fall again. "I was... indisposed at the time of his death."

"I stopped him," Rance said, heavy as a lead coffin. "Mr Allen and me pulled him off her. That fool man of his was there too, bleating and flapping. He'd given Mr James too much poppy juice and brandy. That always made him wild. She"—with a softened glance at his mistress—"paid for it every time."

Grayson spluttered out a "Not James!", but his tone was uncertain. He had flushed a dark red. Darcy took a step away from him, to get some distance between them.

Good God.

Sir William Lucas had said it. *We could do nothing. A man cannot interfere, you know. It is not done...*

Old Mr Harpur, *An unlucky house, that one.*

And Elizabeth herself, at the Longbourn shoot, speaking of Sir William's *...kindness to me, at a time when I needed it most.*

Darcy's stomach roiled and rebelled. He had to swallow down his breakfast again.

What in Hades had James Grayson become? A man who hit his wife? That the bright, merry, carefree boy of Darcy's memory had stooped so low as to abuse the woman to whom he owed the greatest, most sacred duty of care and gentleness, was almost beyond comprehension. Something had destroyed Darcy's old friend, and replaced him with a man Darcy did not know.

Or cared to know.

"We pulled her away from him, Allen and me, and Mrs Allen was there to help her. Never seen so much blood. And then he yelled and when we turned, he was gone over the balustrade onto the floor below. We were on the upstairs landing." Rance took a step into the room, and Miss Lucas had an arm around Mrs Grayson now. "I got to him first. He'd broke his neck. Dead as a coffin nail."

Grayson mumbled something, a bellicose sail with all the wind stripped from it. Darcy closed his eyes for a moment. What a fool he was to be so involved, to lend his countenance to this... this...

Not a farce. A tragedy. A bloody, bloody tragedy.

Grayson made some noise, coughed. Started again. "Who can blame him for hating you? You trapped him—"

"Oh, do stop being such a fool!" Miss Lucas snapped out the words like whiplashes. "He did the trapping, sir! If a young man of your ilk does not wish to be pushed into a marriage of convenience, then he should not assault a young gentlewoman—a very young gentlewoman of only sixteen years!—at a public assembly when she refuses to dance with him because he is so foxed with brandy, he acts as a man possessed. If James Grayson had had even a modicum of gentlemanly conduct, he would have taken the refusal with grace, not create such a public scandal the only recourse was a marriage neither of them wanted. And before you protest your brother's innocence, sir, I was there. I saw it. I saw what he did to Eliza, with her dress... the bruises...." Miss Lucas choked and stopped. She set her jaw so hard, the cords in her neck stood out. "I saw it. So did most of the neighbourhood."

"My brother was a gentleman! He would never—"

"We saw him. He was drunk, and no gentleman. What gentleman assaults a lady barely half his size? What sort of man? What sort of senseless brute?"

"Wasn't the last time, either." Rance took another step into the room, watching his mistress with unmistakable anxiety. "Look, the Mr James who came back from Italy wasn't the man who went out there, all high courage and excitement. He was... broke by it into something as couldn't be mended. He wasn't mad, but he was... in pieces. Different. The days he weren't soused in brandy and poppy syrup were the real rare ones." He glanced at Grayson. "Lord

Kirton made sure I came south with him. His lordship wanted someone he could trust to keep an eye on him. 'Twas me who sent the express for his lordship when Mr James fell. You was still abroad. You never saw him, never saw what he was like."

Grayson, scarlet again, said nothing. He did not meet Darcy's eyes.

The widow raised her chin. "You should thank James, Mr Grayson. It was the anniversary of the battle, where he had suffered so much. I thought to give him something to hope for, a future. I failed. James left me Netherfield on the condition he died childless, and specified it in both his will and our marriage settlement. He did die childless. I lost my son on that upstairs landing, when James fell. If my child had lived, you would not only have no claim on Netherfield, you would not have Graymead. You would be dispossessed entirely. Think on that." She looked at Darcy. "And you, sir? What is your interest here?"

Darcy worked a suddenly dry mouth, to moisten it. "None, except that James was a very dear friend when we were young. I thought only to... Grayson here asked for my assistance to determine how his brother died—"

"I am sorry for the loss of your friend, then, but it does not excuse your deceit. I once thought you a man of honour. It is disappointing to have another proof to the contrary."

She could not have slapped him harder, had she used her balled fists to do it. He gaped at her, shocked into silence.

"Please leave. If you wish to discover more, then I insist you go to the authorities. Mr Harpur is the chief magistrate, and it was he who investigated James's death. He also has full knowledge of James's will and our marriage settlement, since he was a witness to the signing of both." Elizabeth drew in a ragged breath. "Please leave now."

"The magistrates are in session today in the Guildhall. That is a lucky coincidence." Miss Lucas released her hold on Elizabeth and took a step forward to stand in front of her, a barrier of indignant, protective rectitude. Another step, and another, to make Darcy and Grayson fall back.

Grayson looked lost, bewildered; a man who had been planted a facer by an opponent he had reckoned would be weak and easy to overcome.

Darcy swallowed. Bowed his head. "Mrs Grayson, I apol—"

"Not now." Miss Lucas held up a hand, palm out towards him. "No one needs platitudes now."

Rance jerked his head at the doorway. He looked grim. Darcy nodded, grasped Grayson's arm, and between them, he and Rance bundled him out. Just as Rance reached for the door to close it, a soft sound came from within the room, the noise of something broken and wounded.

"Do not think on it, Eliza," Miss Lucas said, her own voice thick with tears. "It does not do to dwell on it."

Rance pulled the door to, shutting them out.

CHAPTER TWENTY-EIGHT

Legal Redress

"A fool! Dear God, I am a gold-plated, addle-pated, credulous fool!" And Darcy kicked savagely at Nether House's brick gatepost as they passed it. Elizabeth Grayson's scorn stung at him, biting at him as he imagined acid would. "I am a damned simpleton for ever getting involved, for allowing you to play upon my affection for James and impose on me with your humbug! You do not care a jot about what happened to James, do you? She had you to rights immediately! When your first words are to complain that you do not have Netherfield in your grasp..." Darcy shook his head, and marched steadily up Meryton's main thoroughfare towards the town square.

"What! Could you see an estate of that magnitude and worth slip from your grasp and not feel hard done by? What man could? It is rank hypocrisy to pretend otherwise!"

"I do not consider," said Darcy, with a deadness of tone of which he was moderately proud, "that is a word you should employ against others." He was pleased to see Grayson redden.

After a moment or two of fulmination, during which Grayson grumbled under his breath and stamped down his boots on each step with such force he splashed mud right up to the turned-down cuffs, he scoffed, "I wonder, then, that you do not wash your hands of the business. I will see the magistrates myself."

"No. I will see this through." And then, Darcy thought, he must abase himself before the widow and crave her pardon. The Lord alone knew if she would grant it.

Grayson merely grunted, and for the next hour while they kicked their heels in a private room in the White Hart awaiting a summons from the clerk of the court, he spoke but little, drinking steadily and glaring at the tabletop as if to set it afire.

"You could never have had any expectation of Netherfield," Darcy said at one point. "It was never part of Graymead's holdings, but is outside the entail."

"Exactly. Hence outside my uncle's control."

Well, that explained things. Grayson must have trustees—the Earl of Rufford, it seemed, was one—until he reached the age specified in the deeds of settlement that governed the Graymead entail, to prevent him wasting his inheritance. Grayson needed money, it was clear, could not touch Graymead, and had an eye on Netherfield.

Darcy could no longer wonder at Grayson's family sending him to the West Indies. He did wonder at them allowing him to return.

They sat in silence until the clerk's assistant arrived to escort them to the magistrates' private chambers behind the main Guildhall courtroom. Mr Harpur, Mr Goulding, and Sir William Lucas sat around one end of an oak table that looked old enough to have been made when the Guildhall was built, with Mr Phillips, the local attorney, at Mr Harpur's left. The table was laden with salads and cold meat, and jugs of frothy beer jostled with coffee pots.

"Good day, Darcy, Saville! Our clerk, Mr Phillips, says you wish to speak with us." Mr Harpur, the senior magistrate, greeted them kindly, waving them into chairs. "I trust you will not object if we take some refreshment. We have but an hour before the next session begins, and this is our only opportunity to stay our hunger. You are welcome to join us."

The pleasant expression on his face, however, did not survive the presentation of Grayson under his real name. Mr Harpur's welcoming smile faded into something close to grave disapproval.

"I see." Mr Harpur removed his gold spectacles, took a silk handkerchief from his pocket and spent a moment or two polishing the lenses. "Your interest in Netherfield Park stems, then, from your relationship with its former owner?"

"I want to understand how James came to marry that woman, and how he died." Grayson's truculence was in fine disregard for the manner shown by the magistrates.

"Do you?" Mr Harpur replaced his spectacles. "Well, perhaps we can aid you. We have full records, of course, including depositions by all the witnesses. I think my memory will serve, however, and what I do not recall, Goulding, who was also a magistrate then, will no doubt remember. First, though, I will send for the apothecary, Mr Jones, since he has an expertise that will aid our account. Mr Phillips?"

Phillips nodded and left the room without a glance at Darcy and Grayson, presumably to instruct his assistant for he was gone but a moment or two before returning to his seat.

Mr Harpur pulled his plate towards him and spoke between delicate bites of roast beef washed down with coffee that looked strong enough to stain the oak if he spilled it. "Old Tom Templeton died around midsummer in the year '06. His boy was twenty years dead before him, and his godson, James Grayson, was his heir. I was Templeton's executor and familiar with his will. A little before Christmas, we heard the heir had come to take possession, but he did not welcome visitors."

"He was the most sociable and easy of men," Darcy protested. "Never happier than being the life of any gathering."

"That is not the man we came to know." Harpur poured himself another can of coffee. "He made his first appearance at Meryton's Twelfth Night ball in the assembly rooms in January '07. He was more than half sprung when he arrived, but sober enough to be introduced to most of the gentlemen present. We were all there, I think. Our wives demanded it." He smiled slightly, but the smile drooped into a small sigh. "Only the two eldest Bennet girls were out then, of course. Miss Jane is a great beauty, but Elizabeth, so bright and lively, shone them all down. Grayson marked her. Danced with her when he would not with any other, but he had been drinking deep all night, and I fear he alarmed her. She refused a second dance. He was not pleased, and retaliated." Mr Harpur stopped and grimaced. "It was a disgraceful attack. You will recall a corridor runs from the assembly room to the supper chamber, with a side corridor off it. Grayson forced her into the side corridor, and while he was prevented from completely befouling her, she was injured and her clothing damaged. You understand many saw this. It was not some made up offence, but a public one witnessed by many in the neighbourhood."

Grayson let out an odd grunting sound, that might have been understanding, or a wordless protest, but Darcy said, with a presentiment that this would go badly, "Miss Lucas intimated as much earlier."

Sir William spluttered. "My daughter? Wha—"

"We called upon Mrs Grayson." Darcy straightened in his chair, and pushed away the coffee he had taken, untasted.

Goulding sat back and steepled his hands before him as if to create a spiky fence to ward them off. Sir William's normally full, florid cheeks paled, distress pulling them into dips and hollows above a downturned mouth. Phillips sat more stiffly than a corpse, his head back, staring at them down his nose; he was the widow's uncle, of course, and could be expected to take her part.

Darcy was more concerned that the slight air of distaste Mr Harpur had worn deepened into unmistakable disgust. The genial old gentleman retreated, leaving the magistrate in his place. Authority and gravitas may have come with his office, but Mr Harpur's character imbued a sense of such affronted honour and outraged morality that would have had Darcy squirming in his seat had he been a little younger.

"Did you, indeed," was all Mr Harpur said, but icebergs would have been less cold and unforgiving. "I cannot imagine that the George Darcy I knew would approve of such conduct in his son."

Nettled, Darcy was swift in rebuttal. "I have been meticulously correct in my approaches to Mrs Grayson. What is more, my father valued his friends dearly—as you should know, sir—and would certainly expect me to value mine. James and I were friends from boyhood, and though I went to Cambridge when we left Eton, and he went to his cornetcy, we remained close friends. At least," Darcy added, not to give a false impression, "as much as that was possible while he was abroad on his military duties, or injured, and I was dealing with my father's sudden death."

"Hmmph," was all the answer Mr Harpur gave. He glanced at the door as a tall, ascetic man entered, and welcomed him, introducing him as the local apothecary, Mr Jones.

Jones took the chair next to Phillips, his bright, intelligent gaze going from one countenance to another. When Grayson's name was mentioned, he grimaced.

"I am recounting the events of the Twelfth Day assembly, Jones, of the year seven," Mr Harpur said. "It is essential that Grayson's brother fully understands the magnitude of what occurred that night."

"When James Grayson attacked Miss Elizabeth Bennet, as she was then? Very well, sir." Jones's nose could not wrinkle more if he had just taken a hearty sniff of his own concoction for a lady's vinaigrette. "I was there, so went immediately to help Miss Elizabeth when she was rescued. She was barely conscious. He had knocked her down with a blow to the face—she was lucky he did not break her cheekbone, though she did have a fearful contusion—then lifted her up and slammed her against the wall, and held her there with his arm over her throat." The sound of his sucking air in over his teeth conveyed repugnance. "I dislike speaking thus of a gentlewoman, particularly in such circumstances, when every word increases her shame despite her innocence of any wrongdoing. To do so to strangers—! Hmmph."

Darcy held up a hand, but before he could speak, the apothecary continued, eyeing them both with aversion.

"I did not see the actual assault—those who rescued her and pulled her away did that—but her injuries certainly tallied with their accounts. I shall just add that the marks of his hands were visible almost immediately on her neck and... and..." He gestured to his upper chest, and glowered.

Matthew Grayson was scarlet. Darcy felt his own face burn. James must have been mad! To have served a gentlewoman so... one barely out of childhood... the same age as Georgiana. Darcy clamped a hand over his mouth, swallowing down the nausea and ignoring the burn of acid. He deserved it.

"My boy made him rue it." For the first time since Darcy had met him, Sir William spoke without the geniality and warmth that characterised him. "John hauled him off her, and he and others dragged Grayson out to teach him a lesson. They beat him soundly before tossing him into the horse trough and keeping him in it until he had sobered enough to know what it was he had done."

"My two helped him," Goulding said. "As they should."

"The Bennets did well enough out of it," Grayson muttered, but everyone at the table heard him. It garnered looks so cold, hell would have frozen over.

"Bennet did everything he could to avoid scandal," Goulding said. "But when the rumours spread as far as Hatfield and St Albans, he had no choice. Like all such gossip, it grew every mile it travelled, until it was utterly ruinous to Lizzy Bennet's good name. 'Tis always the woman who bears the brunt of an ill-natured tale like that. Iniquitous as it was, he had to give Lizzy to Grayson if his other girls were not to be tainted by association. His own wife was the loudest voice bewailing the family's ruin. He had to act."

"Goulding, Phillips and I went with Bennet to talk to Grayson, who, thankfully, was sober. To give your brother his due, Mr Grayson, he was repentant. He admitted the Bennets' predicament was entirely his making." Mr Harpur looked at Darcy, and it seemed to be with more understanding and less blame. "He agreed to a swift marriage under a common licence. He told us his circumstances—that he was estranged from his family, and that his estates were entailed in strict settlement except for Netherfield, which he agreed should be designated for a second son, and if he died childless, would devolve to Elizabeth. Mr Phillips drew up a new will for him to this effect, and also had it written into the marriage articles. We all witnessed both documents. They were married by the end of the month."

Matthew Grayson flashed into anger. "You coerced him into it!"

The petulance had no noticeable effect on Mr Harpur. "It was necessary to protect the good name of an innocent girl who, I would remind you, went to her wedding wearing the marks of her groom's fist on her face."

"Not for the last time." And Sir William sighed.

Mr Harpur inclined his head. "Sadly, no. She knew she would receive no kindness or consideration from her husband, and so it proved. Bennet was not happy to consign his daughter to a man who would, and did, misuse her, knowing that once she was married he could do little to help her. He had no choice. None of us liked the prospect. We had known Elizabeth Bennet from childhood. It was galling no one could help her."

The nausea conquered for the moment, Darcy took his hand from his mouth. "That was the not the James Grayson I knew. There was no merrier, more generous-hearted man alive! He would never hurt a lady! Rance said the war broke him."

"It was the poppy syrup," Jones said, not looking up from his hands, laced together and resting on the table top. "Opium, laudanum… anything of that ilk. They probably gave it to him in Italy when he was injured, to help with the pain, not realising the harm."

"Rance said something about him being soused with brandy and poppy, and it making him wild. But should it not have had the opposite effect? Made him calm and tractable? Sleepy, even."

"For most men, Mr Darcy, that would be the case, but it is well known to medical professionals that, rarely, opium has the opposite effect to that we would expect." Jones glanced up from his hands for only a moment, before resuming his examination of them. "It induced in him a kind of delirium, made his dreams and horrors worse, haunted him with imaginings and magnified them into terror. He told me his nights were sleepless, tormented, riven with bad dreams in which he relived the battle and the horrors he had seen. Mrs Grayson confirmed this to be the case, and that he was very restless, day and night. He tried taking belladonna to counteract it, but that made it worse. He ate little and drank a great deal too much, which did not help. I saw him often jerking with muscular spasms he could not control."

"Dear Lord." Darcy tried to imagine it. "He should have stopped taking it."

"It is pernicious. I refused to give it to him when I realised what was causing his symptoms, but his valet would procure it from other apothecaries, even so far away as Hatfield and St Albans." Jones looked up at last, looking Darcy straight in the eye. An anger simmered in his gaze. The memory of the apothecary's impotence to protect his patients against their own worst natures, perhaps. Or, even more simply, impotence to protect a young girl. "When he took too much, or drank too deep, his wife was a convenient target for his anger."

Darcy winced.

"What happened the night he died?" Grayson asked, more subdued than Darcy had ever seen him.

"The constable called me to Netherfield that night." Mr Harpur looked at them squarely. "Goulding joined me within the hour, and between us we took the depositions of all present at the time—barring that of Mrs Grayson, who was, as Mr Jones can aver, fighting for her life as the result of miscarrying a child. The witnesses were united in the story they told. Mrs Grayson had told him that day she was increasing. Terrified that he was mad and the child would inherit his madness, he spent the day drinking brandy, and, all afire with drink and the poppy syrup supplied by his valet, he made a most serious assault upon her. He was dragging her to the stairs when the servants stopped him and pulled her away to safety. They were all with her, several feet away from him. They heard him call out, and Rance, who was closest, turned in time to see him go over the banister rail to the marble floor of the hall twenty feet below. He broke his neck and died instantly."

"An accident, then," Grayson said, heavily.

No one responded. Darcy met Mr Harpur's compassionate gaze.

Oh.

Even Grayson noted the silence. He looked around the table, grimacing. And, miracle of miracles, said nothing.

Mr Harpur resumed his story. "Lord Rufford and his son arrived two days later and were apprised of all the circumstances. They and Bennet came to an agreement. It was best for all concerned, that they took Grayson to Graymead to be buried, and left Netherfield to Elizabeth, as Grayson had set out in his will. It had never been a part of the Graymead holdings, and they would not contest it. The coroner—"

And here Mr Phillips quirked out a smile and bowed his head.

"—made a determination of accidental death, and so it is recorded. They had the body removed. Since then, the only communication between the families has concerned the legalities arising from the trust Grayson established in his will for the protection of his underage wife—he named his cousin, Lord Kirton, as a trustee along with Mr Bennet and Mr Philips."

"It was not an accident," Darcy said, slowly, to get it all out into the open and understood.

"No. James Grayson met his death while the balance of his mind was disturbed by brandy and opium." Mr Phillips spoke for the first time. "It is not uncommon, as you will know, for a coroner's court to make a judgement of mental imbalance when the evidence points to it, as it did in this case, and hence permit a Christian burial. It is deemed a kindness to all concerned."

Darcy bowed his head. He tugged, surreptitiously, at clothing that suddenly felt too tight, as if arms and legs were too large. Heat bloomed in his face and ears. He had never felt so... so... well, perhaps it was shame.

And perhaps it was deserved.

CHAPTER TWENTY-NINE

Guttered Candles

Miss Bingley was wild to be gone from Netherfield. "We must follow Charles to London immediately and ensure this unhealthy fascination with Miss Bennet comes to nothing. He is blinded by his partiality and cannot see her for the fortune-hunter she undoubtedly is. That mother of hers is, at the very least! He must not ruin his future with a girl who will marry him to oblige her family, and who can do nothing to raise his standing."

Darcy had barely walked through the front door of Netherfield—for the last time, if he had anything to say about it—before he had been accosted by a Miss Bingley whose face had taken on the expression Darcy had last seen on one of the dyspeptic monkeys at the Menagerie. It was not becoming.

"I told Jane Bennet that we were all removing to Town and that Charles was unlikely to return. I would not be proved a liar." She scowled. "Where is Mr Saville? I do hope we are not to be delayed, awaiting his convenience!"

"Already on his way to London. His work here is finished." Darcy had had no compunction in sending Matthew Grayson to Bishop's Stortford to catch the post-coach from Hockerill Crossroads. Nor, to be honest, had Grayson argued. As much as Darcy wanted rid of him, he was eager to be gone. "My valet will pack his belongings."

"Excellent." Miss Bingley nodded emphatic approbation. "Then we may be off within the hour."

"I see no reason to delay."

Indeed, Mr Harpur had been clear he expected Darcy to return to Town as soon as may be. "I cannot think, Darcy, that you will be particularly comfortable in the district now. You were intending to leave for Town, I believe?" And on Darcy's protesting that he must see Mrs Grayson to apologise, the old man had returned a decided negative. "She has been disturbed enough. I will not countenance more. Go back to London, and perhaps consider what has taken place here before approaching her with your apologies."

Darcy had not quite slunk away in disgrace, but in his perturbation of spirits, he might as well have done. Getting rid of Grayson had relieved his sense of shame a trifle. A very small trifle. He would be as glad as Miss Bingley to see the back of Meryton and all who lived there: widows, sardonic fathers, mercenary mothers and compliant daughters in particular.

He would save Bingley from himself. It was the altruistic thing to do.

"Louisa and I are not returning to Town immediately." Hurst shrugged into his greatcoat and strode out of the main door onto the portico, to cast a glance at Caroline Bingley where she stood near the waiting coaches speaking with Mrs Hurst, her whole aspect one of offence and outrage. Darcy followed him. "I have no idea if Jane Bennet cares for my brother Bingley, but I will not rule his life for him. He should be man enough to make his own decisions. Besides,"—and now the cynical glance was aimed at Darcy—"I understand Caroline's objections. The Bennets are lower gentry, of no great wealth and no great connections. No matter Jane Bennet's merits or the state of her affections, she can offer little to raise the Bingleys in society's eyes. Hence the Bennets are obviously below Caroline's, and your, acquaintance, and marriage to such a lady must be a *mésalliance*."

Hurst paused, while Darcy struggled to find words to counter this starkly expressed assessment of what was really a most delicate matter.

"But then, Bennet and I are of a similar rank. If he is of insufficient consequence, then so must Louisa and I be. We will remove ourselves to my estate in Norfolk for the festive season. Since Caroline abhors visiting Chamnhurst, we will have a peaceful few weeks together."

"Hurst! I do not mean—"

"I will not allow Louisa to be drawn into Caroline's machinations. My wife loves her sister dearly, but I cannot but see that association between them is to her detriment. I will end it for now. My brother Bingley will have to stiffen his own spine against you and Caroline, but Louisa's voice will not be added to whatever arguments you make. Safe journey to Town, Darcy. Perhaps we shall see you next year, if you are prepared to accept the risk to your consequence."

"Hurst!"

A sharp nod, and Hurst descended the steps to the wide gravel sweep without allowing Darcy to speak, gathered up his wife with an even sharper "Save your jobations for poor Charles, Caroline! We will have none of it," and, ignoring Miss Bingley's protests, helped Mrs Hurst into their coach. A moment later, and all that could be seen of the Hursts was the carriage as it swayed and rumbled down the drive, rolling off more smoothly as the horses got into their stride.

"But it is not the same at all," Darcy said to the back of the coach, at a loss to understand how his eminently reasonable objections to Bingley's unfortunate entanglement and the Bennets' deplorable circumstances had been so misconstrued.

"Well!" said Miss Bingley, bouncing up to him with explosive wrath. "I had not thought Louisa so disloyal to the family!"

Well, indeed. And with Hurst gone, Darcy had no choice but to escort her to Town. He was not such a gudgeon as to respond to her demure comments about depending upon his strength to support her weakness, though he rolled his eyes when he turned away from her. Instead, he installed her in his coach with her maid, and rode Alastor all the way back to London, despite the cold and the rain.

More than one fortune-hunter would be thwarted that day.

Darcy was summoned to the Bingley household three days after their return to London. Miss Bingley's note, while begging his pardon for her temerity in writing at all, expressed her desire that Darcy reinforce her disquiet over the Bennet entanglement.

Bingley did not look well. As sombre as Darcy had ever seen him, Bingley was… diminished. Darcy had seen guttered candles less worn to the wick. His eyes had a reddish tinge to the whites caused by the thin threads of broken veins, and his rumpled cravat indicated he had dressed with less than his usual care. Indeed, he looked as though he had gone to bed the night before still dressed, and had an uneasy night of it, tossing and turning. The problem with the Bingley family business must be even more complex than anticipated.

Bingley greeted Darcy with a long stare, and a dispirited "Caroline sent for you, did she? She speaks of nothing but the Bennets' lack of connections. You are here, so I expect you agree with her."

"It is a drawback, certainly. You have done much to raise your family, Bingley. Miss Bennet would contribute nothing there and, indeed, the situation of her mother's family is quite objectionable. A tradesman in Cheapside will not add to your consequence. "

"The situation of the Bennets' relations is not such an evil. My family was in similar circumstances not long since."

"All the more reason to look higher. Miss Bennet is an admirable young lady, but she cannot bring you advancement. What is more… Bingley, I hesitate to condemn too quickly, but even if you were to put that objection aside, there are other reasons for not considering Miss Bennet. Her mother betrays a total want of propriety. I have rarely seen such a loud, coarse woman. A gossipy, fortune-hunting mother desperate to marry off her daughters—"

"Not so very different to mothers in society, then."

Darcy brushed off this ridiculous assertion. What mother of consequence would display such naked ambition and lack of decorum? "You cannot want such a mother-in-law, Bingley. Or such a family! The younger daughters are intolerably improper— with the exception of Mrs Grayson, whose manners, like Miss Bennet's, are unexceptionable. Mr Bennet, whose duty it is, does nothing to check them or govern his family or prevent their excesses. You cannot wish to be associated with such people!"

"I would not be marrying her family."

Really, could Bingley be more naive?

"They would be your sisters by marriage. Mrs Bennet will hang on your sleeve and pick your pocket when Mr Bennet is gone. She will leech off you until her own end."

Bingley looked away to one side. He lifted one hand to the wrinkled cravat, pressing it down and smoothing it flat with slow, repetitive strokes. His voice dragged, as if he were too weary to speak with his normal energy. "Caroline insists Miss Bennet does not care for me, but would marry me to meet her mother's desire for a rich son-in-law. She says that you agree with her. Do you, Darcy? What is your assessment?"

"I took great care to observe Miss Bennet," Darcy said, slowly, not relishing the pain he would give this most worthy of friends. "I could not see any sign of partiality in her. Her looks and manner are cheerful, open and engaging—"

"Yes." And Bingley let out a breath in a quiet sigh. His hand stilled, somewhere over the region of his heart.

"But I saw no symptom of particular regard in her. I am sorry, but I did not."

"But she received my attentions with pleasure, I am sure!"

"I would never deny it. But I could not see that she invited them with any participation of sentiment of her own—"

Bingley rubbed his hand over his chest. "I... I thought her to return my regard. Perhaps not to the depth I feel for her, but I cannot believe she was indifferent and accepted my attentions with nothing but the common courtesies a lady would offer an acquaintance. She felt more, I am cert— I thought she did. I thought so indeed."

Dear Lord, this was torture.

"She is so serene, and is so pleasant to all who speak with her, I cannot see that her heart would be easily touched. That she would accept your addresses does not admit of doubt. Her mother would see to that! But you deserve a great deal more in marriage, my friend, than a complacent but unloving wife. If she loved you, then the inequality in fortune and consequence would be of less significance. But I could not see it, Bingley, even after the most minute observation. I cannot believe she has any softer sentiment where you are concerned." Darcy leaned towards Bingley, and laid a hand on his shoulder. "She appeared indifferent."

Bingley winced. "I see. You think I should not return to Netherfield then? There is no question of it in any event, this side of Christmas. I have dealt with the immediate problem, but there are other matters of great importance to the family business that will keep me occupied for some weeks if I am not to lose more than I am comfortable with. Indeed, I have begged my brother Hurst to return to London, and I will travel to Yorkshire the moment I can leave Caroline in his care."

That was unlikely to fill Hurst with delight.

"You should not return to Netherfield quickly, I am sure." Darcy nodded. He had been correct, then, in his speculation that Bingley's subdued demeanour was due to this unexpected crisis of his affairs. "Allow any communication to be through your sister, and take that as your guide. But in truth, I do not deem you have reason to return. Your honour is not engaged."

Bingley was silent for several minutes, sitting with head bowed and shoulders slumped. "Thank you for being honest. You have always been so with me, even when I would have welcomed some dissembling. And now... forgive me, but this business is most pressing, and I should return to it. " He essayed a smile, a poor thin ghost of his usual cheerful demeanour, and gestured to the papers scattered over his desk. "I have not your head for such things, either, so this will take all my powers to understand and master."

"Can I— ?"

"Not unless you understand intimately the workings of Lancashire cotton mills and Yorkshire steel foundries. But thank you, all the same."

"Of course, my dear friend. Of course." And Darcy pressed Bingley's hand and took his leave, sorrowful for the pain he had been forced to inflict.

It was for Bingley's own good. He would master more than this setback to his affairs, Darcy was sure. He would master his heart, too.

Just as Darcy had.

Darcy saw Bingley seldom over the next two weeks, and what little he did see was not encouraging. Bingley was thinner, and his manner remained quiet and repressed. He showed little interest in society, not taking up his usual pursuits and eschewing the gatherings and events that once he had relished so much. The crisis in his affairs absorbed him, and he would go north as soon as could be arranged.

Darcy did not seek him out. Were he in Bingley's place and suffering under such a reverse, he would prefer solitude and quiet in which to reflect and gather his mental strength rather than seek diversion in soirees and balls. Of course, they were not in the same situation. Not at all. Still, it was no hardship for Darcy to forgo the invitations that came his way, and remain in by his own fireside or that of his uncle Ashbourne, where he spent hours with Georgiana. Town was thin of company, and would be until the season started the following spring. That accounted for the dearth of gatherings that appealed to him, obviously. He canvassed the idea of retreating to Pemberley and taking Georgiana with him. If they left soon, they would be home for Christmas.

The one invitation he did accept came mid-month; a short, terse note inviting him to meet Viscount Kirton for a quiet nuncheon at their club, where the viscount had bespoken a private room. Darcy quirked an eyebrow at the note when it arrived. It was unlikely to be a comfortable coze over coffee.

Nor was it.

Kirton, who must have been some six or seven years Darcy's senior, greeted him amicably enough. He had ordered a substantial meal of beefsteak, washed down with claret. They exchanged civilities while the servants were in the room, but the respite, while welcome, was temporary. Kirton dismissed the footmen as soon as they had poured the wine. Darcy found himself poking at the steak on his plate in dispirited fashion, appetite gone, while Kirton spoke.

"You will understand that I have come to Town to scotch any scandal that may affect my family. I have had letters from Meryton. From Mr Bennet; from the magistrate, Mr Harpur; and from Thomas Rance, who was once my cousin's servant."

Darcy nodded. "I rather expected that, and that you would wish to act. You must know I regret, very deeply, that this has happened."

"As do we all, Darcy. The delicate nature of my cousin's death could be ruinous if it were known. My father has political enemies aplenty who would relish such a tale. I believe I have soothed the Meryton people this time. I have apologised profusely and promised to keep Matthew in bounds."

"And me, I suppose."

Kirton nodded and took a hearty mouthful of claret. "I undertook to ensure that the Bennets would not be plagued about James again."

"That is no hardship on my part, I assure you."

"I expect that you will do everything you can to repair this damage."

Darcy tried the claret. Excellent stuff, but it did nothing to ease the tightness at his temple. "I will not speak of it to anyone."

"I have no fear of that. You are known as an honourable man."

Darcy allowed his lip to twist in a self-aimed sneer, but merely nodded.

"And perhaps some communication to Mr Bennet?"

Another nod. He owed that much restitution, unpalatable as it was.

Kirton relaxed visibly. "It may be the fault is with my father and me. We said little to Matthew about the circumstances of James's death, since Matthew was in Antigua at the time."

"He told me so, and that his intention was to discover how James died. That caught my attention, as you might suppose. I had heard nothing of the marriage, which struck me as so unlike James as to be suspicious when young Grayson informed me of it, and nor had I known the circumstances of James's death. I had assumed it to be the progression of illness from his injuries, not… well. At the time, Grayson's misgivings seemed natural."

"Mr Harpur indicated he had explained how the marriage came about." Kirton refilled their glasses. "The James Grayson who returned from Maida was not the young cousin of whom we were all fond. I did not know the man he became, a man warped and consumed with bitterness of spirit. Oh, I understand how the opiates changed him, destroyed him; but that does not make it easier to bear or easier to handle. When my father and I had the full tale of the marriage and how James died, we did not cavil at the way he had settled his affairs in the will and marriage settlement. To do so would have brought out the entire story and that would have been appalling for the family. You will appreciate that as well as spiking political guns, we sought to spare his mother as much as possible. She suffered enough from the death of her son. She did not need to know the truth."

"Of course. I am only sorry that it has resurfaced now to disturb her peace—and yours. I cannot sufficiently regret my own role in this. I have reflected on it, to try and understand myself. You know how close I had been to James?"

Kirton nodded.

"He came home from Maida just as my father was struck down and confined to what became his deathbed. I had one brief meeting with James here in Town, before hurrying to Pemberley. I never saw him again, and less than a year later, I heard of his death. I was very grieved, and, as I said, assumed he had succumbed to his injuries." Darcy raised a hand and rubbed at his temple. "I do not say this to excuse what has happened, but I do believe..." He stopped. Sighed. "James was one of my dearest friends. I cannot but think I failed him. I failed to be the friend he needed, too caught up in Pemberley and all I had to do there after my father's death. When Matthew Grayson came to me in September, the magnitude of that failure struck me hard." He frowned down at his wine. It was merely the first of such failures of care and duty, as Georgiana could attest. He was only belatedly learning his lesson. "I believed I owed him some sort of restitution."

"James was not your responsibility." Kirton regarded him steadily, leaning back in his chair and nursing his glass of wine against his chest. "Or ours, really. He was full grown. But guilt can wrack a man, I know. I have not been free of it myself since James's death. We would not be the men we are if we felt less, but Matthew was able to twist that to his advantage. Matthew is not James's equal."

"Not by any means. He admitted, at the end, that his goal was not to discover what happened to James, but to take the estate James had left Mrs Grayson. I assume he has pressing debts?"

"Oh, yes. He has always been unsatisfactory. We did not send him to the West Indies on a whim, and it was a sad day when my father was forced to allow him to return. Not yet two years at home, and he is completely under the hatches. I dare say he owes vowels to every gamester in Town. He is a hanger-on of your cousin Carsington."

"Carsington? Good God."

The eldest son of Darcy's uncle, the Earl of Ashbourne, Viscount Carsington was a vicious, unprincipled gambler. He and Darcy were not close.

"Indeed. My father and I are Matthew's trustees. So far, we have been able to keep him within bounds, but the trust ends when he is twenty-five and I have no doubt he will run Graymead into the ground. It is entailed under strict settlement, of course, so he may not sell any part of it. He wished to gain Netherfield in order to sell it to clear his debts, and finance his next foray into the gambling hells."

"He would have done better to remain in Antigua."

"Would that we could send him back. I am inclined to allow him to ruin himself and wash my hands of him." Kirton, picked up his fork, and essayed the beef, but he took only a couple of mouthfuls before pushing his plate aside again. "I own to some curiosity about my cousin-by-marriage. I have never spoken to her, though I have seen her. Mr Bennet insisted on that. My father and I went immediately to Meryton when told of James's death, and Mr Bennet was adamant that we saw what James had done. She was not conscious, and the local apothecary feared she might not live after losing the child. She certainly bore the marks of James's fists, poor girl. She was so very young! It was strong evidence that the tale Thomas Rance and the others had to tell, was the truth."

Darcy winced, but said nothing.

Kirton's smile was mirthless. "James named me as one of her trustees in his will, but I agreed with Bennet that my role would be nominal. He and her uncle, the lawyer, did the chief of the work until she reached her majority earlier this year, with my part kept to oversight of the annual accounts."

"You did not think to contest the will?"

"And risk a scandal over James's death? No. My father and I were content to leave matters lie. I have wondered over the years if Mrs Grayson was content with merely being left alone. She has made no claim to be a member of our family."

"I do not think she would." Darcy suspected Elizabeth Grayson harboured such bitterness against her dead husband, and most certainly against his brother, that would preclude it.

Did she harbour a similar bitterness against him?

"What is she like?"

"Lively. Intelligent. Not conventionally educated, I suspect, but with a bright mind and many interests, making her conversation delightful and amusing. Her manners are not those of society, but are less artificial and constrained. I believe her to be kind and considerate, but she does not tolerate poor behaviour. You might ask your cousin about the time she schooled him in how to deal politely with others. She was civil, but censorious when he fell below her standards."

Kirton chuckled.

"She does not have the outstanding classical beauty of her elder sister, but she is very pretty and her manner is engaging." Darcy put down his glass. "I owe her a profound apology."

"Do you fear to give it?"

"I fear I have offended beyond forgiveness."

Lord Kirton's glance was knowing. He smiled. "Well, Darcy, there is only one way to discover whether or not you are right. I believe you are man enough to attempt it."

Darcy was not sure he shared that belief. He could merely hope.

CHAPTER THIRTY

A Contrariety of Emotion

"I have not seen your mother this discomposed for… oh, at least a week. Her nerves must be quite shattered again."

Elizabeth tucked her hand under her father's arm as they walked together out of Longbourn church. The first banns had been called for Charlotte and Mr Collins, to Mama's undisguised fury. After bestowing a poisonous glare indiscriminately between Elizabeth and poor Charlotte, she was already on her way back to Longbourn, her other daughters trying valiantly to keep pace with her unusual speed.

Papa inclined his head to peer under the brim of her bonnet and see her face. "Are you well, child?"

"I will be, Papa." The catch in her voice infuriated her, but her father merely patted her hand and tugged her gently away from the church path to walk among the old grey tombstones. "I was… Oh, Papa, I had thought all behind me, never to trouble me again. I was shocked, I acknowledge. Taken by surprise, despite knowing of the interest in Netherfield shown by Mr Darcy and Mr Saville—my

room at Nether House, then like Jeanne d'Arc, she redonned her armour and presented her calm, gentle serenity to the world. The gossips' ill nature and Mama's loud lamentations made no outward mark on her. What she bore in silence and fortitude was another matter. To Elizabeth's loving eyes, she was thinner and less resilient, quieter and more melancholy. She suffered, and that was enough to make Elizabeth's ire towards Bingleys and Darcys all the hotter and more obdurate.

The militia officers were at most of the events. Mr Wickham came early each time to Elizabeth's side, and they spent many an evening in company. Unlike most gentlemen, he did not pay extravagant compliments of the sort designed to flatter but which, the cynical Elizabeth felt, were so rehearsed and impersonal, they might be made to apply to any woman in the room. Instead, he was more inclined to quiet conversation that gave due deference to her education and wit, discussing the affairs of the day or new books or plays.

"Did you see the Morning Chronicle's review of Mrs Brunton's *Self Control*?" he asked at one such evening party, hosted by the Harringtons. "Have you read it?"

"The novel was quite the most amusing nonsense I have read in years. I laughed a great deal at it, and never so heartily as at the heroine escaping her abductor by tying herself to a canoe and fleeing down some rapids in the wilds of the American continent. I have not seen the review. But then, I suspect Mrs Brunton has seen neither canoe nor rapids, and so we are equal in our ignorance."

Mr Wickham laughed. "The reviewer describes it as an uplifting moral tale with a heroine of unimpeachable moral character and a pleasingly devout adherence to Christian values, but does not mention a canoe."

"In that case I cannot believe the reviewer actually read the book. The canoe is quite the best chapter."

He laughed again, and after a few minutes of discussion of novels and poetry, left to procure her a glass of wine. Lydia at once appeared, to take Mr Wickham's seat.

"It is very bad of you, Lizzy, to keep the most charming man in Meryton to yourself. You have Mr Wickham dancing attendance on you all the time. Other people might wish to talk to him, you know. You do not even flirt! How might talking about books be flirting? He should come and talk to me. I would be infinitely more amusing."

"I shall tell him so, then we shall see if he comes to worship at your feet."

"Hmmph," said Lydia, and flounced away when Wickham reappeared with Elizabeth's wine.

"Have I offended your sister?" he asked.

There was nothing she could say of the truth, as almost every sally might suggest he had some status beyond that as occasional congenial conversationalist. Instead she smiled. "Lydia has no head for books, but seeks more earthy entertainment."

Mr Wickham glanced at Lydia and smiled, and in a moment they returned to their discussion. Elizabeth learned, though, from Lydia's pettishness: she was prepared to accept the gentleman's company as a friend, but did not wish to give any more intimate impression. She wanted no gossip or speculation. Mr Wickham, however, was not always disposed to talk to Lydia or anyone else instead of her. It was vexing.

"You will feel the loss of Miss Lucas when she weds, I expect." Mr Wickham settled beside her at the Lucases' reception a few days after the Harrington's party.

"Yes. Charlotte is a very dear friend, and has been a stalwart support. But who could begrudge her this opportunity for an establishment and eventually a family of her own? I am not so dog-in-the-mangerish."

He nodded, and like her, watched Charlotte for a few moments. Then he sighed. "I envy her, if I am to be honest." He caught Elizabeth's sidelong glance and laughed softly. "Oh, not Mr Collins, of course, or Lady Catherine as a neighbour. But that very opportunity you speak of—to have an establishment, to found and nurture a family of my own. That I envy. It has been denied me, as you know."

"Yes. I am sorry."

"Kympton is not the largest of livings. Some four or five hundred a year, that is all." He smiled. "Derbyshire is not quite so tame as the neighbourhood here. The land is wilder and more difficult to farm, less profitable unless a man has the sort of vast holdings that Darcy does—Pemberley is very large and his holdings diverse. More sheep than wheat, I can tell you! It follows that the parishes are not the richest in tithes, but they are steady and stable. And, of course, the church at Kympton has a large acreage in glebe land, allowing the incumbent a very good livelihood, on the whole." He sighed again. "Ah well. It is gone, and I must not repine."

She gave him a small smile to convey her sympathy. "Would you have liked making sermons?"

"I think I would have liked the life very well." He shifted on the sofa to half turn towards her, his expression one of muted longing. "With the right helpmeet, of course."

No.

She would not be charmed that far. Certainly not.

She said nothing, turning away and keeping her gaze on Charlotte as her friend moved around the room talking and laughing with the Lucases' guests, conscious all the time of Mr Wickham's soulful gaze.

When the silence grew uncomfortable, Mr Wickham straightened up, and changed the subject. "I understand the company at Netherfield Park is not to return."

"Not in the immediate future, I believe."

"That is sad news." But there was a faint note of satisfaction in his tone. "They are missing all our celebrations, are they not? I am struck by the number of gatherings at this time of year, each more pleasant and lively than the last. The acquaintance who told me about the agreeable nature of the society here much understated the case. I believe there are enough events to carry us over the wedding and Christmas itself and well into the new year, to culminate in a ball at the assembly rooms on Twelfth Night. I hope to see you at all of them. You are a social creature, I know."

Elizabeth kept her tone light. "I will be present at many of them, I am sure, sir."

"As you know, I decided not to attend the Netherfield ball since to meet Mr Darcy might be more than I could bear, and that scenes might arise unpleasant to more than myself..."

"Very laudable."

"Perhaps, but I was deprived of the pleasure of dancing with you, and you can be certain I blamed myself most heartily for that folly! While there may be a little impromptu dancing at any of the events we attend, it does not have the cachet of a true ball. I hope that I will see you at the assembly, then, and can prevail upon you for the first two dances. As recompense for my failure at Netherfield!"

Elizabeth summoned up a smile. "I thank you for the honour, sir, but I never attend the Twelfth Night assembly."

"What! Never?"

"Never. Excuse me, sir."

She rose swiftly to her feet, looking around to seek out Jane. As Mary would no doubt have it, it would behove the two wounded spirits to pour into each other the balm of sisterly consolation. He jumped up at once. She dropped him a curtsey and walked hurriedly to join Jane, who sat in silent despondency near the piano. A glance behind her showed Mr Wickham, looking rather silly and startled, had put out a hand as if to restrain her. Even as she looked, he dropped it to his belt, where he rested it on the pommel of his sword.

No. No man was charming enough to inveigle her to that assembly. No man on earth.

The Friday before Christmas, Charlotte sacrificed herself to gain an establishment.

"Well, Lizzy, the wedding was pretty enough." Papa offered the departing carriage carrying Charlotte and her new husband a desultory wave. "And Lady Lucas put on a brave show with the wedding breakfast. I must remember to tell your mama how much I enjoyed it."

"You were ever one to fan flames." Elizabeth whirled her handkerchief around her head in final benediction, in answer to

Charlotte's hand fluttering from the carriage window. "I hope Charlotte will be happy."

Papa considered Elizabeth, while the crowd of neighbours who had gathered on the steps of Lucas Lodge to farewell the newlyweds made a hasty return to the warmth of Lady Lucas's drawing room. "You were ever one to hope, even against all odds. Do you wish to take the carriage to Meryton? It can return for us. I would not mind waiting if I can have another glass of Sir William's port, even if it does mean having to listen to that lieutenant's tale of great woe again."

"Which lieutenant?"

"Wickley, is it? I do not claim close acquaintanceship with any of the officers, since none of them are men of any intellectual substance. The colonel seems a sensible man, though. Or seemed, I should say. Did you hear he is to wed Harriet Harrington? I could tell him how that tune will sound in a twelvemonth if I thought he would listen." And Papa cocked an eye at his own wife, who was at that moment entering the Lodge with Lady Lucas. "I wonder how long before those two come to pulling caps. Perhaps I had better take your mother home directly."

"Lieutenant Wickham?"

"That is the man."

"He told you of his trouble?"

"Oh, yes. I believe it is quite a known thing. Everyone speaks of it and reviles the evil Mr Darcy. You have been quiet at home this last few days, Lizzy, so did you not hear the tale? But that cannot be, since you appear to have some prior knowledge of it, and your astonishment seems to be that I know of it at all."

"Mr Wickham told me a few weeks ago that Mr Darcy had denied him a clerical living. I had not realised it was commonly bruited about. Indeed, Mr Wickham said…" Elizabeth stopped. What was it now? Something about his respect for Mr Darcy's father precluding his defaming the son's name?

"He should write a novel. Add a headless monk and an heiress or two, and I do not doubt he could out-Radcliffe the best of them."

"He was most materially disadvantaged by Mr Darcy, sir."

Papa merely smiled. "And yet, my child, wills are not so easily overset and nor, I will point out, did anyone other than you know of this while Mr Darcy was here to refute it."

"Whatever do you mean?"

He tapped her head with his forefinger. "Use this, Lizzy, and you will know. So, do you and Mary walk or will you take the carriage?"

"What? Oh." Elizabeth shook her head. "Send Mary in the carriage if you will, Papa, after John Coachman has delivered the rest of you home. It is a fine day, and will not be dark for an hour yet, and I would welcome a quiet, solitary walk to clear my head and heart."

"Mary will be thankful. Well, I will speed you on your way, and return to that fine port."

Elizabeth laughed and kissed his cheek, and within ten minutes she was walking briskly under the pale December sun, now declining slowly westward, and enjoying the invigorating wind. When the road was clear, she took a childish delight in kicking her way through the last remnants of the sere, yellow leaves the wind had piled up against the hedges. Every hard motion of her foot helped her shake a little of her unease.

What was Mr Wickham about? Why had he told his tale so widely, despite his claim to respect old Mr Darcy? What could it all mean? She had been a little cooler towards him since the Lucases' party earlier that week. Was that why he had told others, because he had missed her sympathy?

She aimed her boot at a low-lying branch, and smiled when the hard tap shook down the last of the coppery beech leaves in a little shower around her foot.

Oh, what did it matter? What did she care? Neither man was of any import to her.

Laughing, Elizabeth turned from the drift of leaves she had been punting into the beech hedge. Then the laugh died in her throat, and the cool wind leached all the warmth out of her.

The horseman watched her in silence, holding his big chestnut steady. Its mane blew in the same sharp wind that made

Elizabeth's eyes water, but the rider sat like a statue. "Mrs Grayson."

"Mr Darcy." She did not smile. She drew her pelisse in tighter, warding off the chill. "This is a surprise."

CHAPTER THIRTY-ONE

Vain Struggles

Mr Darcy dropped lightly out of the saddle, and looped his horse's reins over one arm. He bowed. "Madam."

Elizabeth stared at him, before recollecting enough of her manners to dip into a slight curtsey. "An unexpected meeting, sir."

"It was a sudden decision to return. I hope you are well?"

"Pretty well, sir, yes. I thank you." Elizabeth forced a smile. "Are you becoming more like Mr Bingley? I thought he was the one for impetuous comings and goings."

"I have business here. I am just come from Longbourn, where I left my card for your father. I had hoped to speak with him, but I understand there was a wedding today."

"Yes. Miss Lucas has married my father's distant cousin, Mr Collins. And is Mr Bingley returned too?" She looked past him, down the Meryton road. There was no sign of anyone else.

Mr Darcy looked startled, his mouth rounding into an O before he recovered himself. "No, I... No. Mr Bingley is not... I do not know when he may return to Netherfield, if at all. I have seen little of him, but I know his business calls him north. Indeed, he left for Yorkshire yesterday and will not return for some time. Weeks, at the least."

Oh. Poor Jane.

Elizabeth thrust her hands behind her back so he would not see her curl them into fists. "Well, perhaps when his business is concluded, we may see him again. He was a cheerful asset to our society here, and his absence is regretted."

Which was as much as she could say, and perhaps was more than she should.

"I have no notion of his returning, ma'am. He has been shown... he has seen that his best interests do not lie here."

Her breath caught in her throat. For an instant she could only stare, then pride had her lifting her chin. "Indeed? I remember a discussion at Netherfield in which we determined that his sweetness of temper may lead him to be influenced by the words of a friend. It was not a mere philosophical debate, then."

They glared at each other. He was completely still. He had clenched the hand on his riding crop so tightly, each knuckle whitened, as though the bones beneath were forcing their way through the skin to take umbrage at her. She hardened her own jaw, and took two or three sharp, hard breaths until her neck hurt from the tension, and she was forced to take the next breath more softly to ease the strain.

After a moment, Mr Darcy unclamped his jaw enough to say, in a tone so constrained his teeth must have bitten on each word as it was forced past them, "It is the office of friends to do what they think is right."

She said nothing. She would not look away. She would not give him the satisfaction of that victory.

He twisted the lower part of his face into an odd grimace, all sagging skin and deep lines from nose to chin, that gave her an intimation of what he would look like when he was eighty. Should he live that long. He swept his free hand over his mouth, and sighed. "Mrs Grayson, I pray you, may we start again? I did not come here to discuss Mr Bingley, but to beg the favour of a private word with you." He glanced around. "I take it you are returning to Nether House? May I escort you there?"

What he saw in her expression, she could not know, but he dropped his voice and took a half step closer. "I wish to offer you my deepest apologies, ma'am, and I would prefer not to be overheard."

Elizabeth continued to look at him. It was, of course, a time of year to be both cheerful and charitable, if she could. In a few short days the world would celebrate the birth of Christ... even when it was hard, she supposed she should try to follow His example.

"Very well. Will you leave that animal here or lead him?"

Elizabeth bit back the sudden urge to laugh at Mr Darcy, who blinked and whose mouth once again formed that O, but soon returned to his usual manner.

"I assure you I can control Alastor easily as we walk."

He hesitated and made a motion as if to offer his free arm, but Elizabeth would not dream of taking it and started off. He had to scramble to catch up with her, and for a moment or two was silent. She said nothing. He had sought this interview. It was for him to begin.

"I have thought of little on my ride here today but how to tell you of the depths of my regret. I am, you understand, very good at planning a conversation in my head, but somehow I always fail in the execution. I plotted many high-flown sentiments as I rode, but I confess I cannot now remember any of them. So I will say only that I would give a very great deal not to have caused you such pain, and I cannot forgive myself for doing so. It is no excuse that I thought I had reason enough when I began this. I have come to see my reasoning was erroneous, and that I compounded old injuries to your peace and happiness is reprehensible. I am heartily sorry. I do not deserve your forgiveness, but I do throw myself on your mercy."

She had pressed her lips together as he spoke, and would not look at him, all the better to hear, and weigh, the tone of his voice. Her chest was tight with a sorrow and anguish she had last felt so deeply more than four years earlier. It made every breath a conscious effort, choked up into her voice and prickled at the back of her eyes. She raised a hand to dash her glove against her eyes to stop the tears in their tracks. That he saw it was obvious, from his muffled exclamation, and, when she could bear to look, the expression of shame on his face.

"Why did you come here? Matthew Grayson hoped to take Netherfield from me, which, much as I deplore it, is something I can understand. Men do not like to lose anything of value, particularly to a woman. But your motives cannot have been the same. What brought you here to cut up my peace so thoroughly?"

His voice was as thick as hers. "I did not dissemble when I named James as a dear friend. He had been so since we were schoolboys together."

She bowed her head and listened as he told her of the guilt and remorse he had felt when James had died, and he had been too caught up in his own concerns to be the friend to James that he should have been.

"I was astounded when Grayson told me James had married. And—forgive me—the circumstances were not clear to me then, and given the relative positions of the Graysons and your own family, it gave rise to the gravest concern. I felt I owed it to James to discover what I could of the matter myself." His mouth twisted. "Grayson assured me that was his object, too. I was foolish enough to believe him."

The relative positions of the Graysons and the Bennets? She might translate that as her father's not being rich enough. "Netherfield is in Meryton parish, not Longbourn, so I am right, I think, in believing you have never been in Longbourn church."

He shook his head, his forehead creasing between his eyes.

"My family's graves are there, the earliest in the church nave. The first Bennet tomb was built in 1487, when Robert Bennet buried his second son. He had been granted the manor of Longbourn the year before, in thanks for aiding Harry Tudor gain his throne. Bennets have been entombed there ever since. We can trace our line through to the Beaumonts, and hence Robert Bennet could claim a distant kinship with King Henry himself. We are old gentry, sir. There is little distance between the Graysons and the Bennets in that regard, and what exists is on our side, I think.

There is merely the issue of wealth, and, I suppose, what some deem our poor connections to trade."

He flushed a brilliant scarlet under her regard, and inclined his head. His colour came and went, leaving duller red stains over his cheekbones.

"Mr Darcy, I too have dear friends I would do much to help." She closed her eyes for an instant, once again seeing Charlotte putting her hand into that of William Collins. Ridiculous to feel guilt over it, but she did. "I absolve of you malicious intent. You cannot have known what James became, and therefore how many wounds you would rip open. I do not believe that you are so... so venomous. I wish, though, that you had just asked. I find it harder to forgive the deceit, the pretence that you were in the neighbourhood merely as Mr Bingley's friend."

"That weighs heavy on me. I assure you that I abhor deceit. I am so very sorry."

Elizabeth nodded. It was hard to breathe. Her face was hot and her nose felt stuffy. Pray the Lord she was not going down with a cold. "Then go in peace, Mr Darcy."

He stopped, and, surprised, she came to a halt and turned to face him.

"And if I do not wish to go?" His voice was low. "What then? What then? I do not wish it. I will not go so tamely. I promised myself I would say nothing, that I would make my apologies and depart back to my old life and learn to live with myself again. But it is impossible!"

"Sir?"

"You must... you must allow me, ma'am...I have struggled against this, as you will expect. Your connections... whatever your family's venerable history, your connections now are to be deplored, so closely aligned as they are to trade. The antecedents of your mother and her relations, the shortcomings and improprieties of your immediate family... they weigh in the balance and had to be considered carefully. They are an obstacle indeed, and for a long time judgement fought against my inclination. Had you been accepted by the Ruffords, it might have mitigated these evils... but I shall say no more on that head. You must understand me. Against all those misgivings, I have struggled in vain. You must allow me to tell you how ardently I admire and love you."

Elizabeth could not speak. She tried, but all that came out was a faint, high-pitched squeak. She took a step back, her entire body prickling and cold ice sliding down her back. She rubbed at the ache in her chest so hard it probably left the impression of the knotted ribbons adorning her dress imprinted on her skin. Despite the touch of winter in her spine, her face burned.

He reached out a hand, and regardless of all he had said earlier about his inability to speak in high-flown periods, he was suddenly eloquent in explaining the pains he undergone as he wrestled with his principles, and the affront a union to one such as her would deal his consequence and standing in the world. Netherfield as a dowry was, he assured her, some compensation to atone for the other defects of her situation in life.

"From this you will see that my attachment is so very strong, so immutable, that I cannot be silent any longer. Do not let me suffer, and be my wife. I pray you will accept my hand in marriage."

Elizabeth gasped in air, and it slid, cool and soothing, down her throat. She was not certain she had breathed for the entirety of his speech. "I... Oh. Oh!"

The impossible man! He should choke on his own pride!

She tried again. "I believe propriety demands I express a sense of obligation for the honour of your proposal. But I have never sought your good opinion. I am astonished that you have such an opinion of me, since I thought your primary feelings were not so much an immutable attachment, as fixed dislike."

He could have looked no more shocked had she pulled a pistol from her pocket and discharged it at him. "Mrs Grayson!"

"I thank you for your offer, sir, but I will refuse it. I would be sorry indeed to wound your consequence to the extent you fear. I would give no man's pride so dreadful an injury. Still, you have bestowed your approbation with such reluctance, I am sure any discomfort you feel will be of short duration."

He was very pale. He drew himself up, throwing out his arms and making his horse shy and dance, tossing its head and showing the whites of its eyes. "You refuse me? Is this the only reply I am to expect? I am to be rejected in such an uncivil fashion?"

"You were hardly civil in making your offer, sir! Having just apologised for one mighty offence, why do you desire to offend and insult me again by proposing in these terms? You tell me your pride is wounded by the thought of having me as your wife. That you struggled against the inclination because I am so low, in your eyes, that marriage to me is a degradation. Good heavens, if I was uncivil, I have some reason for it! You claim to like me, but you do not respect me. No woman who felt an ounce of self-worth could face such an offer with equanimity." She flashed him a sour smile. "We are not all flatterers of Miss Bingley's stamp."

He had been pale before. Now he was truly so white, he looked as though he could have fallen insensible.

"I have lived through one marriage where there was no respect—barely lived through it. We women have no power. We go from the authority of our fathers to that of our husbands. We have no recourse if it all goes ill, so a woman must hope that her husband will at least have as much respect for her as he does for his other possessions, that he gives her at least the same value." She made a sharp gesture at the big chestnut he held by the reins, and the horse snorted and danced back. "And if he does not, if he ranks his other possessions—his horse, say—over the wishes and happiness of his wife, then for all his claims of ardent love, what trust might a woman have in such a husband?"

He fell back a step, shaking his head. Even his lips had paled. "You think I would mistreat you as James did?"

"You respect me as little as he did! And the wounds such disrespect can cause do not have to be applied with a fist. Do you think they hurt the less?"

He gaped, his mouth opening and closing, but he said nothing.

"Even if I may now assume I am more tempting than merely tolerable, there are other reasons for disapprobation. You have suggested—all but admitted—you have warned Mr Bingley away, counselled him that his best interests are not here. What of Jane's interest? Whatever your offences towards me, do you think I can accept you when—doubtless in confederation with Miss Bingley—you have destroyed the happiness of a most beloved sister?"

He stiffened. "I did all I could to separate my friend from your sister. I am glad of it. I would not see him suffer an unequal alliance with a woman who will marry him only to oblige her mother."

"Oh!" Elizabeth's face flamed and her hand dropped from her breastbone. "You accuse us of fortune-hunting? Is that it? And yet, my fortune-hunting mother quite neglected to push any of her daughters at *you*! And you are reputed to have twice Bingley's income. How do you explain that, I wonder? I would remind you whose sister did indeed set her cap at you for your position, sir. It was not one of mine!"

His jaw dropped, and he frowned, as if being forced to see something new and disturbing. "She did not show she cared for him. Towards him I have been kinder than towards myself."

She pulled herself up as high as she could. "And who are you, that Jane must display her feelings to you to judge? Now she must suffer, and counter the derision of having been left without a word from the man who had shown her such attentions, while he gains a reputation for inconstancy and caprice. That is your kindness? Yes, that is all of a piece with the recital I had from Mr Wickham and the high-handed and deplorable manner in which you treated him, imposed upon him his misfortunes, and thrust him into poverty!"

He flushed as red now as he had been white an instant before. "Wickham! You have an interest in his concerns?" He laughed; a hard, unfeeling but humourless huff of sound, raucous as quarrelling crows. "Misfortunes! Yes, they have been great indeed."

"Which you inflicted on him!"

Another hard laugh. "And you believe his tales. I thought better of your quick mind, ma'am. But perhaps none of this would have mattered, if I had not been so honest with you. Would any of this have weighed with you if I had hidden my uncertainties and struggles, and flattered you with ardency and passion? Would I have been answered with more complacency then? I am not ashamed of what I felt, concerning connections so inferior to my own. They are natural misgivings."

"And so are mine! You show always a selfish disdain for the feelings of others. You are arrogant and conceited... you value wealth and connections above all else. Above character, above honesty, sincerity, integrity… How could I trust you? You have behaved in so ungentlemanly a fashion, that I could never be tempted to accept an offer from you. Never!"

He changed colour rapidly, red to white and back again. With a smothered exclamation, he tugged his horse around and prepared to mount. "Enough. Forgive me for having taken up so much of your time, and accept my best wishes for your health and happiness."

He pulled himself up into the saddle, and with one glance that should have burned her to ash, touched his fingers to the brim of his hat and set his heels to his horse's side. The chestnut sprang away, leaving Elizabeth gasping at the side of the road, her hands clutched together under her heart to stop it bounding from its place.

She did not often thank the good Lord for the annoyance of bonnets, when the sides projected forward and prevented her from looking around as she pleased to drink in all the world in one glance. But now she relished the concealment hers offered. When she kept her head lowered as she walked slowly into Meryton in Mr Darcy's wake, her eyes on the cobbles and the few dry leaves skittering over them, the curving sides of her fashionable bonnet hid her tears from view. She was grateful for that much, at least.

CHAPTER THIRTY-TWO

God Bless You

I could never be tempted to accept an offer from you. Never!

Darcy rubbed his hand over his chin, and made himself listen to the landlord's flood of words. The man bobbed and ducked his head, in a single breath extolling the comfort of his rooms and apologising for them not being good enough for the Quality. Not the White Hart's landlord, of course, but the Red Lion's. The militia officers were all quartered at the Hart. He would be content never to see Wickham again, and staying at Meryton's second best inn was no great hardship if it avoided an unpleasant meeting. Perhaps he should have gone to Bishop's Stortford and found a room there rather than take his chances in Meryton.

...all of a piece with the recital I had from Mr Wickham and the high-handed and deplorable manner in which you treated him...

What did she know of deplorable treatment? What did she know of Wickham's lies, his dishonour and debts, the constant scheming always skirting on the edges of criminality, the grief and guilt that had all but consumed Georgiana? What did— Fool that he was! Of course she knew of some kinds of deplorable treatment. Of course she did! Worse perhaps. Who could measure it?

"It will be very well, thank you. No, I will not eat in the common room, but here. Yes, yes… your wife's beef pie… Bring me some ale, would you?"

And he ushered the landlord to the door and closed it on the man with a sigh of relief. He stood at the door, the cross-grained wood only inches from his eyes. He leaned forward and rested his head against its rough hardness. He did it gently, though he would have welcomed the sharp pain if he had been self-indulgent enough to throw a tantrum and bang his head against the oak to knock some sense into himself.

I could never be tempted to accept an offer from you. Never!

At least he could hide himself away long enough to catch his breath. What an utter nodcock he was! Why had he asked her? He had sworn that he would make the reparations she was owed, and give a sincere apology for his doing her so much harm, unwitting as it had been. That was all. He owed her that, and then he would leave her to rebuild her life and find peace. He had sworn to do no more. He had sworn to be stronger than to give in to temptation. He had sworn to keep his distance, as he had all the time he had been at Netherfield, and not raise expectations he could not fulfil. Despite all those oaths, when he fell at that first hurdle, just look where his weakness got him! Abused and sent on his way with her scathing voice sounding in his ears.

…behaved in so ungentlemanly a fashion…

Ungentlemanly! That she, the daughter of a simple country squire dared say that to him. To him! Darcy of Pemberley! She might boast of her ancestors for three hundred years, but his had been landowners and king's men for three hundred before that. His grandfather had been an earl. He was a gentleman born, and a gentleman bred. And she dared! *Dared!*

…selfish disdain for the feelings of others…

With that mother! That loud, vulgar harridan of a fortune-hunting mother, she dared criticise a real gentleman! Probably the only gentleman of his consequence she had ever come across. Not even James had been so wealthy—

... you value wealth and connections above all else. Above character, above honesty, sincerity, integrity...

No! That could not be true. He valued many things more than wealth. Many things.

He pulled away from the door and turned, pressed his back against the oak panels. The room was inelegant, but clean; the furnishings rustic but adequate. An armchair set before the fire, a small table and dining chair beneath the single window that looked out onto Meryton's marketplace, a canopied bed—that, he eyed and wondered about the denizens haunting many an inn's beds, but the mattress was plump and smelled of lavender-fresh linen rather than the sourness of many bodies pressed into it. His satchel lay across the quilted counterpane. He had left it when he had arrived and refreshed himself briefly before setting out on his fruitless quest to Longbourn, leaving the landlord to ready the room for his return.

Damnation! Longbourn. He had left his card. He was honour bound now to visit Mr Bennet on the morrow. Dear God, he had rather flee home to Pemberley and lick his wounds.

He could not settle. He tried the armchair, surprisingly comfortable in the warmth of the flames, but he could not make the tension leave his body. Every part of him, from his neck and jaw to the ache in his calves, was rigid. He felt as taut as a bowstring pulled back ready to release the arrow. The tension made him ache, muscle and bone, as if he had the ague. Sitting still intensified it, had him drumming his feet on the floor, raising them on his toes and down on the heel, again and again in an effort to relieve the strain.

I could never be tempted to accept an offer from you.

Were there people in the world who could release the simple emotions and reactions he was denied himself? He pressed the heels of his hands up against his eyelids until bright shooting-star sparks flashed across the darkness.

...behaved in so ungentlemanly a fashion...

How had it gone so badly? What had he said, but the truth? She was below him in consequence, her connections were deplorable in many respects. Who could relish the thought of a connection to trade, and to Mrs Bennet's brother, too! He must be a fine a specimen, if he were anything like his sister.

Darcy was a gentleman. His first duty was to further his family's standing in the world, and his greatest responsibility was to his name and increasing the family's prestige and fortune. He was duty bound to leave Pemberley to his son in a better state than when he himself inherited it, to root the Darcys deeper in their social sphere through careful alliances and, through his own marriage and Georgiana's, to cement their importance.

There was absolutely nothing reprehensible about any of that! It was an honourable, ethical, prudent way to live one's life. In the normal course of events, he would have achieved the desired enrichment of his family by taking a bride from within his own social sphere. Moreover, with everything he had to offer, he could have looked for a lady with a large dowry. Admittedly, Netherfield offset the need for a cash dowry, but was that enough set against the unbecoming behaviour and poor social standing of so much of her family? Surely she knew it? Surely she understood! How could she not see that weighed against this great duty, her family and connections were wanting, and that by asking for her hand he had offered a marriage far above anything a woman in her position might expect?

You are arrogant and conceited... you value wealth and connections above all else. Above character, above honesty, sincerity, integrity...

He did not. He did *not*.

Although perhaps it may have seemed like it to her. He should have flattered her, not paid her the compliment of expecting her sharp, intelligent mind to understand the depth of his regard, as witness the barriers it had overcome. Perhaps then she would have been kinder.

... that is your kindness?

Wickham. Wickham had poisoned her against him... well, at least there he might defend himself. He had ammunition enough for that! And her anger over Jane Bennet and Bingley—he would defend himself there, too. Her point about her mother never attempting to draw him in, though.... No matter. He had had reason enough where Bingley was concerned. He would show her

It was done.

He did not reread the letter. He had bent over its pages for hours, accompanied for some part of his labour by the muted sounds from the inn's tap room below, or an occasional voice coming from the marketplace outside where some hardy soul braved the chill weather. For the last hour, he had written with only the scratching of the quill on the paper to listen to, all of Meryton quiet around him.

It was done. Though he had told her only about his reasoning regarding Miss Bennet and the main points of his history with Wickham, in truth he had laid himself and all he was before her. His faults, certainly, and his failures; his pride and, he hoped, principles. She could not help but realise his abiding guilt over Georgiana, and perhaps it would acquit him— No. He would not make such false bargains with himself. She would see what he had endeavoured to show her, and if she thought of him a little more kindly, and, most of all, preserved herself from entanglement with Wickham, then he would be content.

His mother had taught him how to lock his letters against prying eyes, but so many pages stacked together were too thick for the more intricate creases. He kept it simple, folding the sheets in from the bottom to meet in the middle, and drawing down the top to cover the edges of the bottom third. The sealing wax was a good rich red, dripping onto the join to seal it in thick, waxy blood. He pressed his signet into it.

His shoulders ached. He had been hunched and cramped too long, and even stretching left a residual twinge between his shoulder blades. The letter lay face up on the desk, and for the last time he raised his quill and wrote her name across the smooth creamy-white space in a spike of inky-black letters.

"Mrs Grayson."

Done.

He straightened and stretched again before moistening his thumb and forefinger, and pinching out his candles. The familiar acrid smell of hot wax filled the room, and thin spires of smoke curled up from each taper in the orange firelight glimmer.

It was the work of minutes to strip to his small-clothes and slip between the linen sheets. He was weary down to his bones, but for hours he watched the shadows under the bed canopy flicker and change, advancing and retreating as the fire flared and died again.

I could never be tempted to accept an offer from you. Never!

CHAPTER THIRTY-THREE

Taking Pains To Get Acquainted

Mr Bennet appeared at Darcy's door bare minutes after the town barber, summoned to shave him, had departed. The town clock in the square was yet to strike eight.

"I thought it best to speak to you here and not divulge to Mrs Bennet the intelligence that you are returned to Meryton. She would be beside herself with curiosity, and I would prefer our meeting be undisturbed. She will doubtless discover it eventually, since your being here cannot entirely escape notice, but I expect you will be long gone before then. And if she does not know I met you, she cannot ask me about it." Mr Bennet quirked up mouth and eyebrows into a smirk, and made himself comfortable in the armchair when Darcy bowed and waved him into it. "I have bespoken us some coffee. It should be here directly."

"I am grateful you agreed to see me, sir." Darcy took the dining chair to a spot opposite Mr Bennet's chair, and seated himself.

"I have had a week or two to regain my temper. And I am, I think, a fair man, and willing to hear you out. I suppose you are here to apologise to my daughter."

"I did so yesterday. I met her on the road as I returned here from Longbourn. She graciously agreed to hear me. But my object is also to explain myself to you, as her father and head of her family."

"You do not look to be at peace. Are you yet unforgiven?"

Darcy had not thought the man so observant. "Absolved of one offence, perhaps."

Mr Bennet opened his mouth to speak, but the maid appeared at that moment with the coffee, and they were reduced to innocuous pleasantries until she was gone again and Darcy had closed the door firmly. They both sipped their coffee, until Mr Bennet once again quirked that sardonic eyebrow. Darcy was reminded of no one more than his grandfather, the old earl, long since dead. He too had had a mocking humour and somewhat less kindness than Mr Bennet had already displayed. Darcy had been rather afraid of him.

"Well," said Mr Bennet, "with this extra intelligence of further offences, perhaps we might take things in order. Shall we begin with your distressing my daughter over James Grayson?"

Yes, very like the old earl. Darcy bit back a sigh, and once again rehearsed the story of his long friendship with James. How many times had he told it over the last few weeks? It had grown no easier with the telling.

He had dismissed Mr Bennet as an indolent father and negligent master of a small estate, little interested in the world around him and unwilling to make the effort needed to keep his family under good regulation. But the man's dark grey eyes—so like his daughter's—were shrewd and knowing as Darcy recited again all the reasons why he had listened to Matthew Grayson's story and allowed himself to be drawn into the younger man's schemes. Having felt the bite of the widow's indignation concerning his views of the unsuitability of a Bennet as a bride for a Grayson, he rather glossed over that part while admitting his surprise at the marriage, but he did not hesitate to otherwise explain his old friendship.

Mr Bennet nodded when he was done. "I see. Young Grayson's blandishments fell on fertile ground, it seems. Yet my son-in-law has been dead more than four years. It seems a little odd to feel such guilt at this remove from the event."

Darcy inclined his head. "I..." He stopped. Sighed. "In summer, there occurred some mischief affecting my own family that might have bitterly harmed one very dear to me. I felt then, and do now, that I did not do enough to prevent it. I can say no more on that head, sir, other than the sense of my negligence and failed duty was most acute. Young Grayson could not know it, but he struck many chords."

"In effect, your besetting sin is to take a great many responsibilities onto yourself, and blame yourself for things beyond your control. My Lizzy accepted the explanation you gave?"

"She absolved me of what she termed malicious intent, though she deplored the deceit I practised. She could not do so more than I do myself, and so she eventually offered her benediction." Darcy swallowed. "For which I was most grateful."

"As any penitent would be. But yet, you then reoffended. That was impolitic."

Darcy looked away. Dear God, he could not speak of that. Not to her father. Not to anyone. Not yet. Not ever.

His mouth was dryer than the ashes the maid had raked from the fireplace earlier that day. "As we talked, further areas of disagreement arose, in which Mrs Grayson found fault with my reasoning, and, I believe, thought my principles are set on false and worldly foundations. I spent much of the night thinking on her strictures." He gestured to the table and the thick letter propped up against a candlestick. "I have written to her to attempt to explain myself better. You will understand that this was not possible on a cold, windy roadway. What is more, I am far more eloquent in ink than I am in speech. I hope to gain your approval to give her the letter, so we may avoid any suggestion of impropriety." A doom-laden thought struck him. "You may wish to read it, of course, as is your right."

That damned eyebrow had a life of its own, it moved so markedly upwards again. "I never read my daughter's correspondence when she was under my authority. I shall not start now." Mr Bennet turned his head to look at the letter. "A thick missive. I see your disagreements with Elizabeth were either weighty in themselves, or many."

Oh, jubilate! That was an escape. He would not like Mr Bennet to read his criticisms of the Bennet family and be gravely offended. And yet he had not spared Mrs Grayson the recital. In the light of a new day, her resentment and anger were all too understandable. "Two areas, sir, but of very great weight. One is not the business of myself alone, and I would prefer not to speak of it further, though I have explained my reasoning to her in the letter. The other concerns one of the militia officers. George Wickham."

"The lieutenant who treats us all to stories of his life as if he were a Cheltenham tragedy in a red coat? A tedious young man."

Heartened, Darcy smiled. "I think so too, but then I have to deal with him. He is something of a Sisyphean stone, constantly rolling downhill to crush my peace." He hitched his chair closer to the fire. "I should tell you of Wickham. Given Mrs Grayson's position as a widow in possession of a fine estate, she is not safe from him."

That made the eyebrow scrunch down into a frown, all the more fearsome for its usurpation of Mr Bennet's usual ironic humour. "In what way?"

"If you will allow, I will relate the whole of our history, to give you a better understanding of why I speak thus."

"I am at my leisure, sir."

Taking that as consent, Darcy spoke quickly, the words coming with ease after his labour of the night before, explaining how Wickham had been treated by the Darcy family. "My father was very fond of him, supporting him at school and through Cambridge to give him the education many a gentleman would envy. But my father did not truly know him. Wickham is adept at showing a genial, charming face to those he wishes to impress. In truth, he revels in immorality and depravity, drawn into a life where cards, daffy-gin and women are all he cares about. That and enriching himself by whatever means he can. He feels cheated that he was raised to be a gentleman, without a gentleman's means. Numerous times at Cambridge I had angry shopkeepers pursue me for

Wickham's debts, or worse, debts fraudulently taken out in my name. And one dreadful day, a town grocer came shouting to my lodgings, his *enceinte* daughter cowering beside him, and I found Wickham had used my name there as well. Only the girl's obvious astonishment at learning who I was, and her avowals that I was a complete stranger to her, proved to her angry father that she had been most comprehensively deceived."

"Awkward and, I dare say, quite mortifying. It seems young Mr Wickham has all the attributes and habits of some our more fashionable gentlemen, if not the income to support his claim to be of their ranks. I would venture to suggest that your family did not, in fact, do well for him and society by removing him from the sphere in which he should have been brought up."

"I do not disagree. What should have been an opportunity to better himself, has been his ruin."

"Yet you did not enlighten your father?"

"No. I cleared up after Wickham every time. I paid his debts, both at Cambridge and after, and I aided women like the grocer's daughter to find a place to begin a new life. My motive was to ensure my father did not see what his favourite had become. After my mother died, he took pleasure in very little. He had always been of a sober temperament, but he became morose and melancholic in his grief, and his health was indifferent. He delighted in Wickham's charm and humour, comforted by him in a way I could not emulate. He was proud of me, I believe, and trained me well to take up his responsibilities. But George was the one to make him smile and laugh. I could not take that from him. He died, still unaware how the charm of the snake hid the poison in the fangs."

Bennet nodded. "It can be hard to find the right way when duties conflict, and we fear to give pain. Still, it would have been better to have told your father the truth. He may have had the means that you did not, to pull the serpent's tooth."

"Perhaps. In truth, I was never sure he would believe me. I have not Wickham's charm."

"You appear to be honest to a fault. Any man of discernment and education should recognise that. However, it is in the past, and done with. Regrets are useless. Tell me of the living he claims your father left him."

"I have several valuable livings in my gift. The largest is that of Kympton, a parish very close to our home at Pemberley. My father's will instructed me to offer the parish to Wickham if he took orders, when it next became available. My father knew that he had done as much as any man could to give Wickham a grounding for a prosperous life by paying for his education, but he also left Wickham a clear one thousand pounds in token of his regard."

"Such a man as you describe? A cleric?"

Darcy agreed. "Exactly, sir. There are men enough in the church who have no calling other than that of their pocketbooks and their disinclination to work for their living, but to knowingly install such a reprobate... I could not do it with an easy conscience. Luckily, I was not required to do so. Wickham himself disclaimed any desire to enter the church, and on reading my father's will asked for monetary compensation if he resigned all rights to the living. He said he had a fancy to study the law. I hoped, rather than believed, him sincere, and after some negotiation, I gave him three thousand pounds in addition to my father's bequest. I have his signature on a deed that sets out these arrangements. I hoped I had seen the last of him."

"I take it that was a hope destined to remain unfulfilled?"

Darcy pushed the chair back with a sharp, angry energy, pushing himself up and striding to the window. He stared out at the marketplace, at the crowds bustling about down there with not thought for his troubles. And why should they? They doubtless had troubles of their own. "Wickham spent the money within a year or two. Gambling and Cyprians, and loose living of all kinds. The old incumbent at Kympton died some eighteen months ago. Wickham was at my door almost before the coffin lid was screwed shut, saying his position was very bad, he had changed his mind about taking orders, and wanted the living." Darcy turned back to face his guest and allowed a faint smile to appear. "Derbyshire breeds large men who make excellent footmen. Two of mine, neither of whom had much cause to love him, saw Wickham to the edge of Pemberley's grounds and, they told me, quite literally tossed him off them. He went, swearing his revenge."

"An unsavoury character, then. And the danger he represents to my daughter?"

"He is an undoubted fortune-hunter. He tried to elope with... with a young heiress of my acquaintance. A very young heiress, deceived by one hired as her companion. She was taken to holiday in Ramsgate, and Wickham followed. It became clear, later, that he and the companion were very good friends."

Mr Bennet grimaced. "I see."

"The young lady was persuaded by both Wickham and the companion to consider herself in love, and had her guardian not arrived unexpectedly in Ramsgate, was on the brink of eloping to Gretna. Had Wickham succeeded, he would have laid claim to her very considerable dowry and she would, I know, have been miserable and ill-treated. His revenge would have been complete indeed."

He and Bennet traded long stares, Bennet's expression one of comprehension and compassion. Darcy's earlier words of the mischief against his own family would have resonated.

"I need no more detail, Mr Darcy. Be assured I treat this entire discussion in confidence."

Darcy could only nod and mouth his thanks. He could not speak.

"I am to assume, then, that balked of one heiress, this lieutenant still seeks easy prey by which he can enrich himself? And of course, my Lizzy has Netherfield. It is a fine estate, and a worthless reprobate could make very merry all his life on more than three thousand a year." Bennet's sharp grey eyes sought Darcy's. "All this is in the letter?"

"Yes. I seek to ensure that she has enough intelligence of Wickham's life and motives to protect herself from him."

"I thank you." Bennet sat back, stroking his chin in meditative fashion, his eyes on the fire. "His proclivity for women... Need we fear for our other daughters?"

"His ambition has always been to marry high and make his fortune that way, so his women have generally been drawn from the professional doxies, or maidservants and the like. I never heard of his ruining a lady of quality. I believe he avoids entanglements with gentlemen's daughters to escape being hounded into marriage with a dowerless or poorly dowered girl. He cannot buy off or ignore a gentleman, as he might an innkeeper or a labourer."

"Entirely mercenary, then. That should protect my other girls since they have small dowries, though I will see what may be done to limit their contact with him. It is difficult, since the militia officers have become an integral part of the neighbourhood and they are popular with my wife and younger daughters, but I will make Longbourn less welcoming."

They were silent for a little while. Darcy stared into the flames for several minutes, wishing he had not been such an utter noddy that he had ruined all hopes of winning Elizabeth. When he looked up, Bennet was watching him, sharp eyes fixed on him.

"I will go directly to Lizzy this morning and deliver your letter. But first, is your friend Bingley likely to return?"

Darcy might have known he would not avoid the issue of Bingley entirely. "The business that drew him from here is most complex and difficult. He has gone to Yorkshire, and I do not expect to see him for many weeks."

"A leak in his canal, perhaps," was Bennet's sardonic comment. He stood, so abruptly that Darcy faltered through a moment of confusion before getting to his feet. "Well, it is always the way of young men, to be hurrying about on business, and I should emulate them and depart to deal with mine. I shall take the letter."

He picked it up and weighed it in his hand. The quality of his smile puzzled Darcy. Sardonic, yes, but there was something of regret in it. Darcy, taking on the unaccustomed role of valet, picked up the greatcoat Bennet had flung over the bed on his arrival.

"I thank you," Bennet said, as Darcy helped him into the greatcoat, "both for this office, and for your honesty in talking to me. While I regret Lizzy's distress, for my own part I can understand your reasoning. Not condone it, mind you, but I do understand." Bennet tucked the letter into the inner pocket of his morning coat, and buttoned the outer coat tightly over his chest. "I have done you the courtesy of not enquiring too closely into the circumstances in which your discussion with my Lizzy took on a contumacious note, and in return I ask one of you. She deserves some peace. Grant her that."

Something invisible had a chokehold on Darcy, but he forced himself to nod. "I wish for nothing but her health and happiness, sir. I will do anything to secure it."

Bennet smiled and shook hands heartily. "Do you know, I believe you would." He opened the door and paused on the threshold. "A benediction, you said earlier? Then I shall add my own. Remember what I said about your besetting sin. Think on that, then go and sin no more. You will find life more pleasant, if you do."

He closed the door behind him.

For the second time in less than a day, Darcy rested his brow against the hard oak door and wished, mightily, to bang his thick head upon it. He had done all he could. Now he had to depend upon her good sense to protect her.

Time to go home. If he left immediately, he could be with the Fitzwilliams and Georgiana by nightfall. And after Christmas they would go to Pemberley, where he would find his own peace.

I could never be tempted to accept an offer from you. Never!

CHAPTER THIRTY-FOUR

More Contrarieties

Elizabeth was alone in the morning room when her father arrived, Mary having already claimed the piano in the drawing room. The sound of scales rippled through the house, mercifully muted by two closed doors.

"You are about very early, Papa. Have you breakfasted?"

"I have had coffee, at least." Her father took a thick letter from his pocket and offered it. "I saw Darcy this morning at the inn, and undertook to deliver this to you. I have a notion it will explain the man to you better than his own performance amongst us permitted. Certainly my discussion with him today revealed him more than I had expected." And when she drew back her hand, Papa caught it and pressed the letter into it. "Do not be missish, Lizzy! I suspect he sat up half the night unburdening himself in cheap ink and parchment. The least you might do to mark his endeavour, is to read it."

"Have you?"

"Certainly not. It is addressed to you, is it not? I have discussed with him some part of it at least, although I do not know the whole. Nor do I wish to know it." Papa gave her his most knowing look, and glanced at the clock on the mantel. "I am going to the bookshop for an hour. When I return, we must discuss the part of the letter that Mr Darcy and I touched on this morning."

Elizabeth wrinkled her nose at the paper, taking in the superscription and the strong strokes of the pen he had used to limn out her name. Miss Bingley had admired his writing, she recalled. It was a good hand, clear and determined-looking.

"I do not often require your obedience, but this time I will. And yes," Papa added as she raised her face to glower at him, "I am very aware that legally I no longer have the authority to do so, but you and I have always been of a like mind and I ask this of you for your own sake. Read it carefully, be open to revising some of your previous impressions and prejudices, and weigh each word. You are a clever woman, Lizzy. I expect you to prove it."

With that he stooped over her and kissed her on the brow, before leaving as precipitously as he had arrived.

Elizabeth turned the letter in her hands. The seal was thick and large, the crest—the Darcy arms, no doubt—clearly impressed into the red wax. She slid her forefinger under the flap and broke the seal with a sharp flick. The sheets, unfolded, were covered front and back. Her father was right. Darcy must have spent half the night on this.

She flattened out the sheets.

"Be not alarmed, madam, on receiving this letter, by the apprehension of its containing any repetition of those sentiments or renewal of those offers which were so disgusting to you. I write without any intention of paining you, or humbling myself..."

The first reading left her breathless.

If the opening lines had reassured her that he would not address her again, the remainder of the letter harrowed her. She had not, indeed, expected it to contain a renewal of his offer the previous day—no man would be so facile!—but she had been right in believing he would excuse his conduct. She was already satisfied with his reasons regarding James, and the part he played in Matthew Grayson's actions against her. Did he, then, hope to placate her ire regarding his interference with Jane?

"I had not been long in Hertfordshire, before I saw, in common with others, that Bingley preferred your elder sister…"

She read on, intent on gleaning every word, barely drawing breath in her eagerness. His first contention, that he believed Jane to be indifferent, had her snorting her derision as to his powers of perception, and giving the close-written papers in her hand an admonitory shake. She jumped up from her seat and walked swiftly about the room, needing the suddenness of movement to stop her shouting aloud at the image of Mr Darcy standing before her with the reins of his horse looped over his arm and the shock of her refusal writ all over his face.

"Indeed! 'No participation of sentiment'! My poor Jane did not perform well enough to your liking, I am to suppose! Who are *you*, that you dare set yourself up in judgement? And is Mr Bingley so bereft of sense that he could not see her inclination for himself? Hateful man!"

It was an effort to keep her voice low, to make sure Mary did not hear her. Not that she truly feared it, as Mary had launched into a difficult piece by Mozart, but Elizabeth would not risk her sister's attention being caught by her ranting like the veriest fishwife just at the moment Mozart, most inconsiderately, demanded his music be played *pianissimo*.

She had thrown herself down into her chair again, when Charlotte's voice sounded in her memory. What was it Charlotte had said? Something about Jane being too reserved and guarded to show her feelings.

"And what if she is? Cannot one sister be a true lady, without that being held to her discredit? Jane is reserved. She is quiet. She is not made in Mama's image." Elizabeth let out her breath in a long sigh, blinked away the sudden stinging in her eyes, and raised the letter again.

Heat burned her face and curled its shamed fingers around her chest at his account of what must be the real objections to the match. She read the damning paragraphs twice, returned the letter to its precise folds and placed it on the small table at her right hand. It was not quite straight. She twitched it into place, its long edge flush with the edge of the table. The blood-red seal stared up at her, the jagged line where she had broken it showing as a deep ravine across its smug face. She had cracked it in the exact centre of the Darcy crest. Good.

How long had she closed her eyes to her family's poor behaviour? Jane was beyond reproach, but the rest all pained and mortified her, even her father on occasion. Darcy could not but see how unrestrained her mother was; how wild and uncontrolled the behaviour of Lydia and Kitty. Neither should be out of the schoolroom, romping about with such restless energy that she feared for the family's good name. Mary... poor Mary's behaviour was of a different kind. She was too desperate to be noticed, to be esteemed for her learning and have people see her the way she was never seen at home. And Papa merely laughed at them all, and did nothing. He saw how improper they all were, how indecorous, but he did nothing. Darcy had seen that too.

Much as she tried to tell herself Darcy's haughty writing was all pride and insolence, it bit at her, worrying at her like a dog snarling over a bone. Her family was ridiculous. They were improper. They humiliated her, even as she loved them. Her face burned again with the remembrance of the Netherfield ball. Dear heavens, one would think they had sat down together and plotted it out. "How can we disgrace Jane and Lizzy the most?" they might have said. "Let us be loud, coarse and unrefined. Let us show those superior Bingleys just what delights will brought by a union between our families!"

Jane owed her heartache to her own mother's lack of restraint and proper dignity, to the wildness of her younger sisters, Mary's pedantry and their father's indolence.

Not that Elizabeth was guiltless either. She had always skirted the edge of decorum when jousting with Miss Bingley. She had shown nothing of her own quality, then.

Or perhaps she had, and her own quality was little better than her mother's.

"Of course Mama is unrestrained and nervous," Elizabeth told Mr Darcy's image. "You are lucky! You are a man. Should you lose everything, as Mama fears she will one day, you have the education and the right to work to raise yourself again. What opportunity do we women have for that same right, subjugated and denigrated as we are, counted as naught in the world of men? If she is over-anxious to marry her daughters to men who can support them, who can blame her for that?"

You did yourself, said the voice of her conscience. *You do blame her.*

Mama had been quick to cry loudly about the shame and the scandal when James had attacked Elizabeth, and saw the compromise as heaven-sent to establish at least one of her daughters in security. She would not listen to pleas to desist, determined not to waste the opportunity. One fewer daughter to concern herself about if she was left with nothing. If the security she sought for her daughter was illusory... well, perhaps Mama should have known, but she was hardly noted for deep thinking.

Poor Jane. She, too, had paid the price for their mother's anxiety for the future.

Elizabeth dashed the back of her hand against her eyes, and picked up the letter. She had read barely half. She would not return to the mortifying sentences about her family, not yet, but press on to the end. Oh. Mr Wickham...

Well, let us see what Mr Darcy has to say for himself in that regard!

"...Mr Wickham is the son of a very respectable man, who had for many years the management of all the Pemberley estates, and whose good conduct in the discharge of his trust naturally inclined my father to be of service to him; and on George Wickham, who was his godson, his kindness was therefore liberally bestowed... My sister, who is more than ten years my junior... she was taken

from school... to Ramsgate; and thither also went Mr Wickham, undoubtedly by design.... he so far recommended himself to Georgiana... that she was persuaded to believe herself in love, and to consent to an elopement. She was then but fifteen..."

Oh, dear heavens. It could not be true. It had to be the grossest falsehood! But no man, not even the greatest villain, would traduce his own sister in such a fashion. It must be true. It must. The connection with the Darcy family... just what Mr Wickham had related himself, but the two accounts of the will...

"Wills are not so easily set aside," her father had said only the previous day, "and nor did anyone other than you know of this while Mr Darcy was here to refute it."

True, on both counts. Her father was right. If Mr Darcy's account was correct, then Wickham had lied about the conditions upon which the living was to be his. Lied! What is more, Wickham had said his loving memories and thankfulness would prevent him shaming his patron's son publicly and yet almost the instant Mr Darcy had left Netherfield, the story of the Kympton living was known everywhere. And Miss Darcy? The girl Wickham had said was as proud and as cold as her brother?

"She was then but fifteen."

Fifteen! A girl of Lydia's age, with such a man laying siege to her childish heart, a man of such extravagance and profligacy. A charming man. He had charmed Elizabeth, too. He had known just what to say, had he not, to confirm her prejudices against Mr Darcy, and she had been a blind fool, allowing his countenance and manner to beguile her into believing that he had all the virtues, and that Mr Darcy was a dishonest, dishonourable villain.

Why was it only now that she could see the impropriety of Wickham's conduct in telling her this tale on their first meeting?

And the impropriety of her own conduct, in listening so eagerly. Lydia could not have welcomed ill-natured gossip with more satisfaction!

"What a ridiculous creature you are, Elizabeth Grayson! Prejudiced, credulous, improper, silly, and absurd! How Wickham must be laughing at you!"

Well, he would laugh no longer. She would see to that.

"Good. You are as calm as I hoped you would be." Papa paused, tilted his head at the sound of Mary's playing in the distance. "And Mary, I hear, is still engaged in pounding Herr Beethoven into submission—"

"Mozart."

"One Teutonic musician is much the same as another." He nodded to the letter in her lap. "We must discuss Wickham."

"A fortune-hunter. Mr Darcy suggests Wickham wants Netherfield."

"Do you think so?"

"I have thought about little else for the last half hour. Yes. If this is to be believed"—she raised the letter—"and I do believe it, then nothing Wickham has said and done here in Meryton has been in earnest, but in pursuit of a fortune. My fortune."

"I agree. I am glad of this warning from Darcy. You are on guard now, and immune to Wickham's blandishments, I hope."

"I always was. I found him a charming and entertaining companion whenever we spoke, but no more than that."

"Good. However, he is likely to be keenly attuned to how his overtures are met, and will notice immediately any change in your manner."

"I have already been a little cooler towards him. He started making sentimental hints, and I wished to depress any ambitions he might have."

"Then you must be careful never to be caught alone by him. No more solitary walks. No walks even with Mary, because she will be no defence. I have spoken with Rance. He will accompany you everywhere from now on, and ensure you are safe." Papa's face was grey, and his age showed in every line and droop of his eyelids and the corners of his mouth. "I would be happier with you at Longbourn. Come now. The Gardiners arrive later today, and you know you always enjoy your aunt's company."

Elizabeth had not planned to remove from her own home until after the Christmas Eve service at church, three days hence. But perhaps her father was right. She would be much at Longbourn, in any event, to join the family party as they prepared for the festivities.

"I have no engagements before Christmas Eve except those with our family... Very well. I will speak to Mary, and we will come today. As for after Christmas, I agree that taking Thomas with me everywhere will afford a good measure of protection. What are we to do about everyone else, Papa? That such a man lives amongst us, and they are unaware... we cannot allow that. The shopkeepers and merchants cannot afford large debts. And many have daughters."

Her father smiled. "Do you think us all so negligent, Lizzy? As soon as we heard about the coming of the militia, Mr Harpur called a meeting at the old Guildhall. The magistrates and gentry reminded the good people of Meryton that 'militia officer' is as fine a synonym for 'impecunious debtor' as might be imagined, and that many of them were all too apt to use their red coats to dazzle silly girls into indiscretion. Of course, we knew nothing then of Wickham in particular, but he is little different to the generality of officers. A sensible shopkeeper will not allow any officer to owe him more than a pound or two and will keep his daughters under tight control. We cannot mandate every man take sufficient pains, however. That there is some debt, I do not doubt, and nor, sorry as I am to say it, do I think every girl in the neighbourhood is safe from presenting their family with an unexpected visitor. We did what we could to warn them."

Elizabeth hesitated, chewing on her lower lip.

"Out with it."

"Lydia, Papa. She is charmed by Wickham and thinks of nothing but officers. Her whole head is full of them. Flirting and dancing with them, being their favourite. She thinks she is the toast of the regiment. Her behaviour is shocking, sir. She is improper, unrefined, loud and... and vulgar. All wild volatility and disdain of restraint... she brings contempt, ridicule and censure upon us all."

Papa cocked an eye at the letter on her lap. "Ah, Lizzy. I must guess at the content of the rest of your letter, then. Chased away the gentleman, has she?"

"You are mistaken in thinking I have any particular offences to resent. I speak of generalities. If you do not check her, Papa, she will be the ruin of us. She should not be out in society. Nor Kitty, who follows her lead."

"Well, that djinn cannot be returned to its lamp. But, you know, you and Jane are respected wherever you go, and appear to advantage against two or three very silly sisters. I think I have done enough. I intend to curtail the appearance of officers at Longbourn, but in truth, Lizzy, you are his target. We have but just agreed that Wickham seeks a fortune. I do not think the thousand pounds Lydia shall have at your mother's death and whatever you have added to it—yes, yes, I know that is what you are doing, and it shames me that you feel you must do so at all. But she has so little in fortune she cannot be of any real interest to Wickham or any of the officers except, as you say yourself, for a little flirting and dancing. They will take no real notice of her. They will be gone again in a few months, and she will be forgotten. That may teach her how insignificant she truly is."

"Or may make her wilder yet." Elizabeth shook her head, and said no more.

She wished she could be as sanguine as her father, but in truth she expected no more of him. It was rather astonishing that he had bestirred himself so much as to meet with Mr Darcy so early in the morning. It was mordantly amusing, in a very faint way, that he was full of the advice he and the other landowners had given the Meryton merchants, but would not follow it himself.

CHAPTER THIRTY-FIVE

Frogge Would a-Wooing Ride

"Until I read his letter, and meditated upon it, I never knew myself." Elizabeth dropped into the chair in Jane's bedroom. "Good Lord, what was I thinking? Mr Darcy wounded my vanity, and so naturally had not one good quality to recommend him and I was perfectly justified in taking so decided a dislike to him. I told myself that every look of his, every intense stare, was to catalogue my faults and deficiencies. I thought him superior and disdainful, believing himself to be far above us. I allowed him few virtues, he could do only wrong in my eyes, and I admit I amused myself being witty with him and about him. Wickham flattered and fawned, and made a show of admiration, and so I listened to his tale and believed even more ill of Mr Darcy, with no thought in my shatter-brained head of how improper we both were to discuss such a thing on first meeting. What a shallow, affected creature I am, with no more intelligent reasoning than... than Mr Collins! I am heartily ashamed of myself."

"Indeed you are not shallow. Mr Darcy was most at fault in wounding you as he did, both in the lesser offence at the Assembly and in deceiving you in his interest regarding your husband." This, from Jane, was as damning a point as she could ever make.

"Yes. He has faults. They are, it seems, merely balanced by my own."

"Though I am sorry for him, as he must have been gravely affected by your refusal. To love you so! It is a great compliment, Lizzy."

"Yes. I suppose it is. He is a very eligible gentleman."

"Do you regret refusing him?"

Elizabeth straightened so quickly the chair squeaked back a few inches on the polished floorboards. "No! No, I do not... at least, not that I refused him, but I do wish I had refused him with less rancour and more civility. That was very ill done of me." She looked into Jane's patient, sweet face. She had said, and would say, nothing of Mr Darcy's communication in respect of Jane and Bingley, though she had reluctantly accepted Darcy's contention that Jane showed little of her feelings. That was certainly true for Jane's public face. But now, in private where Jane could be herself without restriction, seeing her thinner and a little careworn, with lines of patience and suffering around her eyes, stiffened Elizabeth's spine. "He was insulting. He made it clear that any union with me, with our family, would be a degradation. He was most severe upon our family."

Jane closed her eyes and breathed out a soft sigh. "Their behaviour is a little unmoderated at times—"

"It is appalling. Often. But is a loud cheerfulness and a determination to enjoy oneself truly more indecent than a superiority that disdains others, even when all they have done is offer hospitality, friendship and welcome? Oh, no more of it. It is done. He is gone. We shall not meet again."

"Mr Wickham remains."

"Yes, though I am warned of his perfidy and can protect myself."

"What of our neighbours? They are unaware of having such a man amongst them. But to reveal him to their censure... if he is trying to make a new life, I would not make him desperate."

No. A desperate Wickham would be a danger indeed.

"Papa is confident that the precautions all the gentlemen in the district took when they learned the militia were coming should be sufficient. They warned the shopkeepers and merchants, too, that they must be careful where the militia were concerned. To single Mr Wickham out... no. Mr Darcy has not authorised us to make his side of the tale public, and I would not breach his confidence. I would not do so now, but you have always kept my secrets. I will be careful to keep Wickham at a distance. The militia will be gone in the spring." Elizabeth took both of Jane's hands in hers and pressed them. "But enough of me! How are you? You look tired."

"Which is to say, I look fagged to death!"

"No. You are beautiful, even when your eyes are sad and your mouth turns down just so..." Elizabeth freed one hand and pressed a finger gently to the corner of Jane's mouth, pushing it upward to make her smile.

But Jane did not laugh. "I have heard again from Caroline Bingley. I wrote to her a few days after they left, to thank her for her letter and to wish her and all her family the compliments of the season. Her answer arrived yesterday. It seems Mr Bingley is much engaged with Mr and Miss Darcy. So much so, she says, that she barely sees him. She says he seems very content, and she is ever more hopeful of a happy outcome for both families."

"She is lying."

"Lizzy!"

"Jane, that letter is falsehood from beginning to end, particularly if she began it with 'Dear Jane' and ended it with 'Yours, Caroline'. Mr Darcy told me yesterday that he had seen little of his friend, and that the business that took Mr Bingley so precipitously from Netherfield has called him north to Yorkshire, where he is likely to remain for some weeks. He has not been entertaining himself in Town in Mr and Miss Darcy's company. Mr Darcy was quite clear on that head. Miss Bingley is false, Jane. Quite false. Do not trust her."

"Why would she be so deceitful?"

"Because she sees that Mr Bingley loves you. She must be delighted he is gone to Yorkshire, and her intent is to keep him away from Netherfield and persuade you that he does not care for you. I do not doubt his affection. I told you once that we are not grand enough for Miss Bingley, even though we are gentry and she is not, and I own Netherfield while her brother remains unlanded. Do not despair. Though we cannot know when his business in the north is concluded, I do not think Mr Bingley will forget you."

Jane pressed her lips together, but she looked brighter and more hopeful. Before she could speak, the sound of a joyful arrival came from the rooms below. Mama's greetings rang out loudly, drowned in a moment by Lydia's demands about presents from London.

"The Gardiners are here." Elizabeth sprang up, woes forgotten for the moment. "Come, let us go and greet them. The sooner that is over, the sooner we can have Aunt Gardiner to ourselves and seek her wise advice. Other than you, my Jane, there is no one I would sooner confide in!"

Although not, of course, about everything.

As always, Longbourn turned inward for the last two or three days before Christmas, this closing of ranks happening as soon as the Gardiners had arrived on Saturday evening and the Phillipses came from Meryton to join the party for dinner and to stay until the holiday was over. Longbourn strained at the seams with so many extra guests but the Gardiners were lively, intelligent company, a surfeit in themselves, and the Phillipses were always cheerful and obliging. The manor rang with happy voices, gossip and good cheer.

Everyone settled in for a few days of merriment without the need for company manners or the fatigue of entertaining outside the immediate family. After Christmas Day, Meryton's delights would prove too great a draw again, and the combined family party would be convivial at many of the celebrations held in the district until it was time for the Gardiners to return to Gracechurch Street after Twelfth Night. Until Christmas Day, however, they saw no company. Even Lydia was happy to spend Sunday after church talking about fashions with her stylish and sophisticated Aunt Gardiner or playing with her little cousins in the new-fallen snow in the garden, though it was not to be expected that her complaisance would last much beyond that.

Nor did it. On Monday, the day before Christmas Eve, an excited Lydia ushered guests into the drawing room. Most of the ladies of the party were sitting around the fire occupying themselves with stitching and chat, the gentleman having decamped to Mr Bennet's book room with the port bottle. Lydia and Kitty had been romping around the garden with the Gardiner children, Lydia said—although she expressed it as "overseeing their play"—when "Look! Our friends the officers have come to bid us the compliments of the season! Is this not a pleasant surprise?"

She tugged Wickham into the room, followed by her usual entourage of red-coated officers: Captain Carter, and Lieutenants Denny, Chamberlayne and Pratt. Kitty trailed in behind.

The officers were met with blank stares, the surprise Lydia heralded not being so pleasant for those who cherished their few days of insular, familial celebrations. Even Mama took a moment to rally and welcome her visitors. The ladies rose and dropped curtsies. The five young men bowed, and in a moment more, four of them were herded by Lydia into a corner where the number of chairs precluded Kitty joining them. Kitty stood irresolute near the door, flushed to the same scarlet as her cloak, and her mouth turning down.

Wickham came straight to Elizabeth. "My dear Miss Elizabeth! It has been all too many days since we last met!"

Elizabeth resumed her seat beside Aunt Gardiner, laying her book on the table at her left hand. There was no room for Mr Wickham on the small sofa, and he was, perforce, made to stand on the hearthrug where he successfully blocked the warmth of the fire. Perhaps that contributed to the slight chill in Elizabeth's tone. "A mere three days, I believe, sir. Last Friday, at Miss Lucas's wedding. Had you forgotten?"

Wickham laughed, but as one who was not quite certain how his sally appeared to have gone awry. "It seems much longer, I enjoy your company so well. Are you in good health? You look blooming!"

"Very much so, sir. I thank you." And at her aunt's requesting it, she made the introductions. "Allow me to present Lieutenant Wickham to your acquaintance, ma'am. Mr Wickham, this is Mrs Gardiner, our aunt from London. You two have much in common. Mr Wickham is also from Derbyshire, Aunt. In truth, from Pemberley, which is Mr Darcy's estate, you know."

"I do indeed know," Mrs Gardiner said in her usual pleasant tone, inclining her head in answer to Wickham's elaborate bow. "I spent my early years in Lambton. You must know the town, sir, since Pemberley cannot be five miles distant."

Another of those odd, not-quite-at-his-ease laughs. "I know Lambton very well."

Elizabeth squeezed her aunt's hand lightly. "Then I shall allow you two exiles to reminisce with each other!" She jumped up and waved a hand to her vacated seat. "Mr Wickham, please be seated. My aunt, I know, will welcome any intelligence of her home town, and you may have a comfortable coze together talking of mutual acquaintances and exchanging Lambton news."

Wickham could not have looked more astonished if she had tapped him briskly on the nose, the way she would a recalcitrant puppy. He could not escape the conversation without offering grave offence, and giving her an intense, almost betrayed, look, he smiled thinly at Mrs Gardiner and took the offered seat. Mrs Gardiner gave Elizabeth a sidelong glance from under tip-tilted brows.

"Excellent," said Elizabeth, relishing the moment of warmth against her legs now Mr Wickham was no longer acting as a fire screen. "Excuse me. Kitty..."

She contrived to be busy for the next quarter of an hour, whisking Kitty into the hall and helping her out of the damp red cloak, and listening to a fulminating, if whispered, tirade against "Lydia's selfish, greedy, downright *hoggishness* in keeping all the officers to herself even though she knows I like Captain Carter! She will look like a silly pig in five years, too," finished sylph-like

Kitty, dashing the tears from her eyes and stamping her foot. "She eats too many sweet things. She is bursting out of her dresses right now."

Elizabeth considered the bursting to be deliberate and confined to Lydia's upper chest, but did not say so. There was little point, since their mother would never insist on more modest manners. Instead, she winked at Kitty and returned her to the drawing room. Wickham brightened visibly, straightening up and beaming at her, but Elizabeth allowed her gaze to travel over him with no more acknowledgment than a nod and a faint smile. Ignoring his wounded expression, she marched Kitty to the corner where Lydia and the other officers sat. The men, of course, leapt to their feet, and she and Kitty took the seats despite Lydia's glares and huffs.

A few moments of inconsequential chat, and she excused herself again, manoeuvring matters to have Captain Carter sit beside Kitty. Lydia huffed again and folded her arms under her ample bosom, which combined with a heaving intake of breath, was calculated to draw the attention of any blind man in the room who may have missed having her charms thrust into his face. Pratt reddened, Chamberlayne choked, and Denny's eyes popped. Kitty and Captain Carter, however, took no notice. They were engaging in shy conversation when Elizabeth took herself off again to find her father and uncles.

"Goodness, being both careful and nonchalant is exhausting. The officers are here, Papa, and have been for some minutes." She glanced at the clock on the mantel. "The allotted time for a morning call is almost over. Perhaps you gentlemen would care to speed the officers on their way? I do not doubt that they have plans for festive merrymaking that they will wish to pursue."

Her father lowered his book peered at her over it. "Wickham?"

Elizabeth nodded. "He was, he suggests, pining." She looked apologetically at Mr Gardiner. "I foisted him off onto Aunt Gardiner. I will apologise for that as soon as may be."

Uncle Gardiner looked as if he were smelling something most unpleasant. "Your father told us of the man, Lizzy, and the service rendered us by the intelligence of him provided by Mr Darcy. We will come with you, Bennet."

"Let us all go." Elizabeth hooked her arm through that of Uncle Phillips, and allowed the other two to precede them. "I have a small commission for you, Uncle, when the holiday is finished."

He tilted his head to one side. His eyes were bright with the intelligence he masked behind the port-red nose. "Regarding Wickham?"

She had time only to nod before they reached the drawing room. The rest must wait until they had more privacy. Uncle Phillips made a little gesture of understanding with one hand, and went to join his wife. Elizabeth remained near the door where Uncle Gardiner had awaited her, watching as Papa cheerfully sent the young officers on their way. His voice said much about the social demands of the season and that he could not be selfish in keeping them there when he considered how many friends the officers must have yet to visit, while what everyone really heard was the steel-hard message that *this is not the time and place for you, gentlemen, and I wish you gone.* They were military men—of sorts. The song of the steel was unmistakable even to their ears.

Elizabeth smiled brightly and returned farewells and hearty expressions of good will as the five young officers filed past her and Uncle Gardiner, who stood at her side. Captain Carter went with a regretful look and smile for Kitty; the regretful glances from Denny, Chamberlayne and Pratt were for Lydia's assets.

Wickham paused by Elizabeth. "I am sorry we had no opportunity to speak together, Miss Elizabeth."

"This is an exacting time, with so many of my family here and requiring my attention. I am sure you understand."

"Of course." He bowed over her hand, and before she could prevent it, he raised it to his lips, his eyes twinkling at her. "Merry Christmas, my dear Miss Elizabeth."

She kept her smile faint and withdrew her hand, and looked past him to encompass the other officers. "And to you all. Farewell, gentlemen."

Another wounded look, as if he were stricken to the heart, and finally they were gone. Hill closed the door on them.

"You could fuel oil lamps with that charm," was Uncle Gardiner's trenchant comment.

Uncle Phillips looked as a man might, whose last bottle of wine was corked. Papa had words with a sulky and unrepentant Lydia about the sacrosanct nature of a Bennet family Christmas, while Mama and Aunt Phillips fluttered about how handsome and obliging all the officers were, how gentlemanly and "Goodness, sister, does it not remind you of Colonel Miller's regiment when we were girls? I like a redcoat still, I do confess!"

Uncles Phillips and Gardiner went with Elizabeth to the book room.

"Your father told us you had been warned of that lieutenant's fortune-hunting history. Is he always so obviously frog-a-wooing?" Uncle Gardiner asked.

"No, indeed, this is rather new behaviour."

"I cannot like it, Lizzy."

"Nor I. He has been an entertaining, but undemanding, acquaintance until recently. He has not claimed my attention beyond that I would accord any friend—John Lucas, perhaps. But unlike John, these last two or three times we have met, he has, as you saw, tried more overtly to engage my interest."

"You have none, I hope?"

"I am no Miss Mouse, even if Mr Darcy had not taken pains to warn us of Mr Wickham's insalubrious past."

"He is practised enough at this, then, to have a little subtlety. He has taken the time—several weeks now, I think?—to worm his way into your confidence with a seeming honour and honesty, and only now shows his hand."

"As I reflect on it, sir, that is my conclusion too." Elizabeth turned to her other uncle, who stood on the hearthrug, back to fire, his coat tails over his arms as he warmed himself. "Which brings me to the favour I would ask of you, Uncle Phillips. Would you make discreet enquiries with the Meryton merchants and inns, and perhaps in some of the neighbouring towns also? If Mr Darcy has convinced me of one thing, it is that the lieutenant will have debts wherever he can wheedle them. I would not have anyone learn of your actions, as he would then be alerted to them. But I need a tally of his debts, and for you to buy them on my behalf."

Uncle Phillips nodded. "Excellent idea, Lizzy, and I will keep your confidence, never fear. Do you put a limit on expenditure to obtain the debts? You have had a great deal of expense this year with the repairs to Nether House and you will not want to overreach."

Elizabeth had indeed had a great deal of expense. The repairs had bitten hard into the money she gave Mr Gardiner each year to invest and thus enhance her sisters' meagre dowries and support her mother in her widowhood, should it come to it. There would be no profit this year from leasing Netherfield to the Bingleys: every last penny had gone on roof tiles and new chimneys. Her own expenditure would need to be curtailed, if she were to continue the investments.

Yet she shook her head against the thought of moderation. "No. Buy them all, no matter the cost. I need a sharp weapon to defend myself if need be, a weapon even a militia man might fear."

Uncle Gardiner said, smiling, "I do not doubt you will have him quailing, Lizzy."

"That is my intention, Uncle. If I must, I will bring him to his knees." She laughed. "But very definitely not in the romantic pose he fancies."

Poor Frog. It was a sad old song, really. His wooing was always doomed.

CHAPTER THIRTY-SIX

When We Are Led Astray

Christmas Day began with morning service at Longbourn church. The extended Bennet family party filled almost half of the cantoris side of the nave, clustered beneath the pulpit, with the Lucases on the decani side beneath the lectern.

It was the sheer number of people that prevented Elizabeth seeing Wickham. His bright military uniform might have stood out against the sober clothing of the gentlemen there, but the remainder of the church was crowded with tenants and their families, all in their most colourful finery for one of the most important services of the year. A redcoat was less noticeable in such a motley crowd.

She was taken aback, therefore, to walk out of the church at the end of the service, her arm tucked through Jane's and her mind dwelling pleasurably on the midday feast awaiting them at home, to find the lieutenant waiting for her. His dazzling smile and quite blatantly sentimental expression were, she considered, an affront to her intelligence.

Although, perhaps, one she deserved, considering her previous partiality and blindness.

"Mr Wickham! I am all astonishment."

He bowed over her hand, and appeared reluctant to relinquish it. She had to tug it away quite sharply. His expression flickered, the languishing look he evidently intended her to see as admiration, showing an instant of annoyance and chagrin. "I could not resist the chance to wish you a merry Christmas—"

"Again, sir? You did so on Monday." She tempered her sharpness with a slight smile. If the man had the intelligence of a halfwit, he must see its mockery. "I begin to think your powers are failing you, Mr Wickham. You are displaying a shockingly poor memory! I do not doubt that if this progresses, you will not recognise me at all this time next week."

He affected a laugh that did not quite ring true. "You are uniformly charming, Miss Elizabeth! I recall very well... I recall all of our meetings with the greatest of pleasure, you know. I walked out from Meryton today for this chance." He paused, as if waiting for her response.

"That is kind of you," she said, glancing around. Where were her father and uncles?

Seeing the look she was casting about, Aunt Gardiner, who had just left the church porch, came at once. Mr Wickham apparently remembered enough of his manners to greet Aunt Gardiner and Jane, using all his false charm. She watched him with eyes unfettered now by partiality. His was a handsome face, the kind many women would find enough to flutter their hearts and spirits. But where once she had seen an expression of goodness in his countenance, now she looked more closely she fancied she saw the signs of moral weakness and pleasure-seeking selfishness in the chin and thin-lipped mouth, and the eyes that calculated everything to see how he might turn events to his advantage. His mouth smiled; his pleasant voice soothed; his eyes were cool and watchful. He was ingratiatingly flattering to Aunt Gardiner, simpering and smirking and casting many a sidelong look at Elizabeth, accompanied by little smiles and nods, as though to gauge the impact of his charm of manner.

"Did you enjoy the service, sir?" Aunt Gardiner asked.

"Very much. The vicar has a great simplicity and speaks most clearly of the blessing of the day. It was most enlightening." He turned to Elizabeth and the polite smile he had given Aunt Gardiner was increased. The performance of moonstruck lover could hardly be bettered on the London stage.

Mr Wickham had yet to discover that two could play at acting games.

Elizabeth widened her eyes and softened her smile. "Did you wish yourself in his place? You have taken orders, I believe."

Wickham's expression changed on the instant. His jaw dropped a fraction, and it was a moment before he chuffed out a short laugh. "Well, I have my degree, Miss Elizabeth."

"But you are not ordained? Heavens, I must have misunderstood! I thought, from your confidences to me that you had expected the living at... where was it now? Kimble?"

"Kympton," he said, his practised smile fading.

"Yes, of course. Kympton. But surely only a man who had satisfied his bishop as to his suitability for orders can take a parish. My cousin Collins—who is, you know, a rector in Kent—told me that he also had to serve a year as deacon before he was deemed ordained. If you have not done so, I cannot see how you could take the living you say old Mr Darcy wished you to have."

There. Let practised charm meet blithe innocence, and see which prevailed.

His cheekbones flushed a deeper colour, but he should have controlled himself better, to avoid that little grimace he made. "I... In the end, when I knew that the current Mr Darcy would not offer me the living, there was little inducement for me to continue on that course..."

"Oh, that must have been a disappointment! Perhaps you should have considered some alternative as a career where a diligent man may work to raise himself in dignity and honours. The law, perhaps?"

His expression now was not so tender and loving. "I... I..."

"Mr Wickham." Papa appeared behind him. "Good day to you, sir. Your piety must be great indeed to walk over a mile in this biting winter wind to listen to a Christmas sermon here in Longbourn."

Wickham broke the gaze in which Elizabeth had held him. "No, indeed, sir. It was nothing. I came to wish my dear friends the best compliments of the season."

"Very kind of you, Lieutenant." Papa did not so much as grimace as the rest of their party left the church, and Lydia indicated that she had perceived Mr Wickham by emitting a squeal that had all the rooks launching up from their bare-leaved trees to wheel around the churchyard in alarm. "We return the sentiment, of course."

"Excuse me," Jane said, demure as ever, and disengaging herself from Elizabeth, went swiftly to prevent their sister from further auditory expressions of delight. She passed their uncles en route, both walking with determination to join Papa.

"Well, you must excuse us, Lieutenant." Papa nodded a dismissal. "We are for the warmth of home and our Christmas repast with our family."

"Oh. Oh, of course, sir." Wickham looked expectantly from Papa to Elizabeth.

Good Lord, was he expecting an invitation? Elizabeth continued to smile, though her cheeks ached with the effort. "You will have a long walk back to your lodgings, Mr Wickham."

"Yes." He tried one of his melting, tender looks, belied by the glitter of his eyes. "It was worth it to greet you."

"You are most kind. I hope you and the other officers have a cheerful time today." She dropped a curtsey. "Have a merry Christmas, Lieutenant."

She hooked one arm through her aunt's and the other through her uncle Gardiner's, and left Wickham standing before the church. She was careful not to look back, but for all that, she thought he watched her down the short lane until she turned into Longbourn's courtyard gate, and she was out of his sight.

"I am beginning to think I should have gone to London with Jane and the Gardiners," Elizabeth muttered.

For the second day in succession since the Gardiners had left after Twelfth Night and she had returned with her household to Nether House, she was accosted by Mr Wickham as she walked in Meryton. It was tiresome.

Thomas Rance, who was never more than five feet away from her, turned his head to watch Wickham cross the marketplace after calling after her, and moved a little closer still. "Ma'am?"

"Stay close, but do not intervene unless I ask it. I do not want a public spectacle."

The day before, she had been rescued by Captain Carter, who had been looking for an officer for some military task or other and had come upon them just as they were exchanging awkward greetings. He had bowed, sent Wickham off about whatever business he should have been undertaking, and spent a few moments in half-distracted chat before hurrying after the lieutenant. Wickham had not left with such alacrity, it must be said. He had trailed away with many a backward, languishing look to convey his reluctance to leave. Elizabeth pretended not to see them.

Sadly, Captain Carter was not in evidence that day. She was forced by common courtesy to acknowledge Wickham, with no great hope of immediate relief from his attentions. Ladies were severely disadvantaged by being raised always to be the epitome of gracious civility. It was supposed to be indicative of their gentle, compliant natures, or some similar bag of moonshine. Oh, to have Mr Darcy's freedom to be abrasively dismissive! She would employ it in a heartbeat.

"If it were not against military discipline, I should have liked to have sent Captain Carter to... well, to have chastised him most severely yesterday for being so *de trop*! I have not seen you to speak to for an age, you have been so closeted up with your relations. Yours is a close-knit family, Miss Elizabeth. I could wish, one day, for one just like it." Wickham's glance flickered to Elizabeth's right, where Thomas stood, stoic and expressionless. "You are well accompanied today."

"Yes."

"And true to your word, you did not attend the Assembly. I was sorry. I would very much like to have danced with you. Still, there may be a little dancing at the Lucases' house this weekend. You will be there, I hope? I have recently obtained *The Rosicrucian*, and I look forward to discussing it with you."

She might have to be polite, but there was nothing to say she had to tell the truth. "I do not recall reading it. There is so little time at these parties with my neighbours to talk about literature."

He pressed his lips together, and inclined his head. "On other matters, I heard that Darcy had been seen here in Meryton, just before Christmas."

That was unsubtle of him. Perhaps her manner had rattled him.

"Indeed? And yet we had thought him removed to London. How odd that he should have business to bring him back here."

"Yes. Very odd. You have no notion...?"

"I?" Elizabeth put such astonishment into her tone, it imbued its rising inflection with some indignation.

Mr Wickham made an odd sound, a chuffed out short laugh. "Of course. That was foolish of me. May I escort you to your destination?"

"I have an appointment with my Uncle Phillips. It is, as you know, but a few yards."

"They are as miles to a parched man," said Wickham, although what he could mean by it, Elizabeth doubted he really knew. "They must suffice for now."

She laid a hand lightly on his proffered arm, while Thomas fell in behind them. "Mr Darcy's visit cannot affect you, can it, if he was indeed here?"

"I do not know. I have detected a little... coolness, shall we say, in some quarters since then." At her glance, Wickham sighed heavily, and added quickly, "Some of the merchants hereabouts are less welcoming. His envy and hatred... it pains me to say he cannot bear to see me contented. He must always intervene to make my life more difficult, to put barriers to my happiness. I had feared... Well. I have seen so little of you since Christmas. Even when you were back in company, your relations appeared to stay very close."

"As you said, sir, mine is a close-knit family. We spend our Christmases together. It is quite a tradition." She stopped at the foot of the steps to her uncle's office. "And here we are at my uncle's. Thank you for your escort, sir. I must go in, as he and I have business to discuss."

Whether he would have pressed the matter, she did not know. Thomas loomed so close that Wickham took a step backwards. The look he gave Thomas was unmistakably hostile, but it slid into his usual charming, pleasant expression as he bowed over her hand. "Until we meet again, fair lady."

His smile was so brilliant it would have ignited a faggot of wet wood. He bowed again, flung his short military cloak over his shoulder with panache, and strode away. Not without one backward glance to indicate his reluctance, but Elizabeth turned away almost immediately to mount the steps. If there were more yearning glances, he would be directing them to her back.

Beside her, Thomas grunted. It was a wonderfully dismissive sound, one she wished propriety would allow her to emulate, and she was still smiling over it when she was bowed into her uncle's office by his clerk.

"Was that Wickham?" Uncle Phillips asked. And at her nod, he scowled. "Your instincts were correct, Lizzy." He waited until she took the chair before his desk before resuming his seat. He opened a folder to display a sheaf of papers. "The merchants were warned to be wary of the militia, but more than one has been astonished to see that Lieutenant Wickham has managed to build up quite a mound of debt. While the merchants themselves have been careful, it appears their wives and daughters have been more amenable to a smooth tongue and engaging manners. So far" —and he looked at her over his spectacles— "I have not found that any of those wives and daughters have bartered away more than the merchant's goods, but I believe the men are more watchful now so far as those proclivities are concerned."

"How much?"

"A guinea here, thirty shillings there. As I say, it has mounted up. His greatest debts are at the inns. But taking all of Meryton into account, I have papers here for debts totalling sixty-three pounds, fourteen shillings, sevenpence and three farthings."

"Sixty-three pounds! The man has been here just over two months. How in heaven's name has he managed to accumulate so much in so short a time?"

"It appears he is talented at one thing, at least. As you wished, I have bought all the debt. There are a great many merchants giving quiet thanks for your liberality."

"They must not know it was me. Continue to buy his debts, if you will. I shall give you a banker's draft for what you have spent so far."

"Darcy's visit here before Christmas has become well known, and most think this is his work."

"Mr Darcy is proving very useful, then."

Uncle Phillips laughed. "Indeed. What do you wish me to do with the papers?"

"Please keep them in your safe, until such time as I have need of them."

He gave her a quizzical look. "Until such time?"

"Yes. I rather think I will need to make use of them."

Her uncle rose and came to stoop over her, to kiss her on the brow. "Sadly, child, I rather think so, too."

"Lizzy, are you no longer interested in Mr Wickham?"

Elizabeth looked up from fastening the frogging on her pelisse, to smile at Lydia. She had spent her time at Lucas Lodge that evening being very sociable with all her old friends, and giving Wickham no more than the common courtesy of a greeting while avoiding any more intimate discussion. He had stalked the edges of the room and watched her all evening with the same intensity Mr Darcy had shown—the irony of their sharing that habit whilst being so at odds with each other had appealed to her sense of humour—but had not insisted on possessing her attention. She had ensured she was always with too many of her neighbours for that, and perhaps he did not wish to draw everyone's notice to himself. Now the evening was over, the first in his company since Charlotte

Lucas's wedding before Christmas, she was breathing more easily. He must know she had withdrawn from him. Heavens, if even Lydia had noticed, then surely he had!

"My interest in Mr Wickham was never very great, Lyddie. He is an entertaining companion, but that is all."

"You do not mean to have him?"

Elizabeth flinched slightly before she could stop herself. "Certainly not. I have no plans to remarry."

And most certainly not to a man whose sole interest in her was her fortune.

"Oh. He is the handsomest of the officers." Lydia sighed gustily. "And so very romantic! It is hard that his prospects have been blighted by that Mr Darcy."

"We cannot know that is altogether correct."

Lydia stared and snorted out a derisive, mirthless huff of a laugh. "A man as handsome and charming as Wickham would not lie! There was something about old Mr Darcy's will being ignored or unclear or some such—"

"Lydia, I am not nearly so rich as Mr Darcy, but I have a will, and I assure you that Uncle Phillips drew it up very tightly indeed. How much more care would a very rich man take? He would never be so negligent as to leave a will that was unclear in any particular. Wills," Elizabeth added, remembering again her father's words, "are not easily set aside."

Lydia furrowed her brow. Elizabeth tried very hard not to smile at this evidence she was attempting deep thought. If indeed she were, it did not last long.

"Oh well, perhaps it was some other thing. No matter! If you do not want him, Lizzy, I shall add him to my flirts."

And she was off before Elizabeth could protest at the notion of girl who had just turned sixteen having flirts at all, much less militia officers without two ha'pence to rub together. She glanced at her parents, who were taking their leave of the Lucases. Little comfort there: Mama would squeal happily about Lydia's popularity and prospects, Papa would just laugh and call Lydia the silliest girl in England. All Elizabeth could do then, and in the following weeks when Mr Wickham appeared to accept her cool withdrawal from his company with no more than wry smiles and wounded glances, was watch as Lydia coquetted with the officers at every possible opportunity.

She drew comfort from two things. First, that her father must be right, and Lydia, while foolish and improper, was too poor to be an object of prey to any of the officers, all of whom would be looking for a wife with far more dowry than Lydia could offer. And second, that although she watched carefully, she could see no signs of partiality for Lydia on Wickham's part, or for him on Lydia's.

She discovered how insubstantial such comfort was on St Valentine's day.

On both counts.

"... You will laugh when you know where I am gone... for there is but one man in the world I love, and he is an angel... when I write to them and sign my name 'Lydia Wickham'. What a good joke it will be! I can hardly write for laughing! ..."

CHAPTER THIRTY-SEVEN

Mea Culpa

The only Christmas as cheerless as this had been the year Darcy's mother died, only four weeks before the blessed day. That had been a sad Yule indeed. This year was no better. He was just as mired in grief.

Since there was too little time to reach Pemberley before the holiday began, he and Georgiana spent Christmas Day with those of their Ashbourne relations remaining in Town. The earl and his countess had decided to winter at Mapleton, their estate in Derbyshire, leaving with barely enough time to spare before Christmas. Only their three sons remained in Town. Viscount Carsington, the heir, would never willingly spend time with Darcy, preferring wilder companions and the gambling hells, drinking dens and brothels that Darcy abhorred. Darcy despised Carsington for what he stigmatised as weak, self-indulgent selfishness. The antipathy was mutual—in the unlikely event he spoke of his cousin, Carsington contemptuously referred to Darcy as "the monk". Neither felt an instant's regret at not seeing the other. The two younger sons, however, were content to come to Darcy's house for the Christmas feast.

"Your port draws us in," Colonel Edward Fitzwilliam told him that evening, toasting his toes before the drawing room fire at Pember House. "Carsington is a fool to addle his brains and destroy his constitution drinking Old Tom in some foul hell, when there is nectar like this to be had."

Darcy grunted something, anything, in response.

Edward rolled his eyes. "Do try to at least pretend you are listening to me! Or, at least tell me what has you so blue-devilled."

"I am very well."

"That, coz, is doing it much too brown. Something has cut up your peace, and instead of my steady, reliable, reticent cousin who would scorn to show anything to the world of his thoughts and feelings, you are positively Friday-faced." Edward sipped his port, eyes knowing and kind despite his bluffness. "Georgiana?"

"No. No, I am content with her progress. Her spirits are improved markedly since the summer. Ramsgate has left its mark on her, but she is recovering. Her new companion has done much to restore her peace of mind."

"I thought so, too. So, something has disturbed you directly. If it were anyone but you, I would wager the trouble is something in the petticoat line."

"Edward!" Darcy cast a swift, grimacing glance towards the alcove where Georgiana played Thomas Fitzwilliam at piquet, watched over by her companion, Mrs Annesley.

"They cannot hear us. Am I right?"

Darcy cast another glance at Georgiana, but she seemed intent on the game. Thomas, the youngest of the earl's sons, was competitive enough that he had little attention to spare for the conversation of his elders. It was likely safe enough to speak, and Edward was as much of a confessor as his namesake. Darcy trusted no man more. "Do you remember James Grayson?"

"Very well. A good man."

"He was injured at Maida."

"Were not we all?" Edward rubbed his left shoulder.

"He injured his head, chest and arm, I believe; so seriously he could no longer serve with his regiment..." And once again Darcy recounted the whole debacle of James at Netherfield, his hasty marriage and untimely death, Bingley's fortuitous lease on the property, and Matthew Grayson's determination to hold the widow to account. By the time he finished, the port was sour, suddenly, on his tongue, as if its fruity undertones had fermented and spoiled.

When he spoke of James's violence to his young wife, they both looked at Georgiana. Edward winced visibly. No doubt he could envisage as well as did Darcy, the fate that would have befallen her if Wickham had succeeded in his scheme of seduction and elopement, the misery that would have blighted her.

"Poor girl. His head was injured severely, you say? I have heard of that causing such a change in character, in demeanour and temper, that it would seem a new and different man inhabits the same body." Edward winced again. "It rattles the brain, or some such thing."

"Mrs Grayson says that he was wounded in spirit."

Edward gulped down the remainder of his port. His face sagged, as though an older man had slid beneath his skin to change the laughter lines at his eyes to wrinkles and pull down his mouth into a pinched uncertainty. "If a man can come through battle unscathed in spirit, then he is an insensate brute. We are men, and so we do not talk of the things and fears that weigh on us, the things we have seen. But they never leave us." A short, hard laugh. "We rest a while, and say only that we are wearied and tired, and close our eyes to try and shut out the carnage wrought by chainshot, or grapeshot, or sabre... and then we go back again into the fray, because honour and duty demand we do. But we do not forget."

"Do you dream of it?"

"Often. Always. The simplest thing will bring it all back, even here"—Edward swept out his arm to encompass the quiet room—"but I have found the worst is a blacksmith's forge. I have not myself taken my horse to be reshod these five years." At Darcy's enquiring look, he added, "Hot metal and smelted iron—the same stink as when the man standing beside you is shredded by grapeshot and you are drenched in his blood."

Darcy would not offer sympathy: Edward would not welcome it. Instead he refilled Edward's glass to the brim, allowing that simple gesture to say what his mouth must not. "I must assume James was similarly affected."

"I do not doubt it." Edward nodded his thanks and sipped the wine. "How did he die?"

"She told him she was increasing, and fearing he was mad and the child would be tainted, he tried to throw her down a staircase. Thwarted by the servants, he… fell."

Edward raised an eyebrow and Darcy nodded.

"Broke his neck. She lost the child."

"Poor girl," Edward said again, and grimaced. "It must have been hard for her, then, you and young Grayson seeking information."

If Edward had rammed his sabre into Darcy's chest, it could not have hurt more. His breath caught on the metaphorical blade slicing through him. "I have never set out to cause pain to anyone, but I could not have done so more thoroughly if I had planned it for a year. I hurt her grievously, Edward. I am thoroughly ashamed of myself."

Edward's mouth pursed into a silent whistle. "So, it *is* trouble of the petticoat kind."

"We spent two months seeking information from anyone but her. Grayson was convinced she had a hand in James's death, you see. So when, at the end, she charged me with deceit and duplicity, I had no answer."

"You apologised, I am sure."

That was kind of him, to assume Darcy would do the right thing. "I have, and gained absolution for that offence. But then I made the most shocking mull of asking her to marry me."

Edward choked so thoroughly on his port that it caught the attention of Georgiana and Thomas, both of whom turned enquiring faces towards them. Edward waved a hand, his face bright red. "Went down the wrong way," he gasped out.

"A terrible waste of William's port!" Thomas admonished, but he and Georgiana were smiling and returned to their game immediately.

Darcy watched them for a moment, allowing Edward to regain his equanimity. Thomas was making steady progress in his career at the bar. If he and Georgiana continued this good fellowship, Darcy would be pleased to consign her to his care one day.

"She refused you?"

Darcy did not turn from his observation of the younger two. "Emphatically. I had not intended to make her an offer—she is not of our circle, though the daughter of a gentleman—but when she bade me go in peace, I lost my head. Oh, I was a fool. If I had hurt her over James Grayson, I insulted her woefully on her own behalf. Her connections are poor, with an uncle in trade. And as for her family! Some of them are ridiculous. Her younger sisters are loud, vulgar and unrefined, and her mother's sole idea is to see her daughters married as soon and as well as may be, talking improperly and coarsely about it to all and sundry."

"Behaving so very differently from the mothers of the *Bon Ton*, I see." Edward's tone of honeyed acidity could not be bettered, and Darcy felt his face burn. "Your lady's mother reminds me of Lady Catherine, who, I would remind *you*, is also loud and frequently improper. She is only shielded from censure by wealth and position. And by my father, who exerts all his influence to keep her safely out of the way in Kent!"

"It is not at all the sa—" Darcy slumped into his seat. "It is the same, is it not? I have never been blind to our aunt's unrefined behaviour, but I have never condemned it."

"You are hardly the only one. Most will accept Lady Catherine's high-handed offences, yet protest mightily at the same from Mrs Squire in Hertfordshire with no connections and, I assume, little wealth."

"Bennet. Their name is Bennet and they are comfortably situated. The estate, though, is entailed away from the immediate family, to our aunt's clergyman, no less! Their prospects are not of the best. I counted all that more than I did my attraction to her. I spent far more time telling her of my struggles to overcome the scruples that forbade the match, than the reasons I was offering. She was rightly offended. Then, too, she had other causes of disapprobation. I was foolish enough to aid Miss Bingley in separating her brother from Mrs Grayson's elder sister, when any man of sense would have realised it was entirely wrong to interfere. And, I am sorry to say—" here Darcy dropped his voice to ensure Georgiana could not hear "—Wickham has taken a commission in the —shire militia, stationed near Netherfield. He had filled her mind with his usual lies. She tasked me with them."

Edward almost choked a second time. "That blackguard!" he said, the need not to explode with rage in Georgiana's hearing filling his tone with a fury all the more terrible for his quietness. "You should have run him through. Or allowed me to do so at Ramsgate."

"I have warned her. The widowed owner of an estate as fine as Netherfield must be his target. She knows what he is, now."

"We will return to him later," Edward promised, and soothed his indignation with the port. "What is she like?"

Beautiful. Charming. Delightful.

Not mine.

Darcy let his head droop until all he could see was the gleaming leather of his Hessians. "She has not the classical beauty of her elder sister, who would take the *Ton* by storm, but she has ten times the fire, charm, and spirit. Her chief beauty is in her eyes. They are quite astonishing. More than that, she is witty, intelligent, and kind." Darcy raised his head. Edward watched him patiently. "I have never met any woman who comes close to her. She… she delights me."

"She is the daughter of a gentleman, and you are a gentleman's son. I see no disparity there. My father will argue you could look higher, though he will welcome a link to the Ruffords. Mama will be grateful to see you at the altar at all, and as long as your lady—"

"Elizabeth. Elizabeth Grayson."

"—*is* a lady, then my mother will be content. Lady Catherine… well, we all know what her reaction would be to any bride other than Anne. She will combust with rage."

Darcy merely nodded. Of course she would.

"Your Elizabeth owns an estate that I assume gives her some independence?"

"It brings in more than three thousand a year."

"Good Lord, most gentlemen cannot boast as much! The small estate my mother will leave me has nothing near that income. That is a substantial dowry, coz. Consider it as one of, oh, twice or thrice Georgiana's. As for her family... well, I would remind you that Pemberley is a three-day journey north. That provides a mitigating distance." Edward's mouth twitched upward at the corners. "It strikes me that you have not taken long to realise the futility of your first campaign to win the lady. I would have expected far more stiff self-justification from you before you could be brought to see where you erred."

Would he, indeed? That was an unpromising assessment.

"She was most eloquent in listing my faults. I spent that night thinking. Believe me, the scorn of a woman for whom you have a most sincere attachment is a spur to deep reflection. I pray you never experience it. She told me I was no gentleman."

...behaved in so ungentlemanly a fashion...You are arrogant and conceited... you value wealth and connections above all else. Above character, above honesty, sincerity, integrity...

"And indeed, my ungenerous setting out of every objection to the match was anything but gentlemanly. I revelled in my superiority, acting as King Cophetua condescending to the beggar-maid. I am surprised she did not box my ears. When she told me that I respected her as little as James had done, it almost unmanned me that she could think I would treat her as he did."

"You would never hurt a woman."

"I would never hit one. It seems I am adept at hurting them. She told me the wounds left by such disrespect did not have to be applied with a fist. She is right."

"I am impressed. So many women would swallow the insult and take you for your wealth and position. She is no fortune-hunter, that is plain. You realise she saw you as a man stripped of all wealth and connections and position, all of which she deemed the least important things about you. She saw you as you are—the real Fitzwilliam Darcy. That is a rare thing."

"I wish she had seen a better man. It was a harsh mirror she held to my face. You are right. She saw me not as I thought myself to be and it humbles me to know she sees all my pretensions to goodness. I kicked hard against her contention at first, but a night's reflection convinced me that she showed me a true image of how I appear to others. I can only pray I am not truly so arrogant and conceited in my heart."

Edward was definitely smirking. "Your manners would certainly benefit from improvement when you are among strangers or those whom you count as mere acquaintances. You are too often cold and aloof, giving the impression you consider everyone beneath your touch. If she has shown you that, and you have had the fortitude and honesty to listen to her criticism and seen where you must amend yourself, then perhaps she will be good for you."

"I failed to win her."

"Is she worth the winning?"

They looked at each other. What Edward saw, Darcy could not know. He only knew that the faint frail beginnings of hope lightened the darkness a little, small harbingers of an overdue spring, like snowdrops pushing their heads above the frozen ground. He smiled. Nodded.

"Yes."

Nothing more than that simple affirmation was needed.

"Then why are you here, and not grovelling in Hertfordshire?"

"I promised her father I would give her time to restore her peace of mind. Besides, I must wait for Bingley's return from Yorkshire. I must grovel to him first. But when he is back, I will, I hope, have every opportunity to return with him to Hertfordshire. And this time, I will show her that her reproofs have worked a change in me for the better."

"Well, women always like to be right. That alone should start you off on a better footing." Edward put down his empty glass. "But port is not the stuff to soothe aching hearts. Bring out the brandy, man! Nothing else will do."

In the end, Darcy decided not to go north to Pemberley. He had thought to run home and lick his wounds, but Edward's bracingly honest support and good fellowship kept him in London. At Pemberley, he would have no one with whom to share his struggles. Give Edward a glass of port or brandy, and his cousin would listen to Darcy for hours, only the twitches of his mouth betraying a fond amusement.

Darcy was not particularly sociable—but then, he never was—though he took Georgiana to one or two concerts. Otherwise he eschewed dinners and the occasional small balls. Town would be thin of company until the season started in the spring, but it was convivial enough for Darcy's tastes.

He ran into Viscount Kirton several times, mostly fencing at Angelo's and once at Jackson's boxing saloon. Kirton had apparently heard from Mr Bennet and treated Darcy with ease, as if there had never been any cause of disapprobation between them. They fought one very close bout at Angelo's, and Darcy was lucky to come away with a narrow victory.

He saw Hurst, too, more than once. The first time, at their club just before Twelfth Night, he hesitated only an instant before offering his hand and a handsome apology. "I offended you, and you were right to be so. My only excuse, and it is a lamentable one, is that I was so at sixes and sevens, I was positively pudding-headed. I did you a great disservice, and Bingley an even greater one."

Hurst took the hand and the apology with grace. "Although I do hope you know I could see just how pudding-headed you were, Darcy." And with a pointed intelligence that Darcy would have once denied the man had, he asked, plainly, "When do you return to Meryton?"

Had the entire world seen his admiration? Other than the object of it, of course, who had misread it for condemnation; a charge that still, whenever he thought on it, took Darcy's breath away.

"I must wait for Bingley's return, because first I must right the wrong I did him by agreeing with Miss Bingley's views. I had no right to interfere."

"No. Not that it would have stopped Caroline, of course."

"I should have known better. Do you know when we might see Bingley?"

"Not for some weeks yet, I fancy. I do not know how much Charles told you of the catastrophe that took him north? There has been some very ill dealing in the family concerns there, such that their reputation is suffering and it will affect his income if he cannot resolve it. Caroline is chafing at the bit since Charles left her under my authority and Louisa's, and she does not care for that, for Louisa has grown a little more stern and is less likely to allow Caroline free rein." Hurst's smile was diabolical. "Louisa was very much taken with Mrs Grayson, and would like to be, in some way, as decisive and energetic a lady. I cannot say I regret her ambition. It has stiffened her spine against Caroline's wilder flights, that is certain." And the devil inhabiting Hurst's large frame jiggled it with amusement. "We are looking forward to deepening our acquaintance with Mrs Grayson, Darcy."

Were not they all? Darcy merely sighed, and forced a smile.

By mid-February the sharpness of loss had dulled to a constant ache. Oddly, it was harder to bear. If the swift, slicing stabs had been painful, the perpetual misery and anguish wore him down. He was weary of himself and his failures.

Four days after the Valentine's feast, a day on which the lack of a sweetheart with whom to exchange a loving token had gnawed at him like a dog with broken teeth, he had an unexpected visitor. Late in the day, too late really for the polite calls of friends and acquaintances, his butler, Wilkes, appeared in Darcy's study, where he and Edward were battling over the chessboard.

Wilkes carried a dubious expression on his face and a salver with a calling card on it in his hand. "The lady insisted I bring it to you, sir. She is waiting in the hall."

Darcy stared at the card, and was on his feet and almost running out of the doorway before he had time to breathe. It was possible Edward called after him, but he did not stop. The hellhounds could not have stopped him.

She was there. Pale and drawn, she had fixed those glorious eyes, looking bruised and hurt, on the door she must have seen Wilkes enter. Watching for him.

Elizabeth.

CHAPTER THIRTY-EIGHT

An Unfortunate Affair

"Mr Darcy." Elizabeth Grayson dropped into a curtsey. She would not meet his eyes. "I hope you will be willing to grant me a few minutes of your time, sir. I would be grateful..."

She stopped, pressed her lips together firmly. She kept her eyes downcast, as though intent on watching her hands clutch convulsively at each other where she had them clasped together below her breast. She had pretty hands.

She looked at him at last. "I am ashamed to say I need your help, sir."

Wickham.

It had to be Wickham. Darcy swallowed down the rush of hot acid in his mouth—more than once, fighting the thickening feeling in a throat that was held in a choking, icy grip. He could not reply. The silent moment dragged by.

She closed her eyes, her shoulders sagging. "I... Forgive me. I should not have come."

She half turned away, reaching behind her blindly. Thomas Rance was there in an instant to offer his arm, his dark, cold eyes fixed on Darcy.

"No!" Darcy had taken too long to speak. "No, madam. Please." He swallowed the bile again, where it clung, thick and stinging in his throat. "I beg you come in. You are in great distress..."

Edward coughed from the door behind him. He glanced at Edward's face, expressionless in its warning look, and turned back to her.

"Come into my study, ma'am. You too, Rance." He looked to Wilkes. "Have some refreshments prepared."

He offered the widow his arm. Finally, Elizabeth raised her eyes to meet his. It pained him to see her usually direct gaze so searching and uncertain.

"Come," Darcy said again, more gently.

The breath she took was visibly wavering, but deep. "Thank you." She put her hand lightly on his arm and allowed him to lead her in.

Darcy indicated Edward with his free hand. "Mrs Grayson, may I present my cousin, Colonel Fitzwilliam, to your acquaintance? Colonel, this is Mrs Grayson, of Netherfield Park, Hertfordshire. Bingley, you will recall, is leasing Mrs Grayson's estate."

Edward had retreated to the rug set before the fire. He bowed when Darcy entered with Elizabeth, and murmured his polite gratification at the introduction. She curtseyed in return, her face pink.

Edward's sharp eyes grew kind. "I perceive you have some pressing business with Darcy, ma'am. This is obviously no time for strangers, and I will leave you to my cousin's care." And to Darcy, "I will be in the library."

He bowed and was on his way out before she could do more than murmur something begging pardon for trespassing.

"I am sorry, Mr Darcy. I *am* trespassing, both on your good nature and on your guest's. I... I hope you know I would not do so except in the greatest extremity."

"I do know." Darcy settled her into his own chair where it was set before the hearth, and with a jerk of his head, indicated another nearby for Rance. The ex-footman, though, came to stand behind his mistress. Darcy pushed aside the low table with the chessboard, sat in Edward's chair and leaned forward to take her hand. "Did he hurt you?"

"I might have known you would see in an instant where the trouble lies! No. Mr Wickham has not hurt me directly, nor imposed on me. But he has most foully imposed on my family."

He hated to see her cry. The last time, he had caused it and he had cursed himself for an unfeeling fool for weeks. This time, he would gladly throttle Wickham until the bastard's eyes popped.

"You are very distressed. Let me get you something. A glass of wine perhaps? You are ill."

"I am well, I assure you." She pressed his hand and withdrew her own to dab a ridiculously small square of lacy linen to her eyes.

He took his own, more substantial, handkerchief from his pocket and put it close to her hand, within reach should she need it. A glance at Thomas Rance showed that gentleman watching his every move. Absurd! As if Darcy would hurt her.

When she was a little calmer, she explained, "We took your warning to heart, my father and I. In truth, I had cooled my friendship with Mr Wickham even before—" She stopped, and met his gaze. "Even before we spoke that day before Christmas, I had ceased to show him any particular notice. When I read your letter, I made very certain to chill what little remained into extinction. Thomas here accompanies me everywhere, since my father was concerned that once we had made the futility of his addresses plain to him, Wickham might take more direct action. In fact, he appeared to accept it. Oh, not with good grace. I was the recipient of many sulky, reproachful, and wounded looks. But whenever I met him, I treated him with the civility one would give any acquaintance for whom one felt only perfect indifference."

"That was my hope, that you should protect yourself from him. I am very glad you did."

"I do not forget your kindness in warning me. What I had not anticipated, what none of us anticipated, was that he would then turn his attention to one of my sisters." Her clutch on her handkerchief was tight enough to whiten her knuckles. "We thought he had given up the endeavour, but in truth he was merely more cunning than we realised. He did nothing in plain sight, but somehow he has imposed upon—" She choked. "Oh, this is so shameful!"

"Tell me," Darcy said, keeping his tone to the gentle, reassuring one he had found to deal with Georgiana's grief.

"Four days ago, he persuaded my youngest sister to elope."

He jerked upright in his chair. But the other Bennet girls had very little in the way of dowry! What in hell's name was Wickham about?

"I am sorry indeed to hear this. It is most unusual behaviour in him. I have never known him trifle with a gentleman's daughter, unless there was a fortune to be had. In these circumstances, I cannot see what provoked him to such incautious behaviour."

"That, I think, is where his cunning has manifested itself. You understand that I have been little able to think on anything else these last four days, and I am convinced I am right. When their flight was known, my father and Colonel Forster searched north for twenty miles, with no word of them at any of the inns on the Great North Road. John Lucas and Captain Carter searched southward, towards London, and found proof that was the direction they took. Indeed, Captain Carter had no doubt that Wickham never intended marriage. They are hid somewhere here in Town. I am convinced that was always his design in pursuing Lydia—not to marry her, but to encompass her utter ruin and keep us from overtaking them and finding her until that was most thoroughly achieved. I believe his object is to force me to pay over a fortune to him to marry her."

"Good God, that is diabolical."

"The whole family faces ruin and public condemnation. My poor sisters! Their prospects of good marriages were never high. Now…" She shook her head.

"That your sister agreed to this is most disturbing."

"I am not certain that she did. Here—" She took a folded paper from her reticule and offered it. "She left this for Kitty, who is closest to her in age and affection."

A short letter, in a childish, unformed hand.

"Kitty,

You will laugh when you know where I am gone, and I cannot help laughing myself at your surprise to-morrow morning, as soon as I am missed. I am going to Gretna Green, and if you cannot guess with who, I shall think you a simpleton, for there is but one man in the world I love, and he is an angel. I should never be happy without him, so think it no harm to be off! Say nothing to anyone, I beg you. It will make the surprise the greater, when I write to them and sign my name 'Lydia Wickham'. What a good joke it will be! I can hardly write for laughing!

I shall be wed before Harriet Harrington, in any event, and she will not be half so pretty a bride nor half so happy as me!

I hope you will drink to our good journey, and you will soon see your married sister returned to show off her handsome husband.

Lydia"

What a letter to send at such a time! Lydia. Oh yes, the moony one with the corkscrew curls and the loud laugh. Silly, pert, and uneducated, she should not have been out of the schoolroom, much less meeting men of Wickham's stamp. This was a letter from a child in thought and emotions. A deceived child.

A ruined one.

He refolded the letter and handed it back. "It shows, I see, that she at least expected to be married, whatever his plans may have been. I cannot conceive why she agreed to go first to London."

"If the ninnyhammer has any understanding of geography, I shall be astonished. She may not have realised where he was taking her until it was too late. I love my sisters, Mr Darcy, but the two youngest are lamentably ignorant." Elizabeth smoothed the letter and tucked it back into her reticule. "And so, sir, now you understand our trouble. If you will grant me your aid, I cannot tell you the depth of my gratitude."

"What may I do?"

What he wished to do was comfort her, to take her in his arms. But even if he dared, he would not. He could not determine if he wished it for her sake, or for his own. It was an agony not to reach for her, but to sit back and watch her distress with impotent fury at the cause of it. But he would not take his eyes from her. She had feared and misunderstood his silence once. Though he longed to get up and walk about to relieve his feelings, he would not do so lest she misconstrued it into his putting a distance between them. Folly, when he wanted no distance at all, and not even Wickham could force it.

"My father, my Uncle Phillips, and I arrived in Town yesterday. Uncle Phillips is looking into a legal method of hanging Wickham by the heels. My father and my Uncle Gardiner are today searching all of London's hotels and the major inns. But the city is very large, there are many hundreds of inns, and I suspect Wickham to be very well hidden. If I am right in my conjectures, then he cannot succeed unless she is irretrievably ruined, and the longer he may keep her secreted somewhere, the more complete his success. They are unlikely to be found in the better accommodations, even if he could afford them. So I am come to discover if you have any scrap of information from your knowledge of him and your history with him, that might help us discover him... an associate of his who may be approached, or houses and haunts he has frequented in the past."

She sagged where she sat. He suspected only willpower had allowed the flood of words, that she had forced herself to remain calm and coherent until he understood her whole story.

"I will need to give some thought as to how I might best help. But first, you need some refreshments, and also... Mrs Grayson, Colonel Fitzwilliam is Georgiana's other guardian, and he holds Wickham in even less regard than do I. But more than that, he has resources at his command to help with the search. He will be discreet, but he will also be of considerable aid. May I call him in and acquaint him with this problem?"

"Oh... I... I do not..." She stopped and looked him in the eye. Her smile was lamentably lacking in its usual brilliance. "I trust you, sir. I will trust your endorsement of the colonel. Thank you."

He smiled back, and his smile, he was sure, should have ignited the chair she sat upon. She trusted him! She said so with such direct simplicity of manner, it rang with truth. He patted her hand, and went to send a footman scurrying to find the refreshments he had ordered earlier. He fetched Edward from the library himself.

By the time they had returned, the refreshment tray had arrived. Wilkes swept away the chess set and placed the tray before Mrs Grayson, and bowed himself out. She was prevailed upon to dispense the tea and coffee, and taste the little cakes cook had sent up. For several minutes Darcy forgot everything while watching her preside over the tea tray, the living embodiment of so many domestic dreams of late. He started when Edward's elbow connected with his ribs. He suspected only the presence of Mrs Grayson prevented Edward from rolling his eyes and cuffing Darcy about the back of the head.

"Allow me, Mrs Grayson, to explain the problem to Colonel Fitzwilliam. It will, I hope, be less distressing than asking you to repeat the story." And on her agreement, Darcy gave all the known facts to Edward along with Mrs Grayson's opinion of what Wickham was about, showing him the letter which Mrs Grayson once more took from her reticule for the purpose, and noting with satisfaction the lowering of brows and frowns of distaste. Edward truly did abhor Wickham.

"The man is a blight worse than the Ten Plagues." Edward's look when he considered the widow was kind. "I do not doubt your opinion of his scheme for a moment, madam. I am sure he is counting on the notion you will pay him to marry your sister, to save her from disgrace. After four days—and nights—in his company, her ruin is assured, as you will have realised. I must ask, what could you pay?"

"My sisters' dowries are meagre—an equal share of five thousand pounds on my mother's death. For the last four years I have been investing part of my income to supplement this. Lydia's share is perhaps another two thousand—"

Edward chuffed out a short, unamused laugh. "He will look for much more. I doubt he will take her for a penny less than ten."

"That is more than I have been able put aside for them. I cannot rob my other sisters for Lydia's sake. No more than three thousand."

"He will want more. He must know how much Netherfield is worth." Darcy sighed deeply. "Balked of the greater prize when you spurned him, Mrs Grayson, he will look to take as much as possible from you. He is a creature wrought of petty jealousies and envy, and lives for revenge. You have crossed him, and he will try to make you feel the consequences."

"Darcy is right." Edward nodded.

"I am not surprised by this estimation of him." Elizabeth frowned, and put down her coffee cup. "You did not ask me the right question, Colonel. You should have asked how much I was *willing* to pay him. The answer is, not one farthing."

"Not a far— Are you serious, ma'am?"

"Quite serious. Oh, I wish to recover Lydia, and she must be married. She cannot return to Longbourn unwed, and I am sure I will indeed have to pay someone to marry her. I am determined, however, that it will not be Mr Wickham. I will not see him profit from his wickedness. I will find Lydia a husband from my uncle's contacts, perhaps. But Mr Wickham will never claim me as a sister."

Edward stared at her, his jaw a little slack. His smile was slow, but joyous. He stood, and bowed deeply, and there was not one iota of mockery in it. "You are as delightful as my cousin claimed, ma'am. And we shall add to that, sensible and principled. It will be a privilege to help you find the miscreant."

Darcy, skating hurriedly over Edward's infelicitous comments about Elizabeth's more entrancing qualities, chimed in. "Indeed. The question is what we might do to find him, or do we wait for him to contact you or Mr Bennet? If, as we all agree, his intent is to batten on you, ma'am, then he will contact you at some point to start the negotiations, or make Miss Lydia do so."

"I vote that we look," said Edward. "The sooner we find Miss Lydia the better. My concern is that, other than his coming to our notice last summer—"

"Mrs Grayson is aware of that."

Edward's eyebrows hitched up so far it was comical. "Indeed!"

"Yes, Colonel. You are assured of my secrecy on the matter."

"I see." Edward stared a moment longer, then shook his head as if to clear the cobwebs from it. "Well, then. Other than that, it is some years since I concerned myself with Wickham and any associates he may have. Locating them will not be an easy task. The one slight recollection I have is that Carsington mentioned him once. I remember only because of the incongruity of his noticing Wickham at all." Edward turned to Elizabeth to add in explanation, "My brother Viscount Carsington, ma'am, who is quite a man about Town." He grimaced. "I must be frank and say I would not introduce him to a lady, if you take my meaning."

"Perfectly, Colonel."

"Carsington has acquaintances all over Town, in every insalubrious quarter of it. I will start with him." Edward glanced at Darcy. "He may condescend to speak to me about it. He will not speak to you at all."

Mrs Grayson arched an eyebrow at them.

Darcy could only grimace. "We are little in sympathy."

"To put it mildly. You and my brother are in opposition on every point. Well, ma'am, will you leave this to us, to see what we may discover? Where may we find you, if we have information to impart?"

"My father and I are staying with my uncle Gardiner in Gracechurch Street. Number five."

Edward showed no reaction at all to so unfashionable an address, merely inclining his head.

"I shall present myself there tomorrow," Darcy said, "to discuss with your father and uncles how we may work together. Would eleven o'clock suit?"

"Yes, Mr Darcy. It will give me time enough to confess I have approached you, and to recover from the scolding I shall doubtless receive." And there was the hint of the Elizabeth he loved: joyful and teasing and at ease with the world. She smiled at them both, and, dusting cake crumbs from her skirts, rose to her feet. "I must go. I have imposed upon you long enough. Thank you, gentlemen, for your kindness and compassion. Thank you both."

"I will see you to your carriage." Darcy had leapt up as soon as she had moved. He was reluctant to see her leave his house, but propriety forbade that she stay any longer. She had already broken with strict societal norms in visiting an unmarried man without a chaperone. No matter. She would be treated with all due ceremony, as his honoured guest.

She took his arm when he offered it. "I thank you, sir. My father and uncle are using the Gardiner carriage today, so I was able to borrow the Longbourn coach with impunity. John Coachman is awaiting me in the square."

She took cordial leave of Edward, and Darcy escorted her out, sending a footman running to Grosvenor Square to find the Bennet coach. They stood in the quiet hall together for the few minutes she had to wait. Elizabeth glanced at Thomas Rance and nodded, and Rance took several steps to the side to give them at least an illusion of privacy.

"I wished to say something to you, Mr Darcy. I am grateful to you, not only for your help today, but for the generosity of spirit that allowed you to share with me in your letter so much of your history with Wickham. You were under no obligation to do so—"

"I had every obligation. Your safety and happiness were—are—of paramount importance to me." He could not prevent the little grimace. "I told Edward that I had made a shocking mull of speaking to you that day. It has worn on my conscience ever since."

"It was not the most propitious discussion, was it? I wanted to tell you, though, that I have pondered on your letter a great deal these last two months. It has not only brought me to a better understanding of you, but of my own failings. I was loud in condemning you for yours, without consciousness of the beam in my own eye. I regret very much that my pride and vanity, and wounded consequence, made me unkind and uncivil. I should have behaved better."

"I deserved your strictures. It was unconscionably ham-handed of me."

She shook her head. "I do not merit your kindness, nor your generosity today."

"Well, we may argue that until the last trump calls. You merit all I can do or give you."

He kept the memory of her smile with him when, at that moment, her carriage arrived and he was forced to hand her into it and allow her to leave his home. He stood for several minutes on the steps, watching the old coach lumber down the street. Edward's voice in his ear made him jump.

"You were quite right, coz. She does indeed have very beautiful eyes."

"Yes."

The carriage turned the corner and was lost from sight.

"And you are also quite right on another matter. She is indeed worth the winning."

Darcy smiled. "Yes."

CHAPTER THIRTY-NINE

Gracechurch Street

The uncle's house in Gracechurch Street was, naturally, smaller and less luxurious than Darcy's townhouse, but still remarkably commodious. Built from rosy-red brick, it was set back slightly from the street, its frontage level with the houses adjoining it on either side and pierced with long windows. Inside, it had all the plain elegance of the previous century. The Gardiners evidently had an eye for quality: each piece of furniture had been carefully chosen for its beauty as well as utility, and many would not have looked out of place in Pemberley.

Darcy and Colonel Fitzwilliam were shown into a first-floor sitting room where Mr Bennet, his two eldest daughters and Mr Phillips, the Meryton lawyer, awaited them. The lady sitting with them was a few years Darcy's senior. Mrs Gardiner, most likely.

Mrs Grayson came to meet them. "Thank you for coming. Papa has been acquainted with your intention to help us."

Darcy smiled. "I see you survived the scolding."

Her laugh was delightful. "I am not so easily overset." She led them across the room. "This shall be a complicated introduction since Mr Darcy knows some of our company! However, let me begin..." And she made everyone known to Edward, and Mrs Gardiner to Darcy, managing the process with grace. The slight grimace she made when she reached the end was, quite simply, charming. "My uncle Gardiner is at his office and has been sent for. He will be here in a few moments, I am sure."

After the moment of bobbing up and down as everyone rose to bow or curtsey, she ushered Darcy and Fitzwilliam to one of the pair of sofas set facing each other across the hearth. Mr Bennet looked much as he had when Darcy last saw him, but Darcy noticed, dismayed, that Miss Bennet was thinner and paler than he remembered. She sat closest to Edward, and engaged him in the sort of banal conversation that was too often the lot of those meeting for the first time. Edward, who had given Darcy one speaking look when he saw Miss Bennet, responded with such enthusiasm that Mr Bennet watched them with a jaundiced eye, evidently well used to the effect his daughter's beauty had on susceptible men. Mr Phillips being intent on putting a sheaf of legal documents into order, Mrs Grayson and Mrs Gardiner stepped in to fill the conversational gaps.

For the wife of a tradesman, Mrs Gardiner was an elegant, refined sort of lady, as unlike Mrs Bennet's portrayal of a shrieking harpy as might be imagined. Darcy's only moment of doubt was when she claimed some knowledge of his estate and mentioned his parents, but when he discovered her father had been rector of Lambton for several years, he could silently concede that this pleasant lady merely sought to put him at his ease while they talked. She was no encroaching mushroom.

Nor was her husband, when Mr Gardiner appeared a moment or two later. Anyone less like Mrs Bennet could not exist in the world, and Darcy found himself talking easily to an intelligent, very gentleman-like man. Had he not known they were in trade, he would have reckoned the Gardiners to be country gentry, not unlike Mr Bennet in education and breeding. Remembrance of his disdainful dismissal of them, his contention that such connections were beneath him, tinged his already pained memories of his proposal to Elizabeth Grayson with even more regret. She had spoken nothing but truth when she accused him of arrogance and conceit.

Another glance at Miss Bennet's sad demeanour confirmed the accuracy of her charge.

"Shall we retire to my study, gentlemen?" Gardiner said, when he had been introduced.

"Since I will not be left out of matters, uncle, you had better stay here, where there is more room and the chairs are more comfortable." Elizabeth's direct gaze was on her father and uncle, not on Darcy, but he felt the intensity of it. "We have all agreed Wickham's likely motive for taking Lydia with him is another shot in his campaign against *me,* in the hope he will gain some foothold on Netherfield. I will not be patted on the head and sent off to do my embroidery while you gentlemen decide Lydia's fate without me. Or, for that matter, Wickham's fate."

Mr Bennet stared back at his daughter over his spectacles, which had slipped down his nose. "Until we find them, my girl, no one will be deciding anything about anyone. And let me remind you that I am Lydia's father, and it will fall to me to deal with her."

"If we are buying her a husband, Papa, I believe I will have a hand in it." Elizabeth was tart.

"Lizzy," admonished Miss Bennet, in a quiet tone.

Elizabeth grimaced again. It truly was enchanting. "I am sorry, Papa. It is just that I feel so guilty. Wickham is aiming this at me, not at you or the rest of the family. He is trying to force me into providing him with the means for a life of idleness." She turned to Darcy and Edward. "Forgive me, gentlemen. I do know better than to display such improper behaviour, but it grieves me to the heart that he has used Lydia so, purely from resentment and spite. If they had truly loved each other and their passions were stronger than their virtue, I confess I would feel easier. It is his ruthless exploitation of Lydia's girlish fancy that offends and distresses me. No matter what outcome we achieve, she is ruined in an act not of love, but of malice. If I cannot be active in retrieving her, I will run mad!"

Mr Bennet patted her hand. "It is not your fault, Lizzy. No sensible man could blame you for protecting yourself. The fault is mine, for not realising that, balked of his prize, he would employ such an underhand way of achieving his fortune. What a man!"

"If it comes to guilt, then I feel some for misleading you." Darcy's face was hot. "It is true that I have never known him deal with a gentlewoman so, but I am sorry indeed if your reliance on my assertion left your daughter vulnerable to his manipulation."

"It was not your assertion, Mr Darcy, but her nature and mine. Hers to resent all restraint, mine to embrace indolence." Mr Bennet looked suddenly an old man, face sagging with grief and guilt. "Lizzy warned me that Lydia's behaviour required curtailment, but I did not act."

"This achieves nothing." Mrs Gardiner's tone was refined and gentle. "The fault lies with this man Wickham, and, I am sorry to say, with Lydia. To salvage what credit and reputation we may from the wreckage is our task now, not recrimination."

Mr Bennet dipped his head in a queer little half bow. "Well, I should feel my fault, but I do not doubt it will fade swiftly enough. Do you have aught to tell us, gentlemen? Lizzy told us of your generous offer of help."

"Nothing absolute as yet, but we have some intelligence of him that I found very disturbing. Colonel?"

"I spoke to my brother, Viscount Carsington. I recollected his mentioning Wickham once, an unusual enough occurrence for me to seek Carsington out and see if that might give us some clue. I also have a man—Sergeant Oliver, who is a clever, handy sort of fellow—searching out Mrs Younge." Edward hesitated, then added, "She was companion to an heiress unsuccessfully targeted by Wickham, and discovered to be his paramour. If found, she may be induced to give intelligence of Wickham that could help."

Edward hesitated again, and looked at Darcy, who nodded.

"Please tell us," Elizabeth said. "I understand whatever you have to say is disturbing. We will bear it because we must."

"Very well, ma'am. Carsington's 'set' is made up of men of his own stamp. That is, men who are not by any means respectable, but they are, on the whole, of a condition in life far above anything

"Then I comfort myself with the thought that young Grayson now sports a bloodied nose," said Mr Bennet, with beatific smile.

Darcy smiled back. At least a bloody nose. With luck, Grayson would not be able to show his face for a se'ennight. "He wishes us good hunting and asks that I keep him apprised of the outcome. The direction he gives us is The Feathers, 59 King Street, Seven Dials—an inn under the ownership of one Ann Filmer. Seven Dials… a bad place. Notoriously so."

"Dangerous," Edward agreed. "A warren of ramshackle buildings and courtyards, teeming with the lowest class of persons. The area has a bad name, as does the whole of St Giles' parish. It is a very poor place."

"It is the best clue we have had concerning Wickham—" Mr Gardiner began.

Mr Bennet snorted. "It is the only clue. We must decide how to act on it."

It would be some hours yet until dark. Edward looked consideringly at his watch, and said, in decided tones, "I am reluctant to go there without first putting some of my men into place. They can blend in with relative ease. For us to go in daylight… no. We might as well hire the Vauxhall band to march ahead of us playing *God Save The King*. We will be marked within minutes as not belonging in the area, and if Wickham has an ounce of sense, he will be on the watch for anything and anyone unusual. No. We go as evening draws in, dress simply and discreetly, and use the darkness to cover our advance, having put my men in and around the inn."

"And the bailiff's tipstaffs. I will arrange that in advance." Mr Phillip's expression was one of wry humour. "I do not doubt but they will sit happily in the inn drinking ale all evening at my expense until called for."

"That is sensible." Mr Bennet nodded. "Then, gentlemen, I propose we part company and make what preparations we can, though the bulk of that will fall on the colonel and my brother Phillips. Where shall we meet, and when?"

"Perhaps at the Theatre Royal, in Covent Garden, at around half past six o'clock?" Darcy folded the paper carefully and handed it to Elizabeth with a bow. "King Street is but a short walk from there."

"Excellent. I have plenty of time to get my men into position." Edward rubbed his hands together briskly.

Mr Phillips nodded. "I shall go at once to the bailiff's house, and meet you at the inn."

"Then," said Darcy, "we have a plan."

Good hunting indeed. The chase was on.

CHAPTER FORTY

Retrieval...

Covent Garden was a place of shadows intermittently pierced by oil lamps flaming on iron standards set in the streets, and thronged with people. In the Season, the Theatre Royal on Bow Street was one of the most fashionable venues: every night coaches would roll up to decant elegant silk-clad ladies and debonair gentlemen, coming to the play or the opera. With the theatre having only a limited programme over the winter and often closed, the crowds that night were of a lower quality. Most of the women were not at all respectable.

Another reason the men in her family had tried to keep her away.

"With you and Uncle Gardiner, and Thomas Rance with me, not to mention Mr Darcy and the colonel and all the colonel's men, I could not be better protected. If you tell me you are going unarmed, I will be astonished!" Elizabeth nodded at her father's wince. "And if you tell me that you can deal with Lydia in strong hysterics, then I will be more than astonished. I will be incredulous."

This time, her father's wince had been so exaggerated she was hard pressed not to laugh. The thought of Lydia quailed him and, with his grudging, shame-faced agreement, she swathed herself in her aunt's black cloak and got into the coach with him and Uncle Gardiner. Thomas climbed up beside the driver.

A soldier awaited them outside the darkened theatre. "We're for Castle Street, where it meets Cross Lane. There's a yard off the Lane where the colonel says to leave the coaches under guard. They'll be out of plain sight, and safer. 'Tis only a few minutes' walk from there to the Feathers."

At Uncle Gardiner's acquiescence, the soldier hopped up onto the box to show the way. Thomas made room, going to the iron footman's stand at the rear of the carriage, glancing in the window and nodding at Elizabeth en route.

"You could stay with the coach, Lizzy," Papa suggested, but not in a tone that indicated he anticipated much success.

"I will be quite safe, Papa, I am sure."

"You may be. I am not sure I will, when we meet our confederates."

When she alighted from the coach in a cold, smelly little courtyard hemmed about by tall, dark buildings, neither Mr Darcy nor the colonel remonstrated with her father. Elizabeth, though, had to wrap her hands in the warm cloak to stop herself pushing their jaws back up into alignment.

Colonel Fitzwilliam recovered first. "I swear, I will if you do not, coz," he said to Mr Darcy, and although this was incomprehensible to Elizabeth, he did not sound condemnatory. He flashed her a grin in the growing darkness, and bowed.

Mr Darcy, however, appeared to be grinding his teeth. The cords on his neck stuck out. Elizabeth refrained from voicing a hope that this did not indicate an apoplectic tendency in his family. He was vastly improved in civility these last two days, but had not yet learned to be laughed at.

The colonel issued quiet-voiced orders, and they set off immediately. Elizabeth's feet slipped on the slimy cobbles, and she was glad to take her father's arm as they came out onto Cross Lane and walked quickly north to the junction with Castle Street. Several of Colonel Fitzwilliam's soldiers went with them, some a few yards ahead as vanguard, and as many again behind. The colonel treated their adventure as he would a sortie into enemy territory.

They all had longer strides than she did. Crowded into the middle of the group, Elizabeth had to take faster steps, but would not let herself fail to keep up. Thank the Lord she was used to brisk exercise. It kept her warm against the chill air. Mr Darcy walked behind her. The back of her neck burned under the intensity of his stare, and she wriggled her shoulders under the concealing cloak. She slipped again, and suddenly he was there on her other side, taking her free arm.

"Lean on me, Mrs Grayson. It is foul underfoot."

When she glanced at him, he was staring ahead. She could see little but his profile, a silhouette against the frail light of a distant street lamp. She tucked her hand under his arm. Let her compliance be his reward for courtesy.

The colonel paused at the junction. Carts rolled past on their way to and from the fruit market at Covent Garden to the south. "That is King Street." He indicated the street directly opposite Cross Lane. "The Feathers is about halfway up on the right. My men report that the storeys above the tap rooms form one of the meaner sort of lodging houses. It is not certain that Wickham is here, although it is a likely enough haunt."

King Street was darker than the street outside the Theatre Royal, with the flaring lamps set on posts much farther apart. It was narrower, and meaner. The buildings huddled in on each other like a crowd of men jostling to gain the best position at a boxing mill. Some were so old, their upper storeys overhung the narrow footpath. It was as slimy and slippery underfoot as the noisome little court where they had left the coaches.

There were several taverns, the only well-lit buildings in the street, their windows bright with light that gleamed on the swinging signs above their doors and limned the faces of passers-by in a sickly yellow. The Two Spies. The Crown and Anchor. The Horse and Groom.

The Feathers.

No better and no worse looking than any other of the taverns they passed. Light and noise spilled out onto the street: voices, laughter, a raucous song. A man detached himself from the shadows and spoke quietly to the colonel, who smiled.

"Thank you, Oliver. That is indeed interesting. Come with us." The colonel glanced around at them, gathering their attention with his direct gaze. "We will go straight through the tap room to the back of the building, to the office and staircase." He pushed open the door and led the way inside.

"Stay close," her father said in her ear, tightening his grip on her arm. "Keep your face covered."

She kept her head down as they wove a path between groups of drinkers. Swift glances showed her tables set on a sawdusted floor; caught a face here with its dulled, unhealthy skin; an arm or body there, clad in grimy clothing that was cheaper-looking even than that worn by the farm labourers at home. The few women present wore dresses cut so low they might as well have used a ribbon for a bodice.

Mr Darcy at her other elbow was far closer than he had ever been, pressing her against his side. "Mr Phillips is here, with three men. All is in readiness."

A long trestle table took up most of the back wall, two large ale barrels laid on it sideways, shelves behind filled with squat black bottles. The table stopped short of the corner, where a door led to the rooms behind. Colonel Fitzwilliam had the door opened in a trice. One of his men closed it behind them once they had all hurried through, and stayed there to guard it. No one challenged them.

Elizabeth blew out a breath and, released by her father and Mr Darcy, pushed back the hood of her cloak. Immediately before her was a small lobby with one door, and an uncarpeted staircase to the left wound up to the gloom of the upper floors.

The colonel's fierce grin was for Mr Darcy. "Sergeant Oliver's news will amuse you, coz. Let us go and meet Mrs Filmer, the proprietor of this fair tavern." He nodded towards the closed door, and rapped his knuckles against the panels.

A woman's voice bade him enter, followed by an incoherent screech when the colonel flung open the door and the entire company pressed through into the room beyond. Seated behind a rough desk when the door opened, the woman sprang to her feet, her chair skidding back to bounce against the wall behind. Her heavy-set features distorted with anger.

And fear?

"Well, well. Mrs Younge. How fortuitous."

Oh yes. Fear. Colonel Fitzwilliam's genial, happy tone would strike terror into the fiercest Frenchman.

The woman looked around wildly, eyes wide and mouth agape, her hands held rigidly down by her sides and curled into impotent fists. She breathed through her mouth; sharp, harsh rasping breaths that had her bodice heaving. It took her two attempts to speak. "Colonel!" Another wild look, and her gaze lit upon Mr Darcy, at Elizabeth's side. "You, too! What do you want here? Get out! Get out, all of you! Is it not enough you have brought me to this?"

"Tell us what we wish to know and we will leave you in peace." Colonel Fitzwilliam took her by the elbow and returned her to her chair. "Where will I find Wickham?"

She flung off his hand and glowered in silence, drawing thick brows down over her eyes. She pressed her lips together. If a man could die from her Medusa-like glare, the colonel would be measuring his coffin.

"Or," said Mr Darcy, "I could inform the magistrates that a sapphire cross disappeared when you were dismissed. Newgate is an insalubrious place, I am told."

Mrs Younge hissed out something that Elizabeth could only assume was a curse.

"The choice is yours, madam." Darcy could not quite manage the charming geniality of his cousin, but it must have been threatening enough.

Mrs Younge unsealed her lips to grind out, "Front attic."

"With a girl?" the colonel asked.

She nodded, one sharp dip of her head, keeping her eyes on Colonel Fitzwilliam. The whites of her eyes showed briefly, giving her the look of a nervous horse.

"Excellent. We will take him off your hands." Colonel Fitzwilliam gestured to one of his men. "Keep her in here and keep her quiet."

Mrs Younge made a hmmph-ing noise, and for the first time looked directly at Elizabeth. "You are putting yourself into their hands, when you see them treat a woman so?"

"I am capable of seeing their quality," Elizabeth said. "And yours."

Mrs Younge scowled, but wisely kept silent. The soldier the colonel had indicated went to stand over her, and nothing more was said on either side. The colonel snatched one of the lit tallow candles from the desk, and the party hurried up the staircase by its stinking light to the topmost of the three upper storeys, passing the closed doors to several rooms as they crossed the landings between floors. The house was dark and quiet, the noise from the taproom below muted.

The top storey under the house eaves had only two doors leading from the small landing. Colonel Fitzwilliam signalled to Thomas and the man who had met them outside—Sergeant Oliver, was it?—and jerked his head towards the door to the front attic.

"Stay back, Lizzy," Papa said quietly. "Let them subdue Wickham first."

All she could see was a confused medley of backs as the door burst open, slamming back on its hinges, and the leaders of their group surged inside. A squeal, and a man's voice letting loose with a violent string of curses. Noises of a struggle, crashes as something fell over and bounced on an uncarpeted floor, Lydia's voice rising in panic, calling out "George! George!" More deep-voiced curses; a scuffle; a groan of pain; whooping high-pitched, breathy yelps from Lydia.

Thomas appeared in the doorway. "We have him, ma'am."

Elizabeth followed her father in. The single window was obscured by a dingy, torn curtain, and the only light came from the few flames flickering on the hearth until more tallow candles flared in Uncle Gardiner's hand. He set one wooden candlestick onto a rickety table, lit a second candle at the fire and put that on the mantel.

The candles illuminated squalor.

A narrow, dirty room, with rough, cheap furniture of the sort found in small cottages: table, two chairs, a bed bedecked with tattered hangings, half torn down. Wickham was in one of the chairs, held there by the colonel and Sergeant Oliver, their hands clamped on his shoulders. He looked dazed. Perhaps the colonel had given him too hard a blow to the head: he had the bewildered, unformed gaze an infant often showed when it looked on a world incomprehensible to it. He was mostly dressed, at least. A small mercy.

Lydia was in bed under the filthy-looking covers, only her face visible above the edge of the counterpane. Her gaze darted from one person to the next, eyelids twitching. She flung wide her arms, hands flailing and grabbing at thin air, fingers almost convulsive. Her voice exploded out of her, rising with every word, cracking and tight, and as shrill and frenzied as a parrot. "Oh, what are you doing? What are you— Let George go! Let him go!"

Elizabeth moved quickly, landing on the bed on one knee, her other foot bracing her against the floor, using her own body to mask Lydia from everyone's astonished, condemning gaze. She caught Lydia's face between her hands. Hard.

"Stop it. Stop it now." She kept her tone commanding, but even.

Lydia's mouth gaped open. Every breath was a sharp "Oh! Oh! Oh! Oh! Oh!"

Elizabeth pushed her back and down, tightening her hold on Lydia's lower face, pressing her fingertips into the soft, still-rounded, childish cheeks until she could feel the line of Lydia's teeth beneath the skin. "Stop it."

Lydia brought up her hands to push ineffectually at Elizabeth's shoulders. "Oh! Oh! Oh! Oh! Oh!"

The bed smelt of must and a man's tangy sweat. It was not unfamiliar, and Elizabeth forced down the feeling of nausea that welled into her throat. "Breathe. Breathe, Lyddie. In. Out. Do as I tell you. Slow it. In. Out."

Lydia's eyes, wild and dark, stared into hers.

Elizabeth gentled her tone. "Just breathe with me, Lyddie. That is right. That is it. Good girl. Breathe. Breathe."

Lydia blinked, her rigid body sagging into the mattress under Elizabeth's hands.

"Good God," said their father, behind Elizabeth.

She paid him no heed. Left to him, Lydia would be a screaming demon by now. "Good, Lyddie." She was crooning, lilting her voice into the cadence of a lullaby. "Good girl. Slow. Slow. Good."

She released her hold on Lydia's face and sat back keeping herself between the men and her sister's shame. The marks of her fingers were plainly to be seen, little reddened ovals under Lydia's cheekbones. The bile roiled again. To have hurt her little sister so! There was no forgiveness for that. Lydia winced, raised a hand and rubbed at one sore cheek. Elizabeth cupped the other gently, and smoothed it with her finger tips.

A glance behind her showed a collection of shocked faces. Men! Not one of them were ready to deal with Lydia's tumbled emotions.

"Have you come for my wedding, Lizzy?"

Elizabeth leaned forward and pressed a kiss against Lydia's brow. "We have come for you. Thank the Lord we found you. You must get dressed now, and we will leave."

Lydia was not yet quite ready to see reason. Not that Lydia was ever quite ready in that regard. "No! I will not leave George! We are to be married, Lizzy! I will not—"

"We are taking you to Gracechurch Street. It will be better than here."

"No!"

A response in kind would start her off again. Elizabeth strove for the same calm, even tone she had used throughout; a little harder than the motherly crooning. "You have a choice to make. You may walk through the streets to our carriage, dressed and decent and unremarkable. Or I will march you there exactly as you are. Every man out in the streets"—she swept out an arm to indicate King Street—"will laugh, and point, and jeer. They will toss you pennies, the way they do the girls who sell their favours."

She paused. "It is a nasty night with a chill wind. You will likely catch a cold as well as pennies."

Lydia drew a long, wavering breath, her gaze fixed on Elizabeth.

"You must get dressed, Lyddie."

Lydia nodded, stunned into obedience.

"Good. I will help you." Elizabeth raised her voice a little, but kept her gaze on Lydia accompanied by a small, soft smile she hoped would encourage compliance. "Gentlemen, you will all turn your backs, please." Now she glanced behind her. "You too, Mr Wickham."

His expression, two parts smug complacence to one part nervous fear, changed instantly to one of shock and resentment. "I have seen it all, Mrs Grayson," he said with venomous savagery.

"Precisely." Elizabeth turned her attention back to Lydia while feet shuffled, Wickham yelped, and a chair scraped on the floor to indicate he was forcibly turned around by his captors.

Another glance to be sure of Lydia's privacy. Astonishing how much could be read from that row of men's backs. Thomas and the sergeant stood either side of Wickham, forcibly keeping his head turned to the fireplace. Colonel Fitzwilliam's shoulders shook a trifle, but then he was not at all a serious gentleman. Mr Darcy seemed stiff with outrage and, knowing him, discomfort and embarrassment. Her father looked stooped and his rounding shoulders indicated distress, while the back of Uncle Gardiner's neck was red with anger.

She had Lydia back into a respectable-looking state in only a few minutes. Lydia's chemise and petticoat were strewn over the foot of the bed, and a swift hunt discovered a dress draped over a chest in the corner. Her stays were nowhere to be seen. No matter. Elizabeth laced and buttoned her into the sadly crumpled dress, sat her down on the side of the bed, and used both hands to smooth the wild disarray of Lydia's curls. The girl sniffled in the manner of a toddler denied a treat, but she was fit to be seen, at least.

Elizabeth sat beside her and took her hand, squeezing it gently. "Good. We are ready, gentlemen. Now we may begin to resolve this bumble-bath."

CHAPTER FORTY-ONE

... and Retribution

"We are going to be married, Lizzy." Lydia turned a hopeful face to her. "Is that not a fine thing? Will I not have a handsome husband?"

"You certainly *need* to be married." Elizabeth's slight emphasis apparently went unnoticed by her sister, though Wickham scowled.

Lydia confided that "George loves me desperately, and I love him. We will wed as soon as we have a little money. We do not have any, and that is quite a difficulty, you know!", and so the negotiation opened.

Wickham, with more than half an eye on Colonel Fitzwilliam and Mr Darcy, rehearsed some tale of financial woe, assured Papa of his undying love for Lydia, with a rueful "We have acted wrongly, sir, I know, but our feelings for each other are so very strong..."—an assertion that had Lydia tearfully agreeing and sighing, while looking at her paramour with such an expression of infatuation on her face that Elizabeth was forced to look away lest she tell the pair what she thought of them and their conduct.

Wickham made more fatuous statements about his lovestruck state, before shamelessly suggesting a sum of ten thousand pounds would allow him and his beloved Lydia to start afresh. Elizabeth could only be struck by Colonel Fitzwilliam's prescience in the matter of the sum demanded.

Her father countered with the offer of one hundred pounds a year during his lifetime, and Lydia's share of her mother's dowry on Mrs Bennet's demise.

Wickham professed himself shocked and sorrowful that Papa should poke fun in such a way, notable though Papa's sardonic humour was, and repeated his tale and list of wants and needs, almost word for word. He had rehearsed himself, then, for this. The colonel yawned widely and loudly. Mr Darcy, with a muted exclamation of disgust, walked to the window and stared out onto King Street. Mr Gardiner picked up one of the candlesticks and hefted its weight.

Her father mirrored the shock and sorrow, and repeated his offer. "For you know, Longbourn is not so rich as that."

"Ah, but Mrs Grayson will doubtless decide she wishes to see her sister well settled..."

What Mrs Grayson decided, since Wickham had openly drawn her into the argument, was that it was time to play her hand and win a few tricks. Wickham had paused to look at her, expression expectant. He had a particularly ingratiating smile.

"Lydia," said Elizabeth, "are you truly resolved on marrying this poor, miserable creature masquerading as a man?"

Wickham jerked as if she had slapped him. The colonel openly displayed his glee, and Mr Darcy turned back to face the room.

Lydia gaped at her.

"Look at him. Handsome enough, I suppose, in a way that will soon look bloated and coarse, given his dissipations. A man almost twice your age with no income, no profession—"

"He is very handsome! And he would have a profession if that Mr Darcy"—indicated by an angry head-toss—"had not cheated my poor George out of it!"

"Is he still lying about that? Perhaps if he had used the three thousand pounds that Mr Darcy gave him in lieu of the living to make his profession in the law as he promised, we would not now be sitting in this miserable hovel listening to him windbagging us into insensibility."

Lydia mouthed "three thousand pounds" and frowned.

Wickham let out an angry growl, but his attempts to leap up out of his chair were thwarted by the colonel and Sergeant Oliver, who slammed him back into it with military precision. From their expressions and the smug way they looked around for approval, they relished the opportunity.

Held down, Wickham snarled, "The price just increased to fifteen thousand!"

"And thus, Miss Lydia, he condemns himself from his own mouth. He is here for money. He is the kind of man who must have money, but who will not give himself the trouble of earning it." Mr Darcy employed the same cool, non-judgemental tone that he might have used to remark upon the weather, and which carried more conviction than screamed curses could ever do. It earned him an approving nod from Elizabeth. He gave her a slight smile in return.

Wickham's voice rose in outrage. "Fifteen thousand, and we will live in Netherfield!"

Lydia's brows had drawn down in confusion, but she nodded at this. "Well, you do not choose to live there, Lizzy, and we will be nicer than that horrid Bingley woman, or the silly brother who jilted Jane."

"I do not choose to live there because I lease it out, and Uncle Gardiner invests the profits so I can improve my sisters' dowries."

"Oh, do I have more money then? And will you help us? Will you give us money?"

Elizabeth spoke to Lydia, but her words were not for her heedless little sister alone. "You wish me to support you? But that is the man's lot, to work for his family's needs and earn enough to assure their well-being and happiness. Any *real* man would have too much pride, would balk at leeching from another. Particularly from a woman." Elizabeth gestured to Wickham. "This pitiable excuse for manhood will never take care of you, Lydia, nor any children you have. You will never go to balls and parties. You will

make herself believe she was untouched. At rest. She could fold her hands in her lap, listen to the sound of Lydia being coaxed upstairs, to the cries for "George!" and to Jane's soft, soothing voice, and feel that the tears coursing down her face need not have a reason.

"She knows Jane a little better, that is all," Aunt Gardiner said.

Elizabeth took the handkerchief she was offered and dabbed it at her eyes. "I have been thinking of how much James took from me. She and Kitty were such children when I had to leave Longbourn, and I do not know them as well as I ought. By the time I was more myself again, after I was free, it was too late. They had grown away from me."

"Perhaps if you had returned to Longbourn to live…"

"Impossible. I cannot forgive Mama for her part in all my troubles. Even now." Elizabeth dashed away the tears with her fingers and accepted the hands her aunt held out. "Not having their trust and affection is a great loss. It will be best for Lyddie to be with Jane, who comforted all her childish woes when I could not. Jane is a gentler creature than me."

"Was it very bad, how you found her?"

"Yes. A nasty, cheap lodging house, and he so unrepentant, malicious and mercenary." Elizabeth pushed through a small smile, as slow as a spoon drawn through spilled honey. "At least, he was until the tipstaffs arrived. I did not allow her to see that."

"She will come to understand you did the right thing."

"This is Lydia we speak of. She is my mother, writ younger. All she knows is that she caught herself a handsome man, and I have taken him away."

"She is a fool." Her father joined them, her uncles following after. He had a small tray with glasses in his hand and put one glass on the table beside Elizabeth. "Drink that, child."

"My best brandy." Uncle Gardiner rested his hand on Elizabeth's hair for a moment.

Uncle Phillips took a seat and another proffered glass. "A good day's work, niece."

"But not ended. She cannot go home." Elizabeth sighed as the brandy burnt its warmth into her, and let the tension drain away. "We must decide what we can do for her."

"I will keep her here for a short while, but not for long." Uncle Gardiner's looks were very grave. "I have my own children to consider and will not have such an influence near them."

Papa nodded. "She must marry. The question is, to whom? Who will have such a ninnyhammer, soiled as she is? It may have to be Wickham. Perhaps after a few weeks sojourn in the Fleet, he will be willing to marry for less than he demanded."

"I would rather anyone else. Can you help, uncle?" Elizabeth asked.

Uncle Gardiner sighed. "I will do my best, Lizzy. That is all I can promise."

With which less-than-confident assertion, Elizabeth had to be content.

CHAPTER FORTY-TWO

Scritto In Core

Darcy left the Bennet family to itself for three days, arguing that everyone needed a respite from the world to regain some semblance of peace. By Saturday morning, the fourth day, Edward threatened to call for Darcy's carriage and toss him into it.

"Never heed their peace, coz! What about mine? Go, I beg you! Relieve my misery." And as Darcy was donning coat and hat, Edward added, "Give Mrs Grayson my salutations, and be grateful I do not intend to pursue her myself."

If Edward *had* accompanied him, he might have least mollified Miss Lydia with the sight of a redcoat. Instead, she glared when Darcy was announced, and flounced out of the sitting room complaining loudly about wicked people being allowed into the house when her poor George was martyred and forbidden. Darcy paid her no heed, brushing off the embarrassed apologies from her elder sisters, and after the shortest possible time for civility, invited Mrs Grayson out for a walk. His delight when she accepted without hesitation filled him with a warmth no petulant child could temper. That she also chose to leave Rance behind and trust herself to him... his chest swelled so much his waistcoat buttons were in jeopardy.

"I am sorry you heard that," Elizabeth said, as they descended the three broad steps into Gracechurch Street. "It has been a common refrain since we took Lydia from the Feathers, though her childish barbs are usually aimed at me. We are wicked together, it seems."

Mr Darcy tsked. "Is she insensible of everything she owes you?"

"I do not want gratitude. I want her to see her folly and errors, and learn from them. Sadly, that will be as likely as gratitude. Shall we walk up to Moorfields? It is the nearest green space."

This agreed to, they set off northward into Bishopsgate.

"Have any plans been made for Miss Lydia?" Darcy asked.

"Nothing concrete. My uncle is making delicate enquiries amongst his acquaintance, but we are hampered by two things. First, my uncle's friends are very much like him: upright, moral, principled. It will not be easy to find a man willing to take on a ruined girl, particularly a feather-brain with a small dowry and no skills in running a household. Few will deem those disadvantages erased by her being a gentleman's daughter." Elizabeth paused, then sighed. "Second, we do not yet know if she is with child. That will change everything."

Mr Darcy grunted. "Forgive me for asking so personal a question, but do you still intend to give Miss Lydia a dowry? Three thousand was the sum you mentioned."

"Yes. I will not give more. That would rob my other sisters."

"A greater sum would make finding her a husband much easier." He stopped in the street and, realising that a large number of people would have to dodge around him, drew her into the lee of the building at the side of the pavement. "I do not know your father

"Matthew admitted that he arranged for this Wickham person to go to Meryton. He told me he had by then already determined it was unlikely he would be able to deprive you of the estate James bequeathed you. He was bewildered by your good name with the neighbourhood. Having convinced himself that you must be of a particular type..." Kirton paused and winced. "I need not elucidate, I am sure. Anyhow, he could not believe you were as respectable and respected as you are. His notion was to bring in Wickham to encompass the ruin of your good name and show you in what he claims are your true colours."

"Wickham would be willing if he saw something in it for himself. Doubtless Mrs Grayson's estate was enough inducement." Darcy closed his hand into a fist.

"Matthew's reasoning is beyond me since it could no way profit him. No matter. He has failed. As long as my father and I are his trustees, we can shorten his leash. When he is five and twenty in two years, we will lose that advantage. I would not leave you vulnerable to him, Mrs Grayson. I believe he felt free to plot this in part because, when James died, we agreed with your father that we would leave you in peace. In Matthew's addle-pated head, that meant we were indifferent to you. I wish to assure you that is not the case. You are my cousin by marriage, and your well-being is important to the family. No man of honour could think otherwise. I have impressed all this upon Matthew, most forcibly." And Kirton flexed his gloved hands.

Darcy smiled. Kirton was really a *very* fine amateur pugilist.

Elizabeth's smile had the saucy, impudent quality that always made Darcy's blood surge. "Is our meeting today in the way of making a public statement, my lord?"

"It is indeed. It will clip Matthew's wings." Kirton offered his arm. "Will you permit me to take you in? And you must call me Cousin John."

"I would be honoured." Elizabeth dropped a curtsey and took Kirton's arm. But her glance at Darcy was a trifle uncertain. "Cousin."

"Excellent. Shall we join the rest of your party, Darcy? I have a great wish to make the acquaintance of my cousin's family and friends."

Darcy glanced at Miss Bingley. It was entirely likely that a revolution had taken place, and Miss Bingley now shared Kirton's eagerness.

That probably lasted only as long as the introductions, when Elizabeth, quite correctly, turned to her last of all, and added an airy, "Oh, and Miss Bingley of course," before sweeping into the grand saloon on Kirton's arm.

Damn, but she truly was magnificent.

Catalani was in very fine voice, her mastery of her homeland's famous love songs beyond compare. Her glorious singing, her ecstatic expression as she sang of love being written on her heart, added a wonderfully harmonic counterpoint to the pleasure Darcy gained from watching Elizabeth, who sat between him and Kirton.

It was true. Open his chest, and his love would indeed be inscribed on his heart. *Scritto in core.*

Good Lord, but he was become the most romantic fool! Then Elizabeth turned her head to smile at him, and he did not care one whit about how foolish he might be.

could see her face framed within her bonnet's stiffened brim. "Your implacable resentment has a softer side, then."

"I cannot but think he was ruined by my father's regard. It will be my final act of reparation."

"You are very good."

"We both know that is not the case. However, enough of Wickham. How does Miss Lydia?"

Elizabeth brightened. "Good news. Every indication is that she is not with child, and that makes settling her all the simpler. She is calmer, too. That is Jane's doing, of course. Jane has carefully brought her into a better frame of mind. Lydia realises now how dire her situation is, how little Wickham can truly answer to her interest since he is alive only to his own, and how imprudent—in every possible way!—the connection was. She talks of him less than she did. She is less fixed on him."

"Out of sight..." Darcy chuffed out a small laugh. "A true proverb."

"It has given my uncle's search new impetus, to know that she is not so obdurately set now on Wickham, and we are unlikely to have to deal with an unwelcome little stranger."

"Perhaps I may help." He smiled at her eager look. "Colonel Fitzwilliam told me yesterday about a young officer in the First Regiment of Foot—the Royal Scots. Captain Buchanan is the fourth son of a gentleman. He is an excellent man, held back for want of fortune. His father bought him the captaincy, but cannot provide for further advancement. My cousin believes the income from Lydia's dowry will be a welcome addition to the captain's pay. With the added inducement of the purchase of his promotion to major, this could be a very fortuitous opportunity if they take to each other."

"Oh... I had not considered... Yes, Lydia may well be happier with one of her beloved redcoats than a man in trade. Is not the cost of a promotion very expensive, though?"

About fourteen hundred pounds, Edward had said; the difference between a captaincy and a majority. Darcy would not allow her to concern herself about it. "He will sell his captaincy, and there is a difference to be paid. It is nothing of significance."

"I see." She looked rather quizzical, her quick mind doubtless seeing the gaping hole in his argument. If it were so insignificant a sum, why could not the captain's family pay?

"Allow me to investigate further."

Her mouth twitched. "Of course. I suppose it will help, having a captaincy to sell."

"I am sure of it," he said, blandly. "There is some urgency. The majority has not yet been advertised for sale, but given it requires a transfer to the regiment's second battalion in India, there may be considerable interest. India is a great place for making a fortune, and many a man would venture there."

"India! Good Lord." Now she looked thoughtful, brows drawn down. "Such a long way."

"Indeed." Darcy considered distance to be far from the least of the advantages. "It struck me that Miss Lydia might like an adventure."

"Ah, but will the adventure like Lydia?" Elizabeth pursed her lips, which had Darcy looking swiftly away to avoid giving in to temptation. "Do you know much about the captain? Have you met him?"

"Yesterday. He impressed me. He understands Lydia's circumstances, and is accepting of her misstep. His condition is that she must commit to being a real wife to him and eventually build a family, but he is willing to give her time after the marriage to adjust to her new life. Close companionship on the voyage to Bombay is likely to allow for that. It lasts some three or four months."

There was no mistaking her impudent smile. "Oh dear, Mr Darcy. It is painfully obvious that you are inexperienced in the art of selling young gentlemen to even younger ladies. None of that will impress Lydia, even if his red coat is likely to incline her towards him. What is his age? Height? Colouring? Is he fat or thin, indolent or active? Is he a handsome man, and are his shoulders broad enough to adequately fill his uniform without padding?"

He stared. The small noise he made was suspiciously akin to gibbering.

"Ha, Lizzy," she said, sounding good-humoured and merry, "those great mountains will make your Oakham Mount seem naught but a little hillock!"

"A hill near our home, Captain," Elizabeth explained, smiling. "Of no great prominence, but it gives excellent views of our portion of the county. It is a favourite walk of mine."

The talk became more general, then, but Miss Lydia did not revert to the sulks. Indeed, she seemed unusually thoughtful, watching Buchanan throughout the remainder of the meal.

The gentlemen eschewed the idea of separating after dinner if, as Mr Gardiner proposed, they would be allowed to carry their port with them into the drawing room and continue the fascinating discussion. Mrs Gardiner gave gracious permission. Darcy, nothing loath, made ready to escort Elizabeth in, when Miss Lydia stopped them, allowing the rest of the company to go on without them.

"I shall leave you to talk to each other," Darcy said, a touch disappointed to relinquish Elizabeth.

"No," Miss Lydia said, slowly. "It does not signify if you are here. Indeed, I wanted to ask... he lied, did he not? George, I mean. He lied about you not giving him some living or other."

"Yes, he did. Lying, I am sorry to say, is one of his talents."

Miss Lydia nodded, her mouth rather tight. Darcy suspected it was to stop her chin trembling.

"He did not want to marry me. Not without a great deal of money. What you said, Mr Darcy, about him really wanting to marry Netherfield... he only took me with him because he thought he could make Lizzy pay. I am right there, I think."

"I am sorry to say that you are. He is not an evil man. I do not think him violent or wicked enough to do you injury." Darcy kept his tone as gentle as he could. This could have been Georgiana he spoke to. Indeed, it had been Georgiana, and the words he used now were very similar to those he had spoken to his sister. "But he is a man who cannot see beyond his own interest. He is selfish and manipulative. You are not the first he deceived in such a way, Miss Lydia."

"This man, this captain you have brought here tonight. He looks for money too, does he not, to marry me? How is that any different?"

"It is true that Captain Buchanan will be happy to gain your dowry, Lyddie, and the help we can give him in his career," Elizabeth said, with care. "But the difference is that he is leaving to you the choice of accepting him or not. He has not denied you the power of choice by absconding with you to one of the worst areas of London and depriving you of your virtue. Wickham ruined you, dearest. He destroyed your old life as Lydia Bennet, and you cannot go back to it. Captain Buchanan does not pretend to love you yet, but he does agree to treat you well, and honour you as his wife. You can trust him to care for you as a man should care for his wife and family, to work for you and to build your fortunes, the way George Wickham never would. He is as honest as Wickham is not."

"I cannot go back." Miss Lydia seemed to curl in on herself, the way a poor hurt creature would. "I cannot go home."

"Not unmarried, no. But I am certain Papa and Mama will welcome the visit of Captain and Mrs Buchanan before they set sail."

"Mama will not be pleased." Miss Lydia's flash of humour was the image of her elder sister's. "She would not like me settled even so far as Newcastle. Bombay is far beyond her ken!" And in a softer tone, she said, "And beyond mine. It is so very far away, Lizzy."

"But what an adventure you will have! Think of it. You will ride on elephants, and sup with those Indian Princes who have so many jewels, they drip with diamonds like a fountain gushes water. How envious we will be, left behind here while you are off looking at tigers! Think of all the things you will see and do, that you can tell us about in your letters."

"Hmmmpfh. Married women do not have much time for letters." Miss Lydia finally turned to start for the drawing room. She paused when Darcy offered his free arm, then nodded and accepted it. "He is a real soldier, I suppose. Not just a militiaman."

"Very real, Lyddie. And, I think, a brave one. He has seen action, and it has made a man of him."

Miss Lydia paused in the drawing room doorway. "He is just as good looking as George."

"I think so, too." And Elizabeth smiled at her. "Go and talk to him, little sister. Get to know him."

Captain Buchanan looked up at that moment to see them in the doorway, and gave Miss Lydia a nod and a slight smile.

"Just as good looking," Miss Lydia said again, and dropping her hold on Darcy's arm, she walked across the room to sit beside the captain. He turned to her at once, and his smile widened. He looked truly pleased to receive her attention.

A promising beginning.

"She has every ounce of your courage," Darcy said, for the first time feeling something other than vexed exasperation towards the girl.

"More," said Elizabeth, a catch in her voice. "So much more."

CHAPTER FORTY-FOUR

Enter the Baronet's Lady

Following the reading of the banns, Lydia Anne Bennet and William Henry Buchanan were married at St Peter-upon-Cornhill, the Gardiners' church, on the last Monday in March, Easter Monday, almost six weeks after Lydia's ill-fated elopement and some three weeks after their first meeting. The bride was attended by two of her sisters; the groom had Mr Darcy to stand with him, since none of his family could travel from Edinburgh in time for the ceremony.

It was the first day in weeks Elizabeth felt she could take a deep breath. She laid her hand lightly on Mr Darcy's arm as they walked back down the aisle, following the bride and groom and the rest of the wedding party out into the thin spring sunshine to walk around the corner into Gracechurch Street for the wedding breakfast. Jane was taken out by Mr Bingley, of course, who was trying to prove his constancy through demonstration, rather than mere assertion. Jane was blooming as a result.

Which was rather unfair, given an unblooming Jane was still the most beautiful woman Elizabeth knew. Being left in the shade stung sometimes.

"I understand Major and Mrs Buchanan will go straight to Longbourn today after a short time at the breakfast," Mr Darcy said. "It will relieve your mother's anxiety, I expect, to see her daughter safe and well."

"Yes. Mama has written very often, of course, and with Jane sitting over her, Lydia has been induced to respond. Once she had agreed to the match, she had plenty to say about her future with Major Buchanan and all the excitement of outfitting her for the journey and for living in India. Mama is awaiting a meeting with her new son with great interest. They will stay at Longbourn for only five days, before travelling to Edinburgh to allow the Major to farewell his own parents. They must be in Portsmouth by the end of April to leave for Bombay. They may have time to visit Longbourn again on their way south. My mother hopes so, indeed."

"It will be a busy few weeks, much of it spent travelling. It is a great distance to Edinburgh."

"Lydia appears to be thriving on it, though." She glanced sidelong at Mr Darcy, watchful of his reaction. "My uncle Gardiner made up the dowry to the full six thousand, as you probably know, but I am still in the dark about the purchase of my new brother's majority."

Aha. He would not look at her, seemingly taking a vast interest in looking to his left down Leadenhall Street towards—most appropriately—India House. His cheekbones were tinged a faint pink.

"Mr Darcy?"

The pinkness deepened. "Please do not concern yourself about it, Mrs Grayson. As I said when I first mentioned Buchanan to you, with a captaincy to sell, the difference in cost between that and the majority was quite manageable."

"Then one wonders why his family were unable to do it."

He said nothing, merely set his jaw.

Elizabeth forbore to tease him any further. "Do you dine at the Hursts with us this evening?"

"I do." His mouth twitched. "I have derived great amusement watching Miss Bingley make up all the arrears of civility she owes you. Lord Kirton's public acknowledgment upset all her notions."

Elizabeth allowed a little grimace. "I hope I am improved in civility myself. I was shockingly rude that evening at the Argyle Rooms, and it has preyed on my conscience."

"The set down was well deserved."

"Oh, I do not regret that. She did deserve it. But later, when Lord Kirton asked for an introduction to everyone, I was far too dismissive and unceremonious when I came to her. It was badly done of me. I ought to have behaved better. I have tried ever since to be more civil to her."

"It has been noted, I assure you."

"I regretted most hurting Louisa Hurst. She has all the sweetness her sister lacks and I am grown very fond of her. I think we will be great friends, she and I."

"I hope so, indeed. I am pleased to have their acquaintance. I have found my first impressions of the Hursts were mistaken."

She smiled at him. "A common fault with first impressions, I think."

He smiled back, though it looked rueful. They mounted the steps of the Gardiners' house together, the last of the party to enter. She delayed him on the threshold for a moment.

"That matter we spoke of earlier, and which you evaded... thank you," she said, and led him inside before he could deny it.

"I am delighted you are travelling with us." Louisa Hurst sipped her breakfast chocolate. "I am truly anticipating our return to Netherfield. I dare say," she added, glancing sidelong at her brother and Jane on the other side of the breakfast table at the Hursts' house on Jermyn Street, "that we will have much to celebrate."

Neither Jane nor Bingley appeared to hear her. Elizabeth recalled once mentioning to Charlotte the general incivility towards others that appeared to be the hallmark of deep love. She had daily proof of it these days.

"I will relish a closer relationship," she said, and meant it most sincerely. Louisa Hurst had become a true friend. "One can never have too many sisters, I find." They smiled at each other, and both glanced again at Jane and Bingley. "Though I am very pleased your brother and Jane are riding with Miss Bingley in his own carriage. Were I forced to share a carriage with them, I am likely to be so exasperated with their billing and cooing, I would toss them from the coach before we reached Edgware."

"You are not a romantic, Elizabeth?"

"Not at all." Elizabeth kept the smile constant and her tone breezy.

Miss Bingley's arrival at the breakfast table changed the course of the conversation, devolving as it did into general greetings and courtesies. Elizabeth and Jane had arrived at the Hursts' house early that morning in the Gardiners' coach, the entire party then to travel on to Meryton together. Though they came at the time agreed, the Hursts were just starting a leisurely breakfast, and they were still awaiting Mr Darcy's arrival. Elizabeth had declined food, but Louisa Hurst's cook made superlative chocolate, and she relished the cup Louisa served her.

Miss Bingley, being her inimitable self, had greeted everyone, stared inimically at her brother and Jane, and eventually turned to Elizabeth with the enquiry, "Tell me, Mrs Grayson, will we meet *all* your sisters at Longbourn?"

Ah, was the truce over?

The Hursts and Miss Bingley had been told something of Lydia's tale. Jane had been reluctant, at first, to say anything, but even she had to acknowledge that when everyone returned to Meryton, the gossip could not be escaped. The Hursts knew that the marriage was irregular, but, as Louisa had said when she was told, with a wry glance at a Miss Bingley too far from them to overhear, at least Elizabeth had a sister married and everything else would be forgotten, adding "I love Caroline dearly, Elizabeth, but should very much like to see her settled and happy." Elizabeth suspected Mr Hurst would like it even better.

Reminding herself that she was in debt to the Hursts and Bingleys for her travel home, and that she had promised herself to be more than civil, she kept her tone cheerful and careless. "Mary and Kitty are at Longbourn, of course. My brother Buchanan and Lydia are to leave for Edinburgh this morning to visit his family, so I doubt we will see them."

"Oh." Miss Bingley sipped at her tea. "I merely wondered if we would ever meet this Major Buchanan."

She might as well have said "this illusory Major Buchanan", and be done with it.

"Perhaps unlikely, since they will leave for India at the end of the month. Your brother was at the wedding, however, and I assume he will be happy to satisfy your curiosity. Mr Darcy stood up with the major, so perhaps if you remain unsatisfied, you might apply to him for a description."

"Or you might drink your tea and stop delaying us," Mr Hurst said in sharp admonition. "We wish to depart as soon as Darcy is here."

Miss Bingley smiled sweetly.

Oh yes. It seemed the truce was indeed breached.

"Am I to expect Bingley in my book room tomorrow, Lizzy? He seems very attentive to Jane."

"Soon, Papa, if not quite tomorrow. I think the affair is resolving itself to everyone's satisfaction." Elizabeth waved as the Hurst, Bingley and Darcy coaches bowled out of the gates and turned towards Netherfield. She recalled Miss Bingley's sour face. "Well, almost everyone. Those who matter."

Papa glanced at Jane, and nodded. "I am pleased. She was too melancholy before Christmas."

"Mr Bingley's business was protracted, I believe. They were reunited almost as soon as he returned from Yorkshire." As they turned to the house to follow the other girls inside, Elizabeth tucked her hand under his arm. "I was sorry that Mama would not come down. I hoped the knowledge of Bingley's return would cheer her."

"She is much affected by this business of Lydia. In truth, it has brought her very low. She brisked up when we found Lydia, and even more when your Mr Darcy produced a dashing young officer eager for matrimony, but this idea of India has sunk her again. She cannot fathom the distance, and is dreading such a long separation from her favourite."

"I will go up and see her, not that I am ever much comfort to her."

"In a moment." Papa drew her into his book room, and to the chairs set before the hearth. "What news of Wickham?"

"Still in the Fleet. He has accepted Mr Darcy's offer of passage to Australia and the funds to start a new life, with the understanding that if he returns, we will once more prosecute him for his debts. He will remain in prison until he can be escorted to Plymouth or Southampton and the next available transport ship, since he cannot be trusted not to run. Mr Darcy and Colonel Fitzwilliam will personally put Wickham on the ship, and then we may all breathe more easily."

"Mr Darcy has done much for us."

"He has indeed, and we are much beholden to him. He believes his family created Wickham through mistaken indulgence, and that he must remedy the fault."

Papa laughed softly. "Yes. He has a strong sense of responsibility. I can admire it, as much as a man can admire another who possesses the virtues he does not. You have a touch of it yourself, Lizzy. I am conscious of what I owe you. You have worked indefatigably to see your sister creditably established. I am quite shamed by your energy."

"She is my sister, and I want the best for her. The major will be a good husband, I believe. What did you think of him?"

"A sensible man, well read and a good conversationalist. She seemed eager to please him, though she is Lydia still, and a wilful, selfish, fretful creature. Perhaps he will be lucky and she will grow, though I cannot think he has gained the best wife he might have aimed for."

"I hoped you might like him."

"You were right to insist I received them here. I had my doubts."

"Papa, if you had just announced the marriage and that Lydia was going to India, how many of our neighbours would have really believed you, do you think? Allowing the Buchanans to visit and be shown around the neighbourhood, is incontrovertible proof that Lydia is indeed married, there is no further scandal attached to her, and the removal to India therefore is true. The family's reputation is tarnished, perhaps, but restored. I do not think Mr Bingley would have hung back, but it is all to the good for Mary and Kitty. Their futures are rosier."

Papa nodded, smiling. "And what of your future, child? I doubt Mr Darcy is motivated solely by guilt."

Elizabeth's face could not have felt hotter if she had thrust it into the mouth of a volcano. She must be scarlet to the roots of her hair. Even her ears burned. "I have no notion of your meaning."

"Oh Lizzy! 'Tis a little late to be missish!"

Elizabeth rose to her feet and brushed down her skirts. "I am never missish. I shall go and see Mama, sir, if your humour is satisfied. After supper, if you please, I will take Mary home with me to Nether House."

Her father merely chuckled. "Have it your own way. I shall send word so that the Rances expect you tonight. Enjoy your mother's nerves."

"You should not provoke her, Papa. It is very bad of you."

"It is, I own. But your mother and I are used to the situation. I cannot imagine either of us would relish change at this late stage."

Not that he would even try. That was his great failing and sorrow.

And Mama's.

"Lady Catherine de Bourgh, ma'am," Thomas announced in formal, ringing tones, and flung open the door.

Her ladyship swept in.

CHAPTER FORTY-FIVE

Frivolous and Ill-Judged

Lady Catherine was a tall woman, richly attired in a burgundy wool travelling dress of excellent cut. Her bonnet, set back on her head to show the deep, ruffled edge of her lace cap beneath, was an architectural wonder. Elizabeth's mother would covet every thread.

The lady looked to be in her mid-fifties, with a strongly-marked countenance and, although she carried a silver-headed cane, upright bearing. The family resemblance to Mr Darcy lay in the shape and colour of the eyes and the set of the mouth. She must have had some beauty in her youth, and many would consider her to be distinguished still, but, to Elizabeth's eye, the hauteur evident in her manner and expression was not attractive.

She had not liked it in Mr Darcy, either, but he had grown away from it.

She had risen when Lady Catherine entered and now bobbed a curtsey pitched closer to the normal reverence she would accord an older woman than the deep genuflection to which, from the lady's frown, she suspected her visitor felt entitled. "I am Elizabeth

Wickham's smile had all of his old insouciance. "Will you spring for a special licence from the archbishop?"

Darcy could only smile back. "George, if it speeds you on your way and means I never see you again, I will ensure you are married in state by the archbishop, the pope, the chief rabbi, and the entire Society of Friends. Dammit, man, I will see you to the church myself."

He was still occasionally smiling over the first genuine laughter that he and Wickham had shared for, oh, these last ten years, at least, when he returned to Pember House. He had gone first to the Gardiners' for a discussion with Mr Gardiner about investments—and there was an acquaintance he would be glad to foster, no matter what the outcome of his attempt to win Elizabeth—and it was almost four o'clock by the time Wilkes opened the door to him and intoned a greeting. Excellent. He would have time to take tea before settling down to his correspondence.

Except a most unwelcome surprise awaited him. "Lady Catherine? Here?"

Good God.

At Wilkes's nod, Darcy went briskly to the family sitting room where, Wilkes said, his aunt awaited him. Best to get it over with as soon as possible.

She sat enthroned in the largest chair in the room, though it was nothing to the monstrosity she used at Rosings, which was far more ornate than any real throne the king might sit upon. Darcy's staff had attempted to placate the thunderstorm with tea and sweet cakes and pastries. To no avail, if her dark, angry looks were anything to judge by.

"Darcy! At last! Where have you been? I have awaited you this hour, at least."

He bowed. "Good day, Lady Catherine. This is an unexpected visit."

A snort. "A necessary one! Where were you?"

"I had business to attend to, Aunt. If I had received some notice of your coming to Town, I would have been here to greet you. The staff have looked after you, I see."

"Yes, yes! But it is very vexing! I am come on most urgent business myself. Attend me, Darcy. I have heard the most dreadful rumours of a grasping fortune-hunter stabbing her talons into you in Hertfordshire, and I have come at once to refute it—"

"What nonsense," Darcy said, loading his tone with as much contempt as he could muster.

"So I hoped! Mr Collins is quite distraught at having any connection to the woman, but the correspondence he showed me between her and Mrs Collins is quite clear that she drew you into the disgraceful situation regarding her sister's patched-up marriage—"

Darcy had not realised he had such a reserve of contempt to draw upon. It deepened and roughened his voice to the point he barely recognised it himself. "What? I beg your pardon, Lady Catherine, but are you speaking of Mrs Elizabeth Grayson?"

"Whom else? Mr Collins told me how she teased him and flirted and led him on, and only his own consciousness of propriety and goodness kept him safe from her machinations. What—"

"Madam!" And when she stopped speaking, her mouth open and eyes wide at a tone she had never heard from him before, he said, in the same rough voice, deepened by his anger, "Mr Collins lies. You forget I saw his inept attempts at wooing Mrs Grayson when I was in Hertfordshire last autumn, when he made his visit to his cousin. She was never more than polite to him, and to say otherwise is a falsehood that shocks me, coming as it does from a man of the cloth. Mrs Grayson is a respectable and highly respected lady, and your rector is a petty, mean-minded oaf whose pride was damaged when she refused him. That he should lie about her to you—to anyone!—is utterly disgraceful. It is he who should be deeply ashamed of his conduct."

"Dar—"

"Did you say that Mr Collins showed you his wife's correspondence? And you did not chastise him for that disrespect and betrayal? It would fill me with disquiet, if I had appointed such a man to a position of trust."

She bridled with an anger he suspected matched his own. "I trust my rector, nephew!"

"I suggest you think about his unchristian actions."

"His unchristian actions? *His*? What of hers? Do you deny she drew you into the morass of immorality and depravity arising from her sister's shameful elopement? How could you forget what is due to your name? To your family? To Anne?"

"It was Wickham, Lady Catherine. Wickham. A leech and wastrel created by my father's faulty indulgence. Yes, Mrs Grayson sought my help, and no gentleman worthy of the name could refuse to give it, when his own family had been the root of the evil in the first place. Her sister is now respectably married, and there is no scandal to damage anyone. And madam, it has nothing to do with Anne. Nothing is due her in this case."

She drew in a sharp breath. "You are engaged to my daughter! Anything that blackens your name and reputation affects hers!"

Oh, that tired old claim again. Darcy rubbed his fingers over his temples. He had always turned her claims aside, never outright refusing them. No longer. He would set her right. But before he could speak, his aunt went on.

"The woman is shameless, Darcy! She should have had more delicacy than to approach you about the matter, much less use her wiles to draw you in. She refused to consider the wickedness of her actions. A more insolent, impertinent hussy I have never had the displeasure of meeting! I would blush for her, if I thought she knew the meaning of shame. I should have known her kind would be deaf to all morality—low born and grasping, and typical of her class, clawing her way to ingratiate herself with her betters."

Something in Darcy's chest flinched, leapt and jumped. It stopped breath and voice, squeezed his chest into ice, all jagged, sharp edges that sliced and cut. His aunt raged on, adding insult to insult, her harsh crone's voice full of pride and disdain, but he could not hear her well above the thudding in his temples and ears. The ice shrouded him like a second skin. "You have been to Meryton."

"I left Rosings yesterday, immediately after Mr Collins revealed to me the depth of his cousin's perfidy. I could not reach that speck of a town before dark, and spent the most uncomfortable night in a third-class inn in Hatfield. I spoke to the hussy this morning."

"Dear God." He glanced at her, but could not bear to look at her for long. Instead, he turned away and walked to the window. He had never struck a woman. He had never been closer to doing so.

"I told her of your engagement to Anne, and do you know what that... that *woman* said to me? That she refused to promise not to marry you! She will act in a way that would bring about her own happiness, she says, with no regard for anything or anyone else. Selfish, selfish girl! She has no thought for ruining you in the opinion of all your friends, and making you the contempt of the world—no thought for anything but her own self-seeking interest."

She refused to promise not to marry you.

The icy thing inside Darcy's chest leaped again, but this time warmth spread through him, as if the sun shone on his face. Later. He would think of that later. When he could speak without uncontrolled anger, he said, "To my shame, I told Mrs Grayson once that her family was improper and ridiculous; that some of her sisters and her mother, in particular, exhibited unseemly and indecorous behaviour."

"Yes, indeed! So Mr Collins said. The mother is a fortune-hunter, Darcy."

"Her mother seeks security for her daughters against the day that Mr Collins inherits Longbourn and she is dispossessed. She is loud, a little vulgar, anxious, nervous and unrestrained. Familiar traits indeed." Darcy could look out onto the street no longer. He turned and stared into his aunt's smug countenance. "And yet, Lady Catherine, not even Mrs Bennet would travel fifty miles to berate a stranger over an engagement that does not exist."

She flushed. "Darcy!"

"I told her no man would welcome connections which were, as hers are, so decidedly below my own. And yet I have had nothing but courtesy and welcome from her family, and all I have to offer in return—" He broke off, and said over her spluttered, incoherent protests, "I am not engaged to Anne, Aunt. Nor will I ever be."

"You are indeed engaged! It was your mother's dearest wish—"

"One she never voiced to me. I am sorry if this gives you pain, but I am not bound by any fond wish you and my mother may have expressed when I was a child. I will care for Anne as my cousin, but no more." He held up a hand as the lady spluttered some more. "Enough, ma'am. I am grieved to disappoint you, and even more grieved that I have put off this day. I should have made it clear years ago that I would not be constrained into an unwanted marriage because two sisters idly discussed it once."

"More than once! Often! You mother wanted this, Darcy. You cannot deny it!"

"Nor can I tell you she ever mentioned it to me. Enough, Aunt. I am resolved on this."

"But... Rosings. You would have Rosings. Together with Pemberley, your holdings would be unrivalled!"

"I am not a fortune-hunter, Lady Catherine. I do not need Rosings."

"And Anne. What of Anne? She expects your proposal, Darcy!"

"At your contrivance, Aunt. You have never permitted her any opportunity to choose her own path. Well, she may now. I will not be moved by any further representations."

Nor was he. That is not to suggest that Lady Catherine did not try to change his mind by demands, entreaties, exhortations to remember his duty, commands, decrees and downright shrewish scolding, and for a further hour he bore with her, allowing her to vent her passion, anger and frustrated ambition. But not even Lady Catherine could break his resolve, and at last, worn out by his obstinate silences, she took herself off to his uncle's house, shrieking imprecations against him and the vile, mongrel temptress with whom he no doubt intended to pollute his bloodline.

Darcy bowed her out, and as soon as the house door closed and he had spoken to Wilkes about his sister's whereabouts, bounded up the stairs two at a time to the sitting room attached to

Georgiana's rooms. Having returned home from shopping while he and Lady Catherine had exchanged frank views, the wise child had hidden herself away to escape meeting their aunt.

"Has she gone? I could hear her all the way up here. She sounded very angry."

"She is indeed angry, and she is indeed gone. Georgiana, I am for Netherfield tomorrow. I will leave at dawn. Can you be ready?"

Georgiana nodded. "If you wish it, of course. Why such haste?"

"I have a question to ask."

"It must be an important one."

He nodded. "Oh yes. And this time, I hope for a better answer."

She refused to promise not to marry you.

Oakham Mount was truly little more than a large hillock. It barely qualified as a real hill. Its rounded top curved up out of a ring of trees, much like a bald pate out of a fringe of rough hair. A few large rocks broke the surface, forming a natural vantage point over this little portion of Hertfordshire.

She was where her sister said she would be: sitting on the rocks, staring out over Netherfield's lands spread out before them. He sat beside her without speaking, granting her the grace of choosing when to break their silence. He glanced once at her face, seeing little beyond the sides of her bonnet, before turning his gaze in the same direction as hers, to admire the view.

It was a long silence. He found he did not mind it, companionable and calm as was. Sailors felt this, probably, when they came at last into harbour; all storms and mighty seas behind them, home in front.

"I was bitterly unhappy in that house," she said, at last. "Powerless. Helpless. It makes me wary."

"I know. You never thought to sell?"

"I paid too high a price for it. I wore the deepest mourning for a year, but not for James."

"For your child."

"Yes." She sighed. "It is hard for me to trust to anything better."

"That is understandable. And you have turned Netherfield to good account. The care you take for your sisters is exemplary. Admirable."

She turned her head enough for him to see her mouth curve up, before they both resumed staring at the manor house in the distance.

After a long pause, he said, "Once, I knew a man. Very like me in appearance, in family, upbringing, and education. He prided himself on being a gentleman above the ordinary run of the breed—a man of honour, probity and industry, careful for those for whom he was responsible. A man of good principles, he thought; far above the meaner sort with whom he was often forced to mix. He held himself aloof, deeming it beneath him to be anything other than ordinarily civil, and in truth, he was barely that. But what did it matter? The people he moved amongst were nothing to him. He thought meanly of their sense and worth compared with his own, and was not shy to say so, denigrating any behaviours that he considered fell short of his high ideals. After all, these people had nothing but a fraction of his importance in the world. Better they knew it, acknowledged his superiority, and kept their distance."

She turned towards him, fixed her gaze on his face.

"And so he was all his life, until last year. Then he found himself involved in a scheme, a deceit, that shames him deeply even to this day. He counts it as the first step in his awakening, that he could stoop to that sort of dishonour. The one bright spot, the redeeming grace, was the one schemed against." He glanced at her and smiled. "The jewel of the county, indeed. And without thought, in his pride, he stooped to an even greater dishonour—not to him, but to *her*. He told her she was beneath him, that her family connections were a disgrace, but despite this he would raise her, make her his wife."

"Mr Darcy—"

He smiled, shook his head. "Let me finish. She, being a jewel beyond compare, humbled him. He went to her without a doubt of his reception, and she showed him how insufficient he was to aspire to her. She told him *I could never be tempted to accept an offer from you.* And that he behaved in so ungentlemanly a fashion, had such a selfish disdain for the feelings of others, he was quite sunk beneath any hope of her regard."

"Oh do not repeat what I said then!"

"No, listen to me. You were right, Elizabeth, in every particular. You delineated all my faults to a nicety. I was—perhaps still am—a selfish being in practice, for all my delusions of my worth. I have reflected on this a great deal since Christmas, and concluded... well, frankly, I was spoiled as a child, and although I was taught what was right, I followed those principles in pride and conceit. I was arrogant, I was disdainful. I decried your family and connections as beneath me, but you offered me the pleasure and delight that is the Gardiners, and I gave in exchange the ineffable Lady Catherine. For whom, by the way, I cannot apologise enough. But I hope, most sincerely, that the man I mentioned has learned his lessons. I cannot claim he is gone entirely. The bad habits of a lifetime cannot be shed without continued effort and energy, but for the first time in his life he does indeed strive to be better, to be the man he had thought he was."

"You were. You are. Lydia—"

"Oh, I did nothing for Lydia. I did it for you. It was unbearable to see you so broken and hurt by it, when a little endeavour on my part could find a happier ending. Do not credit me with altruism there, I beg you."

She closed her eyes for a moment, glints of tears on her lashes.

"So, let me tell you more about the man who looks like me, the man who hopes he is better now than he was then. He promises that though once he thought he loved the jewel most ardently, that was but a pale shadow of everything he feels now. He would perhaps say his affections and wishes are unchanged, but that would not be true. They are deeper, more powerful. There are no words to say how much more he feels; that she is more necessary to him than breathing. He promises that he understands her fears and trepidation about once more putting herself and all she has into the power of a husband. Whilst once he might have thought that it was right and just that all came to him, now he knows that the oaths he too must take have a deeper meaning than he first believed. This better man promises it will be written into the marriage contract and his will, that while he might be the titular owner, his wife's property remains hers, the income is hers to use to help support her sisters and mother if that is needed, and the property will return to her control if she outlives him. He will help her administer it, if she wishes, but will not take it from her."

She tightened her mouth against the trembling of her chin.

"He promises that she can trust him to care for her, love her, and cherish her. He promises he can think of no finer, more brilliant prospect than to have his family with her, that she need never fear he will turn from her or do anything other than offer his respect, love and worship. He promises they will undoubtedly argue, but he will never demand her unthinking obedience. He promises she can trust him, Elizabeth. And he is not a man who makes promises lightly."

He held out his hand. "Let me help you cross that last Rubicon, Elizabeth. Trust me."

Those brilliant eyes held his, her expression solemn, questioning him. Assessing him. He could see it all: the hope and innocence that not even violence and pain could take from her, the tempering her experiences had given her, the refining. She was the most beautiful woman he had ever known, and yet that was nothing to knowing her character, her worth.

It seemed to take a lifetime, but he held his hand steady, kept his gaze locked with hers. Her smile was a slight thing, but hopeful, and at last, he had his entire heart's desire.

She put her hand into his.

~end~

ABOUT THE AUTHOR

Once I used to do communications work for the UK government, in a variety of departments that saw me do things as diverse as managing national TV campaigns and an internal TV service delivered through everyone's desktop PC. These days I live a much quieter life with my husband in a pretty Georgian vicarage deep in the Nottinghamshire countryside, and I am writing full time. I'm supported in that endeavour not only by the tolerant Mr Winter (bless him!), but also by the Deputy Editor, aka Molly the cockerpoo, who's assisted by the lovely Mavis, a Yorkie-Bichon cross with a bark several sizes larger than she is, but no opinion whatsoever on the placement of semi-colons.

I have been a lover of Jane Austen's works for most of my life. I know it is appalling cheek to use even a fraction of Jane's 'little bit of ivory', but I hope she will forgive me. My only excuse is that of all literary heroines, Lizzy Bennet is the one I wanted to be. Writing Pride and Prejudice variations is the closest I shall ever come.

Julia

Contact me: juliawinterfiction@gmail.com
Website: https://juliawinterfiction.com
Twitter: https://twitter.com/fiction_julia
Facebook: https://www.facebook.com/JuliaWinterFiction

GLASS HAT
PRESS

Made in the USA
Monee, IL
30 October 2021

81095426R00260